Praise for

'A stylish, sun-soaked thriller... destined to be
THE summer read of 2024' **Janice Hallett**

'Sharp, brilliantly observed... had me gasping at every
twist - a scorching summer read' **Sarah Pearse**

'A thrilling study of toxic one-upmanship' **Vaseem Khan**

'You can't look away. Smart, sharp and suspenseful
with characters you won't forget' **Adele Parks**

'Hugely entertaining... full of tension and intrigue' **Liz Nugent**

'If you take one book on holiday this
year, make it this' **Celia Walden**

'Thieving, adultery, addiction, lying and murder...
a perfect holiday read' **Fern Britton**

'Compelling, gripping escapism...
Absolutely loved it' **Jane Fallon**

'Smart, assured, and gripping... an utterly
transportive and suspenseful read' **Lucy Clarke**

Also by Louise Candlish

The Only Suspect
The Heights
The Other Passenger
Those People
Our House
The Swimming Pool
The Sudden Departure of the Frasers
The Disappearance of Emily Marr
The Island Hideaway
The Day You Saved My Life
Other People's Secrets
Before We Say Goodbye
I'll Be There For You
The Second Husband
Since I Don't Have You
The Double Life of Anna Day

Novellas

The Skylight

Louise Candlish is the bestselling author of 16 novels and is published all over the world. Her book *Our House* was adapted into a major four-part ITV drama and won the 2019 British Book Awards Crime and Thriller Book of the Year.

Louise lives in a South London neighbourhood not unlike the one in her books, with her husband, daughter and a fox-red Labrador called Bertie.

For up-to-date news, catch her on X @louise_candlish, on Instagram @louisecandlish or facebook.com/LouiseCandlishAuthor.

our holiday

LOUISE CANDLISH

ONE PLACE. MANY STORIES

HQ
An imprint of HarperCollins*Publishers* Ltd
1 London Bridge Street
London SE1 9GF

www.harpercollins.co.uk

HarperCollins*Publishers*
Macken House, 39/40 Mayor Street Upper,
Dublin 1, D01 C9W8, Ireland

This edition 2024

2
First published in Great Britain by
HQ, an imprint of HarperCollins*Publishers* Ltd 2024

Copyright © Louise Candlish 2024

ISBN: 9780008614652

This book contains FSC™ certified paper and other controlled sources to ensure responsible forest management.

For more information visit: www.harpercollins.co.uk/green

This book is set in 10/15 pt. Sabon by Type-it AS, Norway

Printed and Bound in the UK using 100% Renewable Electricity at CPI Group (UK) Ltd, Croydon, CR0 4YY

To all the readers who've shared the ride
with me these last 20 years

PART ONE

1

Robbie

This is going to sound completely mad, but a house is falling off the cliff.

I mean, seriously, right in front of my eyes.

It's up on the headland on Pine Ridge Road, the highest residential spot in town – the highest prices, too. Exclusive, swanky, *famous* Pine Ridge Road, because if you didn't know it before this summer, you definitely will now and that's partly down to yours truly ('Robbie Jevons is the South Coast's rock star of Zoomer activism' – the *Guardian*, no less).

So anyway. This house is literally sliding out from behind a tall green hedge and heading for the cliff edge, and the crazy thing is I'm the only one who seems to be seeing it! I'm on my own in the dunes behind the stage, the beach to my left, village to my right, the headland a way off but in my direct line of sight. Everyone else has their backs to it as they watch the band – a thousand people or more, all with these blissed-out looks on their faces like they're in the presence of, I don't know, Harry Styles or someone, not some random act from Weymouth doing old rock covers.

'Smoke on the Water'? I mean, come on.

But no. Houses don't move. They don't *slide*. I've smoked

3

a bit of weed and had a few beers, so maybe I'm hallucinating. (I'm kind of dazed from other activities too, but we won't go into that.) To test myself, I look away, focus on a couple at the edge of the crowd. He's knee-deep in the sea, strong as a tree, the tattoos on his pecs gleaming like alligator skin; she's sitting on his shoulders, thighs clamping his neck, arms swaying from side to side to the music. I don't think I know them, but we're all mixed in together, locals and blow-ins and day trippers. Today, like the message on the placard abandoned at my feet, 'NO HUMAN IS TABOO'.

On the count of ten, I look up again and fuck me if the front of the house isn't right over the cliff edge now, like one of those cantilevered balconies on the side of a block of flats. And it's *definitely* real: one storey, wood-clad and slate-roofed, a row of windows shining gold in the dipping sun.

Right behind it, visible through the hedge: a splint of bright yellow.

I get to my feet and stagger down the dune and along the beach to where Shannon's dancing at the side of the stage. 'Fire in the sky,' she chants, all loose-limbed and dreamy, and she reaches out to take my hand. 'Robster! Where've you been?'

'Look,' I shout through the ear-splitting guitars. 'Look what's happening up there!'

She swivels and follows my gaze, not knowing what she's seeing at first. But then the house jerks forward again and she reacts: 'What the fuck? We need to get help. Find one of the marshals or police!'

But it's too late for that. By the time they reach it, it'll be dust.

At that exact moment the song ends and through the applause we start to hear it: a demonic scraping and rumbling, plus the unmistakable throb of something mechanical. As everyone twists to look, the singer's voice comes over the sound system: 'Shit, what's going on up there? Can someone try to . . .?'

He runs out of words.

And into the first pure silence of the day – maybe of the summer – the house tips off the cliff and smashes into the sea.

2

Charlotte

It never got old, the first glimpse of heather as you exited the toll ferry. That blurred ribbon of mauve between the blond of the beach and the bottle green of the pine ridge beyond.

Busy admiring the way the hues had mellowed since her last visit, Charlotte failed to notice a figure step from the verge and hurl red liquid over their windscreen.

'What the hell!' Perry braked and pulled sharply to the side of the road, causing Mango, their fox-red Labrador, to spring to attention in the boot. They climbed out, raising their sunglasses to get a clearer look at the culprit, a wiry young male now scurrying, bucket in hand, towards his cohorts gathered near the toll booth.

'Bloody better not be paint,' Perry said, a flush spreading under his garden tan towards his hairline.

'It's soup, I think.' She extended a finger to touch it. It was disquietingly warm, almost body temperature. 'Or pizza sauce, maybe. It's quite thick. Passata.'

'*Passata?* Are they eco-warriors or something? Like those cretins who threw custard over the Rembrandt?'

'I think they're the Not Just for August crew.' Charlotte craned for a better look at the group, most of whom were either masked or obscured by the signs they brandished, signs with slogans

6

like 'HOLIDAY HOMES KILL COMMUNITIES!', 'GO BACK SUMMER PEOPLE!' and – yep, there it was – '#NJFA!'

'Hey! Stop!' Perry cried, as an approaching Volvo received the same treatment, the liquid splashing into the driver's open window and provoking a furious roar. An old Ford Focus had been allowed to pass without interference, Charlotte saw, even though the tell-tale paraphernalia of the second-home owner was visible through its rear window (no one took a garden hose or an electric drill to a holiday rental), which suggested a grading system that lacked nuance.

Energized by Perry's challenge, the group swarmed closer to chant directly into his face: 'Local homes for local people! Local homes for local people!'

'Get off the road!' he yelled.

'Go back to London!'

'Fuck you!' Perry ducked past them for the toll booth. He was not a tall man and his heft was more marked from behind, arms jerking back and forth as he strode.

Further back, car horns blared at the delay, upsetting Mango, and Charlotte opened the boot to calm her before locating a roll of kitchen towel and removing enough of the gloop to facilitate a safe onward progress. She nodded good-naturedly at a hovering protester who'd become separated from the pack and raised his placard like a shield.

'"Second Home Scum",' she read. 'That's not very welcoming, is it?'

There'd been opposition to holiday homes in one form or another throughout the fifteen years they'd owned Cliff View, but until recently it had been a low-key, fringe affair. Questions raised at council meetings; the occasional march along Old Beach Road and up Bird Lane, where the village's most photogenic cottages were situated; features in the *Voice* highlighting the unfairness of key workers living in caravans while Nimbys blocked plans for new housing estates. A presence, certainly, but it was not what you'd call a campaign. Not coordinated, not militant, as it was now. Not immediately associated with a single group.

She had to admit that as rebrands went, this was an impressive one.

Perry came stomping back, sweating. 'The guy's called the police. Wants us to hang around till they get here.'

Charlotte pulled a face. 'They'll be ages. Why don't I ring them on Monday and they can just log it then?'

'If they even bother. Probably just give the little brats a pat on the back.'

With a resettling of sunglasses and a clunking of doors, they pulled away again. During the entire episode Charlotte's heart rate had not altered. It would have been different had they been travelling at seventy when the attack took place, but as it was, no real harm had been done. And, just minutes away, Cliff View, and her beloved Nook, where this evening they'd drink rosé on the veranda and watch the neon sky dissolve into inky darkness. Then, in the month ahead, dips in the limpid waters of the Old Beach; snoozes in the pine-scented shade; walks with Mango on mirrored sands; and her tax consultancy work shrunk to a single client managed from the kitchen table. Oh, and Benedict arriving in a few hours' time, the first time they'd seen their son in six weeks.

Pine Ridge paradise, basically.

'Wait, it's the first of August, isn't it?' she remembered. Given the name of the protest group, it was no wonder they were out in force. Taken the day off from jobs that in all probability serviced the very people they'd come to harass. Had they begun as soon as the ferry service got underway, at 7 a.m.? If so, their antics would be all over social media by now. 'We obviously chose the wrong day to arrive.'

'Yes, unless they're going to do this every day for the entire month,' Perry said. He applied the wipers to dislodge more tomato smears. 'And they call *us* scum.'

*

Surprise, surprise, there were NJFA daubings on their white-painted front wall – in dripping red for a nice crime-scene effect – and she took photos to submit to the police website, where they would no doubt languish unseen for all eternity.

At least the walls of the house itself were untouched. Cliff View was one of four original clifftop properties built from local grey limestone and slate and easily the best placed, with one aspect to Old Beach and one to open water. It was the largest too, the three smaller ones belonging to – and unlikely to be released any time soon by – two other couples from London and one from Winchester. In between these originals was a collection of one-offs built as and when land from gardens had been sold off, including their direct neighbour, Villa Pino, a Sandbanks-lite edifice owned by Tim and Madeline of Twickenham. Thanks to their sensible decision to install railings rather than a wall, they tended to escape the vandals' paintbrush.

Leaving Perry to unload the car, she took Mango for a little tour, reacquainting herself with the many period features: flag-stone flooring, vaulted ceilings, huge inglenook fireplace. Their cleaner (Charlotte had always employed locals rather than using the Housekeepers agency in Poole that most holiday home owners favoured) had been in to run the hoover around and make the beds, which meant her only job was to slide up the sashes to let in the sea air.

It was divine today. Fresh and salty, almost astringent. Curative.

Next, she headed out back to check on the Nook. Just a few feet from the public footpath and defended only by a low wooden fence, their summerhouse was far more vulnerable to vandalism than the main house, not to mention more exposed to a potential audience; walkers passed frequently along the mile-long path that linked Old Beach to Little Bay and the area's best hotel, The Needles.

It was, everyone agreed, a treasure. Its eight windows and stable door were glazed with antique leaded panes and the lines of the slate roof designed to echo those of the main cottage. Both the cladding and veranda were painted the colour of summer cloud. She'd see pictures of it sometimes on social media, hashtagged #dreamhouse or #coastalcrib, but she wasn't possessive of its image. If you were on public view, you had to expect to share.

Peering through the glass, she saw that the bed had been made up in here too, even though it was unlikely to be used this trip. Their only guests were Benedict and his new girlfriend, who'd be sleeping in the main house.

She stood for a moment on the deck, positioning herself so that all she could see was sea and sky, stainless, limitless. Like this, you could imagine yourself in a wartime vignette, looking out across the blue and contemplating the horrors in France. Thinking yourself – *knowing* yourself – to be one of the lucky ones.

It certainly put the passata into perspective.

*

'You stay here,' she told Mango, closing the gate on her and taking the steps down to the beach, a somewhat hair-raising shortcut to the old part of the village that Perry predicted would soon be closed by the health and safety brigade. No sign of trouble on the sands, only the familiar rows of buttercup-yellow loungers and umbrellas for hire, a patchwork of towels and throws for everyone else. Parents smearing lotion on toddlers' faces while twenty-somethings toasted inked skin (could you still get cancer on skin tattooed with dragons?) and others queued for the Aperol spritzes and locally churned gelato served from attractive wooden counters. What else? Beach tennis, volleyball, that new ball game involving a mini trampoline. A cluster of smiley people in life jackets being briefed at the water's edge before a paddleboard lesson.

Not an activist in sight.

She was queuing at the deli on Old Beach Road when Amy messaged.

> You've landed! Just saw Perry with his paintbrush 😵 LMK when you're free to play.

'Free to play' meant free to invite us over – or at least that was how it had been at Easter, Amy and Linus's first proper visit to their new retreat, a ramshackle bungalow unsuitable for even the most casual hosting. Neighbours in London – Charlotte and Amy had met almost a decade ago at the newfangled hot yoga studio on Lordship Lane that they'd both tried and quickly abandoned for the unheated original – and now here in Pine Ridge, they were going to be seeing more of each other than they did their own families. But, as Charlotte pointed out to Perry, you *chose* your friends, didn't you?

She searched the shelves in vain for NoLo options for Perry, who no longer drank, and hoped he'd remembered to bring his own stocks of Lucky Saint from London. She imagined him ranting to Amy about the ferry shenanigans. The Shaws had travelled down at the weekend – when it was still July – and likely been spared the mayhem, which was ironic because you had to assume they were part of the influx that had inspired the NJFA to up their game in the first place. Like other city folk, they'd only been reassessing their priorities when they'd bought a second home, reshaping their work-life balance following the Covid lockdown, but from down here it had looked suspiciously like they'd taken advantage of suffering.

It looked cruel.

'Can I help?' said the girl at the till, who had fine gold-red hair and a distinctively English high colour. Did she share her fellow locals' anger? She looked so placid. A tag on her apron bore the name Shannon.

'Hi Shannon. Are you new?'

'Been here nearly a year,' the girl said, her tone bright but impersonal.

'Ah. Well, it looks like it's going to be amazing weather for the next few weeks, doesn't it? Have you got any of that crab dip with the samphire? I couldn't see it in the chiller.'

'We're sold out. We've got the mackerel and horseradish, though?'

'I'm not so keen on that. Not to worry.'

The girl scanned her items. 'That's £45.43.'

For a couple of dips and a box of cheese straws! Charlotte tapped her card with a grudging respect. For a community that harboured so many anti-wealth fanatics, there was some seriously good business sense on show.

*

'They're putting in a summerhouse,' Perry said. 'Disruption will be minimal.'

Charlotte dumped the shopping inside and took a seat next to him at the terrace table. 'Amy and Linus? Is that still hot?'

She helped herself to coffee from the French press, even though she normally cut the caffeine at noon. It was Le Creuset, Marseille Blue, one of the items she associated so strongly with Pine Ridge she could experience an almost erotic sensory lurch if she came upon it in John Lewis.

'It's a flat-pack number that goes up in a few hours. If they can get it delivered quickly, they might even sleep in it this trip,' she said – or let the kids. Huck's got a French exchange student coming and one of their bedrooms has still got a boarded-up window, apparently.'

'Linus hasn't got a clue about DIY,' Charlotte said. 'Maybe you could help him out?'

'Maybe.' Perry was rather less keen on Linus than he was Amy, the two being on opposite sides of the current South London controversy involving Low Traffic Neighbourhoods and equally resistant to compromise. Other rivalries were at play too, Charlotte knew, with Linus's cycle insurance business taking off at exactly the same time as Perry had semi-retired, which was just the kind of hierarchical rupture Perry struggled with.

'Look, she sent me a pic.' Perry passed her his phone.

'Well, that looks familiar,' Charlotte said, studying the chalet-style edifice with its wraparound veranda and sloping slate roof.

'I know. Wait for this: she's going to call it the Niche. Imitation is the sincerest form of flattery, I suppose.'

Charlotte was untroubled by this. Eight years older than Amy, she had been happy with the tone set early and naturally in their warm, frank friendship. She shared her wisdom and Amy received it – it would be churlish to resent her acting on it. In any case, the Shaws' new garden room could not be exactly like theirs because the Nook was a vintage treasure, a one-off salvaged from an estate in Sussex and restored by specialist craftsmen.

Perry's and her phones now pinged in unison and they tended to their notifications like surgeons on call. Hers was a new message from Amy saying much the same as the first.

'What time shall I say to come over?' she said and Perry looked up, startled.

'Who?'

'Amy and Linus, of course.' She cocked her head, intrigued. 'Why, who's *your* text from?'

He pocketed his phone, holding her gaze in that unyielding, almost brazen way he did when he lied. 'No one,' he said.

3

Amy

Hi Tim & Madeline,
If you're here, I'd love to keep you in the loop about our
building works. There shouldn't be too much disruption
over August, then we start properly in September. Pop
round any time to discuss,
Amy, the bungalow x

How much of life was spent in activities you knew to be futile, she wondered, posting her note through the stainless-steel letterbox of Villa Pino, the cool white new build that separated their bungalow from Cliff View. She'd continued to think of them as 'the people in between' long after she'd learned their names: Tim and Madeline Rickman.

They only came in July, Charlotte said, adding that they'd moved to Southeast Asia for Tim's work, which had something to do with the evil oil industry and involved a fat tax-free salary, and their kids' earlier school holidays meant they could avoid the British August bunfight.

Nor did they choose to rent to holidaymakers while away, which was good in that there was no noise from partying groups or young families with screaming toddlers, and bad because second homes standing empty was the very reason for local antipathy.

Back at the bungalow, she found her son Huck standing in the garden, mostly immobile, only his hands and feet twitching, as if he'd just been beamed there from the starship *Enterprise*.

'That's where it will go,' she said. 'Right where you're standing.'

He half turned, reminding her that he'd recently grown a man's jaw and long bony nose. 'What will?'

'The Niche. Our new summerhouse.'

His lip curled. 'Why are you calling it that?'

'I just like it.' She hoped Charlotte wouldn't think the name copycat and weird. She'd been on Thesaurus.com and everything.

'French for kennel,' Huck said.

'Really? I might put up a "Beware of the Dog" sign then. Or get Julien to bring us one in French when he comes. What would that be?'

'*Attention au chien.*'

'Your French *has* improved. Maybe you should think about doing it for A level?'

But this drew the same glower his sister produced whenever academic study was invoked. Out of the corner of her eye she could see Beattie at the window of her bedroom, changing her clothes (she did this constantly). As the girl pulled her top over her head, she turned, naked, to the glass. There was no one coming along the path, but still, Amy would need to have a word with her. With only the picket fence defending their rear garden from the public footpath, security was minimal.

As Charlotte had explained, it was a straight choice between your privacy and the view and since Pine Ridge was virtually crime-free and they'd all bought the houses expressly *for* the view, it was a no-brainer.

As if reading her mind, Huck advanced to the fence and eyed the water below with an air of not quite believing it was there. They all did this and presumably would continue to do so for months, maybe years, because it really wasn't something you could be blasé about: the sea right there, a powerful force at your service. Even Linus agreed it was sensational, dismayed though he was that the path was too narrow to cycle.

Both Huck and Beattie had declined his offer to go cycling this afternoon. When they were younger, they'd enjoyed this dedicated activity with Dad, but since he'd joined the cult of Strava and basically become deranged (what did Perry call them? Stravassholes, that was it), he was on his own. His kit had travelled with them from London and was sharing space in the old garage with their DIY stores and general crap, which was a lot to ask of a space designed to hold one narrow 1960s car. She'd yet to figure out where everything was going to go when it was demolished at the end of August to create the access necessary for the build to begin. The council's rule that noisy construction work could not take place between the May and August bank holidays meant they could do very little before then and were resigned to summering in virtual dilapidation.

'They'll level the ground, won't they?' Huck said, turning.

'I sincerely hope so, or it might slide off in the rain! I was thinking, Huck. If it's up and ready by the time Julien comes, maybe one of you can sleep in it? I know it's a bit tight in the house.' When Huck had stayed with his French counterpart earlier in the year, he'd been hosted in a historic property in Rennes. Not super-grand, but it had certainly boasted a full complement of windows. 'Or you could camp out,' she added. 'The French love camping, don't they?'

Huck made no reply. She patted the pouch of her dungarees for the tape measure she often carried, but found only a wodge of leaflets she'd picked up from the doormat when they'd arrived.

She added 'no junk mail sign' to her mental list for the B&Q run tomorrow.

Other than offers to trim hedging or clear guttering, most of the flyers involved calls to action against the very people they'd been delivered to, which struck Amy as another act of futility.

Triple council tax for holiday homes!

Sign the NJFA petition to stop second homes!

In preparation for their month in the spotlight, the NJFA activists had left their mark on several of the front walls up and down the street, including Charlotte and Perry's. Poor things. Just awful to have to deal with graffiti on the first day of your summer holiday – not to mention that business at the ferry that Perry had told her about.

'They've stepped it up,' he'd said. 'Got themselves a proper game plan. But if they think they can intimidate me, they've got another think coming.'

In its current state, the bungalow didn't attract the vandalism directed at the flashier holiday homes. Maybe that was why the flyers had been posted through their door: hopes of a cuckoo in the nest, perhaps. A double agent right in the seat of privilege.

She continued through the flyers:

Join Citizens Against the Elite!

Vote Vicky Marks for councillor if you want the DFLs out!

She hadn't even known what DFL meant when she'd first seen it. 'Is that like "do not resuscitate"?' she'd asked Charlotte, who had chuckled.

'They wish. No, it means "down from London".'

'But how could they get us out? I don't understand.'

'They can't. Last time I checked, English councils can't actually seize a person's property. What they mean is no more. Cap the numbers.'

'What, so me and Linus might be one of the last to be allowed to buy a house here?'

'If they get their way, yes. They have a register of second-home owners, you know. Like a sex offenders' register, Perry says.'

'Is that legal?'

'I suppose it must be. It's a handy resource for the haters, anyway.'

Amy had overheard some of the haters talking in the Gull when she'd come down on her own in May to meet with the builders. A copy of the *Voice* had lain open on the table between the group, four of them, as they chatted, the headline visible: 'First-Time Buyers Kicked Off Coastal Property Ladder'.

'In Cornwall they say "emmets",' someone said in a briefing sort of tone. 'It means ants.'

'What do you say?' a second voice asked, evidently an out-of-towner.

'Grockles.'

'Grockles?'

'Yeah. Or cunts.'

They'd all howled with laughter.

Charlotte had advised soon after that the Gull was best left to the locals. They had the beach bar till 7 p.m. or, better still, the bar at The Needles, which was five minutes away by car or a short stroll along the clifftop path. Amy and Linus had gone there for lunch at Easter and it was all golf buggies and kitchen gardens and yoga on a decked dais. A gorgeous stone pool lay between the manor house and the beach, a separate building housed a spa and gym, and the rooms looked sublime, palatial yet boho. Linus had made a quick mental calculation: with the stamp duty they'd paid on the bungalow they could have spent six months in the hotel. But only in a standard room, he conceded.

At the buzz of a text notification – Charlotte: *Drinks at the Nook at 6?* – Amy surfaced from her reverie and finally located the tape measure in her back pocket. 'Huck, could you do me a favour and hold the other end?'

Silence. She hadn't noticed that he'd sloped off.

She opened the gate to the footpath and stepped out. Instantly she had the feeling that something was out of kilter, the path more exposed than the last time she'd stood on it. Had something been removed? A tree or an old fence post? The low wall of rocks looked the same, the grasses and what she thought might be samphire growing in between. To the right, just visible at the outermost point of the cliff's curve, was a concrete pillbox from the war.

'Huck? *Huck?*' She peered over the edge and down to the water, half expecting to see her son clinging to the rock. Or worse, bobbing, lifeless, in the water.

Nothing. Just the sea, rolling and curling. An animal in a state of stress, frothing at the mouth.

4

Tate

'Thought you'd be sat outside,' Ellie said, entering the caravan's bedroom, or, more accurately, hovering in the doorway about six inches from the only piece of furniture, a mattress enclosed on three sides and plonked on top of a set of drawers that provided their main storage.

'I was gaming.' The console was on the duvet next to him. He'd been, for the last half-hour, catatonic, just staring at the ceiling.

'Right.' She leaned across and flung open the curtains, her face creased with disapproval, as if it were a crime to close them. As if she were his mother, not his lover.

'It got hot,' he said, blinking. For a few hours a day you had the double whammy of the sun beating down on the aluminium roof and streaming through thin windows and it was all you could do not to bake like a spud.

'Then go out,' she snapped. 'It smells rank in here.'

He eyed his girlfriend with wariness. Somewhere beneath the almost nun-like severity of the high-necked overalls and pinned hair required by her employer was the girl with sexy raven hair and wild eyes he'd lusted after and pursued the previous summer. Who'd wanted only to please him. None of this moaning and criticising.

Seeming to read his mind, she changed tack. 'You weren't arrested then?'

He pulled himself up with a satisfying display of core strength. 'No. Just got a warning. I think the police agree with us, to be honest. Look at Ethan, still in his mum's spare room.'

'I forgot he'd started his training. Was he there?'

'Yeah. Looked about twelve in his uniform.'

'Wish I could've come.' This was an ongoing frustration for Ellie. Though she helped NJFA behind the scenes, her boss at the Needles spa would not take kindly to an employee being seen to attack their own clients. Not that it was the hotel guests they targeted, of course, it was the second-home owners, but both groups arrived in high-end cars and it wasn't easy to tell them apart. The compiling of a list of registration numbers was underway, complicated in its own way since a lot of these rich DFLs had second cars as well as second homes.

All right for some.

'How was work?' Following her into the living area, he saw how knackered she looked in the light. She'd come back for her lunch break, which she didn't get till four on Fridays and Saturdays because treatments ran back-to-back till 9 p.m.

'Fine. Had this woman just now for a full body. She goes, "It was much more vicious in the Thai spa I went to." She kept saying that word. "You can be more *vicious*, Ellie."'

'Hope you were.' He slid onto the bench at the fold-down table and opened his tobacco tin to roll a smoke, thinking it had been a while since he'd felt her trained touch on *his* body. Weeks, maybe a month. *Full body*: the words made him shift on the bench seat.

'Did you pick up the gas?'

'Not yet. There's still enough for a shower,' he said. Hoped. Running out of hot water mid-shower made a shit experience

22

soul-destroying – Robbie's description. Robbie was a bit of a word-smith. Alongside his job at the garage and role as leader of NJFA, he was frequently asked to quote to media outlets covering the housing crisis.

Hoping Ellie wouldn't start on about the laundrette – he'd failed in that task too, on account of not having the right coins – he dug in his pocket for a lighter.

'Not in here,' she said sharply. 'I can't go back stinking of smoke.'

'I was going out.' She had no choice but to submit to his touch as he eased by (it was impossible to give someone the cold shoulder in a space measuring 300 square feet). 'Chill, babe.'

'Chill, babe?' she scoffed, less like his mother now and more like her own. 'Are you listening to me?': that was Tracey's catchphrase as she henpecked Phil, who, sap that he was, gave every impression of getting off on the arrangement.

Well, Tate didn't. *Don't say it*, he thought. *Don't say it or I'll be out of here and you'll never see me again.* (Fine, so she'd be able to find him easily enough at work at the beach bar.)

Seeming once more to read his mind, Ellie settled on an instruction. 'Get the gas while you're out, yeah?'

*

Normally, he smoked at the white plastic table and chairs under their awning, but this time he felt the need to put some space between Ellie's mood and him. His own mood was harder to escape as he walked down Adventure Way (what 'adventure' did they have in mind, the clowns who designed this place?), lined on both sides with the fifty or so tourers, occupied by a mix of summer workers, illegal permanents like them, and actual holidaymakers, before turning onto the main gravel road through the site (Paradise Avenue, what a joke). On his left was the statics section, housing mainly older people, who would sit outside in their tiny decked squares, sometimes all day long, in the heat and dust, like there weren't beaches and dunes and meadows less than a mile away. They were noticeably friendlier to young locals like Ellie and him than they were to the seasonal workers, though the most hated group – according to Robbie and Shannon, who'd experienced the arrival of a ten-strong convoy in the neighbouring field earlier in the year – was the travellers. After a brief battle with the perman-ents, they'd moved on, leaving behind a ton of litter and shit.

Tate was in range of the shower block and toilets now – easier to go there than use their own chemical toilet, which involved yet another chore – and the office and shop, which was often closed and usually out of gas or whatever else it was you needed in a hurry. He'd drop in on his way back.

He noticed how his legs knew how many paces there were between his van and the gate, how comfortable he was here now, like *this was it*. Tragic, as if his body had stopped resisting. Stopped striving. Even the NJFA stuff, he couldn't say what was in it for them, besides the political protest, the being on the right side of history. No more second homes? Fine, but if those properties were offered to the market as long-term lets, would their rents ever come down to anything near the £400 he and Ellie paid here?

We're paying it forward, Robbie said. Doing it for the next generation. For all his knowledge of the facts and figures, and his own family history, which was totally undeniably grim, Robbie retained a capacity for optimism.

Speak of the devil, he was already at their favoured picnic table on the mound across the road from the entrance, smoking. The garage closed mid-afternoon on Saturdays.

'Yo.'

'Yo.' The choice of greeting was not so much ironic as ingrained: they'd been addressing each other like this for two decades (Ellie's dad called them Beavis and Butthead, which, if Tate could be bothered to take offence, which he could not, he would say was fucking rude).

'They can't take this away from us,' Robbie said, gesturing with his fag to the view of the sea, a thick band of blue curving south from Pine Ridge to Little Bay and beyond.

'Well, they *can*,' Tate said. 'They could sell this land to some developer.'

'No one would want to build a house twenty feet from a caravan park.'

'They could sell the whole park. Push us back even further. Back by the A-road, probably.'

'Someone's full of the joys,' said Robbie, whose wry, knowing tone – he had no accent either, or at least it had been so neutralized as to no longer register to Tate's ear – contrasted with his dangerous, bulldog looks. He slipped out his phone and began thumbing. 'This'll cheer you up if you haven't seen it already.'

It was the video posted on social media of the morning's stunt. A thirty-second clip of an Audi A8 crawling into range, then the sudden, shocking bloom of red. Brakes, angry voices. 'What are you doing? You're a disgrace!' Then a voice Tate knew to be their mate Rio's: 'No. *You're* the disgrace. Twat!' A chorus of 'Not Just for August! Not Just for August!'

'Golden,' Tate said. Robbie was right, it did cheer him up. It also answered his question about what he got out of this. Tribal energy. The release of frustration.

'How many cars did you get?' Robbie asked.

'Loads. This one bloke rolled down the window and got it in his face. What a loser. How was the garage? Any slashed tyres to sort?'

This remained a preferred method of Crowland-based pressure group Citizens Against the Elite. There'd been a time, before Robbie turned a bunch of resentful barflies into a pressure group who understood realpolitik (well, *he* understood it, anyway), when it had been theirs too. But Robbie had seen that what got attention now was not rendering vehicles immobile, but throwing stuff at them – the brighter the better – and trying to get the video of it viral. In London, the 'Just Stop Oil' people had just spray-painted the windows of a showroom full of Lamborghinis neon orange. It was all over the news.

First rule of NJFA: no death threats. Not for them the stories coming from other coastal hotspots of councillors too intimidated to eat in local restaurants or estate agents calling the police about suspicious packages slung on their doorsteps.

As well as the food-throwing, graffiti was acceptable, and stickering, yes, but not smashed windows or other destruction. No dogshit through letterboxes either, that was beneath them. Above all else, Robbie said, any act had to involve words. If the message wasn't evident, it was a wasted opportunity. They were laser-focused activists, not some rent-a-mob.

Robbie pocketed his phone. Glancing up, he gave a low whistle. 'Look at this, mate.'

A tall, slim girl of about twenty, maybe late teens, was strolling up the lane. She wore flared jeans, tight as a second skin on her thighs, and a tailored shirt with a psychedelic pattern unbuttoned low enough to give a glimpse of bra. Her hair was long and shiny, like someone had poured maple syrup over her shoulders and her face was . . . Well, now it came closer, it was lovely, dazzlingly lovely. It was *perfect*.

Tate felt a whoosh of adrenaline and lust – possibly his favourite pairing of bodily sensations. But, at the caravan park gates, the girl stopped and looked about her, and the dismay on her face as she clocked the site punched him in the gut. This was how normal people reacted to this crap, low-grade place. To his *home*.

Robbie seemed not to have noticed. He called down to her, all cheerful: 'You all right there? You look a bit lost.'

'I think I am, actually.' Posh voice, easy smile, straight teeth. Figured. Some influencer staying at The Needles.

'Where're you headed? The Needles?'

'Yes.'

Maybe she was the chick who'd wanted the vicious massage. Tate felt a response in his groin at the thought.

'Sorry to have to break it to you, but this is about as far from there as you'll get,' Robbie told her.

'Really? But my mum . . .' She corrected herself: 'I was told it was only fifteen minutes away and I've already been walking longer than that.'

'I meant aesthetically,' Robbie said, smirking. 'Philosophically.'

Tate flicked him a look. He liked to do this. Display his knowledge, his vocabulary. *I might be a mechanic living in a caravan, but that doesn't mean I'm not* educated. Tate, on the other hand, was the looker. It had been this way since the two of them were at school together. Smart cop, hot cop.

He was aware that he needed to speak; if he didn't, she'd forever know him as Robbie's mute friend. 'Tell you what, you can check in here and we'll only charge you a tenner. Special rate for models.' He gave her his best smile: helpless, boyish, a touch of brooding.

She blushed. 'I'm not actually staying at the hotel. I just wanted to see what they've got there.'

'What they've got? They've got *everything*.'

27

'His girlfriend works there, so he should know,' Robbie said, with a hint of slyness only Tate would catch.

Why did he have to go and say that?

Robbie stepped towards her and gestured to the way she'd come. 'If you came up from the village and down Crowland Road past the Meadow, you must have veered off to the right instead of keeping straight on. Go back down here, then take a sharp right. A few minutes' down and you'll see the sign for Little Bay and the hotel's right there.'

'Okay. Awesome. Thanks.'

They watched her retreat. Her bum was incredible, probably the best Tate had ever seen and in his line of work he'd seen thousands. When they turned back to each other, he gave his friend an unimpressed look.

'What?' Robbie said.

'You know what.'

'Horny bastard. She looks a bit young, d'you think?' The caution in his voice was mild but unmissable. 'Gorgeous, though. I'll give you that.'

I'll give you that: the phrase struck Tate as profound, though he couldn't say why. But he sensed it then, within himself, the knowledge that he was going to do something this summer that he would almost certainly come to regret and yet had absolutely no capacity to prevent.

'She's a fucking goddess,' he said.

5

Charlotte

Benedict's taxi pulled up just as the first bottle of rosé was uncorked and plunged into the ice bucket. The unerring instinct of the student. They greeted him at the door with tight hugs – he smelled of the crowded Saturday train he'd arrived on, of clothes and hair in need of a wash – before turning to welcome the petite dark-haired girl by his side.

'This,' he said, and he paused for effect, 'is Tabitha.'

'It certainly is,' she said, and the two of them dropped dusty swollen backpacks to the floor with the air of wanting nothing more to do with them. 'Hello, doggo,' she added, spying Mango, who remained aloof, as she always did with newcomers.

Tabitha, who was two years older than Benedict and about to start her master's at Bristol, had an intriguing sense of contradiction about her, Charlotte thought. An impish smile to soften the impact of a sharp, intelligent gaze; a well-cut playsuit of pink and silver vertical stripes undermined by battered yellow Crocs; fine white fingers sharpened with punky, dark green fingernails. She looked fragile but, Charlotte could already intuit, was anything but.

'Welcome to Cliff View. Benedict's been coming here since he was little.'

'He told me. It means a lot to him.' She had an attractive voice, melodic and warm as she complimented the sequence of cosy rooms she was now steered through, finishing in the kitchen with its view of their beautiful garden, of the ornamental grasses and rugged stone paths and slender pines. And, of course, the glittering water beyond.

She turned to Benedict. 'What trees are they?'

'Um, pines. Pine Ridge, yeah?'

'Is this the ridge?'

'No, that's at the back of the village,' Charlotte said. 'You probably came the beach road way, did you? There's an upper road as well, over the ridge. But the pines are everywhere.'

The students seized the glasses of rosé Perry handed them. 'Yay, bitch diesel,' Benedict said. 'You'll be drinking a lot of this while you're here, Tabs. How was your drive down?' he asked his father in that new adult way he did since leaving home. Sometimes it was hard not to feel wonder for what was natural, even mundane.

'Fine until we got off the ferry,' Perry said. 'Then we met a load of troublemakers. Or social justice warriors, as I believe they prefer to be known.'

Benedict sniggered. 'Watch what you say, Dad. Tabs is one of those.'

'I am,' she agreed. 'You're looking at the new chair of the Bristol Uni Progressives Society.'

'Oh.' Perry's gaze narrowed. 'Were you one of the ones who tipped the Colston statue into the harbour during lockdown?'

'No, I was back at my mum's place then. We were online that year. Wish I *had* been though. They were total legends.'

'Where's your mum based, Tabitha?' Charlotte asked.

After she had replied – near Rutland Water and, yes, they had done the full-circuit hike many times, though a disappointing portion of it was not on the water – Perry said, 'What issues are you interested in?', as if the women's exchange had not taken place, and Charlotte had a sense of where this evening – this holiday – might be going.

'I guess I'm drawn to anything to do with DEI,' Tabitha said.

'That's diversity, equity and inclusion,' Benedict translated.

'Thank you, darling,' Charlotte said, 'but I did just do some work for a protein drink brand whose MD is thirty-five. An uber millennial. So rest assured I've been re-educated.'

'Hard to know how humanity managed its moral compass before millennials,' Perry said.

'I'm not sure it had one,' Tabitha said with a glorious smile.

'Why don't you take your drinks down to the Nook?' Charlotte said. 'I'll organize some snacks.'

'Good plan,' Benedict said. 'Wait till you see it, Tabs, it's dope.'

'Are you coming, Mango?' Tabitha cajoled, and the dog took a pace back.

'Stranger danger,' Benedict said laughing. 'I hope this isn't one of those, like, *tropes* where the baddie has everyone fooled except the family pet.'

'I'll win her over,' Tabitha said.

*

The tide had that effervescent quality it sometimes did, rousing in Charlotte a false sense of camaraderie as she approached the summerhouse, as if it were rallying expressly to support her and not simply going about its business as a deadly expanse dominating most of the earth's surface.

(Interesting that she should already feel in need of support.)

The tray of nibbles heavy in her hands, she arrived on the veranda just in time to catch Perry's defensive growl in response to

31

something Benedict was saying. She was going to have to remind him to go easy on the youngsters, especially Tabitha; Benedict was, after all, smitten with the girl. In every conversation they'd had this last term, however brief, he'd brought up her name.

'*Are* you, Dad?' he teased. 'I bet you are.'

'Bet he's what?' Charlotte said. The deck was deep, the rattan seating arranged in a sea-facing crescent around a narrow drift-wood table, upon which she now placed the various bowls and plates before settling next to Perry. Their son, taller than both of his parents, was on the sofa, his outstretched legs a tripping hazard, and Tabitha sat next to him, cross-legged, barefoot. Her toenails were the same green as her fingernails.

'Trolling Sadiq Khan on Twitter,' Benedict replied, scooping baba ghanoush with a breadstick and crunching down on it.

Perry placed his phone face down on the table. 'I admit he's top of my list of public servants I'd like to send to the Tower, but no, I wasn't trolling anyone. Just having a quick shufti.' He began rolling up his shirt sleeves. 'Wait, can I still use that word? Is that cultural appropriation?'

'Just quaint boomer slang, Dad. I told you he was addicted,' Benedict added to Tabitha.

Charlotte had looked at Perry's feed once or twice to see what kind of thing he posted and his echo chamber appeared to be one of motorists who despised cyclists:

ffs are there ANY boroughs left in London where you can still drive at 30?

This is discrimination, pure and simple. Cyclists should pay road tax as well, no exemptions.

> @MayorOfLondon Sadiq Khan, you are a hypocrite and
> a bellend.

Still, at least he wasn't going to be stopped for drunk driving.

'What's that white on your elbow, Dad?'

Perry rubbed at it. He bit his nails and so wouldn't be able to pick it off easily. 'Oh, it's just a bit of paint.'

'He's been covering over the latest hate,' Charlotte said, explaining to Tabitha, 'Every time we come down now, there's graffiti on the front wall.'

'Who by? The same people who were at the ferry?' Benedict lifted the bowl of olives and balanced it on the arm of the sofa. 'What did they write?'

'"NJFA". Short for "Not Just for August". That's their name now. Meaning "A house is for life, not just for August". You know,' she told Tabitha, 'as in "A puppy is for life, not just for Christmas"?'

'Oh, right. That's quite clever,' Tabitha said.

'If you consider criminal damage clever,' Perry said, with a visible clench, and Tabitha pulled herself upright, the wine in her glass sloshing.

'No, it's just from *their* point of view, it's justified, isn't it? It must be *terrible* to see outsiders buy these amazing houses in your home town and only use them in the summer, when you can't afford one to live in all year round.'

'Sure,' Perry said. 'I feel the same when I walk through Kensington and Belgravia. No one there from one month to the next. That's *my* home town, but I don't daub obscenities on their wall because they can afford it and I can't. I go back to my own less valuable home and get on with my day.'

'Okay.' Tabitha's expression remained agreeable. 'But *your* home is, I don't know, a really nice place in . . . Dulwich?' She turned to Benedict for confirmation and he nodded, still munching. Eager fingers caressed the back of her neck and Charlotte imagined them depositing flecks of dip in the girl's hair. He'd always been a finger licker, Benedict. Both father and son had an oral fixation, which was not a pleasant thought.

'*Their* home might be someone's living-room floor,' Tabitha continued, earnestly. 'Maybe even a *tent*.'

Charlotte focused on the sky, on the fluorescent blue that preceded sunset. A single bird moving across it, a hobby perhaps. Birdlife in August was sparse, most skulking in the trees before waiting to migrate.

'So what do you suggest?' Perry said. 'That we swap? I can assure you they'll take one look at the running costs of this place and beg to have their tent back.'

'Then maybe the running costs could be part of the deal,' Tabitha said, with the air of being happy to run with a good idea when she heard one.

'What deal is that? Can't I just fund the system that pays their benefits like I always have? With my decades of higher-rate tax?'

Before Benedict could rile him by pointing out that he currently paid no income tax at all, Charlotte intervened. 'The locals aren't on benefits, Perry. They work incredibly hard. In tourism for example. Making our holidays more enjoyable.'

But it was too late, Perry had hit his stride. 'Levelling down, that's what you young people seem to want. Here's a question for you. Who was it who said the problem with socialism is that sooner or later you run out of other people's money to spend?'

Benedict shot Tabitha a look of comic long-suffering. 'Er, Churchill?'

'Nope.'

'Orwell?'

'Orwell *was* a socialist,' Charlotte said. 'Though he was alert to the corruptive nature of all types of power, obviously.'

She wished she hadn't added the 'obviously' when Tabitha looked like she might not know who Orwell was, much less what he'd been alert to. This should have beggared belief, but sadly did not with this generation. The girl had not, after all, been able to identify a pine tree.

'It was Thatcher.' Perry spoke with excessive satisfaction and Charlotte read the looks Benedict and Tabitha now exchanged – *Is our whole holiday going to be like this?* (hers); *I did warn you* (his) – and even though the interpretation was entirely her own, she couldn't help feeling a little betrayed by her son.

'Right. Thatcher. Okay.' With an air of magnanimity, Benedict helped himself to more wine and Charlotte was pleased when Perry let the debate end there. They were going to need to find some other topics of conversation as a four because going at it hammer and tongs on the culture wars was not how she intended spending her precious holiday with her only child.

Meanwhile, let the youngsters share their outrage at the wealth hoarders while drinking £20 rosé supplied by said group. They were students. It would be far worse if they were hard-hearted, dreaming of boots stamping on a human face forever.

Congratulating herself for remembering a quote she'd committed to memory over thirty years ago, she peered up the footpath and wondered what was keeping Amy and Linus.

6

Amy

'Guys,' she yelled. 'Time to go!'

Beattie appeared first, coming out of her bedroom and making a big song and dance about checking the soles of her feet for splinters. Though Amy had laid out a crazy paving of cheap rugs where the previous owner's carpet had been pulled up, they slipped easily out of place. 'Can you not shout, Mum,' she said, her face displeased. 'Like, we're in the world's smallest house?'

'Hardly.' Amy watched her daughter put on a pair of sandals she'd not seen before, Ancient Greek-style, with braided gold straps. 'And be careful who you say that kind of thing to around here. It could sound a bit tone-deaf.'

'Why? Who would want to live here? I'm getting total condemned building vibes.'

In a disappointing reversal of her original position as Amy's chief ally when renovation plans were first discussed, Beattie had developed misgivings when confronted with the reality of staying in the 'before' model. There was no way she was inviting her friends here, she'd declared on arrival, having initially liked the notion of bringing them to hang out on the beach after dark with the local talent. Italy would have been better, obviously, because Italian boys were so fucking hot, but yeah, it'd be sick or fire or whatever the latest import was.

It was all an act, her dumb *Love Island* thing. She was an A-star student, an academic scholar at her academic school. At first it had irritated Amy, but Charlotte had advised a different approach. As long as her grades didn't slip, let her try out these different personas. In the end, it was only clothes, make-up, language. It wasn't her *soul*.

It still ranked as one of the best days of Amy's life when the scholarship offer from Spencer had come through and they were able to share the news with their circle, exchanging shining prideful looks with the fellow successful and groans of commiseration with those whose children had not made the cut.

'I knew she'd get in,' she'd said to Linus. 'She always makes really bold eye contact with authority figures. They love that in a candidate.'

Sometimes, Amy felt embarrassed by how unquestioningly she'd bought into the Spencer cult in those early days. There'd been, she realized, a lack of self-awareness on her part. A renewed focus on her own work as an administrator had helped her restore a sense of balance, albeit now paused on account of her project management duties down here; gradually, she'd learned to give Beattie the space to develop (into what? Best not to think about it).

With Huck, who went to the local comp, she was just glad to see him leave vaguely on time in the morning and come back in the afternoon the same gender.

'How was your wander?' she asked. 'Did you pick up the treatment list from the Needles spa?' It had been her idea that Beattie should go and take a look at the hotel, to satisfy herself that there were plenty of glamorous, structurally sound places to retreat to in Pine Ridge.

'No. I didn't even get there. I took a wrong turn.'

'But it's a straight road.'

'I know. But it kind of forked off and I wasn't concentrating. I ended up by a caravan site maybe?'

It was hard to see how there might be any doubt. 'Up near the ridge? That's Golden Sands Park. I think Charlotte said some of the summer workers live there. Well, we can check out the hotel tomorrow if you like?'

But the mere inference of a mother-daughter expedition was enough to silence the girl. *Never commit*, that was Beattie's motto (which was ironic because the motto of her school was *Always commit*). At least she was ready to leave for the Tuckers', done up to the nines in the knock-off designer gear she'd recently adopted. The Seventies jeans, shirt and grey-framed sunglasses propped on her head were all fake high-end labels, but when you were seventeen and gorgeous you didn't need the real thing. She'd looked just as good in her previous incarnation, a kind of ironic granny chic that had involved penny-pinching thrifting on her part and expensive dry cleaning on Amy's.

'Boys!' Amy advanced through the ramshackle kitchen and took a bottle of wine from the fridge.

'Here, Miss,' Linus said, arriving just ahead of Huck. Both had showered, nut-brown hair combed, pale skin newly charred. Unlike Beattie, both were underdressed to the point of downright disrespect, Huck in the same shapeless clothes he'd travelled in and made dusty schlepping around the garden, Linus in fraying shorts and a T-shirt pasted to his back. It made Amy feel a bit squeamish to see the muscles and sinews bulging in his oversized cyclist's calves.

'I was thinking,' she said. 'Why don't you ask Perry if he wants to go on a bike ride with you?'

'You're having a laugh, aren't you? There's more chance of hell freezing over than him saying yes to that.' Owing to his mild delivery, with its trace of a Scots accent, Linus had the ability to present the steeliest of criticism as gentle fun-poking.

'I just thought it might be nice if you did some activities together.' She and Charlotte had agreed this first summer together offered an excellent opportunity for the men to bond. 'Besides drinking.'

'Why? He's fine with that, I thought.'

'I didn't mean him.' Perry, a reformed alcoholic, had been more than fine on the occasions they'd had dinner together in Dulwich. Sometimes, when a debate was raging, Amy suspected him of goading the less clear-eyed. 'I was thinking about us, actually. We're here for more than four weeks. I don't want to booze every night.'

'Really?' Linus said. '*I* do.'

*

As they approached the beautiful corner plot of Cliff View, the Nook resplendent on the near side, Amy wondered why it was that she always thought of the house as Charlotte's, as if some old-money inheritance had paid for it and not Perry's bonuses from his years in the City. In any case, though the house was ten times grander and more covetable than their bungalow, the Tuckers had paid less for it than they had theirs. No point being galled; they'd all benefited from soaring house prices in London. Respect to the Pine Ridge pioneers, that was Amy's attitude.

'You're here!' Charlotte cried, in imperial holiday mode, her expensively streaked bob freshly tousled, yoga-slim waist accentuated by the smocked bodice of a floral-print dress (designer, no doubt; she worked her Net-a-Porter loyalty card hard). She made introductions for the benefit of the slight, pretty girl cosied up to Benedict, and Amy, Huck and Beattie squeezed into the remaining seats. Linus stayed standing, however, his back to the railing – and the sea – as if he didn't intend staying long.

'Heard about Passatagate,' he said to Perry.

'Let's not confer a grandeur on the episode it doesn't warrant,' Perry said.

'What would you call it then?'

'I'd call it infantile nonsense. I blame Greta Thunberg for all this food throwing. It's tantrums, basically. I mean, why in God's name would you want a teenager as the leader of a global movement?'

'I agree,' Charlotte said. 'What about Roger Federer, now he's retired? No, wait. Hasn't he got a private jet? He'd have to give that up.'

'Not at all. Hypocrisy is overlooked, if not actively encouraged.'

This was standard Tucker banter, but Amy could tell Linus was going to play it straight to rile Perry.

'It wasn't about the climate, though, was it? This protest at the ferry?'

'No, it was about HHH,' Perry said, casting a glance at Benedict's new girlfriend. 'Holiday Home Hostility, for those unaware of the phenomenon.'

'You need to drive down in your Peugeot,' Linus said. 'Range Rovers are always targets. Can't think why.'

Amy sent him a warning look before turning to Tabitha. 'Tell us all about uni. Beattie's about to apply, we'd love your advice.'

'What subject are you thinking of doing?' Tabitha asked Beattie. 'Maybe economics? Or business studies?'

'I thought you wanted to do natural sciences,' Amy said, and Beattie just flicked her hand at her, as if it were none of her business.

'I didn't decide until I was literally filling in the UCAS form,' Tabitha said kindly. 'Like, how are you supposed to know at seventeen how you want to spend your time even a year later?'

'One hundred per cent,' Beattie agreed. Amy had long given up campaigning for the reintroduction of the word 'yes' into her daughter's vocabulary. The way she arranged herself, one arm hooked around a weathered wooden post, the dusk sky behind her, she looked like a starlet magnanimously opening her home to *Architectural Digest*.

Her mind wandered to their own summerhouse. She'd offered it to Huck or his exchange student, but maybe she and Linus could sleep there. Let the kids have the two habitable bedrooms in the bungalow and make the Niche a kind of love nest. Would Linus go for that? Watching his eyes flash as he described to Perry and Benedict the episode in which he'd been knocked off his bike by a rogue cockapoo, resulting in his threat to report the animal to the police, it felt less a stretch than a full-blown Disney fantasy. And since Perry was not only a cyclist-hater but also a dog fanatic, this was not a story to charm his host.

Mango, possibly the most handsome animal she'd seen in her life, lay under her master's chair with outstretched legs and bent elbows, watching the cliff path for intruders.

She tuned back into the girls' conversation; Tabitha was talking now of her extra-curricular pursuits at Bristol, recommending societies, recalling the past year's protests. She had a lovely natural look, Amy thought. Pale skin with a pretty pink flush, navy-blue eyes with feathery lashes.

'You don't have these crazy false eyelashes all the girls have, Tabitha?' she said, when the girl drew breath.

'Mum, don't be judgy,' Beattie said.

'I've got hypersensitive skin,' Tabitha said. 'I actually think they look really great though.'

'I'm quite tempted myself,' Amy said. 'Mine are stubs.'

'They'd look stupid on you,' Beattie said. 'They're not for old people.'

Amy felt no hurt – or at least countered the hurt with the

reminder that to declare it only fuelled the teen's appetite to punish harder. Better to focus on the fact that Huck was laughing with Benedict – actually, really laughing. She wished her two had had more of Benedict's influence these last years, but since the advent of exam season – first his, now Beattie's – the families had rarely come together like this in London.

All the more reason to celebrate this new era.

'That's not what I said,' Perry objected, on her other side, sounding far from celebratory. 'Course I'm in. Looks piss easy.'

'We're going to get paddleboarding lessons together,' Linus told her, with a mischievous smirk. 'Me, Perry and the boys, a nice shared activity.'

'Oh. Great.' She couldn't help wishing the one he'd chosen did not involve taking Huck out to sea; he was not as strong a swimmer as his father.

'*I* want to come,' Tabitha said, but Benedict overruled her.

'Just the boys.'

'That's exclusionary.'

'Not exclusionary, *exclusive*,' Perry corrected her in a tone that struck Amy as a little sharp. 'I don't see why men shouldn't be entitled to a safe space like every other group.'

'What, the middle of the English Channel?' Charlotte said, hooting. 'They're welcome to it, aren't they, girls?'

Tabitha gave a surprisingly girlish giggle, Beattie laughed her sardonic drain laugh, a nice girl acting mean, and Charlotte began telling them about the history of Cliff View, how it used to have a garden twice this size until the previous owners sold half the land and, a generation later, the Rickmans bought it and built Villa Pino.

'It's very nice inside. Quite understated and Scandi. They're out of the UK, so you won't meet them this time.'

'They must be able to charge a fortune on Airbnb,' Tabitha said, which made Amy think of her own bullish financial projections for the bungalow.

'Oh, they don't do holiday lets,' Charlotte said.

'Why not?'

'They don't want the hassle.'

'A choice they are fully entitled to make,' Perry put in.

'So you think their place will be empty for the rest of the year?' Amy said.

'Why?' Charlotte chuckled. 'Thinking of asking if you can rent it while you do your building work?'

'Over my dead body,' Linus said, before Amy could answer. 'We're already paying for two houses. No way are we paying for a third.'

*

It was almost dark by the time they left, dim enough for them to have to pay attention to their footing on the rough path back to the bungalow, their steps inaudible thanks to the noisy slosh of the full tide below. Lights inched across the horizon; a ferry, Amy guessed, bound for France or the Channel Islands.

As they passed Villa Pino, it occurred to her what the weird sensation she'd felt earlier might have been, when she'd checked Huck hadn't fallen over the edge. Because she was having it again now, fainter this time, but definitely the same strain of anxiety.

It wasn't the feeling of something bad having happened, of someone having slipped or fallen. It was more a sensing of *in*action. A cold, deliberate stillness.

The feeling of being watched.

7

Robbie

Instantly, people are yelling to each other in panic. Running, barefoot, shoes snatched up or abandoned. Some are even shielding their kids with their bodies, like a plane just broke up in mid-air and an engine's about to smack down and make a crater of them and their family.

Seems like a bit of an overreaction, if you ask me. I mean, I'm the one who's going to be in the firing line for this, not any of them.

'I think they think the cliff's collapsing,' I tell Shannon, and we stay where we are for a minute and just watch the spot where the house went in, where an almighty fountain exploded from the water. It's actually kind of satisfying the way the sea jumps and sloshes as it rearranges itself around this new entity. A ship gone down. A dog swallowing a treat. In a second, there'll be a bigger wave than usual on the shore. Then there's going to be smashed glass washing up; timber, tiles, furniture, God knows what else. They'll have to close the beach and clean up.

'I can't believe this, Robbie.' Shannon casts me a fearful look. An out-of-her-depth kind of look. 'That's right where we were the other night.'

'I know. Up goes Plod, look.' One of the police officers working the festival is taking the steps up to the cliff path, his hi-vis jacket

44

vivid against the dark rock, while a second positions himself at the foot of the steps, presumably to bar entry to gawkers. There are more of them than in previous years. They've been expecting something, some climactic high jinks, they just didn't know what.

And now they'll think this is it.

'Can't see anyone else rushing up. You'd think the owners'd be up there like a shot.'

'Right. Where are they?' Shannon doesn't question the assumption that the owners must be here on the beach. August bank holiday Monday, great weather, a festival for all the family. This is *the* Pine Ridge experience. 'Unless they've already gone for dinner?'

Sounds about right. They hung around long enough to judge (correctly) that the band was crap and hightailed over to The Needles for a last lobster burger and thrice-cooked truffle fries or whatever they serve down there, before hitting the road back to London first thing tomorrow. Because they're DFLs of course. Even if we hadn't had the interaction with the Pine Ridge Road residents that we have, we all know what they are.

A voice that isn't the singer's comes over the system: 'I'm very sorry to advise you that for health and safety reasons we need to end the festival early. We apologize for any disappointment this causes. Please be patient exiting the car park.' There's a hideous screech of feedback and then the mic cuts out. After that, the band starts packing up and the remains of the crowd start making their way to the car park and bus stops.

Looks like the bar's stopped serving, pints left on the tables half drunk or dropped on the sand. There's no sign of Tate, so he must be out back or – not ideal – on his break.

Just so long as someone can vouch for him.

I fish my phone from my pocket and put in a call to him, but it goes straight to voicemail. 'Let's go to the Gull,' I say to

Shannon. 'I'll see if the others are around. Rio was here a minute ago, wasn't he?'

As we head over the dunes towards Old Beach Road, I look back across the beach and notice a new arrival at the foot of the cliff steps. Young, female, up on tiptoes as she cranes over the shoulder of the officer – even from this distance, you can see how self-assured she is, how determined.

I know who she is, of course. She's been a presence this summer. She's been a presence today.

'By the way, your flies are undone,' Shannon says. 'You didn't piss in the dunes, did you? That's so gross.'

I zip myself up. The flush in my face is purely from the alcohol, I swear. 'Seriously,' I tell her. 'You don't want to know.'

8

Charlotte

Earlier in August

As Beattie Shaw got to her feet and began flicking grains of sand off her long bare thighs, Charlotte thought of that old Stranglers song about beaches and peaches, because there was not a male eye in range that did not swivel in the girl's direction.

She'd been in jeans and a long-sleeved top the previous evening and it was only now she wore a swimsuit that you could fully appreciate her metamorphosis. When it had taken place, Charlotte wasn't quite sure, for Beattie had been absent for most of Easter, away on a school trip, and in any case it had been too cold for swimwear, but last summer, when the Shaws had rented a cottage on Bird Lane, she'd been fleshier, paler, draped in oversized hoodies even when on the beach. Now she was the product of regular gym workouts, fake tan of some sort (high quality, no smears) and wore an extraordinary plunging black halterneck swimsuit with a horn buckle at the waist. Her honey-coloured hair was partly pinned on her head, partly loose on her shoulders, with cute bleached tails.

Truly, it was like Bardot had rocked up in Pine Ridge. What must Amy think? What must *Linus* think?

Well, nothing right now since they'd driven on this glorious August afternoon to the B&Q in Bournemouth. Charlotte remembered those early months – years, really – of holiday-homeowning.

Everyone assumed you were sitting at the water's edge shucking oysters and knocking back the bubbles when in reality you were standing in the queue of a DIY superstore or plumbers' merchant wondering where you were going to find the washer you needed to fit the shower since they'd inconveniently sold out and didn't have the first idea when it would be back in stock.

'I love your sunglasses, Beattie,' she said. 'Can I try them on?'

'Sure.' The girl handed them to her – they had large amber lenses and a fine, well-crafted feel to the frames – and said how nice they looked on her, even as Perry laughed out loud.

'You look like you're in some Seventies am-dram production.'

'What's am-dram?' Beattie said and Charlotte explained.

'Two generations divided by a common language,' Perry quipped, which meant nothing to Beattie either. She took back her shades and picked her way across the sand to the water. As she entered the shallows – famously clear, Caribbean placid – there was something very sensuous about the way she put one foot in front of the other, as if savouring the drag of the water on her shins. Really, the cut of that swimsuit at the back was stunning, contriving somehow to extend the girl's legs while preserving her modesty. Too many other women (and, God forbid, men) were wearing thongs this summer.

'What's stunning?'

She turned at the sound of Benedict's voice behind her – she hadn't realized she'd spoken out loud – and looked across her husband's prone figure towards the two students. Benedict was on his front, Tabitha her back, her head propped up on a wedge-shaped inflatable. Their legs were intertwined, Benedict's longer limbs overshooting the beach blanket, his bony toes digging into the sand.

'Beattie's swimsuit,' she said.

'It's fake designer,' Tabitha said. 'She gets stuff online from Vietnam. She's going to send me the link.' She seemed to catch herself, presumably realising that consuming counterfeit fashion was a little unethical for someone with her credentials. Charlotte vaguely remembered seeing an article about students marching in protest down Counterfeit Alley in Manchester or wherever it was.

'Wouldn't mind having a look myself. Honestly, she looks just like that famous *Vogue* shoot with Jerry Hall.'

'Who's Jerry Hall?'

She suppressed a sigh; clearly this holiday was going to involve a fair bit of explaining cultural references to the Zoomers. 'You know, the model. Tall and blonde and Texan? Married to Mick Jagger and Rupert Murdoch – maybe someone else as well, actually. Not all at the same time. That would be polygamy.'

'Polyandry when it's the woman who's doing it,' Perry said.

'Well, she's got an amazing wardrobe, that's for sure. I only ever see her in her school uniform at home.'

Beattie was submerged now, a bobbing golden head in the glitter. Not far beyond her, a jet ski was weaving through the yellow buoys, treating them like slalom poles. It was far too close to the swimmers. At the lifeguard station, two guards chatted, necks bent over a phone. There'd be a horrible accident if they didn't watch out, Charlotte thought. Banned on Old Beach but hired out from other centres on the coast, jet skis were, in her view, a menace.

'What's the subject of your master's, Tabitha?' she asked, regretting the question even before learning the answer, which had something to do with the persecution of non-binary groups in North Korea. She didn't blame Perry for draping his forearm over his face, his hand covering the ear closest to their guest.

'Oh, I didn't know that was a thing there,' she said.

'I wouldn't call it a "thing",' Tabitha said. She was extremely precise about language, Charlotte had noticed. 'The problem of inherited gender roles is a lived experience across the globe.'

'You don't plan on going out there, do you? To do your research? It is possible, isn't it, if you get on one of those government-sanctioned tours?'

'Maybe. I'll probably just reach out online,' Tabitha said. 'It's terrible how people don't care,' she added, casting her gaze beyond their own group, not so much critical as wounded. Benedict gave her arm a little squeeze.

Just so long as *he* didn't book himself a flight to Pyongyang, Charlotte thought. She was starting to wonder about an Aperol from the beach bar, but she tried to avoid daytime drinking in support of Perry. She admired his sobriety, of course she did, she depended on it, knew how hard it had been to achieve and continued to be to sustain, and yet there were times when she secretly admitted to herself that he was a less appealing playmate for it. A bit *diminished*.

Shameful, but true.

Voices carried from the shore, posh London ones, a mum and a dad:

'Move your arms, darling! *That's* it!'

'Well done, Isabel!'

'Look at your sister swimming! Isn't she clever? *Clever* Isabel!'

'She's going to be in the Olympics one day!'

Had she and Perry been this emphatic, this public, in their praise of Benedict? She was fairly confident they had not. Certainly not as a couple, anyway. Perry, if he'd been there at all, had been on his Nokia or Blackberry or whatever the device du jour had been back in the Noughties. Beer in hand, or something stronger, leaving Charlotte to do the heavy lifting.

Not that she minded, particularly. The problem with men being involved in things was the positive reinforcement *they* required. Just children by another name.

She felt the tickle of hot sand on her legs as Benedict and Tabitha tripped past her to join Beattie in the water.

'Pity the poor North Koreans,' Perry groaned. 'How long's she staying, do we know?'

Charlotte checked that Huck was safely out of earshot – he had earbuds in and his head nodded gently to music – before replying. 'At least two weeks, I think. Their plans are "fluid".'

'I bet they are.'

'She's harmless,' Charlotte said. 'Let's not fall out with them, Perry. We can save our outmoded views for when we're on our own.'

'Outmoded,' he scoffed, and removed his sunhat to reveal a band of sweat-dampened hair. 'I notice our bank account's current enough.'

'Ha.'

As Perry flopped back, Charlotte stood to adjust her parasol. The sun was fierce and there was not the breeze they got up on the headland. Before resettling with her book, she reached to touch the sarong Beattie had left on her towel in a jewel-coloured pool. Expecting to feel something cheap and synthetic, she was surprised to find it was pure silk. And as beautifully stitched as a made-to-measure wedding gown.

Which made no sense at all.

She scooped up her phone and took a picture of the label.

9

Amy

Settling in the hollow where the top of the cliff steps met the barrier of granite chunks that protected pedestrians from the drop, she pinched the screen of her phone and zoomed in as closely as the camera app would allow.

She wasn't the type to spy on her teenagers, God no, but occasionally she burned with the primitive need to know they were still alive.

Maybe it was to do with that weird turn she'd had last night. It had occurred to her on waking that there might be an obvious explanation for this feeling of being watched: the Rickmans might have let Villa Pino after all and one of the occupants been standing at the window. But when she'd tried the bell that morning, there'd been, once again, no response. The windows had plantation shutters, so it was impossible to peer in.

The scene on the beach looked innocent enough. The couples on the posh yellow hire loungers, some sharing with toddlers in sunsuits and hats; elsewhere, round-bellied, spindly-armed older men and their younger counterparts with the reverse: narrow waists and bulked-up arms. The middle-aged women in impressive nick, their daughters lean and lovely, except for their terrible tattoos. Tattoos were Amy's greatest parenting fear, bordering on a phobia (she'd googled it and found it was called tatouazophobia, which sounded made-up), to the extent that she could no longer watch dramas involving yakuza or look at those photos of prisoners in El Salvador's mega-prisons.

The breeze blew a strand of pale hair over the camera and she tucked it behind her ear. Ah, *there* was Charlotte. Stretched out on a lounger in a blue swimsuit and straw Panama hat, hardback novel propped on her bent knee.

And Huck, only half parked on a ruched-up towel, relaxing with his music. She hoped it wasn't grime, like the vile song she'd heard coming from his room about main hoes sucking elephants or whatever it was. Linus had had to have a word.

It had been the effect on Huck when they'd first come to Pine Ridge for a weekend with Charlotte that had led Amy to set up the alert for the Coastal Home Agency and the other property sites. Withdrawn and sullen for the whole of Year 9, he'd been relaxed and cooperative during their stay, with significantly fewer disaster documentaries consumed. A subsequent ten-day stay in an Airbnb on Bird Lane had elicited a similar boost to his mood.

Once the decision about the holiday home had been made, there had been quite a wait for a property to come up. Agents were getting thousands of calls a day, the media reported, sharp-elbowed city folk buying places sight unseen in a bid to base themselves somewhere more bucolic. She still remembered holding her breath as she read a travel piece in *The Times* entitled 'Ten Best Beach Villages for Lockdown Leavers'. Mercifully, Pine Ridge had missed the cut.

It was only as people were trickling back to the office that the bungalow had come up. Having not been modernized since it was built in the Sixties, it was not listed on Coastal Home or the smarter sites, but that hadn't stopped it from being grossly overpriced. Amy's friend Julia, who worked for one of the big estate agencies in London, said that even though everything that came up for sale on the south coast was either vastly overpriced or disastrously flawed, it still went under offer instantly. It was literally money for old rope, she said.

'Well, only if the house is made of rope,' Amy said. (Actually, the bungalow *had* had rope incorporated into its garden design but she'd already torn that out. Nautical styling was the ultimate holiday home cliché, according to Charlotte.)

Predictably, Linus had baulked. 'That can't be the right price. For a place that size? One floor? I'd expect a massive beach house with a pool for that.'

'Come on, even Perry and Charlotte haven't got a pool. They devalue a place, I read. The running costs put people off. Plus, this is right on the cliff path. It would destabilize it.'

'Wait, Pine Ridge Road? Then it must be right next door to their place?'

'Not right next door. There's a house in between.'

'Oh well,' he said, 'in that case they won't find it creepy at all.'

'I genuinely think it will make all the difference to Huck. The only times in the last year I've seen him look happy were when he was down there. London can be very harmful to more sensitive teens and we all know how demonized middle-class boys are right now. We don't want him rebelling, Linus. Getting mixed up in county lines or something. Doing drugs.'

Linus's eyebrows shot up. Drug abuse – the dead-eyed injecting themselves between their toes – was to him what tattoos were to her. 'Then let's talk about moving out of town. Get somewhere decent, not this wreck.'

'We can't take Beattie out of Spencer. Besides, all their friends are here. And ours.'

'True.'

A business plan had been produced to illustrate the vast sums

54

they could earn in holiday rental once the place was done up. For the next three years, their visits would be restricted by school terms, which left most of June, July and September to let it out at high season rates. A few reminders about the challenging cycling routes inland and Linus was persuaded.

The mortgage was added to the existing one on the Dulwich house, swollen with equity. The cash deposit, a series of small inheritances that had become quite sizeable with investment, was supposed to be for the kids' first flats, but they were only seventeen and fifteen and Julia said the average first-time buyer in the UK was now thirty-four. Plenty of time to build the fund up again.

*

Finally, she thought. *There she is*. Beattie, up by the water sports kiosk, at the centre of the cluster of young people that included Benedict and Tabitha, all with wet hair and sunburnt faces. She was in her new black swimsuit and that lovely teal and pink sarong Amy had admired that morning.

'Pareo, not sarong,' Beattie corrected her and even though Amy suspected they were the same thing she'd thought to herself, imagine knowing the word 'pareo' at seventeen. Perhaps Beattie was destined for a career as a fashion entrepreneur, which would be a shame given her talent for science, but the girl wasn't quite so self-involved as to have missed the growing profile of her father's start-up and was likely inspired by that.

She was certainly proving adept at sourcing bargains.

Her pulse picked up: just a few feet from the group stood a man who was weirdly, unnaturally still. Watching Beattie intently and not even hiding the fact, shading his eyes with his fingers to get a better look.

'All right there?'

She jumped at the weight of a palm on her shoulder. Perry, hot-faced from the climb up the steps. 'Perry. Hi. You gave me a fright. You're not on the beach with Charlotte?'

He gave her an amused smile. *Well, obviously.* 'Checking on Mango. Poor thing, cooped up up here. Charlotte mentioned the petition about allowing dogs on the beaches all day, did she? The 10 a.m. rule is absurd.'

'Yes, I've signed it,' Amy said.

'What're you doing? Getting a few pictures for the socials?'

'I just . . . Actually, I'm a bit worried there's some guy staring at the girls.'

'Sorry to have to break it to you, but males are biologically hardwired to stare at totty.'

Totty? Sometimes he lapsed into what she assumed was his Nineties banker parlance. Banter, mockery, casual misogyny. Stories of when he and the boys got spangled on private planes to Vegas, a hooker on each arm at the roulette wheel. (Charlotte had confided that he'd been known to refer to #MeToo as #MeNeither – purely for shock effect, of course.)

'I don't care. There's a point where it's harassment.' She handed him her phone, guided it to the man in question. 'The one in the turquoise shorts. A vile staring pervert.'

'There are pervs everywhere, Amy. Especially on beaches. If you go down past The Needles, there's a nudist beach. Did Charlotte tell you that? Not that I'm saying nudists are perverts, just, you know, more *liberated* than most. That's where I'd go if I really wanted to stare.' He gave a hoot of laughter.

Amy suppressed a sigh. 'Do you know him? Is he local?'

'I have no idea.'

For a couple who'd had a holiday home here for fifteen years, the Tuckers knew very few people beyond their neighbours on Pine

Ridge Road and the other second-homers. Their policy was to keep themselves to themselves and avoid local politics unless it involved campaigning for an arthouse cinema or for dogs' rights to pee on sandcastles 24/7. Linus was shaping up into broadly the same beast, bar an interest in local road races, but Amy had different instincts. In her five months of ownership to date, she'd already attended two community meetings and planned to go to another this month that, according to the *Voice*, offered the opportunity to pose questions directly to the council's housing committee.

The incidents at the ferry, the graffiti, the flyers: it couldn't be more obvious that there were serious issues.

Perry handed her back her phone. 'He'll be gone by the end of the day. Supposed to rain this evening.'

As if rain deterred a sex offender! She tried to ignore the prickling suspicion that this man might have something to do with yesterday's mood of unease.

Perry headed on and she allowed herself another minute before returning to the bungalow, where Linus would by now have taken stock of the B&Q haul and be wanting to share the news that they'd forgotten something crucial and needed to go back. She reactivated the camera. The stalker was on his way to the water, while Beattie was on the move in the other direction, to the beach bar, where she joined the queue. Coke Zero was her tipple, she'd be getting one for £3 even though Amy had stocked them in the fridge to save unnecessary expense.

Heading home, she noticed open shutters at the windows of the top floor of neighbouring Villa Pino, the ones that opened onto a little sun terrace. It had views to die for, Charlotte said, though it was not for those with a fear of heights.

Strange, Amy could have sworn all the shutters had been closed when she'd passed earlier.

10

Beattie

She recognized him straight away, the dude from the caravan site. So he worked at the beach bar: *that* was a nice surprise, since she planned on hanging here on a daily basis. There was nothing else to do, after all; staying up at the bungalow only got her roped into cleaning or helping her brother with some science project he would never have bothered with if their mum hadn't been totally fixated and constantly threatening to get him a tutor.

Queuing, she thought how much hotter he was than she remembered. A total snack. Not super-tall, but an inch or two more than her five-nine, with wide-set dark eyes, straight brows, a mouth that curled at the corners. He looked just like that singer from a million years ago who got screwed over by his creepy manager and they just made a movie about it.

Elvis, that was it.

There were two of them working the bar, but she got Elvis while his colleague served the group behind her.

'Hey. You're not lost today then?' He spoke in a low growl lifted by a cute local accent.

'Not yet. Nice office,' she said, with a half turn to the idyllic setting. She saw him check out her bare shoulders – she'd crossed her pareo over her swimsuit and tied the ends in a halter-neck, which made her shoulders look muscular and strong.

'Best beach on the south coast, they say.'

She detected scepticism in his tone. 'What, you don't think so?'

'Hard to say when you grow up here. You're just used to it.' He shovelled ice cubes into the plastic cup for her Coke Zero. He had amazing Japanese tattoos all up his arms, with masks and blossoms and some kind of cool fish with perfectly drawn scales.

He handed her the drink, held out the card reader. Beattie paid and took a slurp. The ice bobbed against her upper lip. There was no one waiting, so she stayed where she was, swaying slightly to the song playing on the bar's speakers: 'Female of the Species'.

'Cool playlist.'

'Yeah. My boss is pretty wedded to his Nineties dance. Says it makes the Gen Xers spend more.'

'So are there any, like, clubs in this place?' She already knew the answer, of course, because Benedict had been coming here for years. Last summer, she'd gone out with him a couple of times and it had all been beyond lame.

'Probably not anything like you're used to,' he said smiling.

'Which is?'

'London clubs. They're a million times better.'

She flared her eyes at him, aiming for playful, maybe a bit wicked. 'How do you even know I'm from London?'

'It's just obvious.' He met her gaze, challenging her to hold it, to look at him properly.

'Where do *you* hang out then?'

'Me and my mates go to the Gull. Far end of Old Beach Road?' He leaned across the bar to gesture to the newer part of the village, coming close enough for her to feel his body heat. The pub was in the distance, slightly elevated. Grey and ugly. 'You should come. They might ID you, mind. How old are you?'

'I've got ID,' she said evasively. Not that being seventeen was a problem as far as she was concerned, but he looked a bit older, mid-twenties maybe. She saw him glance over her shoulder, where some old guy waited to be served. 'You want me to go?'

'No. No. Stay. I'm almost on my break anyway.' He directed the waiting man to his colleague, then returned his attention to her, mouth curving. A lick of black hair fell onto his forehead and he pushed it back with long tanned fingers. 'Missing your boyfriend, then? Up in London?'

'No.' Let him decide whether that meant no she wasn't missing him or no she didn't have one in the first place. She already knew he had a girlfriend because the guy he'd been with when they met had said so. 'Your girlfriend, who works at the hotel. What's her name?'

He drank from a bottle of water before answering. 'Ellie.'

'Do you live with her?' It was bold to ask, but useful to know since she had no meeting place to offer and, in any case, she'd found boys responded well to direct questions. Then, when he nodded, 'What, at the hotel?'

He chuckled. 'No chance. I mean there *is* some staff accommodation, but we're in a caravan – in Golden Sands Park, opposite where we saw you yesterday? She sublets it from her parents' mates. I'd be homeless if I wasn't shacking up with her.'

This was a surprising admission, and she was fairly sure not just a line to make her think he wasn't *really* attached but in fact a free agent. It was more like an unplanned confession to a stranger.

'Why would you be homeless? You've got a job.'

'Yeah, but there's nowhere to live. No rentals, no council properties. Not in Pine Ridge, anyway. They're all holiday lets now. You grow up here and you either stay with your mum forever or you leave. We're not even meant to be in the caravan longer than a month, but management turn a blind eye. And the council. To keep us off their backs because when there *is* a rental there's like two hundred people going for that one place.'

'That's terrible!' Beattie knew better than to ask about the possibility of buying because she knew from her parents' endless discussions that prices down here were almost on a par with London, even for the dump they'd bought. Her mum had already hinted that she'd get help for her first flat. 'Is it all right? I mean, is there water and electricity and stuff?'

'Yeah. Though apparently the pipes freeze in winter, so it can get pretty rough. I've only been there since April, so we'll see. Where are you staying? You said you're not at The Needles? Are you at the Staywell then?'

'No. My mum and dad have just bought a house here.'

'Seriously?' He gave a short laugh, not bitter, more ironic. 'I shouldn't be fraternising with you then. I'm a member of NJFA.'

'Oh.' She knew this was the anti-second homes group, but couldn't remember what the initials stood for. 'Is that the people who throw, like, ketchup over cars? Down by the ferry?'

'It's soup. But yeah. We're against people buying houses and only using them in the summer. They're empty the rest of the time while locals have to, like I just said, slum it in caravans and shit.'

'Wow.' She breathed out, gave him an apologetic smile. 'Looks like we've got a conflict of interests here.'

His gaze lingered on her mouth. 'I'm all right with that if you are.'

It wasn't a question and was so much sexier that way. Behind her, a tremendous shriek rose from somewhere on the beach, human or seagull she couldn't tell, and neither she nor he looked up to find out.

'So how long are you around for?' he said.

She shifted her weight from one foot to the other, felt her thighs meet. 'The whole month.'

'Amazing. If you give me your number, I can let you know if I hear about any parties. What do you girls call them? Motives?'

Her smile widened. 'If we're time-travelling back to 2018, er, sure. I'll bring my Glossier Boy Brow.'

'I have no clue what that is. Remember I'm just a yokel.' He grabbed his phone from behind the bar, held it aloft, smirking back at her. She told him her number and he tapped it in. 'I'm Tate, by the way.'

'Beattie,' she said, spelling it out. She wondered if his girlfriend checked his phone for female contacts. He had to be the hottest guy in this place, she must be a *bit* possessive. Beattie was unusual, though, so maybe he could pass it off as male.

'Promise I won't send you dick pics or any of that crap you probably get at uni,' he said.

'Sixth form college,' she said and watched for his reaction. He looked cool with the information.

His gaze left her to take in a couple who'd arrived beside her and were surveying the drinks list. The woman was wearing a gorgeous bikini. Beattie had three, one white, one pink and a multi-coloured one with swirls, but this one was nicer, black with red and white beads on the ties.

She picked up her drink. 'Bye then.'

'Bye, Beattie,' he said, and he gave her a sexy slow-burn look she knew she'd bring to mind later when she was alone.

As it was, she tripped away feeling really quite woozy, the beach and everyone on it lost for a moment in the post-Tate dazzle.

*

God knew where they would hook up, if they did, because it was impossible to imagine him in her horrible little bedroom next to the kitchen, even if the bungalow was empty, which it never was.

In her absence, a new blind had been fitted to her window. Her mum was in dungarees again, her thin blonde hair scraped back so you could see bits of grey in the roots, which made Beattie feel a bit queasy.

'Make sure you keep it closed when you're undressing. You can see in from the footpath.'

'What are you talking about? There's no way anyone's looking from all the way down there.'

'Well, there're neighbours as well. I thought I saw someone at the window next door. Gave me the creeps a bit.'

'Uh. You're really selling it, Mum. Anyway, Benedict's mum said next door's empty all summer.'

'Hmm. I'm not sure about that.'

At the sight of her mum's pinched expression, Beattie felt a bubbling of irritation. 'You always do this!'

'Do what?'

'Get all paranoid.'

'When have I ever been paranoid?'

'Like when I lost my passport and you thought someone was going to steal my identity and run, like, frauds in my name.' After a short period of crisis, the passport had been found in Beattie's rucksack from her biology trip to Costa Rica.

'Scoff all you like,' her mum said, 'but one day you'll cross paths with one of these fraudsters and you'll wish you'd taken me seriously. These people are sociopathic, Beattie. They empty bank accounts and destroy lives without a thought.'

'I'm sure they do, Mum.' Beattie turned away. Honestly, her parents were maniacs. 'I'm sure they do.'

11

Tate

After his shift finished, he took the path along the dunes to the far end of Old Beach for the NJFA meeting in the Gull. With every step his eyes drifted to the right, to the girls still splayed out in the evening sun, and it seemed to him that every flick of the hand was an invitation, every glance his way a come-on. Seriously, there were times when doing this job, spending all day handing iced drinks to women in bikinis and watching drops of condensation slide down their wrists to their elbows, made you feel like a fucking sex addict. His boss Gav said it was the opposite with him. All that nudity, summer after summer, had desensitized him; he was a surgeon who'd learned to overcome his natural revulsion for human innards.

Tate thought that made him sound like a real psycho.

It helped, sometimes, to focus on the marks on the bodies rather than the bodies themselves: moles, insect bites, patches of leg hair missed by the razor, tattoos. He saw a lot of ink in an average day. Birds on buttocks, flowers between shoulder blades, barbed wire around ankles. Snakes and circles and love hearts. Occasionally he'd recognize one as the work of his friend Des, who'd done most of Tate's own.

He knew that his interaction with the girl – *Beattie*, God, even the name had an erotic ring to it – had upped the heat for sure. Got his hormones racing. The sex drought at home was also

64

a factor. No, not 'home' – since that horrible realisation that the caravan park had wormed its way into his muscle memory, he'd made a point of never calling it that. *We're not meant to be there for longer than a month*, he'd told Beattie, and yet he'd been there for four so far!

Toeing bits of shell and pine cones from the sandy path, he wondered about the alternatives. The winter kipping in the box-room at Rio's mum's hadn't been a total disaster; he'd only left because Ellie had asked him to move in with her, not because he'd been thrown out. Des had taken his place, but there were other boxrooms and it wasn't like he'd be sleeping rough.

He left the dune path and crossed to Old Beach Road. The Gull was heaving. He beat his way through the mob in the main bar to take the stairs to the smaller bar upstairs where the group met. This summer, NJFA meetings had become so frequent they were almost an every-other-day routine, those absent through work or other commitments updated by Robbie on their WhatsApp group after the event. Management was cool about hosting activists; most of their customers being locals or day trippers, they had nothing to lose. The enemy drank at the beach bar (Gav knew about Tate's 'radical tendencies' but was prepared to overlook them, Tate being such a babe magnet) or, till late, down at The Needles.

This evening, there were about ten of them, mostly on their feet for a view of the TV screen on the far wall, and Tate soon saw why: Robbie was on the regional BBC news. It happened now and again, when reporters were doing a segment about the housing crisis in coastal communities and couldn't be bothered to travel to Cornwall or Wales. He remembered now Robbie telling him about it a week or so ago. Ellie had given him a haircut specially for it.

They had him standing outside his old house at the top of Bird Lane, with a reporter asking questions from off camera.

Reporter: So this is where you grew up?

Robbie: That's right. This is the foot of the ridge, so you've got the woods behind and the sea down below. From that top window you get an amazing view of the dunes and the water.

Reporter: When did you move out, Robbie?

Robbie: When I was sixteen. My mum got the eviction notice when I was doing my GCSEs and we had to move to temporary accommodation. The landlord sold to the highest bidder, a couple from London who turned it into a holiday lets business.

Reporter: What's the harm in that? We all need a break, don't we?

Robbie: Yes, absolutely. It's not that we begrudge city people their holidays, but by definition it's seasonal. For at least half of the year this place is empty. And you have to remember that every time the usage changes like this, it's one less family that gets to grow up here. Follow that to its logical conclusion and eventually you have no permanent population at all. No families, no school, no library. No real community. It's basically extinction.

Tate had to admit his best friend was TV gold. He looked like a bit of rough but sounded refined – intelligent and reasonable. He was never impatient, even though he'd been asked these questions a hundred times before, or so angry he risked being dismissed as a crank or a gammon.

When they'd formed NJFA during the pandemic, he'd been the natural choice for leader. He put in the hours. He knew the stats.

And, besides, he was a real victim of all of this. It was horrific what had happened to his mum and typically discreet of him not to weaponize it on camera.

Now he was walking down the path of the cottage and knocking on the door, the house number pixelated, though easily identifiable by any local. There was no answer – they were probably out paddleboarding or eating £5 gelatos – and he peered through the front window, turning to the interviewer with a rueful smile.

Robbie: It looks nothing like it did when I lived here with my mum. They've knocked the downstairs rooms through and done it up. I can see a lot of beach knick-knacks, you know what I mean? I'm not sure I'd recognize it if it weren't for the number on the door. It used to be a home, but if you ask me, what it is now is a trophy. Hardly different from an elephant tusk or a tiger skin.

Reporter: That's quite a disturbing image, Robbie.

Robbie: I know. It's quite a disturbing situation.

Tate had known the cottage almost as well as his own home. Birthday parties, sleepovers, all-night gaming marathons. Smoking weed out of the window in the turret room, polluting that fresh pine air with their illicit toxins. After a while, the view used to go all fuzzy, like the horizon was swarming with swallows or something. Not even ten years ago and yet it felt completely distant, unreal.

Robbie had been all set to go to uni, but when his mum died, he had to scrap that and stay to sort things out. Went full-time at Jevons Motors in Crowland, which was owned by his uncle and where he'd previously had a Saturday job. Lived with his

67

uncle's family as well for a few years. Then he'd started going out with Shannon, who'd been living with her parents in their static in Golden Sands Park, and they'd kept an eye out for one of the tourers coming free. Just temporary, of course, but they all knew what that meant.

Tate had passed his friends' caravan last night on his way back from the shower block and it had been creaking, very faintly. You could tell what they were doing in there.

Stop bringing everything back to sex!

He returned his attention to the news segment, in which a couple of dissenting voices had been rolled out, among them Gav. Figured. He had an 'I'm all right, Jack' attitude and had built his own house in Poole.

Gav: Obviously, here at the beach bar we're part of the tourist industry and our policy is to treat every customer the same. People just want to have a good time, not be lectured about who's entitled to be here and who isn't. This is a free country, isn't it? Pine Ridge has always been a holiday destination – everyone's welcome, as far as I'm concerned.

Next came was the familiar face of Katy, owner of Fleur, the boutique around the corner from the deli where Shannon worked.

Katy: It's up to the council to decide on housing matters. They're our elected representatives. To my mind, it's not right what the protesters are doing. We don't want Pine Ridge associated with violence and abuse. Local businesses value holidaymakers' trade. Why would we want to bite the hand that feeds us?

There'd be no reprisals for public dissent like this, not from NJFA anyhow, because Robbie said infighting was a distraction from the main cause. They would not fall for the old divide and rule tactics, oh no; their fellow Pine Ridgers were not the enemy, whatever their views. No, the enemy was the rich second-homers, people like the owners of Robbie's former home.

People like Beattie's parents.

The feature ended with video of the NJFA group assembled on the roadside, placards lowered as Robbie addressed them, like Gareth Southgate giving the lads a half-time pep talk. Not unlike the scene in the pub, where the group now clapped and whistled and cried out in celebration.

Robbie held his hands up, modest, resigned to their adulation. 'It's never too late to get our homes back,' he said, more emotional than usual, and the cheer went up again. Then he outlined his latest idea: to name and shame the houses standing empty this month via time-lapse videos released across social media. *Empty in August*, they'd call it (he was keen on sub-brands), targeting the bastards who hadn't even bothered coming down in the height of summer.

More approval from the troops. But Tate struggled to feel the same unquestioning zeal as his fellows. Robbie's mantra was that it was never too late, but it seemed to Tate that this was exactly what it was, not least because none of the locals ever squared up to their own complicity. The people of Pine Ridge, people like Robbie's mum's old landlord, born and bred in the village, had not had their properties seized by a fascist state, they'd not had family members held hostage till they signed on the dotted line. They'd willingly sold to the highest bidder, simple as that.

He tuned back in. 'Wait till you hear the *really* genius idea,' Robbie was saying, drawing fresh energy from the group. 'It's gonna take a bit of persuasion, mind.'

'Who of, Rob? The council?'

Robbie snickered. 'No, the missus.'

*

Tate left the meeting early, claiming to be meeting Ellie but in fact going back down to the beach and hanging out by the water sports hut. It was closed for the evening, the kayaks and pedalos stored on the sands in multi-coloured stacks. He watched the last of the girls roll up their beach blankets and slip on their flip-flops and smooth their long hair over burnished shoulders and all the other things girls did and he thought again of Beattie. She was up for it, that much had been clear.

He took his phone from his back pocket and texted her: *What u doin?*

Maybe he could get her to come and meet him. Get to know each other a bit. There were plenty of hidden places in the dunes, as well as the pillbox on the clifftop down past the Meadow. There was not a person who'd grown up in Pine Ridge who hadn't taken refuge there for one reason or another.

He waited for a reply, his foot tapping. He thought of Robbie and his innate command, the way he oozed purpose, and it made him feel aimless by comparison.

He waited a bit longer but there was still no reply.

The last of the girls were walking towards Old Beach Road, so he got to his feet and went after them.

12

Perry

'Right. Everyone ready?'

'Yes, Rio,' they chorused, and his ear singling out Linus, Perry was pretty damn sure he detected a challenge in his tone.

They and their sons stood on the shore in a ragged little sun-beaten squad, life vests fitted, paddles adjusted to the correct length, while Beattie and Tabitha took photos from the water and mocked them. He tried not to think of his pale breadstick legs being disparaged by strangers on Instagram. His nerves felt disproportionate to the experience ahead, as if they were about to be whisked to a crocodile-infested island for some survival reality show. Who of the four of them would triumph in a male-only arena? Would father sacrifice son or son father? Would Linus savage Perry or Perry Linus?

It had been too much to hope that talk of paddleboarding remained just that – or even just a one-off. Linus, not content with racing the country lanes on his eight-grand bike (it hadn't taken long for him to drop that little nugget), had booked a course of four and paid in full. Non-refundable.

Their instructor dragged his eyes from the girls, now sauntering past and back to their towels, and led the group into the shallows. (Rio: too young to have been named after the Duran Duran song, Perry thought, so it must have been Rio Ferdinand.) They waded after him, getting used to the sensation of the leash around their ankles, and copied his technique for mounting their boards and finding a kneeling position.

Perry had kayaked a bit with Benedict when he was younger and had forgotten how peaceful it was once you got past the pedalos and the swimmers. Only the louder voices carried: 'The water's so clear!' 'My turn!' 'Can you still touch the bottom?' Then, causing a pang that felt unique in its treachery: 'Time for a beer!'

And Rio's voice, closer. 'Everyone feeling steady? Stay spaced out,' he called as Benedict drifted a little too close to Huck.

As the shore shrank, you really appreciated how undeveloped the coastline was, the ugliest buildings being the Gull and the Staywell, the latter up behind the new village, the mostly 1970s zone where the locals lived – and even that was discreet enough not to impinge on the ridge skyline. Best was the view of Cliff View. You could tell it had been there for centuries, it owned its spot – unlike the Shaws' bungalow, which was scarcely visible beyond the pines, a nondescript slug of a thing, the street's poor relation by anyone's standards.

He wondered if Linus was looking up and thinking the same. Probably not, since he was struggling to keep afloat, in contrast to Huck, who'd picked it up fast and was the first to his feet. Meanwhile, Benedict's height seemed to disadvantage him – or maybe he was exhausted by all that sex with Tabitha, the sounds of which were unmissable every night.

Probably the only time she stopped going on about the oppressed. It had been too much to hope that the girl's well of causes might run dry once she'd surrendered to the luxury of privilege. On the contrary, it appeared to be a magic porridge pot, perpetually refilling itself. Only that morning she'd made breakfast pure torture by outlining her role in the university's 'IncBid' movement – or was it 'BidInc'? Either way, it was basically a campaign for inclusion that seemed to involve finding new ways to exclude anyone who disagreed with them.

'Would it not be in the spirit of inclusion to listen to the other side's views?' Perry had asked her.

'Not if they cause people to literally break down,' she explained, in her warm, husky, helpful voice. 'People have a right not to be challenged.'

Perry and Charlotte had exchanged a glance at that. *People have a right not to be challenged*. Okay, not quite the motto of student life in their day – or, indeed, of a democratic society committed to free speech – but it did have the potential to become a summer catchphrase. He'd work on that.

Sometimes he thought that what he missed most about office life was the catchphrases, though likely they were censored now, even in the City. According to his old friend Charlie, emails were now subject to secret HR scans and Stasi-like programmes had been put in place to encourage colleague to shop colleague with evidence of problematic bias. Surely that could not be true?

'I wonder if you're still allowed to say The Old Lady,' he said. 'Does she need to declare her pronouns, d'you think?'

'The Old Lady?' Tabitha queried. 'Well, I hope so. It can really affect your mental health if people get it wrong.'

'I wondered when the mental elves were going to get a mention,' Perry muttered, not quite under his breath.

'Dad,' Benedict protested.

'He means the Bank of England,' Charlotte told their guest. 'The Old Lady of Threadneedle Street? Where the Bank of England is located?'

'Oh,' Tabitha said, with a show of goodwill, as if getting into the swing of their vintage brand of conversation.

Under the table, Perry saw, Benedict trailed his fingers over her thigh.

*

Linus was noticeably frustrated as they returned to the shore, his scowl an anomaly among the ranks of carefree holidaymakers. It was obvious he'd expected to be a natural: what was cycling if not balancing? It didn't help that Rio said they'd need another session, maybe two of their remaining three, before they could safely venture beyond the still waters of Old Beach and into more challenging currents.

Perry couldn't help crowing. 'Not as easy as it looks, is it?'

'Yeah, you're holding us back, Dad,' Huck said to his father.

'*Everyone* will benefit from more tuition,' Rio said. 'But by your final day, we'll be confidently heading down to Little Bay and beyond.'

'You were great,' Benedict told Perry as they returned their boards. 'Solid as a rock.'

'Must be those extra pounds around the middle,' Linus said in his joking-but-not-really way. 'Natural stabilizers, like the QM2. Steady as she goes.'

He was such a sore loser, and quick to add that he had to rush straight off for a Zoom 'with the board'.

'Hope you get on better with that kind than this,' Perry said, matching his faux-affable tone.

Huck wanted to get ice cream, so Perry and Benedict wandered back up to the house on their own, zigzagging past the parasols and blankets and cool boxes, avoiding a quartet of vigorous sleek-bodied athletic types playing Spikeball. Near the cliff steps, a table had been set up by the NJFA to collect signatures for a petition and Perry stopped to see what it was all about. As if there could be any doubt: *No more property sales for holiday homes!*

He scanned the signatures – they'd collected a fair few so far. 'Just seeing if there are any names I recognize,' he told Benedict, winking. 'Names beginning with T, if you know what I mean.'

'Dad,' Benedict said. 'Don't get all triggered, but can you ease up on Tabs a bit. Like, you don't have to challenge *everything* she says.'

'Because people have a right not to be challenged?' Perry said, thrilled at so early an opportunity.

'No, because people have a right not to be challenged *constantly*.'

'A firm concur to *that*. Especially if it involves foodstuffs being thrown at windscreens.' They waited while a line of walkers came down the steps, boots dusted with sand, and continued. 'You know I had to take the Range Rover to the garage for a valet clean?'

'Oh my God,' Benedict groaned, 'could that *be* any more the kind of thing people would expect someone like you to say?'

'Someone like me? I'm not apologising for having a decent set of wheels, Ben.'

Perry thought for the thousandth time how strange it was that people should object to success. Yes, envy was natural, but emotions – or deadly sins – aside, didn't people know that it was the taxes paid by the successful that funded the services they took for granted? And by successful he did not mean the superrich, everyone knew they were tax evaders, registered in the Bahamas or Luxembourg or whatever. No, the middle classes, paying more than half their earnings to the government and getting diddly squat in return. Just a load of abuse.

Obviously, people *didn't* know. Let's face it, there wasn't a great deal of understanding of economics in this country – it wasn't a compulsory subject in schools. Young people like these passata-throwing, graffiti-spattering vandals thought money grew on trees. They thought they could put nothing in and yet take out whatever they needed.

Well, one thing was for sure. If Comrade Tabitha *did* sign her name to any of this anti-holiday home stuff, she'd be out of Hotel Cliff View on her ear – no matter how in lust Benedict was.

They took the steps, steep enough to give Perry a vertiginous feeling when he looked down at the beach, even as the tableau gave him a pleasing sense of responsibility, for who were they, the nearest residents, if not protectors, custodians, latter-day lamplighters?

At the top, his son made a fresh appeal. 'You know what, Dad? Maybe it's not a bad idea to admit things have swung too far one way? You of all people know how important it is to have a roof over your head. I mean, you volunteer at Helping Homes. Tabs didn't even know that till I told her this morning.'

'Because I don't go on about it,' Perry said. 'Charity creates a multitude of sins, after all.'

'Thatcher again?'

'Oscar Wilde.'

Benedict rolled his eyes. 'You never quote anyone from this century.'

'That's not true,' Perry crowed. 'I *literally* just quoted your girlfriend.'

This, at least, drew a grin of concession from the boy.

*

'I need to head back to town tomorrow,' he told Charlotte that evening as they shelled prawns for a salad. Through open doors,

76

shouts of laughter could be heard coming from the Nook, where Benedict and Tabitha were chugging beers with the Shaw kids. Beattie had already been sent up to the house for restocks, tripping into the kitchen in a minuscule dress and trainers with peculiar patchwork uppers and corrugated soles that looked like they'd been designed by a blind man.

'Why?' Charlotte asked. 'We've only just got here.'

'The charity needs me. Just for one day.' That made him think of 'Heroes' and he sang the line, treating her to a few Bowie moves.

'Thank you, Perry.' Sometimes, just occasionally, she spoke to him as if she were an infant school teacher and he the gobby boy at the back. 'I thought the whole point of volunteering was that you dictated your own availability?'

'Well, I'm not sure that's the *whole* point. I told you I'd probably need to go back once a week.'

'Did you? I don't remember you having to last year.'

'I was new then.' He pulled a face. 'Not quite so indispensable.'

She was cool about it, of course. It suited her that he was involved with a housing charity, supporting the less fortunate in a bodily, quantifiable way. It was good optics. Benedict had virtually said the same thing a few hours ago.

Seriously, how had they reached the point in society when private citizens needed to concern themselves with optics?

The prawns done, he took the red peppers his wife handed him and sliced into the first. A tickle of chill entered through the open door, not what you'd expect after such a roasting day. 'I was thinking, with all this Not Just For August crap, there's actually no reason for us to *be* here in August, not now Ben's at uni. We should come down earlier, when the natives are less restless.'

'Hmm,' Charlotte said. 'Honestly, these avocados are still rock hard. I wish they wouldn't label them ready to eat when they're obviously anything but.'

'Better weather as well,' Perry added. 'It was stunning when we were here in June.'

She glanced up. '*We*? You came on your own. I was in the office.'

He felt a flush creep over his face. Turned to the cutlery drawer, even though he already had the knife he needed, a single, stark thought rising: *I'm a bastard and a fraud.* He imagined himself saying it out loud, seeing Charlotte's confusion and denial.

'Anyway,' she said, 'everything's set up for August. The night market, the bank holiday festival. We'd miss it all. What about your paddleboarding? Haven't you got a lesson tomorrow?'

Perry recovered himself. 'The next one's not till next week. We're having to work around Linus's global Zoom schedule. You'll be okay with just the Moke, will you?'

The Moke had been Perry's gift to her the last summer he'd been earning, a vintage Austin in green and white, perfect for trundling to The Needles or to the beaches beyond or down to the farm shop in Crowland.

'Benedict and Tabitha are using it tomorrow, I think. I'm fine though. Always happy to get my steps in.' She raised her left wrist, displaying the narrow black Fitbit she wore day and night. It made Perry feel a bit claustrophobic to think of a device monitoring your heart rate and REM and the rest of it. The kind of voluntary surveillance that could end up getting you fingered for a crime.

'Well, don't let them hog it if you need it.' Trust Benedict, he thought. This time next year he'd probably have taken their bedroom as well. Moved the young Marxist in with him. Seized their property as reparations for thoughtcrimes detectable exclusively by the young, like those high-frequency alarms audible only to teenagers and dogs.

'Will you be back for dinner tomorrow?' Charlotte asked. She was on her phone now and Perry glimpsed a shopping page of trainers like the ones Beattie Shaw was wearing. He hoped his wife wasn't going to order them for herself; if a teenage hottie struggled to pull them off, he didn't fancy *her* chances.

'I don't think I will, no.' He gathered the last of the pepper slices and released them into the salad bowl with a satisfying splash of colour. 'It makes more sense to stay over.'

13

Charlotte

Oh dear, it was becoming a *thing*. Amy's suspicions. First there'd been the sex offender on the beach and now she was convinced she'd seen someone on the upper floor of Villa Pino. She wasn't on edge like this in London, so Charlotte could only assume it was new-second-home owner anxiety, the natural by-product of the stress of holidaying in a house twenty times less comfortable than the one you'd left behind in the city.

In which case, did she *really* want to add to it? They were close, that went without saying, had been mutually candid from the off in the way women destined to be good friends were, but even so . . . Was what Charlotte planned to say – what was the phrase Benedict used all the time that meant out of order? *Out of pocket*, that was it. Was this out of pocket?

'They do have an alarm, don't they?' Amy said, her dainty features crinkling with concern. 'The Rickmans?' Her mood was at odds with the anarchic holiday cheer of the Needles conservatory café. It was the first Friday in August and every seat was taken, weekenders newly arrived and ready for fun, having booked their rooms in deep midwinter. It was mostly the Chelsea-on-Sea crowd, of course, the men dressed like yacht crew, the women Talitha Getty wannabes whose drug of choice began and ended with Brad Pitt rosé. Younger children running riot, melting down.

'Yes, I'm sure they do,' she assured Amy.

'I wonder if they've got cameras so they can keep tabs remotely?'

'I doubt it. They're not very techy.'

'Do you and Perry?' Amy asked.

'No. It's always been very safe here. Mind you, he's talking about fitting something now we're getting all this graffiti. Wants to catch the vandals red-handed, take the footage to the police, but I told him they probably mask up. They're not stupid. I really do think they must have left the shutters open by mistake, Amy. Either that or the Housekeepers girl was doing her rounds.'

'What's Housekeepers?'

'An agency that services holiday lets.' Charlotte adjusted her seat a fraction to avoid a sunbeam. There was something vaguely colonial about the way the ceiling fans made the bamboo blinds flutter. 'They're based in Poole, but they do a lot of the properties here. Madeline's probably asked them to look in every now and then, air the place.'

'You haven't got a key?'

'I don't, no. Amy, listen.' Charlotte leaned in, feeling rare trepidation now. 'I wasn't sure whether to say anything, but . . . I mean, I don't have a daughter myself, obviously, but if it was Benedict, I think I'd like to know.'

Amy lowered her coffee cup. 'Know what? Something to do with Beattie? Has she been rude to you?' She placed a palm on her heart, her expression pained. 'She's usually quite nice to people who aren't her parents.'

'She is. She's charming. Absolutely. It's just . . . Well. Those clothes she's wearing this holiday. The shoes and bags and sunglasses. She didn't have them at Easter, did she? They all look very expensive.'

'I know.' Amy exhaled in relief. 'Best fakes I've ever seen.'

'The thing is,' Charlotte said, 'I'm pretty sure they're *not* fakes.'

Amy frowned. Her fingers went to the pendant at her throat, 'Boss Mum' spelled out in cursive letters. 'They must be. How could she possibly afford the real thing? That fake Fendi tote she takes everywhere, that'd cost hundreds, wouldn't it?'

'Over a thousand, I'd say. I thought maybe with Linus's business taking off?' But Charlotte suggested this with little hope; the Shaws were not ones to spoil their kids.

'No,' Amy said. 'We haven't upped their allowances or anything. And even if we wanted to, all our spare cash is going on the build.'

'Some side hustle, maybe?'

'She does a bit of babysitting, but that just covers her gym membership.' Amy paused. 'You don't think . . . Oh my God, you don't think she *shoplifted* all these things?'

'No.' Charlotte bit down on her lip. 'They'd have security tags on them. Is there a boyfriend? Maybe someone older, with money?'

'Not that I know of.' Amy took a moment to consider. 'No. I really don't think so. She goes out at weekends, but just to house parties or the pub.'

'That could be when she goes off and meets him?'

Amy looked doubtful. 'But she usually comes back with a girlfriend who stays over.'

'So maybe he's only wooing her at this stage,' Charlotte said, then realising she needed to be more explicit, 'Maybe what I mean is groom? Or something a bit more active on her part? There's this thing I read about in *The Times* a few weeks ago. Findoms. Have you heard of them? They're girls who . . . *interact* online with men who want to be dominated.'

Amy's mouth fell open. 'Dominated? Like with whips?'

'No, not physically. Financially. Some of the girls have wish lists on shopping sites and the men buy things for them from the list. It can be very lucrative, apparently.'

At the sight of Amy's misting eyes, Charlotte reined back. 'I'm sorry, Amy. I'm not accusing her of anything. I'm just trying to think how she might have come to afford these things.'

'"Might" being the operative word,' Amy said, retreating to the safety of denial. 'But how can you be so sure they're genuine designer?'

'I saw the label on her beach wrap the other day. It's Erdem, definitely genuine. And not really an obvious one for the counterfeit industry. And the sunglasses are Chloé. I tried them on myself in Liberty.' She'd googled them and brought up an image on her phone. 'Are these them?'

'Yes.' Amy scanned the details and exclaimed, 'Three hundred and fifty pounds!'

'And the Birkenstocks she was wearing last night, I'm sure they're—'

'Oh, we gave her the money for those. For her exam results.'

'Did you give her five hundred pounds?'

'What? No! They cost less than a hundred.'

'Not the ones *she's* got. They're a collaboration with Manolo Blahnik.' Again, Charlotte showed her the photo online. It was obvious Amy recognized the match. 'And those trainers she had on the other night, I'm pretty sure they're Loewe. They're *six* hundred.'

'Loewe? How would she know these brands? Let's look up the Fendi bag.' As Amy scrolled, her eyes grew wide with disbelief. 'There's not a single one under a thousand pounds. Here it is, with the embroidery. Bloody hell, Charlotte, twelve hundred pounds!'

She gave back the phone, her hand trembling. 'I think I'd better look into this.'

Charlotte nodded. 'I would. Maybe start by taking a proper look at the labels. Are they made in China? Check what the authentic labels look like online and compare.'

'She's been doing her own laundry,' Amy said suddenly. 'I thought it was weird that she wanted to, but it's not like I'm going to turn the offer down.'

'Of course not.' No need to rake over old complaints of Beattie weaponizing homework assignments to get out of domestic chores. Benedict had been just as sneaky. 'Do you have access to her bank account? She's still under eighteen, isn't she?'

'She uses an app. She'd never let me see.'

'But did you help her set it up originally? You might have the login details somewhere and you could get in via the website. Make sure you use the same device you used to sign her up, so she doesn't get an alert.'

'My laptop. I've got it back at the house.' Amy brightened a fraction.

'Good. Then you can look at the statements, see exactly how much she's spending and where the money's coming from to fund it all.'

'But if it was this wish list thing you just said, the transactions would be the man's?'

'That's just one possibility,' Charlotte said. 'This is a process of elimination.'

Amy nodded. 'The only problem is the folder with the login details is back in London.'

'I could get Perry to go round and pick it up? He's up in London today.'

'That would be brilliant. Our neighbour's got a spare key.' She gave Charlotte directions for finding the file and Charlotte relayed them to Perry by text.

'All sorted,' Charlotte said, both relieved that she'd put investigations in motion and sorry she'd single-handedly added to Amy's troubles. 'What about a glass of rosé? The Miraval's lovely.'

14

Perry

In the event, the capital did not offer a warm welcome, at least not at first. The Friday traffic was typically blood pressure-raising, with lanes closed for roadworks – not a worker in sight, naturally – and a filthy, almost acid drizzle smearing his windscreen as he crawled from red light to red light around the South Circular.

Their house on Masefield Road, a gently curving stretch of grand redbrick Edwardians overlooking the playing fields of Spencer School, was exactly as they'd left it, their trusty Peugeot runaround in the off-street parking space, bins present and correct in the wooden shelter he'd built in the first weeks of his return from rehab. He let himself in, glanced at the post and did a cursory tour of the downstairs rooms, before collecting his toolkit and departing in the Peugeot.

He never took the Range Rover to Keeler House. Unlike well-heeled Masefield Road, with its robust neighbourhood watch culture, Ryland Street was in a pocket off Tulse Hill best described as 'vibrant'. Which was to say in no position to defend itself from undesirables, like the drunks on the corner – there again today – whose spare clothes were spread out on the pavement like a picnic blanket, or from whoever had fly-tipped the skanky old sofa two doors down from Keeler House. (The winos should relocate to the sofa, he thought, like in *The Wire*. There just wasn't enough joined-up thinking on Ryland Street.)

He parked up just opposite. Since his last visit, someone had sculpted 'BLM' in the hedge and he chuckled at the thought of activists taking to topiary art in Pine Ridge, on their hedge that screened the garden from the beach steps, perhaps? 'NJFA' was too fiddly, hopefully, especially if they wanted to include the hashtag.

He approached Keeler House and pressed the bell for number 2. It was a converted Victorian house with twelve units and he'd been in all of them at one time or another to fix skirting boards, hang shelving, draught-proof sashes and so on. When he'd initially volunteered with Helping Homes, a charity dedicated to resettling the homeless and facilitating independent living, he'd had in mind bookkeeping or fundraising; but those roles were held centrally and the moment he'd revealed his rudimentary DIY skills, his fate had been sealed.

The lock released and he made his way down the narrow hallway, given a lick of paint last year but already badly scuffed, to the rear ground-floor unit. The door was opened by a boyish chestnut-haired figure, who blinked and smiled before stepping aside to let him in.

'Hi Jordan.' Perry closed the door behind him, gently, carefully, and lowered his toolbox to the floor.

There was nothing gentle or careful about the way he manhandled the other man towards the unmade bed, pinning him to it with his full weight as he kissed him on the mouth.

*

They'd met in recovery. Not the rehab bit – Perry had been to a private clinic for that – but in the sessions at the local community centre that he'd come to rely on since and still attended when at home. He'd noticed Jordan straight away for he was easier on the eye than most, good-looking in a pale, fine-boned way. He spoke in private, under-his-breath tones that meant you had to lean in to catch even half of what he said, which generally opened with a negative: 'Nothing else to do,' he'd say, or 'No one told me,' or 'Never heard that.' At twenty-five, he was both heartbreakingly world-weary and almost juvenile in his helplessness, not an uncommon contradiction in those who attended the meetings but the only instance that provoked in Perry the desire to intervene.

'Where do you live?' he asked him.

'Nowhere.'

'Nowhere?'

Jordan shrugged. 'I'm on a mate's couch in Brixton. Just temporary.'

'Then I think maybe I can help,' Perry said.

Soon after, he'd had his new friend rehoused by Helping Homes, who arranged for a support worker to check in on him weekly. In retrospect it had perhaps looked all too easy, given Jordan the idea that Perry was not so much a mentor as a fixer.

As for anything more intimate, there'd been a sense of come-on from the day he was installed, but Perry had assumed flirtation was the young man's standard operating procedure, as it usually was with the physically blessed. But given their age and economic differences (plus, let's face it, little chance of their getting shitfaced together and benefiting from the magic of disinhibition), he'd had no sense that it might ever transform into the carnal.

But it did. In this very room.

Jordan had been leaning out of the window, smoking a roll-up while smouldering over some perceived injustice, every inch the young Sean Penn, when he turned to stare at Perry as he completed his task (plugging gaps with wire wool, if he remembered, following the sighting of a mouse).

'What?' Perry said.

'What?' Jordan repeated.

'I asked first.'

He'd tossed the fag end out the window and moved towards him, not so much self-assured as lacking the belief that he had anything to lose from rejection. Almost too surprised to resist, Perry did not. Jordan tasted of cigarettes, his tongue rough, halfway between human and cat, and his touch infectiously lewd and satisfying.

It had become a regular thing.

It was unsavoury, obviously. Not the gay bit per se – even an upper-end Gen Xer like Perry knew this was a sexual preference to glory in (all the champagne socialists of Masefield Road flew the Pride flag with, well, *pride* on designated days) – nor even the fact of the adultery, how Charlotte or Benedict might feel if they discovered the existence of this double life. This first affair, first gay relationship, for previous dalliances had been a case of too few to mention and had occurred without exception when Perry was out of the country (as a student, travelling in South America and doing so many drugs he would have slept with an alpaca if someone had suggested it; once, thrillingly, with an escort on a work jolly to Monaco).

No, what was unsavoury was that Jordan was technically vulnerable and Perry's liaisons with him a clear abuse of his position within the charity.

While Jordan had not yet said what their relationship meant to him and Perry was wary about asking, for him it had developed into something all too familiar: a craving.

Something to feel incomplete without. Not quite alive.

'I was gonna ask you a favour,' Jordan said, next to him on the slender single mattress, standard issue throughout the centre, as was the small chest of drawers and freestanding wardrobe. Perry had fixed the wardrobe doors for the previous incumbent when they'd been hanging off their hinges.

Is that what I'm doing? he thought, his hand resting on Jordan's chest, feeling its rhythmic rise and fall. *Waiting for someone to put me back on my hinges?* (He'd found that there were useful metaphors to be found in DIY.) There was no warden or live-in helper at Keeler House, not since last year's cuts, and residents had to call their off-site support worker if they had an issue. Luckily, Jordan's was not one to go the extra mile, which meant no inconvenient unscheduled visits.

'Oh yes? What favour?' He could hear how artificially cheerful he sounded, like he used to when Benedict would try to tell him about his geography homework and his tone would belie his sinking feeling because he knew it was going to be something really boring to do with carbon cycles.

'This job's come up. Delivery. Super flexible, so I choose when I want to work. Thing is, I need a car.'

A shiver of disquiet passed through Perry. Oh God, was he going to ask to use the Peugeot? In the room directly above, dialogue thundered from what he knew to be a super-sized TV. You couldn't complain directly because the guy – Trev – was an intimidating specimen. Weight-trained, inked to within an inch of his life, and homophobic too, if Jordan's rather hammy accounts of verbal abuse were to be taken seriously. He was also known to hog the bathroom, taking hour-long soaks in the residence's only bathtub.

Keep out of his way and stick to showers, Perry advised, stopping short of promising to arrange alternative accommodation.

'There's this Astra I can have. My mate Tom's. He says I can have it for free. It's just an old banger.' Jordan paused. 'I was wondering, could I register it in your name?'

Perry frowned. 'Why not yours?'

'My licence never came back, did it.'

He'd complained about this before. Something to do with a renewal that had not been dealt with, the suspicion that his licence had been lost in the system.

'Have you rung the DVLA to chase it up?'

'Couldn't get through. Didn't want to use all my data getting put on hold for hours.'

'Use my phone,' Perry offered.

This, they now did, but there were over an hour's worth of callers ahead of them on the helpline and Perry didn't have all day, especially now Charlotte had messaged him to ask him to pick up something from the Shaws' place, an errand he could have done without, even if he would enjoy having a little nose to see what high-end toys Linus had treated himself to now his annoyingly well-marketed bike insurance business was turning a decent profit.

'It's an absolute disgrace,' he said, cutting off the call. The passport office was the same, he'd read; the UK was sliding into a banana republic. (Wait, were you allowed to say 'banana republic' these days? He'd ask Tabitha. She'd soon let him know if it was now deemed a slur against Hondurans or fruit eaters or whatever. Instruct him on the correct terminology.)

'As soon as I get it, I'll change it to mine.' Jordan shrugged the duvet from him; he overheated easily. 'But I need to take it now or he'll give it to someone else.'

Pointless to suggest he ask a family member: he'd estranged

himself from them during the drinking years and suggestions by his support worker that he might make efforts to reconcile had been met with caution. 'This address or mine?' Perry asked.

'Suppose it'd need to be yours, would it?'

Hard to think this through with a naked body jammed against his and fresh stirrings of arousal under the covers, but Perry tried. The whole thing could be done online, he imagined, but even if there turned out to be a couple of letters from the DVLA, he was confident Charlotte wouldn't open them. She was the breadwinner now, but certain traditional gender roles still applied and cars were his department. MOTs, services, insurance, breakdown coverage, parking fines, the whole shebang.

He had a sudden flash of his wife and the rest of the Pine Ridge gang, limbs shiny with sunscreen as they floated on their backs in the crystalline waters of Old Beach, and it was like experiencing interference from life forms on a planet far away. He couldn't tell if the bleak feeling in his stomach was love or guilt or disgust.

'Sure,' he told Jordan. 'If it's just for a few weeks, I don't see why not.'

15

Robbie

We're sinking the pints like there's no tomorrow, trying to sedate our racing hearts, make sense of this carnage. From our table in the upstairs window of the Gull, we can just make out the emergency vehicles gathering in the beach car park, the cluster of police at the top of the cliff steps, silhouetted against a tangerine dusk sky that's all wrong, like it thinks it's the backdrop to a marriage proposal. The wind's picked up and it's got to be tricky navigating the tide, on its way out now, but still lashing at the headland, so my guess is they'll wait for it to go right out before attempting any proper clean-up.

I can't see any media yet but they'll be here by first light, you can be sure of that. *Cliff House Tumbles in Festival Horror . . .* The police won't be the only ones wanting to interview us.

There's four of us so far: me, Tate, Rio, and Shannon, who's on the phone to her cousin Ethan, a police trainee who's on shift today and with any luck part of the response crew. Des and Ellie are still at work and missed the whole thing.

'It was surreal,' I tell Tate, who wants to hear for the second time exactly what I saw. They don't have a view of the cliff from the bar, so it took them a minute to figure out why people were dumping their drinks and getting hysterical. 'It was like it was on wheels or something.'

'I thought the cliff must have fallen away,' Rio says. He's got the worst sunburn on his face and neck, livid against his white neckline.

'No, it's not going anywhere, that cliff,' I say. 'They stabilized it a few years ago, remember.'

They all ask, apparently, the rich Londoners who view houses on Pine Ridge Road. Is the cliff *solid*? How bad is the *erosion*? You inbreds do know there's a *climate crisis*, don't you? If it's safe enough for the coastal path, it's safe enough for the houses, the agents parrot.

Shannon gets off the phone, bright-eyed with news. 'It wasn't a house,' she announces. 'As in the main, *actual* house. It was one of those summerhouses at the bottom of the garden. Got to be one of the ones we hit the other week. I'm trying to remember, there were two right next to each other at the beach end, weren't there?'

A summerhouse. If I'd been sober, I'd have worked that out for myself. We all know most of the second homes have additional buildings: garden rooms, guest cottages, shepherd's huts. Up by the ridge, someone's done up an old horsebox as a cocktail bar.

As we suspected, the property belongs to a posh couple from London, though Ethan is either unable or unwilling to confirm any names.

'Maybe it's the bloke who lamped you?' Rio suggests, and my tongue explores the swollen side of my mouth. Pretty much healed now.

'Maybe.'

'Good job you were on the beach. Otherwise, you'd be suspect numero uno.'

'Probably still will be,' I say, chuckling. 'They'll say I was a digital avatar and the real me was heading for the M3 in the JCB.'

'JCB?' Rio looks confused.

'Yeah. Large objects don't move by themselves, do they? That summerhouse wasn't pushed off the cliff by a mobility scooter, I'll tell you that for nothing. So, if it wasn't one of us, then it must have been the Citizens.'

'I was thinking that,' Shannon says. 'Explains why they've been so quiet this summer. Been saving themselves.'

'So you don't reckon it could've just been an accident?' Rio says.

'An accident involving a JCB? Yeah, sure. In which case, someone take back their licence before they shovel the whole fucking village into the sea.'

We snigger into our drinks, all except Tate, who's gone very quiet. Grey around the gills as well. Finally, he breaks his silence: 'There's been construction kit up there this weekend. At the old bungalow, I think.'

'The bungalow?' Rio grimaces. 'That's my paddleboarding guy's place. Linus.'

Who's married to Amy, who just happens to be the DFL I dislike more than any other. It's unusual for me to differentiate one from another, to think in terms of an individual rather than group dislike, but from the minute she arrived, back in the spring, she got my goat.

She came down more often than they usually do, mostly on her own, and that seemed to be all it took to make her feel like a proper native. That and reading the *Voice* and turning up to council meetings, where she talked about the environment and – what was it again, at that last one? – *understanding our plight*, that was it.

Back in May, there was an open forum about the rental crisis and she stood up, her face all twisted with sincerity, and went, 'I'm new to the community. Tell me what I can do. I want to be part of the solution, not the problem.' Silence is violence: all the clichés. She wanted us to know she considered Pine Ridge her first home, her *spiritual* home, even if, formally, for tax and stuff (i.e. everything except holidays), her London place would continue to be her main residence.

I thought *yeah right*. One thing I'll say for most of them: they don't pretend. They're not acting like it's some quirk of fortune they got their second home and now they need to wear a hairshirt or whatever. They're more like, 'I've worked hard, I've got the money, so why shouldn't I have a holiday place by the sea if that's what I fancy?'

But she wants it both ways, this Amy, which is so next-level elite.

Anyway, I looked up her London house online. Easy enough to find out the address, down Dulwich way. And I can tell you for nothing that it's enormous. I mean, you could *almost* get the whole two homes thing if they were in some shoebox the rest of the time, like the people trapped in tower blocks during lockdown, but no, it's massive, must have four or five bedrooms. It's the Pine Ridge house that's the shoebox.

'Robbie?' Shannon's speaking in my ear really loudly, almost yelling. 'Stop doing that!'

Resurfacing, I blow air like I've been holding my breath. 'Doing what?'

'Going into a trance!'

'Sorry. Still a bit wasted. What were we saying?'

'The JCB. Tate's seen one up at the bungalow. *And* they've got a summerhouse.'

'Oh. Yeah. Well, it *could've* been them. It was hard to tell which garden it was, the way the cliff curves, you know? Could've been any of them.' I try to catch Tate's eye, but he's staring into his glass, eyeballing the last inch of his pint as if it's all that stands between him and survival. And I have a really strong instinct there's more to come. More news.

More damage.

'Well,' Shannon says, into the void. 'Whosever it is, they're not putting it back together any time soon, so let's hope they were insured.'

'Or let's hope they weren't,' Rio says, with a wicked little smile.

16

Amy

Earlier in August

Yes, she celebrated, but under her breath because Linus was in the room, inconveniently spending his Sunday morning on work emails (the kids, at least, had hightailed it to the beach at the first suggestion they might help with a spot of dust containment). The login details buried in the file Perry had brought back from London yesterday had worked and she was into Beattie's bank account and scrolling through the last six months of transactions.

Most of the payments were under £20. Starbucks. Grind Coffee, their local pusher. Uber. TfL. Amazon. Debits to friends that she guessed were for drinks bought by those who'd already turned 18 (the account had an automatic lock on payments to pubs and bars).

No cash withdrawals – the Zoomers didn't use cashpoints.

As for clothing, there was one purchase at Urban Outfitters, another at a Cancer Research shop, but no retailers of designer clothes and not a single payment out over £50, much less the hundreds, even thousands, charged by the labels Charlotte had identified – and others she had been able to authenticate with minimal research.

As for deposits, there was only Beattie's monthly allowance, plus the £100 they'd given her after her latest stellar exam results.

Gifts from grandparents and other relatives on her birthday back in April. The occasional payment from local families for babysitting jobs, though Amy knew many paid cash.

She scanned the debits a second time, reassuring herself that there was indeed nothing rogue afoot. How then to explain the mystery of her daughter's luxury shopping habit? Logging out, she reread the article in *The Times* that Charlotte had forwarded.

'Paypig' Loses Home after Debts Spiral

A man who became embroiled in the BDSM world of findom – or financial domination – has declared himself bankrupt and lost his home after debts to a 'domme' spiralled out of control.

'I was addicted,' John Gibbs told Warwick County Court on Tuesday. 'I willingly gave away control of my bank accounts. I have no one to blame but myself and I am very sorry to let my creditors down.'

It read slightly as if someone had written the apology for him (his domme, perhaps).

Men like Gibbs are known as 'paypigs', part of a consensual relationship that involves the transfer of financial power from the submissive to the dominatrix.

'The motivation is predominantly erotic,' explains sex therapist Reena Powell. 'The submissive finds the dynamic sexually arousing, despite their not meeting the other party in person.'

Thank God for that!

The transactions involved in findom relationships vary from one-off payments to regular transfers of money and even, as in Gibbs' case, the surrendering of login details and passwords, allowing the domme to take total control of their bank accounts. A domme may construct a strict punitive budget for the submissive or create a shopping wish list from which she 'permits' the submissive to make purchases for her.

Amy paused and read the last sentence again. This must have been the point that caught Charlotte's eye too.

While Gibbs picks up the pieces of his life and hopes that psychotherapy will curb future urges to enter into similar relationships, his former domme, whose identity was protected during the court proceedings, will not be charged. Whatever her motives, she has committed no crime – providing her financial gains are declared to HMRC.

Closing the laptop, she walked out of the bungalow, down the back garden, along the clifftop path and up the Tuckers' garden to the open door of their kitchen, where Charlotte, dressed in yoga top and wide-legged pants, sat in front of her laptop, the screen split into multiple documents.

'Are you working on a Sunday as well?'

Charlotte had commented more than once that while people envied them their month-long vacation, the reality was she worked more weekends down here than at home, what with the beaches teeming with day trippers and the restaurant service harried. 'I can do this later,' she said and gestured to Amy to take a seat.

'I've looked at Beattie's bank statement and there's no sign of anything suspicious,' Amy said, plonking herself opposite. 'So

I think what you said about the findom thing could be right. Hi, by the way.'

'Hi. You know you said she did some babysitting?' Charlotte had the ability to enter a conversation with minimal warm-up. 'I was thinking, is there anyone who might have given these things to her? Someone who works in fashion, maybe?'

'No, they're just regular families. They barely want to pay the going rate, there's no way they're handing out designer clothes as a tip. I have to face it, Charlotte. Beattie's got use of some saddo's account or these items are on a wish list and he's buying them for her.'

Charlotte nodded. 'I have to agree it might be something like that – though I'd question whether we're allowed to use the word "saddo" any more. Self-esteem-non-normative?'

But Amy couldn't laugh. Instead, she felt a horrible fluttering in her heart as adrenaline surged through her. 'The question is, exactly what does she have to do to get a Fendi bag? Even if it is just online? There must be images involved. He buys her the clothes and wants to see her in them? Or taking them off? Oh God, are there videos of her out there? You read about this stuff turning up on Pornhub without girls' consent and ruining their lives. Driving them to suicide. Should I get on to the police, do you think?'

'You have no evidence whatsoever that there are images of her out there,' Charlotte said calmly. 'Not even in the possession of this one individual – if he exists in the first place. It's all just a theory at this stage.'

They looked at each other and Amy was touched to find her own pain reflected in Charlotte's eyes. This was a young girl who'd somehow got herself in the clutches of something – someone – at best not quite right and at worst dangerous.

She had a new thought. 'You know I saw that man watching her on the beach? I'm wondering if he has anything to do with this. Maybe he's found out where she lives and is stalking her?'

'Let's not let our imaginations run away with us,' Charlotte said, meaning *your*, but Amy appreciated the adjustment. 'The good news is she seems perfectly happy – I saw her earlier, laughing away with Benedict and Tabitha. You haven't noticed she's been more anxious or angry than usual?'

Amy considered. First off, Beattie was never anxious. Unlike 99 per cent of her peers, she gave no impression of harbouring self-doubt or of disliking her appearance or personality; on the contrary, she seemed a little too thrilled with her assets, her delight in male attention positively old-school (last night, when Tabitha had cheered news of the outlawing of wolf-whistling, she'd looked amazed). Angry? She'd certainly been annoyed by the state of the bungalow. Also irritated to discover you had to be eighteen to use the gym at The Needles. But she had brightened when Amy offered to drive her to the branch of GymLads in Bournemouth, which would be covered by her membership.

'If anything, I'd say she's grown in confidence. A bit of humility wouldn't go amiss, to be honest.'

'Good,' Charlotte said. 'Then whatever's going on, it isn't making her feel victimized. We need to get into her messaging apps. Benedict's great with IT, I could ask him?'

'No, she'd never forgive me if I involved one of her friends.'

'Linus? He must know all the tech tricks?'

'I think I'd rather not escalate it quite yet.'

'What then?'

Amy took a breath. 'Crazy as it sounds, I think I'll just ask her direct.'

'Wow,' Charlotte said. 'When?'

'Maybe tomorrow morning, when the boys are out paddle-boarding.'

'Good plan,' Charlotte said. 'Till then, hold your nerve.'

*

As she left Cliff View, a seagull took flight from the roof of the Nook and plunged towards her almost in attack. She felt silly for cringing when it angled away at the last moment, especially when two walkers passed by on the cliff path and laughed.

Passing Villa Pino, she noticed the gate swinging open. Okay, she was *definitely* not imagining this. And if Charlotte was right about there being agency workers going in and out, then she'd simply introduce herself and ask for a business card; this time next year, she might need their services.

She padded up the garden, a chic, low-maintenance design with broad stone paths winding through beds of shrubs and lavender, and approached the back door. This too gave way, so she took a breath and stepped inside.

'Hello?'

She walked through a vast sky-blue kitchen-diner towards the door on the far side. Even in the dim shuttered light you could tell the place had been professionally designed, one of those interiors they described as a symphony, all the elements – colour, texture, shape – conceived as a whole. If she hadn't been trespassing, she might have taken out her phone and got some shots for her mood board.

Moving deeper, she reached the hallway, where a heap of mail sat on the doormat. On instinct, she gathered it up and stacked it neatly on the jade-coloured console table at the foot of the stairs. Then, hearing a hoover starting up overhead, she called out again: 'Hello! Housekeepers?'

A young woman in grey leggings, cleaner's smock and white plimsolls appeared on the landing. 'You gave me a fright!' She spoke with an accent Amy couldn't place.

'I'm so sorry. Are you from Housekeepers?'

She descended a few steps, giving Amy a searching look. 'Sorry, who are you?'

'I'm the next-door neighbour. I shouldn't have just walked in, but the gate was open and I know the Rickmans are away so I thought I'd better check. I'm Amy.'

'Ah. Yes, that's right. Housekeepers.'

'You work Sundays?'

'Weekends are our busiest times.'

Which made sense. Holiday let changeover days, second-homers arriving late Sunday evening when the traffic had eased. 'Is it a regular time you come or just whenever you're passing? I'm probably being silly, but I've just had a feeling someone's been in here. Like yesterday, were you here then?'

'I don't think so. We're only here once a week and the house is locked up the rest of the time, with the alarm on.' The girl looked a bit sorry for Amy, who could feel her worry lines deepening. 'I'll give you my mobile number and you can phone me if you think it happens again?'

If you think. 'Thank you. Yes. That would be great.' Amy added the number to her contacts.

Back at the bungalow, she checked in with Linus. 'I just saw inside Villa Pino. It's *really* nice.'

'Villa Pino?'

'Next door?'

'Oh. Right,' he said vaguely. It was clear he had not yet fully engaged with this trip.

'I was thinking, let's go out for dinner tonight, just the four of us. We haven't actually done that yet. I'll see if they've got a table at The Needles.'

'Sure,' Linus said, returning his attention to his laptop. 'Wouldn't mind a break from the Tuckers.'

It was maybe a *little* early in the holiday for him to be voicing this sentiment, but Amy said nothing, just opened her contacts – still showing the Housekeepers girl – and dialled the restaurant.

17

Tate

'I need to talk to you about something,' Ellie said in a low, grave voice, and he saw apprehension in her eyes, which he knew from a lifetime's observations of female dynamics ought to make *him* apprehensive too.

She'd made a big deal of tonight. The comped meal in the brasserie (food only, not drinks, which were double the price of the beach bar), some kind of reward for having attained a certain level of client satisfaction. The great table her mate would fix for them on the terrace, which was obviously the prime spot. The view across the sloping lawn to the pool and sea had a Mediterranean glamour to it, with fairy lights twinkling everywhere you looked, strings of them wound around the trunks and branches of the trees – not just pines, but imported palms as well.

They clinked glasses. He had a vodka cocktail and she had a glass of very pale pink wine that caught the light as she raised her glass and glowed like a gemstone.

'Never seen such a tiny amount of wine in such a massive glass,' he commented.

'It's fine,' Ellie said. 'I'm not up for a session.'

Shame. He hoped what she wanted to talk to him about wasn't to do with his flirting with the girls at the bar, which was not only encouraged by Gav but also an impulse beyond his own control. To ask him to stop was like asking him not to breathe. 'Did I tell you I saw Robbie earlier? He's decided on Thursday for his stunt. Says he wants it front of mind at the housing meeting the week after.'

'Where's he going to do it?'

'Up on Pine Ridge Road. There's a couple of places that've been empty all season, apparently.'

Despite being the resort's premier road, Pine Ridge Road hadn't had much of NJFA's attention this summer, other than the first-day-of-the-month graffiti, partly because they'd been concentrating on the new builds at the edge of the village, up past the Staywell. It was far less picturesque a zone than the main village, but nowhere was safe from DFLs now, not since The Needles had opened. It was their gateway drug: they came for weekend and left with thoughts of a permanent habit.

It was paradise, this place. Or, as Robbie said, paradise lost.

'I'll see if I can swap my shift so I can come along to that,' Ellie said.

'Great.' Tate rubbed at an itch in his nose, smelling beach bar lager on his fingers. You couldn't get rid of it with tepid showers. Same for Robbie with oil and petrol from the garage. There were worse smells. Imagine working in a sewage plant or something.

He smeared butter – *green* butter, what the fuck? – on a piece of warm bread and popped it in his mouth. 'So what did you want to talk about?'

But the hostess was seating people at the next table and Ellie seemed to want to wait for this to finish before spilling. A couple in their forties, the woman gushing about how *heavenly* the terrace was, the guy agreeing as if conceding the point, and a teenage boy, dressed like he surfed but who had probably never seen a wave over five feet his entire life, making no comment. And now, appearing in Tate's eyeline, oh fuck, the girl from the beach. *The* girl. Beattie the Beautiful, in a white dress with bits cut out at the sides like those paper snowflakes they'd made at infant school.

In the days since they'd first chatted, they'd exchanged a few texts – and pictures – that had fired his imagination in a big way, made him sweat, in fact, but had not yet led to a plan to meet.

She saw him straight away, clocked who he was with, what this was, and looked away.

'What?' he asked Ellie a second time and she gave a nervous laugh.

'I genuinely have no idea how you're going to react to this.'

'To what?' How many times did he have to say it?

'I'm pregnant.'

It was how he imagined being taken down by a sniper. Out of nowhere. Fast and deadly, robbing him of breath, of a heartbeat.

'Say something,' Ellie said.

Think. I can't deal with this. I definitely can't deal with this when the girl I'm obsessed with is sitting right there, almost in touching distance. *Say something. Anything!*

'You can't have a baby in a caravan,' he said finally.

She frowned. '*You?*'

Big mistake. 'We. *We* can't have a baby in a caravan. It's not a proper home.'

'Okay. Well, I was thinking we could see if we could move to a static? Shannon's on the waitlist and I thought if one came up, she might let us jump the queue . . .'

He grimaced. A static. The same but fixed. Not just for now but forever. Pensioners for neighbours, or middle-aged people like Shannon's parents, who were nice enough but deathly dull. The smell of nappies on top of the stink of the chemical toilet and the food odours that never cleared no matter how hard you scrubbed.

He took two huge swallows of his drink, basically finishing it.

'Or we'd get on the council's emergency list, probably,' Ellie said. 'A couple with a baby gets priority. It wouldn't be in Pine Ridge, obviously. More likely Crowland.'

The council's emergency list: it was so fucking sordid. Not to mention surreal, discussing it in this high-class place, where a room for the night probably cost more than whatever their monthly rent would be in said new emergency accommodation. *A couple with a baby*: he wasn't sure he even wanted the couple part, let alone the baby.

At the next table wine was being tasted, approved, poured. Even the younger kid – Beattie's brother, he assumed – was allowed some. Tate would be sacked if he was caught serving alcohol to an underage kid at the beach bar, but here it was different. No one challenged posh parents.

He rose to go to the loo.

'You're not leaving?' Ellie said in alarm.

'No, just need a slash. Order some more drinks, will you?'

The loos were quite a distance from the restaurant, through the bar and down a corridor that smelled of something sweet, caramel maybe, and down a short flight of stairs. In the men's room, he stared at himself in the mirror. A father? The idea was ludicrous – he'd barely stopped being a child himself. He had a seasonal job earning minimum wage, one step up from a kid's paper round. Ellie said it herself sometimes, and not always as fondly as she might: he needed looking after.

When he came out, someone was waiting to the side of the door and fingers fluttered in front of his face. Fingers with long baby-blue nails and clusters of rings. Beattie! Even standing at a gawky angle, her legs crooked, she looked wildly sexy in the dress with the cut-outs that flashed her tanned skin. Her feet were in pimped-up Birkenstocks, velvet and jewels and whatever.

'Awkward,' she said and he had no idea if the shyness in her smile was real or a total act.

'You look incredible,' he blurted.

'I know.' She reached out and took his left hand, using her other hand to push open the door to the ladies. Pulled him into the cubicle nearest the entrance so violently he banged his hip on the edge of the door.

Then they were kissing. Frantic, savage, as if someone had told them they had five minutes left to live. He had one quick rational thought – how could it be that this was the best he'd felt in his entire life when he'd just heard possibly the worst news? – before allowing physical sensation to obliterate it. Their hands were everywhere on each other, under their clothes, on the skin. His fingers inside the scooped-out bits, then under her bra, inside her knickers. Both of them were moaning, getting past the point of no return, but there was no way they could have sex here, in this cubicle.

'We have to stop. Someone's gonna come in.'

'I know. We need somewhere to meet,' she said, a hot, breathless whisper. 'Your place?'

He thought of the caravan, Ellie's work rota on the corkboard. Was it possible? She never missed a shift. You couldn't keep rich clients waiting even five minutes.

Ellie was pregnant! Knowledge only minutes old and already the most haunting thought in his entire head.

'Yeah,' he said finally. 'Friday daytime should be all right.' If he remembered correctly, this was the next time Ellie was working and he was not.

Beattie opened the door. 'Coast's clear. You go first.'

But opening the main door, he bumped into a punter, who looked at him askance.

'Gender fluid,' he said, and he heard Beattie giggle behind him.

'Of course,' the woman said, all earnest. 'No problem.'

*

His lips felt chewed and swollen. He hoped he didn't have make-up smeared on his face as he rejoined Ellie, thanked his lucky stars for the fading light.

'You okay?'

'Yeah.'

'We don't have to talk about it if you don't want to,' she said and he averted his gaze, frightened by what he suddenly saw across the table, saw behind her eyes: a maternal, sexless care giver, under the skin of a pretty young woman. A cute avatar to catfish him.

Their food arrived then, which bought him a few minutes. He was both ravenous and nauseous as he plunged his knife into his aged steak and watched red juice leak from it. His hip throbbed and he had a residual ache in his trousers that was not going to subside until he had her. Beattie . . . Shit, she was back at her table now, he could hear her saying, 'You are such a *worm*, Huck.' Then the dad was berating her and the brother grumbling and the mum snapped: 'Let's just try to get on, shall we? We're supposed to be on holiday.'

'I'm having a great time,' Beattie said, and Tate didn't dare catch her eye in case Ellie picked up on it. She'd have to do a one-eighty, but still. She probably had an enhanced radar for rivals now she was pregnant.

'I know it's a shock,' she said, because she hadn't meant it when she'd said he didn't have to talk about it. She'd just meant that she would spoon-feed him his lines if he wasn't capable of delivering them independently.

'You could say that,' he said through a mouthful of fries.

III

'We just need time to get used to it.'

'Hmm.' He used the arrival of their drinks to sneak a glance at Beattie. She was forking fingernails through her hair, sucking in her lower lip before letting it slide slowly back. She was so exactly the solution to his chronically frustrated libido he feared he might have imagined her.

Ellie noticed him looking, turned as well. God, he'd been right about her radar.

'That kid's checking you out,' she said.

What the fuck!

But she meant the boy. 'Likes your tattoos, I reckon.'

The mum followed the kid's gaze and said, 'Over my dead body, Huck.'

'What? Dad's got one!'

'His is tiny and on his ankle. Not covering his whole arm like *that*.'

'Nice,' Ellie said, flaring her eyes at Tate. Her second drink was water, he noticed. 'We'll be all right though, won't we?'

He knew what she wanted to hear and it wasn't complicated. Just reassurance, three words or, better still, an extension of them: *I love you – and I'll love our baby too.*

She needed it. She deserved it.

But he couldn't say it.

18

Amy

Of all the trepidations that a lifetime of Monday mornings had flung in her path, none quite matched this one. Ideally, she'd have waited for Beattie to emerge from her room of her own accord, but the paddleboarding lesson was only an hour long and she didn't want to risk it. As soon as Linus and Huck left, she made two oat flat whites and knocked on her daughter's door.

'Beattie?'

She was stretched out on top of her duvet in pale blue cotton pyjamas. On her phone, of course. Every hour spent on a screen took thirteen minutes off your night's sleep, Amy had read, but tell that to the digital natives. At least she looked her age first thing in the morning, make-up removed on little reusable pads she left lying around the bathroom. It had been hard at dinner last night to watch her in her little dress, lips pouting, eyes glittering, drawing glances from all the men. She'd wanted to hustle her aside and say, 'Who are you, you siren, and what have you done with my daughter?'

'I brought you a coffee.'

Beattie reached to take the cup. 'Hey. Thanks.'

'Do you have a minute? I wanted to have a chat.'

Instantly, the girl's gaze darkened. She made no attempt to help as Amy cast about for somewhere to perch. The only available chair was heaped with clothes and so Amy transferred these to the foot of the bed and sat on it.

Beattie took a sip of her coffee before speaking in a husky drawl. 'Seriously, whatever you want to say, I've already covered it in PSHE.'

'Have you covered findoms?'

There was a beat of surprise. 'What?'

'Findom. Financial domination.'

'I have no idea what that is.' Beattie sounded genuinely puzzled. 'Wait, is that like coercive control? We had a talk about domestic abuse and raised money for that shelter in Streatham.'

Was she bluffing? Amy couldn't tell. 'No, this is girls who have online friendships with men who want them to control their finances. Sometimes they have access to their banking and dictate all their spending. They call the girl a financial dominatrix and the man a paypig and there's a sexual element to it. In no way would the girl be to blame,' she added, 'especially if she were young and had entered into it sort of accidentally, you know? If she'd been groomed.'

Beattie continued to frown. 'Is this, like, OnlyFans? Mum, whatever site you mean, I'm not on it. I swear.'

It was the trace of pity in her voice that made Amy believe her. Pity for the tragic middle-aged woman diving headfirst down another internet rabbit hole. Out of touch, clueless.

'What social media *do* you use these days?'

Beattie proffered her phone and Amy itched to take it, but she knew it was a trap: to accept only signalled her mistrust, inviting potentially terminal consequences. She'd already trawled through the girl's banking, which had been risky enough: what if Beattie had been alerted to the access?

'It's okay,' she said. Before it was withdrawn, the screen lit up with a notification. Too fleeting for Amy to read the message, but she caught the sender's name: *Tate*. 'Who's Tate?'

Beattie shot her a defiant look. 'Just one of hundreds of skanky old men I'm findom-ing – or whatever it was you just said. Want to give him a call? Ask him if I've taken control of his bank account and paid his gas bill on time?'

Amy felt her cheeks flame. 'There's no need to be so challenging, Beattie.'

'You're the one who's challenging me.' The girl's eyes flashed with outrage. 'Why would I even want to do something weird like that?'

Amy breathed deeply and took a beat. She remembered how decisive she'd sounded when discussing it with Charlotte: *I'll just ask her direct*. It struck her that she'd asked the wrong question. 'Can we start this conversation again?'

Beattie slurped her coffee. 'If you want.'

'I need you to tell me where you're getting all your expensive clothes from. I know you don't have much money of your own, so I'm worried someone is buying them for you. Hence my questions about findoms, which I obviously got wrong and I'm sorry. But I *do* want to know how these things came into your possession and I think it's reasonable to ask.'

Beattie lowered her cup. A flush rose in her face as she glanced at the heap at her feet. Amy looked too: sod's law the top item was a cheap nylon top from H&M. Her gaze returned to Amy, steady again. 'I told you. They're fakes.'

'I don't think they are, Beattie. At least they may have been sold as fakes, but they are actually genuine designer. The Fendi bag, the Chloé sunglasses. And before you object, I haven't been snooping. You leave stuff all over the place and I've just used my eyes.'

Or Charlotte had. In any case, there was a fractional concession on her daughter's part. 'I suppose *some* could be. The ones I got from charity shops. In fancy places, you know, like the Kings Road and High Street Ken.'

Amy remembered the Cancer Research item on the bank statement – just one. Had there been several she might have gone along with this undeniably attractive line of defence. Lord knew she didn't *want* the answer to be sordid.

'There's loads of like billionaires out there,' Beattie continued. 'Arabs and Russians and stuff. They buy something in the wrong size and they don't bother taking it back. A thousand pounds is like, I don't know, 50p to them. That's how I got the bag. The shop didn't even know it was worth so much. *I* didn't.'

'How could a bag be the wrong size?'

'I don't mean literally every single thing. Just, that's how these people think. They buy something, it's not right, so they give it away.'

Amy found this hard to believe. No wealthy person she'd crossed paths with deposited untouched designer handbags in charity shops. 'What about the Birkenstocks? I can't imagine you wanting to buy shoes second-hand.'

'I got those new. You and Dad gave me the money?'

'Come on, Beattie. I looked them up and they're limited edition and on sale for five hundred pounds. Please be honest.'

'I *am*,' she said with a flare of indignation. 'They're seconds and not even this season. I got them on an auction site. I told you this when you gave me the money.'

Amy was certain she had not and nor had anything resembling an auction site appeared on the bank statement, but she could hardly say this. 'What auction site?'

Beattie scowled. 'It's called Amiss. You won't know it.'

'Okay. If you show me a receipt, that would put my mind at ease.'

'I can't. Lexi ordered them on her account. I paid her back. In cash from babysitting,' she added, with pre-emptive pique. 'You're always making everything into some mystery. Like you *want* me to be in a crime ring or something.'

A crime ring? That took Amy aback. It also dislodged a distant memory of a movie about teenagers in LA who broke into celebrities' houses and pilfered their clothes and jewellery.

'I don't want to talk about this any more,' Beattie said, returning to her phone. 'I'm getting, like, weird obsessed vibes here.'

Amy considered her position. She was by no means any clearer on the source of her daughter's shopping budget, but she was at least satisfied the girl wasn't being sexually exploited and that was enough of a win for now. 'Okay. But just be aware that if you're going to swan around Pine Ridge like a Kardashian, there's tension between us and some of the locals. Economic tension.'

It was a pathetic, cowardly swerve of focus, and again Beattie looked at her with pity.

'Fine, Mum. I'll try not to let my shoes cause social unrest.'

*

Since Linus was not one to hide his light under a bushel, his glum mood on returning from paddleboarding could only mean that this session had been as inglorious as the first. Amy didn't dare ask if Perry had once more proved to be a natural.

'When's the next one?'

'Not for a few days. Rio's booked solid.'

'Well, at least you can practise in his absence.' This was the sort of remark that made the kids bristle, but worked well with Linus, especially if she invoked one of his cycling mantras as she now did: 'Hate it now, love it later and all that.'

He nodded. 'Pain is temporary. Everything okay with Beats? I haven't seen her today.'

'Fine.' Feeling guilty for excluding him from her investigations, Amy reached instead for the consolation of a secondary mystery. 'Linus, you know I told you I met the woman from Housekeepers? When I went into the house next door?'

'Oh yes.'

'Well, there was this huge pile of junk mail on the doormat, including the note I posted the day we arrived. I recognized it because the envelope is pink.'

'So?'

'So why didn't she pick it up?'

A touch of impatience crossed his brow. 'I don't know. Maybe she does stuff in a certain order?'

'But it wasn't pushed to the side by the front door opening. The back gate was open, so I think she came in that way. Which means she came up from the beach or all the way along the cliff path from the Meadow. Why would she do that? Everyone comes the road way except the residents themselves. *Ourselves*.'

But Linus just gave her a droll look before turning from her, his mind already on the next task. 'The riddle of the cleaner's routine – there's an episode of *Sherlock* right there. On the cutting-room floor.'

19

Beattie

This was going to be the last time, definitely.

Okay, so *last* time was supposed to have been the last time, because there'd been that notice up that had literally made her heart stop, but she'd been looking online and there were a few more things she had to have. If she was going to do this, if she was going to have sex with Tate when they met tomorrow, she knew exactly what she wanted to wear under her adidas x Gucci dress (the most expensive item in her collection). What she wanted him to remove.

And that underwear was not available in Pine Ridge or Bournemouth, even if the conditions in the branch of GymLads she'd used down there had been right, which they had not. She'd ended up just doing a workout and leaving.

'I have to go up to London,' she told her parents. 'I've forgotten some textbooks I need.'

'Can't we just get new ones delivered down here?' her dad said.

'They're too expensive to buy again. Plus I want to see Sienna.'

She was careful to reference a different friend from Lexi, in case her mum started going on about S&M gimps and receipts for shoes again. She got the feeling her dad wasn't in on these pervy suspicions, but there was no way her mum had worked out that the stuff was properly designer on her own. Her idea of a luxury brand was the Sweaty Betty sale. No, someone was onto her and the sooner she shut this down the better.

It turned out Benedict's dad was driving up to London again and he offered to give her a lift. He was okay, Perry. One of the less handsy dads. Even though he *literally* worked as handyman, which was pretty funny.

'Why's he going up again?' her dad asked her mum. 'He's already been once.'

'He's needed to do stuff for his housing charity, I think.'

'What stuff? He just puts shelves up! He's not even paid, he's completely economically inactive.'

'Don't say that,' her mum said, meaning not in front of Beattie, which was such a joke when everyone knew how judgy parents were. 'I'm economically inactive as well. It doesn't mean we're not valued citizens.'

Her dad looked caught out, which was always fun to see. 'You're just taking a few months off while you sort out this place. It's game over for him.'

Beattie's mum sighed. 'I feel for him, Linus. It can't be that easy.'

'Looks pretty fucking easy from where I'm standing,' her dad said.

*

The Tuckers had a seriously posh car, with creamy leather seats and air con you could barely hear. Everything was clean and soft and swishy. With her pods in, she wouldn't need to speak to Perry, but they weren't even at the ferry when he was already trying to get the conversation going.

She plucked the pod from her right ear. 'Sorry?'

'I just said, do you want to listen to the same music? Since it's just the two of us? We always do when it's just me and Benedict.'

'Er, okay.' *Idiot.* She should have said she was listening to a podcast for school. Adults never questioned schoolwork because they were all so super competitive. It was the one thing that was untouchable.

'You choose,' he said, kind of pathetically pleased. 'Do you have a playlist or something?'

'No, whatever you want is cool.'

He fiddled with the display and chose a radio station called 'Eighties Smash'. Some weird folky thing with fiddles filled the car. 'Do you know Dexys?' Perry asked.

'Um. I don't think so.'

'This wasn't their best, actually. I was just a kid when they were big. In case you're trying to work out *just* how prehistoric I am.'

She wasn't, but she smiled politely. They managed the ferry crossing and drive through Poole without any more chat, but then they stopped at a red light just as the radio signal went all crunchy, and Perry took this as his cue to try again.

'Got a lot of reading this summer, then, have you?'

'Not much.' Then, remembering this was the reason she was so urgently returning home, 'I mean, yeah, quite a bit. I've got uni applications next term, so I've got to say what I'm reading in my personal statement.'

The light changed and the car reared forwards, making her stomach flip.

'I'm sure Benedict will help if you need any advice on that,' Perry said. 'No, wait, you're an academic scholar, aren't you? It's all coming back to me, your amazing GCSE results. You must have been over the moon.'

'Yeah, super gassed,' Beattie said. GCSEs were a hundred years ago.

After that there was a good hour, maybe two, when Perry didn't say much, just hummed along to the songs. The occasional bit of commentary: 'I'm not sure this one's stood the test of time,' and 'We used to think Adam and the Ants were the dog's bollocks.'

There were sweets in the glove compartment, he said, if she fancied one. They were the fruit ones in a tin with icing sugar, like you'd have if you were in a care home or something. She took one shaped like a raspberry and had a lovely daydream about Tate while sucking it.

'So what are you youngsters watching on TV right now?' Perry asked. 'That druggie one? *Euphoria* is it?'

She squirmed a little. 'Loads of stuff.'

'Like?' He was getting all animated, like he did when the families were together and he argued with Benedict and Tabitha. 'Go on, what was the last thing you watched.'

'Um. Probably *Dahmer*.'

'The serial killer guy? You didn't find it a bit disturbing?'

She shrugged.

'Wow. That blows my mind.'

She waited for him to explain.

'I mean, I'm just surprised you're not sickened by something like that.'

'I'm not *not* sickened,' Beattie said. 'I just think the show is good. Makes you see how he came to be this weirdo monster.'

'Are you doing psychology at A level?' he asked.

'No, why?'

'I just thought that might be why you're interested. In serial killers.'

It was bizarre the way parents thought you were only interested in something because there was a link to what you were doing at school. It was the opposite mostly.

'I'm doing maths, biology and chemistry,' she said.

But it seemed like he hadn't heard because he checked his mirrors and made an aggressive overtaking manoeuvre before saying, 'I've developed a bit of an interest in psychology myself. You probably know I used to have a problem with alcohol. Still do,' he corrected himself.

'Oh.' *This* was interesting. She turned to him, the sweet tin in her lap. 'What's it like to be, you know, an addict? I mean, do you still get, like, tempted?'

He nodded like she'd said something really insightful and his eyes checked the mirrors. 'The simplest way I can describe it is it's like a wound that's going to take your whole life to heal. You have to know the tools to stop yourself from picking at the stitches.'

It was a horrible image and she didn't reply, just looked at the cars weaving in and out on the motorway like this was F1. She'd like one of those vintage Porsches, she thought, and imagined herself gliding past all the middle-aged people, with their questions and their 'tracks' that hadn't stood the test of time.

'It's always there,' Perry continued, as if minutes had not passed since he last spoke. 'That yearning. Like a lover lost at war or something. You miss them. You didn't get a proper goodbye.' Hearing himself, he laughed. 'Listen to me going on.'

She took another sweet and held the open tin close to Perry so he could take one without crashing the car. Benedict liked the lemon ones, he said, but he chose his randomly and it was so coated in icing sugar she wasn't sure which one it was. He crunched it rather than sucked it and when she looked at him in surprise, he explained, 'I don't like that feeling when you've rubbed away your upper palate.'

Again, she could think of nothing to say in response. They didn't speak again until they were in London and she recognized the A-road off which Sienna lived.

'You can drop me here,' she said. 'I'm seeing a friend before going back to the house.'

'Sure thing,' Perry said, pulling over on the red line so the driver behind got mad and blared his horn, and even before she'd jumped out and closed the door again, he turned the music up and gave this freaky little cry of joy, like *finally* there was a song that made him feel how he wanted to feel.

20

Charlotte

When the trespassers arrived, her first instinct was relief that Perry was out of town – even if she did suspect him of disappearing this second time purely to demonstrate to Linus that he too had work to do, clients to service. Of all of them he was the most easily wound up, the most apt to overreact.

Then again, there was such a thing as being *too* tolerant, *too* passive, in the face of invasion.

She happened to be out front when it came lumbering into view: a caravan about twenty feet long, towed by an old Skoda Yeti. At first, she assumed the driver had taken a wrong turn and would now set about making a painful reversal or three-point turn before continuing up to Golden Sands Park. She even lingered in case they needed any help judging clearances.

Instead, they drew to a halt opposite the Shaws' bungalow and a young man jumped out of the passenger seat, a pair of bolt cutters in his hand. He crossed the road to Villa Pino and, without a glance in either direction, broke the chain holding the padlock on the driveway gates. He then opened the gates and, as the Skoda's engine roared back to life, gestured for the driver to enter.

Charlotte strode towards him, thinking there was something familiar about his hustling, tenacious demeanour. 'Hello? Can I ask what you're doing?'

But he held up a palm to her and continued directing the vehicle into the crescent drive, until the tourer was satisfactorily positioned, pretty much parallel with the front of the house. The driver killed the engine, got out, and joined him. He was older, with similar colouring, possibly a relative.

'What's going on?' she asked again, though it was as plain as the nose on her face that they were disconnecting the tow. Once that was done, they set about securing the caravan's wheels with yellow clamps, intending, presumably, to leave it there, immobile, immovable.

They were staging some sort of sit-in.

The younger one, who'd broken the lock and now directed the clamping, finally looked up and deigned to engage with her. 'Nothing to worry about,' he said, his eyes squinting in the sun. He had the calm and persuasive manner of the born liar.

'Well, I think it *is* something to worry about,' Charlotte said. She was starting to sweat under her cotton leopard-print dress. 'You can't just abandon a random caravan here.'

'It may be random to you, but it's not to me. It's my home. And I'm not abandoning it, I'm very much staying with it.'

It came to her then who he was: the leader of NJFA. She'd seen him on TV and in the *Voice*. She spoke more forcefully: 'Unless you have the owners' permission, this is trespassing. And criminal damage.'

'What criminal damage?'

'I *saw* you break the padlock – and so did your friend.'

'Didn't see nothing,' the friend said laughing.

She noticed they didn't address the trespassing accusation. There was probably no such thing when you were a Trotskyist or whatever they were. Private property must be abolished and all that. Everything for Everyone, that was the Soviets' cry (or, wait, was it the Welsh?)

'I know you're from Not Just for August. Robbie something, isn't it?'

'My fame grows.' He straightened and thanked his compadre. 'Sorted, mate. You head, yeah?' Moments later, the car departed and Robbie unlocked his caravan door and went inside.

Charlotte glanced down the empty street. It was one of those unsettlingly still days where the sky looked more like a ceiling fresco than a real cloudscape. As if she might not be flesh and bone at all but a figure conjured out of pigment and lime plaster. She wondered whether to call Amy and get her back from IKEA in Southampton, but that seemed a bit of an overreaction. She noticed a woman emerging from a house further down – not the owner, who Charlotte and Perry had had drinks with many times, but a stranger in a beach kaftan and flip-flops – and she waved to get her attention.

'Hi there. Have you seen this?'

The woman waved back. 'We're just here for the week,' she called apologetically, for who would want to waste one of their precious seven days involved in some neighbourhood wrangle?

'Not to worry.' A few cursory knocks at other doors revealed exactly what you'd expect of a beautiful afternoon in August: everyone was out. Returning, she found that a banner had been affixed to the Rickmans' railings: '*Empty In August #NJFA*' in huge red letters. That explained the selection process. And to know Villa Pino was empty, they must have been watching the place.

She went inside to find her phone and call the police. By the time she came back out, Linus had arrived home from a bike ride and was in discussion with Robbie, sweat rolling down his face. Joining them, she found they were talking not about the flagrant act of audacity taking place in front of the residents' eyes but the lightweight beauty of his bike.

'Eight kilos,' Linus said in a proud, boastful tone.

'You're joking me,' Robbie said.

'No, seriously. Some of them only weigh seven.'

'That's mad, that is. How do—'

'Can I have a word, Linus?' Charlotte interrupted, and steered him towards his own driveway. He was giving off serious body heat and smelled very animal. 'That man is the leader of Not Just for August and this is some sort of stunt.'

'I gathered as much, Charlotte.'

'Well, you don't seem very bothered.'

'I'm not. He says he's only here for a short while.'

'What does that mean?' Until the stunt served its purpose, she supposed, which must mean media coverage. 'Do you think he's planning on staying overnight? He's got no utilities.'

Linus paused to ponder this. 'They use gas canisters, if I remember.'

'What about the loo? And please don't tell me you're going to offer your facilities. Amy wouldn't like that. She's already worried about Beattie getting attention from the locals.'

This at least elicited a flicker of concern, but no more. 'Amy worries too much. Anyway, they've probably got one of those chemical loos. Perry not back from London yet?'

'Not till tomorrow morning.'

Linus nodded, satisfied, and Charlotte tipped her head, trying to figure him out. Pragmatism was one thing, but there was something about his manner that suggested he was taking a perverse pleasure in this turn of events. It felt like an extension of his tendency to support Tabitha in her political disagreements with Perry.

As she'd anticipated, supporters were now populating the street and Robbie soon began lobbing soundbites to people filming with their phones. God knew who they were; it was hard to tell these days if someone was bona fide media or just a moocher with nothing better to do.

'What message are you sending to the council, Robbie?'

Robbie thrust his hands in his jeans pockets and raised himself onto the balls of his feet, instantly taller. 'The message I'm sending is we'd like a little less conversation and a little more action, if you know what I'm saying?'

'What sort of action?'

'For starters, we'd like to see the licensing of all second homes in Pine Ridge. We're also calling for the piloting of a scheme that allows locals to access unused accommodation.'

'Are you for compulsory purchase?'

This was met with a friendly chuckle. 'In an ideal world, yes, but we have to be realistic about what the law will allow. I think we can agree that to have a house like this standing empty is heartbreaking for those working families crammed into a B&B or, like me, confined to a small caravan.'

It soon became apparent that all photography and video was set up to showcase a shocking contrast between the ancient discoloured caravan in the foreground and the gleaming new villa behind it, with grand Cliff View to its left. There was no mileage in having the bungalow represent millionaire's row, so the photographers set up on the Shaws' drive for their shots. Linus did nothing to stop this, even stepping aside to allow more of the mob access, and Charlotte approached him once more.

'Linus, you do realize this is bad news, don't you? For us, I mean. For all second-home owners.'

'Not us, Charlotte, just these people in between.'

He didn't even know their names.

'But you know they twist things to make us all look guilty. You've heard what they say: we're selfish and greedy, complicit in hollowing out communities.' She frowned, felt the sting of SPF in her eyes. 'I don't understand, why would you support them and not your own neighbours?'

'I'm not supporting anyone.'

'It looks like you are, Linus. What's going on? Is there something I need to know about?' Then, finally, she guessed. 'Wait, is this to do with the paddleboarding?' She'd gathered from Perry's preening that they'd developed a rivalry, one they were struggling to keep amicable, spending more time bickering about the scheduling of the sessions than actually out on the water. Perry was frustrated by Linus's work commitments, Linus (according to Amy) by Perry's 'unnecessary' trips back home.

A terrible thought struck. 'You didn't . . . You're not feeding NJFA information, are you? Is that how they knew Villa Pino was unoccupied?'

He gave a scornful laugh. 'This isn't *Bridge of Spies*, Charlotte. Seriously, can you back off? I get more than my fair share of conspiracy theories from Amy.'

She gave him a last hard stare. 'Well, as far as your new friend is concerned, I seriously advise you to develop a few of your own. He might not be interested in the bungalow now, but he sure as hell will be once it's done up.'

She turned from him with a parting shot: 'And when that happens, you just might find you need your neighbours after all.'

21

Beattie

She had no intention of visiting Sienna – not least because her friend was in Corfu with her family – but took the Tube to Bond Street and continued by foot to the Marylebone branch of GymLads. As she tapped in and eased through the barrier, she thought about her first time in her home branch in South London. Not that it had been much like what she did now, because the bank card had just been sitting there under the bench in the changing room, presumably having fallen from someone's pocket or bag. She'd had no idea if the woman whose name it bore – Miss Joanne Whittaker – was in the next room busy on the cross trainer or had already done her workout and left.

As if controlled remotely by someone else, she'd snatched it up, slipped it into the pocket of her hoodie and left. Walked across the park towards Brixton, where there was a department store with a ton of brands, mostly lame. She flipped through the racks of clothes, struggling to find something she wanted, then just as she was giving up saw the pink UGG fuzzy slides. The contactless worked like a dream.

She worked her way down the high street, buying bits and pieces. It was a confusing escalation of feelings because she was getting both more confident as each transaction cleared and more nervous as time ticked by and poor Joanne Whittaker got closer to noticing she'd lost her card and decided to phone her bank.

She'd binned the card before getting on the bus.

At home, she told her mum she'd spent her birthday money.

'You got a lot,' her mum said in a praising tone.

'There was a sale on,' Beattie said.

She found out later that after a certain number of contactless payments they asked for your PIN, so she must have been lucky. She'd have crapped herself if that had happened.

Maybe it would have put her off trying anything again, who knew.

Now, in the changing room of GymLads Marylebone, she could see at once that the conditions were perfect. August, not too busy, but not so empty that there'd be only three of them tapping in and out if anyone bothered to check. She went to do a quick workout – leaving within ten minutes of arrival would be a dead giveaway – before returning to survey the women getting changed and using the lockers. Quite a few yoga bunnies, undoubtedly here for the ninety-minute advanced class that started in fifteen minutes. They liked to go in ten minutes early to get the spot they wanted or to fuss about with layering mats and arranging bricks or whatever, then afterwards, they'd stand around with their water bottles, chatting about how centred they felt.

All in all, she could count on having almost two hours.

Once the changing room emptied, she approached the chosen locker and took out her shim, sliding it into the gap to force the lever aside. Inside was a kit bag and a handbag, in which phone and wallet were conveniently stored together. She took the phone and selected the debit card for a well-known high street bank, checking the name was an ethnically plausible match. Susannah

Rice: good. She left the wallet where she'd found it, having learned that most people didn't go immediately to their wallets to see if everything was there. Their phones, yes, but she knew that if it were her, she'd just think she'd left it at home.

Well, she *wouldn't*, obviously, not now that she knew what evil geniuses like her got up to.

The entire time she acted exactly like this were her locker. If someone came in, which had happened once or twice, she knew to slip off her hoodie and shove it in. Do up her shoelace or something.

Leaving the gym, she noticed the same sign she'd seen in a previously visited branch – 'Thefts have been reported in branches of GymLads! Keep your belongings safe!' – and asked herself a tough question: would it have deterred her if she'd seen it on the way in?

Maybe. Then again, she did *really* need this spree before tomorrow's meet with Tate.

She dipped into a Starbucks and picked up a skinny caramel latte with extra and surprisingly nice vegan whipped cream (her victim's treat) and set about downloading the relevant banking app to the secret iPhone she'd bought with cash saved up from babysitting jobs (going rate in her neighbourhood: £12 an hour. Average job: four hours, usually rounded up to £50). Up came the message, always a variation of the same: *We have detected a new device. A security passcode will be sent to your registered device.* Instantly, the notification popped up on the stolen phone. It was only visible for a second, but long enough for her to memorize the code. Sometimes people had their notifications turned off, in which case she had to ditch the phone and be content with the contactless purchases on the card, with its frustratingly low £100 limit.

She tapped in the code, reset the access details and Apple Pay security, and checked out the available balance. Shit, this Susannah Rice bitch had over £20,000 just sitting there! She indulged a brief fantasy of transferring the whole lot to her own account – of course instantly traceable since she only had her young person's account, not some, like, offshore thing – before slipping from her seat, phone and latte in hand.

Selfridges was her chosen store today and she went straight to the underwear department to buy the Agent Provocateur corset and knickers she'd seen online, plus a bra or two that caught her eye. A pair of zebra-print silk pyjamas, a cute silk eye mask. She'd need to cut the labels out and tell her mum she'd got them at the market or something. She didn't need another interrogation like the last one. At the till, the total was £1,570 and the girl didn't bat an eye. Rich teenagers came in the whole time and dropped thousands.

Emerging into Oxford Street, she didn't feel entirely sated. Could she risk going down to the Apple Store on Regent Street and getting some new AirPods? Maybe another iPhone to sell or stash.

She did. Her haul included phone, AirPods, a few silicone wallets, and a couple of HomePod minis that would be good birthday presents for friends.

Afterwards, with barely an hour on the clock – Ms Rice would still be doing her warrior poses or whatever – she deleted the banking app from her phone and turned it off. The stolen one she ditched in a bin. She always felt bad about the phone, knowing how her own life would basically be over if she lost hers, but it was too much of a risk to return to the gym and deposit it somewhere (maybe even hand it in and say she'd found it – how twisted would that be?) Also, for all she knew, it might have recorded information about the new device it had sought verification for. Yes, she'd bought the phone with cash, but it might still be traceable to the Apple store, where old security footage could be requisitioned.

You had to be one step ahead in this game.

She took the steps down to Oxford Circus Tube, picturing herself at home in an hour's time, getting rid of the packaging and labels in a neighbour's bin before stuffing everything into her daypack with the textbooks she had no intention of reading. Perry was staying in town overnight, so she'd need to use her own money for the train fare back to the south coast.

All in all, seriously exhausting for the sake of a date with a man in a caravan – even if he was the hottest dude she'd laid eyes on in the entirety of her seventeen years and four months.

As she approached the barriers down to the Victoria line, she became aware of someone behind her, a second before feeling a tap on her shoulder.

She turned, heart jumping, to find a tall slender woman in her twenties, dressed in normal work-type clothes, blonde hair tucked behind her ears. Store detective? Police? Not . . . oh God, not *Susannah Rice*?

'What?' Beattie said, wondering if she should bolt and if so, whether up or down would be better. In movies, when people were chased into subways, they were always lucky and the train was right there on the platform, the doors snapping shut in the enemy's face.

'I'm with Fire Talent. I was wondering if you'd ever thought about modelling?'

She was a scout! Trying to give Beattie a business card and smiling, all gooey and sincere, like that was all it would take to persuade her to sign up. Had it been the first time, Beattie might have been tempted, but she'd been approached before, both in person and via Instagram, and after discussions with Lexi and Sienna had decided to wait until she was eighteen, when she'd have more followers and, more importantly, her mum wouldn't be able to interfere. Like, insist on accompanying her to a shoot for Nike or whoever and start accusing them of scamming her. What a freak.

'Maybe when I've left school,' she said politely, pocketing the card. 'My mum says I have to concentrate on my exams this next year.'

And she gave the woman a little shrug, like *obviously* she was going to do what her mum said. A girl like her wouldn't dream of breaking the rules.

22

Charlotte

As the press and hangers-on finally began to drift away, she ventured back out. Terrible electronic music was coming from the caravan, not at an anti-social volume, but still irritating in its tinny, insistent way. Through the window, she could see Robbie at his laptop, his expression intent, every inch the keyboard warrior. She imagined him posting the kind of ripostes she'd seen online under newspaper guides to finding the perfect holiday home:

Stop promoting community destruction! This is obscene. Shame on you.

Why are you encouraging the rich to steal from the poor? These people are Second-Home Scumbags.

UK's property Ponzi is only going one way . . .

She could no longer put off texting Madeline Rickman:

Sorry to report that you have visitors. I've called the police. Will keep you up to date.

Her attention switched to a weary figure in work overalls strolling down the street. Her flat shoes squeaked with each stride and she had a plastic carrier of food shopping that looked like it might break under its own weight. Another familiar face.

'Excuse me,' she called, as the girl took a right into the Rickmans' drive and approached the caravan door. 'You work in the deli, don't you?' The name came to her (she was very good with names): 'Shannon, isn't it?'

The girl spun, her face impassive. 'That's right.'

'Do you know Robbie?'

'He's my boyfriend.'

'You mean you live in this caravan as well?'

Shannon nodded. Charlotte couldn't tell if her glacial expression masked wariness or dislike.

'Did you know about this . . . this change of pitch?' She must have, of course, or she wouldn't have known where to come. 'What he's doing is illegal, you know. I wonder if you could have a word with him.'

To her surprise, the girl's face broke open and she laughed freely, as if Charlotte had made her day with so enjoyable a quip. 'You don't know Robbie.'

'Who doesn't know me?' Here he came, down the steps, all cocky, like Mark Rylance in *Jerusalem*. Then, realising who it was his girlfriend was talking to, he gave Charlotte an insolent look as if to say *Still here?*

The very question she should be demanding of him!

'Since the police don't seem to be coming, I thought maybe I would call a breakdown service for you,' she said in a level tone. 'Or I could ask at the garage in Crowland if they could come and tow you away.'

'That would be theft, though,' Robbie said affably. 'It also happens that that's where I work and we're a bit short-staffed, you know what I mean? Not sure we'll be able to get anyone out to you before the weekend.'

The little shit had an answer for everything.

As Shannon climbed into the van, a cab pulled up at the bungalow and Beattie's tanned legs emerged, her feet in scuffed black plimsolls. The rest of her lacked the usual high fashion regalia too: black denim shorts, grey hoodie, hair scraped back.

She clocked the caravan and held up a hand to Robbie. 'Hey.'

He stepped towards her, smiling broadly. 'We meet again. You been off somewhere?'

'Just back to London. I needed some books for school.' She patted her backpack.

As the cab roared off, Robbie lit a cigarette. His manner was easy, avuncular. 'What are you studying?'

'It's just biology stuff,' Beattie said, and grimaced. 'A-level year coming up.'

'Tough one,' Robbie said, exhaling smoke to one side, and as he proceeded to advise the teen on study techniques Charlotte gave a huff and retreated inside. This was absurd. What was wrong with the Shaws? It was one thing to show face at the council's meeting about housing next week, as she knew Amy planned to do, but quite another to fraternize with the enemy like this. To sanction criminal damage.

She poured herself a glass of wine, a surprisingly powerful white from a local vineyard Perry had supported before – and partly during – his dark days, and tended to her thread with Madeline, who must have been thrilled to have been woken in the early hours with news of drama six and a half thousand miles away.

Wtf? Have they broken into the house?

No, on drive in own caravan. They've damaged the gates, but otherwise peaceful.

Are they travellers?

No, locals. Activists.

But the police are there?

Not yet. Maybe call them too?

Will do. Thanks, Charlotte, really appreciate this.

Soon after, Benedict and Tabitha came back from a trip down the coast. When they appeared in front of her, sandy and sun-kissed, she felt suddenly weary, disconnected. Their carefree laughter felt like something from ancient times.

'Whassup out front?' Benedict said.

She felt her mouth twist with irritation. 'Whassup is those activists have decided to squat in the Rickmans' drive.'

'Why?'

'It's about the house being empty in August, which is evidently tantamount to evil.' She heard Perry's outrage in her phrasing. 'Yes, yes, I know they have a point to make about their lived experience, but I'd prefer it if they made it somewhere else. Now our house is going to be plastered all over the news.'

'Sounds like doxxing to me,' Benedict said.

'If they've identified the owner,' Tabitha clarified.

'They've identified the house and the street, isn't that enough?' Charlotte said. 'We're private citizens, we have rights like everyone else.' Oh God, she really was channelling Perry, which begged the question of whether she needed her husband's contrary spirit nearby to activate her own level-headedness.

But no. She was perfectly calm and wry in other situations, such as the workplace. Known for her sangfroid. This was about Robbie the activist and his infuriating sense of entitlement to disrupt *their* hard-earned holiday. To treat them as mere emblems, to make an example of them, when he knew nothing about them and their private struggles, nothing at all.

'Are we still going out for dinner?' Benedict said, and this too irritated her.

'I think we'll just fend for ourselves now that this emergency has arisen. I need to liaise with the Rickmans if the police come.'

Since the police had *not* come, it seemed unlikely that they were treating it as an urgent matter. Perry would be back tomorrow, in any case, and unlike Linus, whose dynamism began and ended with his featherweight bike, he was a man who rolled up his sleeves and got things done.

If he had to, he'd remove the wheel clamps and tow the damn thing away himself.

23

Perry

He was singing along to 'Feeling Good' as he cruised at eighty between speed cameras on the M27, because he was, well, *feeling good*.

Driving on his own was possibly his favourite pastime. Not that he hadn't enjoyed chatting to young Beattie on the way up; he much preferred her type to student radicals like Tabitha. Happy to dress like a female. No guff about heteronormative fragility or unconscious decolonisation or whatever other gobbledygook they came out with. She had something about her, a confidence, an air of hedonism, that he could relate to, that was how youth *should* be experienced. Enjoy it while you looked good and someone else paid the bills. Don't look for reasons to be miserable.

Her father was a twat, but you couldn't have everything.

As always, he'd synchronized his rendezvous with Jordan with genuine errands at Keeler House, one of which had been for alpha neighbour Trev, who had a taste for the monstrously oversized, be it in his own musculature (the words brick shithouse sprang to mind) or in the TV screen that filled the whole of one wall of his room. The space smelled like a locker room, a consequence, presumably, of the impressive set of weights in one corner.

Normally when Perry got going with a job, especially if it involved his electric drill, the resident would slope off to the kitchen for a cup of tea or out to the garden for a roll-up, but this guy stayed right there, breathing audibly.

'Don't touch my stuff,' he said, when Perry eyed up the weights.

'I'm going to have to move them so I can get to the wall behind. Perhaps you could do it for me?'

This Trev did, grudgingly, before sitting on his bed and watching Perry through narrowed eyes as he removed the damaged section of wall (God, had it been kicked with a hobnailed boot or something?) and began fitting a new piece of plasterboard.

The job didn't take long, and as he got back to his feet, he was startled to find the guy's face right there – he hadn't been aware of his having moved – and Trev jeered at his surprise. His teeth were like something out of Dickens, tongue studded with silver.

'All sorted,' Perry said, unable to stop his heart from hammering. 'The plaster's wet so be careful for a few hours.'

'Hours?' Trev echoed, as if Perry were out of his tiny mind if he thought he was going to inconvenience him to this extent.

'Hours,' Perry confirmed, and made no further eye contact.

'He's not right in the head,' he said to Jordan later.

'I *told* you,' Jordan said with a shudder.

*

He stayed overnight in Jordan's room, which he'd never done before, slipping away early and going back to Masefield Road to switch cars and shower before getting back on the road to Pine Ridge. Sixties Smash Radio pounded from the stereo, hence the Nina Simone.

There'd been the usual sullied skies in South London, but on the coast the sun blazed from an immaculate dome of blue and the air sizzled with dry heat. On the ferry, he scrolled through his Twitter feed. A post from NJFA was getting a lot of shares: pictures of a caravan parked almost flush against the front of a smart white house, a young man standing next to a sign on the railings that read: '*Empty In August!*'

Wait, that wasn't Villa Pino, was it?

He zoomed in. It bloody well was!

He checked his messages. Not a dickybird from Charlotte. No doubt she hadn't wanted to bother him while he was busy or, more likely, not wanted to set in motion a mad dash back and risk a fireball on the M3. The NJFA post was from last night. Checking, he found an update from that morning, the same chap barbecuing sausages, coffee mug in hand. A link to a TikTok reel of his overnight stay, complete with shots of Cliff View outlined against the dusk sky, all to the soundtrack of 'Two Tribes' by Frankie Goes to Hollywood. For Christ's sake!

He rang Charlotte.

'Hi Perry. Are you on your way? Where are you?'

'On the ferry, just about to dock. Is that caravan I'm seeing on Twitter parked outside the Rickmans'?'

Charlotte tutted. 'I *knew* it was going to be possible to identify the address.'

'Is it still there?'

'Yes.'

'Why the fuck haven't the police moved them on?'

'They didn't come yesterday when I phoned them, but I've just tried again and said I write for the *Daily Mail* and they claim they're on their way. Honestly, I thought yesterday was a circus, but it's all happening now. There's even a TV crew. This guy knows what he's doing. I actually think he *wants* to be arrested, maybe he even arranged it with the police. Listen, if I were you, I'd park the car at the beach and walk up in case they film you and show the reg on the news.'

'Are you serious?' Perry spluttered. Anyone would think *they* were the criminals.

'Well, at least you won't get attacked at the toll booth. The entire group is in the street for this.'

'Is Benedict with you?' Perry asked.

'He's still in bed. Amy's here, but her summerhouse has just arrived so she's dealing with that. Linus is out on his bike again.' Her voice lowered. 'He was *very* unhelpful yesterday. I could really have used his support, but he was almost obstructive.'

'I bet he was. Listen, I have to go.' The barrier was up and cars were moving off the ferry. Charlotte was wrong about the activists; a couple had been dispatched to pelt eggs, one of which cracked on his windscreen in a cartoon explosion.

He rolled down the window and yelled 'Piss off!', seeing too late that a masked figure held her phone up, filming.

The slime of the egg had created an annoying blind spot, but he gunned the engine and pulled away with less care than usual. There was a long queue waiting to enter the village via Old Beach Road, so he indicated right for the ridge loop. He was damned if he was going to do as Charlotte had suggested and park at the beach. He had a right to drive down his own road and park in his own drive and if any bugger presented his licence plate onscreen in a derogatory light, then he'd sue them.

He made the gentle ascent to the ridge on autopilot. Having not checked his rear view for a few moments, he didn't spot the bike till it swerved in front of him and he braked abruptly. But he could feel the car's speed exceeding that of the cyclist and made the split-second decision to swing onto the grass verge, which caused the seatbelt to cut painfully into his shoulder. At least the airbag didn't deploy. A second or two later and he'd have smashed into trees, seriously injuring himself.

He waited for the cyclist to loop back and check on him, but the bastard just kept on climbing. Perry fired up the engine and sped after him, pulled in front of him, blocking the lane sideways in a manoeuvre he'd seen in police documentaries. *Now* he had to stop. He dismounted, gesturing furiously at Perry, and began unstrapping his ribbed helmet.

Perry jumped out of the Range Rover, mouth already working: 'You ran me off the road, mate! Did you not see?'

'Calm down, Perry, for fuck's sake.'

'What the . . . Linus!'

They paced towards one another, mismatched boxers squaring off in the ring, Perry as conscious of his superior bulk as he was his lack of height. In his poncy cycling Lycra, Linus was lean to the point of spidery, his hair flat and dripping, face burning with exertion and anger.

'You were going way too fast! What were you thinking?' The accusation had a puritanical note to it which only intensified Perry's glower.

'I was well under the limit. This is a sixty and I was barely doing that.'

'No, Perry, it's not a sixty, it's a forty. It switches at the bottom of the hill, presumably because it's a difficult gradient and you're about to hit woodland.'

The fucking know-it-all. He'd been here five minutes and was telling Perry, a home owner of fifteen years, where the difficult gradients were.

'What's that on your windscreen? No wonder you had a blind spot.'

'It's egg, courtesy of our friends at the ferry. Why aren't you at the house dealing with this squatter business? Charlotte says it's a three-ring circus, press crawling all over the place.'

Linus shrugged, his bony shoulders almost reaching his ears. 'What am *I* supposed to do about it?'

'Well, not leave it to the girls, for starters. You know I've been away. For Christ's sake, Linus, be a man.'

'What, like you, you mean?'

This took Perry aback. Was that . . .? No, it couldn't be a dig at his extracurriculars, could it? How could Linus possibly know about Jordan? 'Yes, like me. I'm on my way there now to do what you should have done and protect the women and children from these fucking revolutionaries.'

Linus scoffed at him. 'D'you want to dial down the rhetoric a bit, mate? We're not dealing with Che Guevara here. Last time I looked, the bloke was sitting on his step having a cup of PG Tips.'

Perry had had enough. He climbed back into the Range Rover and crawled off comically slowly, Linus pointedly stepping off the road, arms raised, as he'd passed.

Over the hill, progressing at a painful 40 mph, he approached Golden Sands Park and was surprised to spot another member of the Shaw family: Beattie. She was wearing an ankle-length blue dress with stripes down the side, a plunging V neck revealing quite a bit of black lace. The quilted flip-flop things on her feet seemed a strange choice, like something a rapper would wear to relax backstage.

He rolled down his window. 'You need a lift somewhere?'

She gave him a tight smile. 'No, I'm cool.'

'You dad's just behind on his bike. We had a bit of a near-miss, actually.'

'Oh.' The girl looked completely unbothered, had no questions about her dad's welfare when he could be lying on the roadside, ploughed down by Perry or some other motorist. He began to feel a little remorseful for the altercation. Quite apart from the friendship/neighbourhood politics of the thing, there was also the possibility that Linus had one of those cameras on his handlebars – or built into that snazzy helmet of his.

'You want me to wait with you till he comes along? Make sure he's okay?'

Beattie's gaze fell just beyond him. 'No, it's fine. I'm meeting someone.'

'Okay. Well, I'll love you and leave you then.'

She looked faintly disturbed by this farewell, perhaps did not know the phrase, and he hoped he hadn't blundered across yet another of life's new lines, offending with pleasantries that had previously and for as long as he could remember been, well, *pleasant*. Either way, the exchange was humiliating and when he rolled up his window, he felt the desire for a drink hover around his head like a fly. As he visualized a rolled-up newspaper and swatted it away, he saw in his rear-view Linus appear on the ridge, hurtling downhill at well over forty.

Bloody hypocrite.

24

Beattie

Beattie watched Perry's car roll out of sight before ducking into the entrance to the caravan park. She had no intention of waiting for her dad to ride by, seeing the stupid way he crouched over the handlebars like he was in the Tour de France or whatever. No, she was here for sex and she could do without images of his big sweaty face popping into her head and scarring her psychologically for the rest of her life.

She studied the park map by the office. The central avenue of the park was clearly the most direct route to the tourers section where Tate lived, but he'd recommended taking the perimeter path, where she'd be less visible to the gossips. En route, she took a selfie by a static and sent it to the girls – *Tryst with local in a caravan* – and giggled at the flurry of 'lmho' and 'omds' comments it provoked.

Some of the caravans were really small, not much bigger than the summerhouse being assembled in her garden right now. Her mum had been in a state of excitement—

Stop. She needed an image of her mum in a state of excitement about as much as one of her dad dripping sweat onto his handlebars.

Finally reaching the right pitch, she found Tate standing in the open doorway of a stained, old-looking caravan, a dinky set of steps between them.

'Hey. Come in. Quick.' He moved aside, making no contact with her as she entered, which was somehow sexier than if he'd gripped her straight away.

Inside, it was all a lot nicer than she'd expected. Retro and feminine, with cheesecloth curtains, vintage cushions and cute little lanterns. 'This is actually quite cool.'

'Yeah. Ellie's into these makeovers. It's a big thing in the community.'

'You make it sound like you're travellers or something.' She giggled. 'The police just arrested your friend Robbie by the way. You know my mum and dad's place is right next door?'

The whole scene had been crazy, with neighbours watching and a whole bunch of people who might have been Robbie's squad or journalists or maybe just tourists filming on their phones as Robbie was guided into the back seat of a police car, just like on TV. He'd grinned like on TV too, at one point catching Beattie's eye and she'd found herself smiling stupidly back at him, like *fangirling*. Mortifying.

If Tate noticed her blushing at the memory, he didn't let on. 'You've been up to London,' he said.

'Yesterday, yeah.' Beattie leaned against the tiny kitchen unit, one foot flat against the other calf. 'What's going to happen to him? He didn't seem very worried.'

'He'll be out later today,' Tate said. 'Tomorrow at the latest.'

'How do you know?'

'He's been arrested before. I have as well.'

'Seriously?'

'Yeah. Goes with the territory. We may look like pussies living in these pimped-up doll's houses, but we're criminals, me and Robbie.'

'Wow,' Beattie said. 'I'm feeling the gangster vibes here.'

'Come here and feel them properly.' He slid open a door behind him to reveal a mattress. The bedding wasn't crumpled, but it wasn't smooth either.

'Wait, there's an actual bed?'

He smirked. 'How did you think we slept? In hammocks?'

They smashed together then, nose-diving onto the mattress. It was too weird to think that this was where he slept with his girlfriend, the sad girl she'd seen him with at The Needles, and so she banished her face as she had her parents'. Better not to see at all, perhaps, only to feel, so she closed her eyes and enjoyed the feel of Tate's teeth biting her lower lip, his fingers at the front of her dress, fumbling for fastenings.

The alliteration of that made her want to giggle again. *Stop thinking.*

'Jesus. Fuck. Wow.'

He'd seen the lacy corset. She opened her eyes and looked at his face. It was like something less than human, stripped back to the animal. 'You like it? I bought it in London yesterday.' She started to wriggle out of her knickers.

'Keep the top bit on,' Tate breathed. Something seemed to occur to him then. 'Wait, you're not . . .?'

'Not what?'

'You know, a virgin?'

'Why?' Beattie inhaled, every nerve super-sharp, sensations overflowing. 'Would you not be cool with that?'

'I'd be cool, yeah. I'd just want to know is all.' He was breathing very heavily. 'Maybe you'd want to rethink if this is where you'd want to, y'know, lose it.'

She felt an exhilarating infusion of power as he paused to await this unexpected new level of consent that seemed to be to do with the caravan.

'Well, I'm not,' she said. 'And I'm not rethinking anything.'

*

Afterwards, he fetched beers from the world's smallest fridge.

'Do your mum and dad live around here?' Beattie asked.

'My mum, no. She's up north now. No idea where my dad even is. Haven't seen him since I was, like, five.'

'Oh.' She had a weirdly maternal feeling then, like she wanted to cradle his head against her breastbone, blended with guilt for having not waited to see if her own dad was unharmed after whatever it was that had happened with Perry. 'But your mum, when did she move?'

'Few years ago now.'

'Because of the housing situation?'

'No, because she's got really bad taste in men. I tried to take over her flat, actually, but the landlord decided to switch to an Airbnb.'

She slurped her beer, felt the malty froth expand inside her mouth. 'Where was it?'

'The estate on the other side of the village. Behind the Gull?'

'Do tourists stay over there as well?'

'They stay everywhere.' Tate ran a sunburnt hand through his floppy fringe, clearing his forehead. The skin was paler there and baby soft.

'But you don't target them. Only the ones who own somewhere, right? The second-homers. They're always talking about it, you know.'

'What do they say?' Tate asked.

Sometimes they said it was the politics of envy, but she didn't tell him that. 'My mum says it's a complicated ecosystem.'

'You could say that.'

'So did the same happen to Robbie? Is that the reason he's in a caravan as well?'

'Worse.' He snuggled close, snaked an arm around her ribs and she admired the contrast between the blacks and reds of his tattoos and her smooth, unblemished skin. 'His family got put in this skanky B&B. The damp was really bad and his mum got this respiratory illness, had to go to hospital. Caught Covid and died.'

'That's terrible. How old was she?'

'Like, fifty?'

'No wonder he's, y'know, motivated.'

They had sex again and then he checked his phone. 'We should put some clothes on. You know, just in case.'

'Sure.' She wondered if Tate had had a fling with a tourist before; it would be useful to know if he was practised in the logistics of deception. 'When's Ellie back?'

'Not for ages, but if they let Robbie off with a caution, he'll probably come straight round. His uncle will be towing the van back any minute.'

Beattie's eyes went wide. 'That's it then? He just gives up?'

'He's made his point. He won't want to spend a minute longer with the . . .' Tate caught himself, remembering who he was with.

'With the what?' Beattie said laughing. 'What do you guys call us?'

He sent her a mischievous look. 'A lot of names. Blow-ins. Grockles.'

'Grockles?' She laughed. 'Sounds like goblins or something. Aren't there any nicer ones?'

'Summer people, maybe.'

'*That's* better. Yes. Thank you.'

Dressed, they pressed together again to kiss goodbye.

'Feel like we've wasted a bit of time here,' Tate said. 'I mean, you've been down here already, I don't know, how long?'

'Maybe ten days? But I don't go back till the end of the month, so if we . . .' Beattie let the thought drop. *See each other every day*, that was what she wanted to say, what she wanted to happen. To see him here, every day, in his tiny caravan, where it was humid and confining and breathless, claustrophobic in the best way.

'Loads more time then,' he said, his thought processes evidently briefer.

She retraced her steps to the exit, her body aching where his had been, her mood never better. But at the top of the hill, just clear of the caravan park, she watched as a Needles-branded golf buggy pulled up and a woman climbed out of the passenger seat. Fuck, it was Ellie, Tate's girlfriend!

'I hope you feel better!' the driver called.

'I'm sure I will,' Ellie said. 'It's just a stomach upset. Thanks so much!'

Woah. Tate was going to get a serious shock. He'd probably have smoothed out the sheets and stuff by now, but would he have showered?

She messaged him: *SOS ur gf is here! U hve 2 mins!*

This was *so* not going to work as a regular thing. They needed somewhere else to hang – and pronto.

*

The dilemma lasted all of the walk home, which ended with her turning into Pine Ridge Road just as the caravan exited. Hopefully its return would be a helpful distraction if Tate's girlfriend was experiencing any suspicions.

On arrival at the bungalow, she found the summerhouse already up and her mum testing paint colours on the sea-facing side. It was actually very cute, kind of Alpine-looking.

She slipped a hand round her mum's waist. 'Looks really nice. When will we be able to use it?'

'As soon as it's painted,' her mum said, giving her a flashback to girlhood, the way she used to answer Beattie's incessant questions in a patient, adoring voice (well, mostly). 'It'll take a couple of days. Fancy helping with the painting?'

'Maybe. Will it have electricity?'

'Not till the extension's done, but I've got some gorgeous LED lamps. I'll show you in a minute.'

'I was thinking,' Beattie said, 'maybe I could use it as my bedroom?'

'It's *my* bedroom,' a voice protested and it took her a second to figure out that it belonged to Huck, speaking from inside the summerhouse.

'*My* bedroom,' she mimicked, irritated.

'Oh,' her mum said. 'I thought maybe Huck and Julien might sleep in it. I'm not sure I'd be comfortable with you being down here on your own.'

This was not good, not good at all. Inspiration struck. 'It's way too small to share. Julien could have my room. Close to the bathroom and everything. I'll clean it for him?' There wasn't much chance of her mum believing in this sudden altruism, but she was fairly confident the true reason for her need for privacy remained unguessable.

'I don't know, Beattie.'

'Mum!' Huck yelled.

'*Mum!*' Beattie echoed, even meaner now. It was crucial she crush his challenge. His pesky prior claim could not be allowed to trump her firstborn status.

'Well, it could work, I suppose,' her mum said. 'If it's properly secure.' She pulled the sentimental face that meant an embarrassing declaration of love was forthcoming. 'Honestly, darling, I don't think I could live with myself if anything happened to you.'

Both pleased and revolted, Beattie stepped away from her and out onto the footpath. Laughter from the beach carried on the breeze, followed by the rumble of a rogue wave rolling in, and the sky was a rich, flat blue, like it was in a Ghibli cartoon or something. She almost expected to see a magic castle up there.

She was startled from her reverie by a more urgent call from Huck. 'Mum? I can't get out! The bolt's stuck!'

'Why did you lock it?' her mum called back.

'To see if it worked.'

'See,' Beattie said, satisfied, as her mum switched to fire-fighting mode and began issuing instructions through the door, an edge of hysteria to her voice. 'It's totally secure already.'

25

Robbie

'Robbie? You need to hear this!'

I've been dreaming about my mum. A good dream, thank God. They were horrendous at first – for years, actually – like some VR horror game. I'd be trapped under her corpse, my breath getting thinner and thinner, or I was the surgeon who cut into her chest and saw the dead lung tissue. Smelled the rot. But recently the darkness has lifted and I see her as she was when I was young and she was a normal mum with a house and a job and a body still free of disease.

'Robbie, wake up!'

I groan. Whatever she's got to say, I'm pretty sure I don't want to hear it. Especially if it's to do with refilling the water barrel or details of the latest domestic between the couple next door. 'Fuck, Shannon, I'm sleeping . . .'

Caravan living is fine, better than people think, but it does mean you're in each other's faces – literally. When I open my eyes, hers are right there, inches from mine. She's urgent, agitated, and surprisingly not recoiling from my stale lager breath. We're in the living room, not the bedroom, both still dressed. The TV's playing an old *Married At First Sight*.

'What time is it?'

'Just after eleven. You dozed off the minute we got back.'

As I lift myself off the bench it feels chillier than it should. There's the roar of rough wind up on the ridge and I have an awful memory of last winter, how fucking freezing it got. Wiping the condensation off the windows with icy fingers. And it's not even September yet. The weather's been gorgeous – until this last week, the problem's been the heat.

My next thought is unexpected: Tate's not going to be able to hack the winter. It's too grim. For me, everything we do with NJFA is about the principle as much as the personal, it's about the integrity of Pine Ridge, preserving its identity as a home town, a community. But for him, it's *all* personal. He wants a roof over his own head, a roof made of local slate, sprinkled with needles from ancient pines and dusted with salt from the ocean. He wants girls and vodka and music. He wants to live like the summer people – all year round.

'There's news,' she says, and perches opposite.

'News about what?'

'About that house.'

It takes another moment for my feeble brain to catch up. The house – summerhouse – falling into the sea. The aborted concert. Beers in the Gull with the gang after a bit of a session on the beach.

A session on the beach – well, that dislodges another fragment of memory that I instantly dismiss. *Concentrate.*

'Well?' I say, and she sucks in her breath, nervous. I can tell it's real nerves, as well, not just her stringing out a bit of gossip for effect.

'Ethan just texted me. Apparently, there was someone in there.'

There's a silence. Though she could hardly have been clearer, I don't want to acknowledge what I've just heard. I don't want to face this. I want to rewind to five minutes ago and dream about my mum.

'I don't understand. I thought the family were out?'

'They were. Out of the main house. But it turns out one of them, *someone*, was in this building in the garden.'

We stare at each other for a moment, arms by our sides, keeping our balance in a tilting world. 'How are they only just discovering this?'

'The tide, I suppose,' she says. 'It'll be out by now, won't it? They've been able to get to the wreckage.'

I replay the action in my mind. The summerhouse nudging towards the cliff edge, those agonising seconds when I assumed I was hallucinating. Ten, maybe twenty, when it hung in thin air before dropping.

'How many feet is that? Must be thirty.' And clear as a bell I hear my mum's voice cut in: 'You're like goats, you lot,' she used to say if she found us hanging above the seawall as kids. Further down past the Meadow, where the pillbox is. More times, she'd call me her brave lion. I'd forgotten that. *My brave lion.*

I blink, swallow the grim dehydrated saliva that's pooled in my mouth, blink again. What word did she just use? *Wreckage.* They've been able to get to the wreckage. 'Could you even survive a drop like that?'

'I don't know.' Shannon's eyes go all shiny, like she might cry. 'But not in this case. Not according to Ethan. Whoever it is, they're dead.'

PART TWO

26

Robbie

Monday 28 August, 11.15 p.m.

We're outside the van, both of us smoking, but the pain in my chest is nothing to do with the cigarette. It's the vice-grip of dread. Because whatever that was up on the clifftop today, that prank, that stunt, someone is dead and this is serious fucking shit.

Shannon agrees that we need to get everyone together – now. Tomorrow morning will be too late. We have to be prepared to account for our every move before we get hauled in by the police. One by one, starting with me.

I text Rio that we're on our way down to his place and then we pick up Tate and Ellie from across the way. I feel a weird kind of sadness in the moments before we tell them, like we're about to corrupt their innocence.

They react pretty much the same as I did. Disbelief. Horror. In Tate's case, borderline panic.

'Who is it?' he asks as we fall into step and start marching down Paradise Avenue to the exit. 'Does Ethan know?'

'I don't think so,' Shannon says. 'But there's no way he'd tell me even if he did. You have to notify family first. Right or left?' she asks, at the exit.

We choose left for the more direct route over the ridge and through the pine forest to the new village, where Rio's mum's place is. The road's unlit and what feels like a fragrant canopy in daylight is seriously creepy at night. We bunch up, trying not to infect one another with Blair Witch vibes.

'Were they talking about it at The Needles?' I ask Ellie.

'About the house falling in, yeah. Most of the guests were at the festival. Came traipsing back early, straight to the bar.'

'We need to find out who it is,' Tate says, persistent, way more keyed up than the rest of us.

Which fucking worries me, to be frank.

We hit the upper reaches of the village and start the steep trek down. Rio's mum's place is just up from the Gull, where there are still lights on and voices carrying as the staff clean up. Best trade of the summer for them, corpse or no corpse.

Rio comes to the door and we give him and Des the news. They exchange a fretful look, chests rising and sinking, and I know they wish I'd just leave them to crash out. Des in particular looks shattered, like he's worked one shift too many, his normally close-trimmed hair growing over the Mohican tattoos that encircle his ears.

Rio's mum and her boyfriend have gone to bed and we cram into the front room and close the door. There's not that much more space in here than in the caravan, but it feels more sheltering. Jammed in its terrace, it's not going to rock in a gale. A light sprinkle of rain won't sound like bullets from a Kalashnikov.

I settle on a wonky old dining chair by the window and all heads turn to me. Normally I enjoy being the leader, the ideas man, but not this time.

'Right. I know what we said in the pub, but now I need to know the truth. Does anyone need covering for?' I spell it out: 'This could turn into a murder charge, so we need to make sure we've got everyone's back. Let's just go round the room. Anyone got any gaps we need to know about?'

'No.' Ellie speaks first. She was working a shift at the spa, back-to-back treatments, completely out of the picture.

'No.' Des only got back from work at eight-thirty and he took the bus and ferry, which means there'll be CCTV visuals of him somewhere between Poole and here.

'No.' Rio was on the beach; when not with Shannon or me, he was with his mum's partner and a whole bunch of their mates who can vouch for him.

'No.' Tate was working at the beach bar, which closed soon after the concert was aborted, at which point he came to the Gull and joined Rio, Shannon and me.

Finally, Shannon, who I don't even need to ask. I know for sure she was watching the band when it happened because she was right there in my line of sight. Not that she could operate heavy machinery anyway. She's never even learned to drive.

Des speaks up: 'Whoever did it . . . I mean, if the idea was just to destroy this garden house thing, then they might not've known there was someone in there?'

'Yeah, but it still counts,' Shannon says. 'It'd be manslaughter, not murder, but that's still years in prison.'

I wonder if the victim died of their injuries or by drowning. I hope, at least, they were unconscious, with no clue that cold salt water was invading their lungs, claiming them.

'I don't get it,' Ellie says. 'If you were in a building that started moving, you'd get the hell out, wouldn't you?'

'There was definitely enough time to escape,' I say. 'It's not like it suddenly blew up. Maybe the door got stuck? Maybe they were hammering at the window but there was no one around to hear?'

'Or they were asleep?' Shannon suggests. 'Had a bit too much to drink?'

'You'd have to have ODed on smack to sleep through the noise of a JCB,' Des says.

'Or the band,' Rio says. 'There was more feedback than actual music.'

A couple of us snicker: he's not wrong.

Tate clears his throat, focused once more on Shannon. 'Ethan didn't say which house it was? What number?'

'They don't have numbers up there,' I point out. 'They have names. The summerhouses have got their own names as well.'

'That's right. The one on the end's got a little wooden name-plate.' Shannon tries to remember. 'Something beginning with N, maybe?'

'I spy with my little eye, a death trap beginning with N,' Rio says, with a little yelp of guilty laughter.

'That's not funny,' Tate says. 'Ask Ethan,' he tells Shannon, way too curt, and she shoots a look at him, like, *Don't tell me what to do.*

I check the 'official' NJFA WhatsApp thread. There was an exchange earlier, right after the house fell, a few images shared, but nothing in the later part of the evening. Of course, it was a dawn start for many; they'll be asleep.

'We're definitely the only ones who know,' I say. 'Us and the police.'

I select a contact from the thread I haven't texted individually before and fire off a quick line:

Just checking you're OK?

The ticks pop up. It's been read. That's enough.

'I'm thinking it's bound to be someone I've served,' Shannon says.

'I know,' Ellie agrees. 'I might've had them in for a treatment as well. Trying to think who I've seen around this last week.'

I'm ashamed to admit this to the group, but I'm thinking that if the dead person is a local and not a DFL, then it would at least take the heat off us. We would never knowingly harm one of our own. But, then, what would a local be doing in a posh guest cottage?

I notice Tate's left knee jerking, a spasm he can't seem to control.

'If I could choose . . .' Ellie continues, but changes her mind. 'No, I'm not gonna say it.'

'Go on,' Des says. 'We don't care.'

'Just, if I had to choose, it would be that posh cow.'

'Which one?' Rio says.

'From earlier? She accused me of stealing? A complete bitch.'

'Like I said, which one?'

We all crack up. All except Tate, who's glowering at Rio like he's going to smack him in the teeth. 'Why are you even laughing about this? What's wrong with you?' Next thing, he's on his feet and striding out the door.

'Tate!' Ellie's up now, tearing after him. We hear her call his name again in the street before she comes back in, hands upturned in despair. 'He's gone in the wrong direction. He's got the key, as well!'

For God's sake, I really don't want to deal with the drama between those two. 'Let's all get some sleep,' I tell the others. 'Tomorrow's going to be a nightmare.'

'Walk back with us,' Shannon says to Ellie. 'If he's not home, you can stay over at ours.'

'What's up with him, anyway?' Rio says.

'Fuck knows,' I say. 'He's been acting off all night.'

'I know what it is.' Ellie's got tears wobbling in her eyes. 'It's nothing to do with this.'

And suddenly, like an attack of cramp, I get it. Whatever she thinks it is, she's mistaken, because it *is* to do with this.

You twat, Tate. You devious, horny twat.

'I'll go and find him,' I say, sighing.

27

Amy

Earlier in August

Everything was ready for Julien's arrival. The Niche was painted – a shimmering oyster grey to absorb the changing moods of the sea and sky – and Beattie installed, freeing up her room in the bungalow for their guest. The garden was prepped for the welcome barbecue, the dirt under the pines covered with an oversized kilim and dotted with what bits of garden seating she'd been able to cobble together. The effect fell some way short of the safari chic Amy had been aiming for, but at least the raincloud that might have put it in jeopardy had rolled obligingly inland. The evening light was limpid and silky.

She couldn't believe they were two weeks into the trip already. Halfway through their . . . their what? 'Holiday' it wasn't, at least not in her case. She'd swum in the sea precisely twice, her city pallor improved only by the flush of stress. What then? Exploratory visit? Extended recce? Soft launch?

Waiting for Linus and the boys to return from the train station, she had her first – and always, *always* best – glass of rosé while scanning the new edition of the *Voice*, which had on its front page a report on the NJFA caravan stunt. Out till late at IKEA and a string of decorator's merchants, she'd missed most of the drama, which was probably just as well because she'd only have been strong-armed by Charlotte into opposition when she really did have mixed emotions about this issue. As she'd tried to explain to the kids, it was complex.

By all accounts – including his own – Linus had not covered himself in glory in her stead.

She peered at the main image, a rather beautifully composed photo of the activist's caravan sitting plum in front of Villa Pino.

Activist Highlights Injustice in
Pine Ridge Property Market

Tensions between locals and incomers reached fever pitch in Pine Ridge last week when activists staged a sit-in at a holiday villa left empty for the summer. Crowds gathered on Thursday to support Robbie Jevons, leader of the Not Just For August pressure group, as he spent 24 hours in the driveway of the house on prestigious Pine Ridge Road – occupying a caravan usually pitched in Golden Sands Park.

Arrested on Friday by the police on suspicion of 'residing on land without consent in or with a vehicle', Jevons was released the same day without charge and insisted he had no regrets. 'I think everyone gets the point I was making,' he told the Voice. *'The house in question is one of dozens left empty all year round, even in summer – we have documentary proof of that – while locals suffer insecurity and even homelessness.'*

Well, Amy thought, at least it solved one mystery. That sense of being watched – it turned out they *had* been, by activists monitoring their properties, making lists of which houses were occupied and which empty. Perry and Charlotte were right: this was getting sinister.

The property targeted is a lavish beach house with five bedrooms and 2,500 square feet of accommodation. According to local agent Carolyn Goode, its value could be as high as £2 million. 'All homes on the headland carry a premium because of their spectacular views. If one were to come onto the market today, it would be out of reach to all but the wealthiest one per cent'.

It is thought that there are over 270,000 homeless people in England, whereas an estimated 770,000 households own second homes in the UK, which is just under one in ten of the population.

But in high-end holiday resorts like Pine Ridge the percentage is significantly higher. At least half of properties are second homes or holiday rentals, claims Jevons, who recently appeared on BBC South to talk about the loss of his childhood home to a holiday let landlord. 'If this is the situation for working people like me, imagine how tough it is for those who are vulnerable and unable to work,' he said. 'What we have here is an iniquitous two-tier housing system and we will challenge it as long as it continues.'

Having missed the BBC story referenced in the article, Amy got up to hunt for her phone. She was struck, as she was several times a day, by the fact that everything she touched felt gritty; the sand and the soil, the pervasive dust: it was as if the world had been pulverized, reduced to fine grains.

According to Charlotte, the dust hung around for years, as she'd told Linus that morning.

'Amy, do you release that every other sentence that comes out of your mouth begins "According to Charlotte",' he said.

'Well, tell me stuff yourself and I won't need to hear it from her,' she'd retorted.

For instance, according to Charlotte, he and Perry had almost come to blows up on the ridge road – when had he been going to tell her about *that*? She supposed that given the men's ideological differences on road usage, it had only been a matter of time, and neither had been physically harmed, which was the main thing.

She left the house and powered through the dirt to the Niche, rapping on the window rather than the door because the external paintwork wasn't quite dry.

'Beattie?'

The blind was raised, allowing Amy a glimpse of the interior, which, while not exactly a suite at The Needles, had a pleasing cabin-like charm. A sofa bed with a nice thick topper and lovely washed linen covers. Cute mushroom-shaped cordless lamps in aquamarine and amber. Beattie couldn't fit all her clothes in the narrow wardrobe, so the excess had been moved into Huck's room (Amy wouldn't allow her creeping subterranean worries about the provenance of said items to surface today. She was far too busy).

Beattie opened the door wrapped in a towel, make-up brushes in hand.

'Can I use your phone to call mine? I can't find it anywhere.'

'Can't you use Dad's?

'He's out, picking up Julien.'

'Huck's then.'

'He's with Dad! For goodness sake, I'll bring it straight back!'

A solid day of painting until she thought her shoulder might dislocate, not to mention another trip to the emporia of Bournemouth for furnishings *for Beattie*, and now, moments after finishing, the girl wouldn't even lend her her phone for two minutes!

Beattie surrendered it with her customary doublespeak challenge: 'Feel free to look at my socials. I know you're dying to.'

'Thank you, I will,' Amy said, though she knew they would have been sanitized of anything of interest. That had been the risk of the confrontation about the clothes: she'd alerted her to the need for enhanced privacy.

Okay, so maybe she *was* going to think about the clothes – but only for as long as it took her to find her phone. Since their little chat, she'd not been aware of anything new arriving in the teenage wardrobe, with the exception of a pair of pyjamas with the labels cut out that Beattie said had been a birthday gift from her friends that she hadn't worn yet. A potentially suspicious trip to London had proved innocent, Perry having dropped her at Sienna's in Putney and, according to Linus, her having returned home on the promised train with a bagful of textbooks.

She called her own number several times before finally catching a snatch of its ring – in the garage, where she'd been cleaning her paintbrushes earlier. Ending the call, her thumb hovered over the Chrome icon. The young 'uns didn't google things like they did, preferring TikToxic, as Perry called it, but Amy knew Beattie used Google for academic research and she'd certainly claimed to be studying when she'd asked for help making salads earlier.

Sure enough, a page from *The Biologist* website popped up, an article about genetics. That would be to do with her reading for her personal statement – a reassuring sign. She tapped the back arrow and found the search that had led Beattie there. She tapped it once again and found another term in the search box: 'gym theft'.

God, I hope she hasn't had anything stolen at the gym, she thought. Charlotte wasn't the only one capable of recognising a costly designer item when she saw one.

*

At the sound of the car pulling into the driveway, she went out front to greet their house guest. She'd met Julien when delivering Huck to

Paris earlier in the year, a service that now looked embarrassingly overprotective compared with the insouciance her opposite number had shown in expecting her son to travel alone from his home in Rennes to Paris to St Pancras and then across the city to Waterloo to catch the train down to the coast.

Well, she *said* insouciance, but it was presumably just trust.

'Julien, you're here! *Bienvenue!* I'm so sorry about the mess. I'd hoped we'd be a lot further along by now.'

Julien gave a *de rien* shrug and made polite noises about the bedroom he'd been assigned, which was at best functional, its sea view rendered partial by the installation of the summerhouse. He wore shorts, a T-shirt and Sixties-style trainers, in contrast to Huck, who was dressed basically in camouflage gear.

The boys helped themselves to Cokes and she began shuttling the side dishes from the kitchen while Linus handled the grilling. There was enough food for twelve, though they'd only invited the Tuckers and Tabitha. This was the first – and likely last – time they would host this summer; no one wanted to stand around in the dirt when there were idyllic alternatives in all directions.

Theirs would be idyllic too, of course. This time next year, the bungalow would be a cool L-shaped retreat with a mid-century Palm Springs vibe, each bedroom with its own doors opening onto a terrace of potted citrus trees.

Somehow, paradoxically, Amy felt further now from the point of actualization than she had months ago.

As she assisted Linus at the grill, the boys sprawled on the kilim and Huck connected a rap playlist to a cute little orange speaker shaped like a lantern – Amy would have preferred something more mellow, but knew better than to interfere – before showing Julien the widely circulated clip of Perry shouting 'Piss off!' to the activists at the ferry. They both creased up.

'I'm weak,' Huck said, panting with laughter.

'Don't say a word when he's here, okay?' Amy warned him. 'Is that one of those Apple mini pod thingies? When did you get that?'

'It was a present from Beattie,' Huck said, which roused her suspicions at once. Then she felt guilty for being sceptical that the girl might treat her sibling once in a while for no reason other than that she loved him.

Speaking of Beattie, was she *still* not ready?

28

Charlotte

'Do we *have* to?' Perry said.

'Yes,' Charlotte said. 'We're welcoming Julien. But we'll come back as soon as we've eaten. Benedict and Tabitha are going out, so we can have an early night.'

He looked at her with a certain fear and she wondered if he thought she was suggesting sex. She chose not to examine her response to that.

'Come on, you don't have to talk to Linus.'

There was, two weeks into the trip, an undeniable antagonism between the two men, the flames of their paddleboarding strife fanned by that skirmish up on the ridge. Mind you, she wasn't exactly clamouring to see Linus herself. He'd been pathetic, if not downright malicious, during the activists' Villa Pino stunt, not least because the Rickmans (had they been in residence) would have been the first to leap to his defence had it been the bungalow targeted. Linus needed to decide which side he was on here.

It was, she realized, the first time she'd begun thinking in terms of sides.

Benedict and Tabitha materialized, skin and hair gleaming with a rude health that made her ache for her own lost youth, and the four wandered up the path.

'I'm going to miss the sea when we go back to uni,' Tabitha

said, waggling her fingers over the cliff edge towards the blue. 'It's just *so* beautiful.'

'You do know there's such a thing as the Bristol Channel?' Unlike Perry, Charlotte had warmed to the girl, whose every dispiriting pronouncement about food insecurity or period poverty was matched by a life-affirming appreciation of Pine Ridge. She'd fallen hard for their village, reminding Charlotte of her old self, their early years here when she'd fantasized about relocating full-time, but of course WFH had not been a thing then and wild horses couldn't have dragged Perry from the work hard, play hard hellscape of the City.

They arrived to find Amy on the veranda of the new summerhouse, thumping on one of the windows. Beattie was in there getting dressed, she explained, so they couldn't look inside for now.

'It's super cute, Amy,' Tabitha said.

'I love the paint colour,' Charlotte said, wondering if it was an exact match with the Nook or simply approximate.

'Let's just hope the activists don't come and raze it to the ground,' Perry said.

'Well, they haven't touched yours,' Linus said, approaching, tongs raised. 'And that's a lot more ostentatious.'

'Ostentatious?' Perry scoffed. 'The Nook's hardly Versailles.'

'Linus,' Amy said.

'Perry,' Charlotte said at the same time, and the two women exchanged a weary look.

'Come and have a drink and meet Julien,' Amy said.

Julien was dark and slight, limber in that French way that spoke of his having swum and sailed and played tennis since he was knee-high, and with a swagger that suggested he was fully aware that it was only a matter of a summer or two before he'd be irresistible to the opposite sex.

'Cool camo,' Benedict said to Huck.

'Careful or you'll find yourself deployed to Ukraine,' Perry said.

'You're on fire tonight, Perry,' Amy said.

'Speaking of which, the barbie smells great,' Charlotte said. 'Did you get the meat from the Crowland farm shop?'

'Yes, thank you for the tip. We've kept the fish completely separate,' Amy assured Tabitha, who – somewhat remarkably – was pescatarian and not vegan.

Drinks were distributed and they passed a few minutes in harmless small talk before Linus looked up and said, 'What the actual fuck?' and they all turned to see Beattie step down from her new digs and walk gingerly towards them in a pair of six-inch wedges.

But it was not these, Charlotte suspected, that were the problem as far as her father was concerned, or at least not so much as the tiny white boob tube top with the word 'VIBING' on it in pink and the cut-off denims no larger than knickers. To complete the look, she wore her hair in pigtails, with heart-shaped sunglasses with rose-gold frames perched on her nose. Her lips were a glossy bubble-gum colour, nails a Dulux chart of pinks. All she was missing was the lollipop.

'Let's eat first,' Amy warned Linus. 'She's in her own garden, not parading around town. Beattie, you've finally joined us! Come and meet Julien . . .'

Julien recovered from a moment of bodily arrest to raise a palm in Beattie's direction, only faintly colouring when she singled out his trainers for praise. She raised her sunglasses to inspect them, exposing a professional make-up job involving red eyeliner, violet eyeshadow, false lashes and stick-on gemstones. 'I totally want those in licorice brown.'

Linus, vibrating with disapproval, served up the barbecue and they settled to eat on the scatter cushions and beanbags on the huge kilim laid under the trees.

'Tell me again what your plan is for the garden,' Charlotte encouraged Amy, who took the opening and ran with it. Not liking the previous owner's rock garden – Charlotte remembered rotting duckboard paths and rope dividers that burned on contact – she'd cleared most of it in time for this visit, doing the work herself with shovels and wheelbarrows, which must have been back-breaking. The builders hired to bulldoze the garage could have done it in a tenth of the time, but she'd had an unstoppable instinct to *get things underway*.

On she ploughed, half an eye on Linus, who managed to sustain a mutinous expression even while chewing, until a noisy trail of walkers passed along the footpath and drowned her out.

'What is this?' Julien asked, astonished.

'Just a wowdy wabble of wamblers,' Perry said.

'Dad,' Benedict said.

'What? It's just a line from Monty Python.'

'Tabitha's brother has a speech disorder.'

'Of course he does,' Perry muttered under his breath.

'Very poor taste, Perry,' Linus said smugly, but his ire was soon reignited by his problematic firstborn – for Beattie, it emerged, intended joining Benedict and Tabitha on their night out. Hence the regalia.

'Can Huck and Julien go with you?' Amy said.

'Mum!' Huck shot her a look of mortification. Julien said nothing, his upper body rocking to the music as he wolfed a second burger.

'We're going to the Gull,' Beattie said in a withering tone. 'They'll be ID'd.'

'Won't *you* be?' Amy said.

'I've been there a few times, so no.'

'But were you dressed like Lolita on those occasions?' Linus asked, in such a Perry-like way, Charlotte found the instinct to defuse as strong as if it *had* been him.

'I'm not sure how friendly it is in there at the moment, guys,' she said, in a level tone. 'You know, with all the protests. It's very much a locals' hangout.'

'Maybe you can take them, Linus,' Perry suggested. 'I hear you got very chummy with the natives when they set up shop next door.'

'We don't need anyone to "take" us,' Beattie said. 'We're not twelve.'

'Did you not hear me?' Linus snapped. 'You're not going to the Gull dressed like a . . .' He struggled to locate the right word, which was probably just as well, and now Amy was chipping in with what Charlotte instantly identified as an ill-fated attempt to walk the tightrope between supporting her spouse and mollifying her daughter.

'Is this that sexy baby trend? I actually just read about that. I'm sure Tabitha would agree it's a bit objectifying, wouldn't you, Tabitha?'

'I don't believe in victim-blaming,' Tabitha said, at the same time as Beattie shot Amy down:

'Mum, stop! You're embarrassing yourself.'

'How?'

'Everything you say. You sound so *dumb*.'

'Oh, I'm sorry,' Amy said, sarcastically. 'Is it cringe? No, what's that other word, cheugy? Big yikes? You can't have it both ways, Beattie. If you're not too self-conscious to waft around town in that outfit, then you're not too self-conscious to hear an opinion that isn't to your liking. I don't care what Tabitha says, it's not "victim blaming" to advise a teenage girl not to flaunt herself half naked in a pub full of older men, and the Gull is . . .' She faltered, suddenly aware of the open mouths at so fierce an outburst, and Beattie pounced.

'It's what, Mum? Somewhere working-class people go? People who live in caravans?'

'Don't be ridiculous,' Amy said, flushing.

Beattie tossed her pigtails over her shoulders and stuck out her jaw. 'They only live in caravans because we've bought their houses! There's not a single long-term rental on the market at the moment, did you know that?'

Perry snorted. 'Don't tell me you've been drinking the NJFA Kool-Aid as well, Beattie? I thought you were one of the few who *hadn't* been woke-washed.'

'Er, meaning what, Dad? Benedict protested.

'It's true,' Beattie said. 'Robbie's mum died because she was rehoused in, like, a slum and got this chronic lung disease.'

Tabitha's fingers flew to her mouth. 'I didn't know that. That's terrible.'

'Yes, it is,' Perry conceded, 'but perhaps she should have sought accommodation in a different area instead. I've said it before and I'll say it again, it is not a birthright to live in the place you grew up. Millions of Londoners discover this every year but *they* don't go around sabre rattling.'

'Sabre rattling?' Benedict said. Even his gentle eyes were flaming now. 'Come on, Dad. Don't be that guy.'

'What guy?'

'You know.'

'No, I don't know,' Perry said.

'The boomer who hates on everything his kids say. Like this guy I was just reading about who ran over his own daughter. They'd been arguing about climate change and he just lost it. Mowed her down in their own drive as she tried to leave.'

'He was a total denier,' Tabitha confirmed.

Charlotte scratched an itch on her calf, the skin grey with dust, and drained her glass of rosé.

'What happened?' Amy asked.

'*She* died. *He* went to jail.'

'At least he won't be in a position to observe the rising sea levels there,' Perry said, but only Huck and Julien laughed. No one besides them ate much either and soon Beattie was hustling Benedict and Tabitha to depart.

'Benedict, will you make sure you get the girls home safely?' Charlotte said.

'Of course,' Benedict said.

'That's okay with us, Linus, isn't it?' Amy said, as if presenting a compromise to a wilful child. Her own explosion seemed to have subdued Linus's objections, however; it was the classic dual instinct of parenting: never *both* scream.

'Back by twelve,' he told Beattie tersely. 'Or I'll come down and find you myself.'

'Careful on the cliff steps in those shoes,' Amy added. 'Sorry about that,' she said to Charlotte when they'd gone. 'As you can see, clothes remain our Achilles heel.'

Charlotte checked Perry was not in earshot; she could hear him asking Julien where his family stood on wealth tax. Would Julien even understand? His English *was* excellent; he even appeared to be fluent in the rapper speak or whatever it was that Huck sometimes deployed.

'I was going to ask about that,' Charlotte said. 'Any news?'

Amy splashed more rosé into their glasses. 'Nada. But when we get back to London, I'm going to monitor her deliveries. She mentioned this website, Amiss, so I thought if I can get a reference number, then I can contact the retailer and see whose name the account is registered under.'

This struck Charlotte as a rather slim lead. Hadn't Beattie claimed to buy things through a friend? Following the rule that the best lies contained a grain of truth, it was likely the items were being sent to someone else's address.

'I wish this Not Just For August stuff would calm down. Are you still going to the housing meeting on Tuesday? I thought I might come along as well. I overheard the woman who owns Housekeepers – Claire, she's called – telling the manager of Fleur that they're making some sort of announcement.'

'Interesting. I wonder if it's—' Amy broke off at the sound of raised voices. Perry had moved away from the kids to harangue Linus, who was scraping the grill.

'I *know* it was you. I mean, who else could it have been?'

'Believe it or not,' Linus said, matching his volume, 'I have more important things to do with my time. Like run a business?'

'This might be about the speeding complaint,' Charlotte said to Amy. 'I told him not to say anything. He had a call from the police yesterday.' She raised an eyebrow. 'Seems they *can* find the time to investigate crime when it suits them.'

'What happened? He didn't get points on his licence?' Amy asked.

'No, they don't have cameras in the village, so it was just a warning following a verbal complaint. I assumed it was a local, but he's convinced it was Linus.'

'Linus wouldn't do that,' Amy said, and looked forlorn when her husband retreated indoors while Perry pulled a none too subtle 'Can we go now?' face in Charlotte's direction. She thought about protesting that she'd just got a new drink, but remembered their agreement and put her glass down.

'Wanna go down to the beach and play some beats?' Huck said to Julien.

'Bussin,' Julien said. They too got to their feet and two minutes later, Amy had been abandoned, last seen decanting Charlotte's wine into her own glass.

'More important things to do, my arse,' Perry said to Charlotte, as they strolled back to Cliff View. Then, not liking her lack of agreement: 'What? It's not my fault he suffers from the disease that defines his generation.'

Charlotte was puzzled. 'Covid?'

'No, narcissism.'

'Ah.' She sighed. 'I agree he can be annoying, but he's our friend, Perry.'

'Friend?' Perry snorted. 'He wouldn't piss on us if we were on fire.'

29

Tate

Fans whirred in all four corners of the community hall, but they might as well have had their plugs ripped from the sockets for all the difference it made. It was the midpoint of August, the hottest day of the summer so far, and his shift at the bar had been one long stream of requests for ice – plus two fainting episodes and a parade of the heat-struck past the bar to the first-aid hut.

It was going to be impossible to sleep in the caravan tonight, Ellie radiating heat beside him. He pictured himself lying on the grass outside, arms and legs flung out in a star.

On the stage, purple upholstered seats awaited the rear ends of the council's housing committee. A screen had been rigged up, which suggested a presentation of some sort – most likely stats manipulated or even fabricated to make the housing situation look less dire than it was.

On the floor, all the factions were well represented: the business community, including Gav; both NJFA and the Citizens Against the Elite crew; permanent residents, some home owners, some renters. A fair few second-home owners too – it being August, they were mostly in town, after all, but if Tate had to guess, he'd say they were rattled by the 'unprecedented season of activism', as Robbie put it.

'They get it now,' he'd crowed, high on the drama of his caravan stunt and the resulting front-page photo of his arrest in the *Voice*, followed by a rehash on *Mail Online*. 'They finally get that this is more than just a group of resentful layabouts mouthing a few slogans. It's a fucking reckoning.'

What with his bar shifts and the need to stay put for his liaison with Beattie, Tate hadn't had a chance to go to Pine Ridge Road to witness the event in person, so his friend now pointed out a few of the disgruntled residents he'd tussled with on the day. The well-dressed busybody with the highlighted bob was from Cliff View, on Robbie's case from the moment of his arrival with questions and threats but quick to duck out of sight when the news people came looking for quotes. According to Robbie, that stank of guilt. There'd been a husband, as well, a right old ranter, but he'd only turned up after Robbie's arrest, so Robbie's uncle had had that particular pleasure when he'd gone to tow the caravan back. And the tall woman with the blonde hair and pinched expression was the mum of the hot girl they'd seen in the road that time and who'd been drinking in the Gull with a posse of Londoners a few nights ago. He couldn't remember the girl's name – could Tate?

Tate pretended he couldn't. Also left unmentioned was that he and said hot girl had slipped off to the dunes for half an hour that night. When they'd got back, sand in their hair, some student bloke had been looking for her, but he was just a friend, she'd assured Tate. Not that he had any right to demand fidelity given his own situation.

Though Ellie had not been working that night, she'd opted out of a session in the Gull, feeling a bit nauseous. Ditto tonight. At this rate, people were going to guess she was up the duff before they'd even made a decision about whether they were keeping it.

What was he talking about? A decision *had* been made. Just not by him. Her instructions echoed in his ears: 'Talk to one of

186

the councillors and find out how long the Crowland waiting list is for couples expecting a baby.' Also, 'When do you want to tell my parents? Your mum?'

As Robbie pressed the flesh with a few supporters, Tate watched in surprise – and slight dread – as Beattie's mum bore down on him, her manner a mix of indignation and apology.

'I just wanted to say, I know how passionately you feel,' she began and for an awful moment he thought she was talking about Beattie and him. But it was the issue that drew them all here this evening, of course. *Idiot.* 'You *are* part of NJFA, aren't you? I do understand your plight, but there are other aspects to bear in mind. It's quite nuanced, all of this, you know.'

She had a pendant at her throat that said 'Boss Mum' and Tate wondered if it had been a gift from Beattie.

'I mean, on paper it looks like we're snapping up all the best places, but that's not necessarily the case. The house *we've* bought was virtually condemned – I don't think any of you would have wanted to live in it even if it *was* up for rent.'

I think we probably would, Tate thought, but he let her get it off her chest. He could see very little in her of Beattie, who must take after her father's side, but the accent was the same, even if the mum was very sincere, almost pleading, while Beattie had a too-cool-for-school drawl.

School. He had not allowed himself to consider whether the schoolgirl factor was part of the attraction. On the one hand, he'd assumed she was older; on the other, she mentioned it a lot herself and he'd responded, well, positively. Nothing weird, like her calling him sir or him threatening detention, just a nice erotic frisson.

'Plus we had to spend a fortune on emergency wiring before it was even safe to set foot in there,' her mum continued, and he wondered what this earnest woman would say if she knew he had an arrangement to fuck her daughter in her new summerhouse. He'd snuck up yesterday during his break to christen the 'shed with a bed', as Beattie described it. She'd locked them in and joked about false imprisonment—

'... and ploughing a lot of money into the refurb, using local builders and craftsmen.' She broke off, suddenly inspired, to ask, 'Where do you work? I'm trying to think how I know you. Is it The Needles?'

'The beach bar. But you're probably remembering me from the Needles restaurant a while back? You were telling your son not to get inked like me.'

'Oh. Okay. I knew I recognized you.' She flushed faintly. 'I'm Amy, by the way.'

'Tate.'

He saw the recognition in her eyes. 'I think you might know my daughter, Beattie? I saw your name come up on her phone the other day.'

What? Thank fuck Ellie wasn't here to hear this.

'Oh. Right. Beattie, yeah, I know her. Met her in the Gull with her friends.'

'That'll be Benedict and Tabitha,' Amy said as if they were normal everyday names and not ridiculously posh. 'Tabitha's here, actually. Talking to your friend? They had a good chat apparently when he was our temporary neighbour. She's very concerned about the housing issue. We all are, believe it or not.'

On this defensive note, she returned to her party and moments later Robbie slid into the seat next to him.

'Uh oh, see you got stuck with whatsherface. Did she have a moan about the caravan?'

'No. She was sympathetic. Says she understands our plight.'

Robbie chuckled. 'It's a plight all right. And sympathy gets us nowhere if people like her don't change their actions. Their entitlement.'

It always came back to that word. Entitlement. Who was entitled to a life here, a home here. Who deserved it most. Robbie was right: Amy 'understood' but she didn't want to give up her house, before or after the refurb by 'craftsmen'.

(Even if he *was* grateful for the shed with the bed.)

'She's the worst kind of DFL,' Robbie continued. 'Total hypocrite. Got a massive house in Dulwich.'

'How d'you know that?' Tate asked.

'I know a lot of stuff.'

'What else d'you know?'

'I know how much they paid for the bungalow. Eight hundred grand. Before they even do it up. And the London place must be worth a couple of million.'

'Sheesh.' They were fantastic, unreal, depressing amounts of money. For a moment he felt like getting up and leaving this latest crap, waste-of-space showdown, but right then the councillors trooped in and one of them, a woman often wheeled out to reassure the have-nots that they took their concerns very seriously and were doing everything in their power to bring them into the haves' fold, thanked them all for coming along.

An agenda was displayed on the screen, but they'd scarcely had a chance to scan it when Robbie sprang to his feet, arm raised. This was a strategy of his, to pre-empt the standard platitudes with a provocation of some sort.

'In light of recent protests, and my own, how shall I put this, *reacquaintance* with the fuzz' – there was a smattering of laughter at this – 'what new proposals does the Housing Department have to tackle the ongoing problem of rental shortages for local people?'

Something very unusual happened then. As they all engaged

autopilot, expectant of the usual banalities, the woman didn't fob them off, but actually had some new information.

'I'm glad you asked, Robbie, because we're pleased to announce that we've just obtained planning permission to use the local authority land next to the caravan park for a new community of cosy cabins. This will be a ground-breaking development – in every sense of the word.'

Instantly, the atmosphere fired. What did she just say? What ground-breaking development? As a presentation began, Robbie sat back down, exchanging querying looks with Tate. 'What the fuck is a cosy cabin?' he murmured.

Well, for starters, it wasn't 'cosy cabin' but 'KosyKabin', as the first slide made clear. A 'stylish, affordable, sustainable solution' to the housing crisis, apparently.

'These will *not* be offered on the open market,' the councillor announced, 'but will be reserved for those either born in or who are long-term residents of Pine Ridge, with the rent capped at affordable levels. Sublets and holiday lets will be strictly forbidden.'

Computer-generated images were now shared: exterior shots of sleek, minimalist accommodation, with the pines of the ridge standing guard behind, as well as interiors and floorplans; there was to be a mix of one-beds for singles or couples and two-beds for families. An email address was given for locals to register and start the application process. Tate whipped out his phone and made a note. Ellie would be all over this like a rash.

By his side, Robbie was blindsided, which was a first, and it was left to others to lead the follow-up Q&A.

'When will the cabins be ready for people to move into?'

All going well, early next year. Modular micro houses like these could be put up in a matter of weeks.

'How are the council going to pay for the scheme?'

Eco grants would be applied for, plus funds borrowed and paid back after 2024, when Westminster allowed local councils to double the council tax of second-homers, which was expected to be unanimously approved.

Tate checked the DFLs' reactions to this, expecting them to be up in arms at the notion of their council tax doubling; it was, after all, already several thousand a year on top of the tax on their principal residence. But they all looked okay with it, almost like they'd been expecting worse. The girl Beattie had come to the pub with, Tabitha, looked genuinely elated.

In a brief lull, a voice from the back could be heard – a cut-glass, middle-aged voice, presumably commenting privately to one of her own kind: 'Brilliant. Lovely. Now can we get on with our holiday?'

*

Afterwards, in the Gull, everyone needed Robbie to tell them how they should be feeling about this unexpected new development. He stood in the bay window of the upstairs bar, the sunset orange and fiery behind him, lighting his pint like it was radioactive.

'Well, they kept *that* on the down-low,' he said, with grudging respect. 'Cosy is the word. Did you clock the floorplans? They're not a lot bigger than caravans really. But it's a start. Yeah. It's got to be better than sofa-surfing.'

'I'm definitely getting my name down,' Des said. 'No offence, Rio.'

'Me as well, mate,' Rio said. 'Hey, we might all be neighbours.'

Tate could just see it: a stylish, affordable, sustainable NJFA ghetto. 'So, what, we've won, then?' he said. 'Do we shelve the rest of the campaign?'

'No, no, no.' Robbie didn't like that. 'That's exactly what they want. For all we know, this could be a sop to gag us for the rest of the summer while they all rake in the money from their tourist businesses. I mean, it's a bit of a coincidence there were no rumours or leaks, isn't it? It's come straight out of the blue – almost like they pulled it together specially for this meeting. After all the amazing media we've been getting.'

'Well, I *hope* it's true,' Rio said.

'So do I. But, if anything, we need to ramp up the pressure to make sure it actually happens. What we don't want is them quietly dropping the whole thing once the grockles have gone home.'

He had his ideas face on.

'What are you thinking, Rob?' Des said.

'I'm thinking it might be time to break out the super sticker.'

Of all their fly-posting activities, the one that drove the council and property owners – everyone, really – most out of their minds was the stickering, because Robbie had a contact who supplied them with heavy-duty adhesives, the kind you could only remove with power tools.

'I'm thinking there're already a fair few "cosy cabins" about the place,' he added, his fingers twitching to make air quotes. 'We just haven't called them that.'

30

Perry

The mail on the Masefield Road doormat was supremely unwelcome. Enough to make him regret this week's overnighter in town, if not *quite* to abort it.

A parking ticket for the Astra – rather a reminder that one had not been paid – and the date suggested it had been incurred within days, if not hours, of Jordan having taken possession of the car. It came back to Perry with a cold, plunging feeling, the moment of indecision when he'd registered it online and dithered over whether to name Jordan as the keeper of the vehicle. He'd decided not to and not only because he didn't have Jordan's details to hand; there was also the risk of Charlotte alighting on its existence somehow and explaining an extra car in his own name (purchased for Benedict as a student run-around, perhaps?) would be a whole lot simpler than explaining an extra car in a stranger's name.

He leafed through the rest of the post. Bloody hell, here was a second violation! This one was for driving in a bus lane and included photographic evidence: definitely Jordan's Astra, alone in an empty bus lane as cars queued bumper-to-bumper in the correct lane beside it. The fool. Two fines in the space of a week. If he meant to go on as he'd started, it would cost him a grand a month.

And by 'him', he meant himself, of course, because it was obvious that he was going have to settle these fines. Jordan didn't have a bean and had already complained that the money he'd earned so far from his delivery gig had been swallowed – if not exceeded – by petrol costs. He'd had no idea fuel was so expensive, he wished he hadn't taken the car in the first place, zero-hours work was a con. And while he was at it, he hated Trev and the other tenants and his room was too hot or too cold and the water pressure in the shower was too weak or too strong.

Of course, rather like the young people closer to Perry's home, he was never personally at fault, had no sense of accountability. Just handed his mistakes to the nearest grown-up to deal with.

He would need to use his individual account to pay the fines, Perry thought, pocketing them. Charlotte checked the app for their joint account regularly and might question the payments.

God, what if he started getting speeding tickets? That meant points on his licence. Or else denying he'd been the driver and declaring the person who had been.

Did Jordan . . .? Oh fuck. Was he *quite* sure Jordan had organized insurance?

*

It wasn't possible to raise the issue on arrival because Jordan had a preoccupation of his own. He shut the door behind Perry with a paranoid flourish, speaking in conspiratorial whispers.

'Almost had a drink last night, didn't I?'

'No! Why?'

It transpired that a row had kicked off in the kitchen between Trev and Jordan over the use of the kettle. 'I swear I thought he was gonna pour boiling water over me. Put sugar in it and all, make that prison napalm stuff.'

'This isn't the Scrubs, Jordan.' Perry noticed the dozen or so butts in the ashtray on the windowsill under the open sash, further evidence of his friend's agitation. Beyond, at the end of the garden, two residents sat on the only bench vaping in silence. He pulled the curtain across, not wishing to be seen. 'Anyway, he's all talk. The minute he assaulted you or anyone else, he'd be out on his ear. It's all in the code of conduct he signed when he took his room.'

Like Trev gave two hoots about the code of conduct. Perry sincerely hoped he wasn't monitoring his comings and goings, since the residents weren't supposed to have visitors stay over.

'I keep telling you, just avoid him. He's looking for aggro, don't give it to him. Listen, Jor, I don't wish to add to your woes . . . What?' The way Jordan began scoffing, you'd think he was quoting Shakespeare. 'But you've had two fines for the car. One's for going in a bus lane and the other's a reminder for a parking ticket.'

'What?' Jordan was outraged, his pale skin colouring.

'Did you not see it under your windscreen? A bright yellow plastic thing?'

Jordan lowered his gaze. 'Oh. Yeah. Maybe.'

'Well, where is it?' Perry said, exasperated. 'You need to pay parking tickets straight away or they double the charge.'

'How much?'

'A hundred and ten quid. Plus a hundred and thirty for the bus lane.'

'I haven't got that.' Jordan looked sorry for himself, persecuted even. He was, Perry was finding, a person who took the weather personally.

'It's okay, don't get upset. I'll pay it.'

'Great. Thanks, Pez.'

'Just checking, you did get yourself insured, didn't you?'

'Thought you put me on yours?' Jordan said.

'No! How can I do that? I have a wife, Jordan. We have a shared policy.'

'Why?'

'Because we're married. That's what marriage is. Everything is shared.'

Jordan shook his head as if in ideological disagreement with this, which was fair enough given Perry's manifest penchant for secrecy. 'How long are you down south for?'

'Till after the bank holiday,' Perry said vaguely.

'You sleeping in that little house on the edge of the cliff?'

No need to ask how he knew about the Nook, because – yes, another regrettable mistake – Perry had taken him there. Twice, in fact. The first time, out of season, Charlotte had asked him to go down for janitorial duties and he'd thought why not take Jordan with him, it wasn't as if there'd be any neighbours around to see them. The leaking radiator he'd fabricated on his return accounted for the second trip. On both occasions, he'd been quite clear that it was a terrible idea and yet . . . Well, he'd lived his whole life succumbing to terrible ideas.

On their first visit, they'd slept in the guest room. It overlooked the street, which seemed a shame when the other two bedrooms had such impressive sea views. And, he had to face it, he *did* want to impress Jordan. But he wasn't about to install him in the master bedroom, or in Benedict's room, and so for their second stay – in June – they'd shacked up in the Nook. It had been, he had to admit, pretty special. The murmur of the tide, the flutter of the sheer muslin drapes, the creak of timber and scent of seaweed and salt. Like being adrift together on a boat.

Of course, if Charlotte ever found out, she'd shove him off the cliff and happily do time for it. The Nook, unlike the houses, the cars, the rest of it, was hers.

'You'll sort out the insurance then, will you?' he said. 'First thing?'

'Course I will,' Jordan said.

'And no more fines, right? I mean it.'

31

Amy

Charlotte's rap at the kitchen door was uncharacteristically sharp, not to mention early. It was barely eight and she was normally out walking Mango at this time. Amy supposed she must go out even earlier on weekends, when the battle for beach space started straight after breakfast.

'Amy? Linus? You need to come and see this!'

She sounded quite distraught, Amy thought, which was also unlike her.

Linus wasn't dressed and so she went out alone. Charlotte was halfway back down the garden by then and Amy soon saw where she was headed – and why.

'I don't believe it!'

All four sides of the Niche, plus the entire veranda, were covered in stickers. Big garish yellow ones, with two words stamped in black capitals: *THIRD HOME*. A glance to the left revealed that the Nook had suffered the same fate; the way the contrast quivered in the hazy morning light gave the sense of a gargantuan swarm of bees having descended and made it their home.

'They've done it all the way up,' Charlotte said. 'Alison and Humphrey's shepherd's hut, even Gerry and Leanne's old garden shed. I mean, how can that possibly offend them?' She was choking up and Amy gave her a hug. Her own attachment to the week-old

Niche was strong enough, so she could only imagine how Charlotte must feel about the desecration of her long-standing beloved Nook. Unsupported, she suspected, since Perry was in London again – for the third time this trip at Amy's count.

'Oh!' Adrenaline seized her system as she remembered Beattie was inside the Niche and must also have been when the guerrilla attack took place, sleeping right through it. Unless . . . Images of abduction and assault flashed before her and she thumped on the door. 'Beattie? *Beattie!* Are you there?'

Groans confirmed the girl was alive.

'It's okay,' Amy called. 'Don't worry. Go back to sleep.'

'Third Home?' Linus said from behind them. He peered closely at the lettering as if missing something. 'I don't get it. Who did this?'

'The same people you were all pally with when they broke in next door,' Charlotte said coolly.

'I thought you said that was all resolved?' Linus said to Amy. 'They're getting those micro houses.'

'Which has obviously given them ideas,' Charlotte said. 'They want to make it clear it's not over, not until they have the keys in their hands. Maybe not even then. You know, I was just thinking when we arrived how stupid they were to miss a trick like this. They've never come the back way before.'

'Said the vicar to the tart,' said Linus, who couldn't have expected a laugh and didn't get one.

Amy tried in vain to loosen the edge of a sticker with her thumbnail. A super-strength adhesive of some sort had been used – they were going to have to use a steamer and scraper to get these off, which meant a whole new paint job. 'Should we call the police?' she said.

'Already done,' Charlotte said.

When the officer arrived – a man-child who she'd put money on still living with his mum and having his washing done for him – Charlotte took charge, giving their names and leading the tour of the affected properties.

'It's obviously linked with the news about the KosyKabins,' she told him, meeting a blank look. 'You do know about the council's new housing plan?'

'I'll be sure to catch up on it,' he promised.

'Well, you'll find it's just the latest in a long and exhausting month of abuse. I have a log if you'd like to see it?'

'A log of . . .?'

'All the incidents.' Charlotte sighed. 'The caravan squat next door, you know about. That got dealt with reasonably quickly. There's also been graffiti on the wall, a petition set up on the beach that created a really intimidating atmosphere. And the business with the passata at the ferry, you definitely got called out to that. There've been eggs, as well, if you're interested.' Her voice had a new tough edge, Amy thought. They'd made a mistake, the activists, targeting the Nook. It would be, for Charlotte, unforgivable.

They returned to the Niche. Out on the water, flat and glossy this morning, a chain of kayakers came gliding into view from the direction of Little Bay. At the same time, music drifted from the beach bar, where they always played Nineties classics: Groove Armada, 'At the River'. It felt surreal to be up here with the police while others frolicked. Disconnected, derailed.

'I really think you should be patrolling more visibly, Constable,' Charlotte told the young officer. 'Before it turns violent.'

'What makes you think it will turn violent?' he asked.

'Because that's the nature of escalation, isn't it? If you've damaged property, what's the next logical step? To damage people.'

*

In the space of an hour, they'd unearthed the electric steamer and cable extension and taken up Huck and Julien's offer to do the work for a not inconsiderable fee. What Julien's family would make of him spending his holiday in manual labour Amy wasn't sure, but he seemed very keen to earn.

'I really don't think we can let Beattie sleep down there any more,' she said to Linus, when their daughter returned to the bungalow in a foul mood, far more indignant about being inconvenienced than about the criminal damage itself. Amy decided to delay breaking the news of a longer-term eviction.

Linus had a presentation to work on, so she took her coffee round to Charlotte's, finding her on the kitchen terrace with her back to the garden and the acid yellow of the Nook.

'I can't look at it, Amy. It's sacrilege.'

'The boys will be down in a few hours. The stickers are coming off quite quickly with the steamer.'

'I'm worried about the glass. It's original and quite fragile.' Charlotte poured coffee for them both from her blue Le Creuset pot and Amy wondered fleetingly what colour she would choose if she were to get one. 'Honestly, there's been so much hassle this summer. Is this how it's always going to be from now on? Is it . . .' She let Amy guess the rest: *Is it over?* Are the good times gone? The glory days of haring down from the big city and doing whatever you liked in your little seaside playground. Acting like you owned the place.

Was it over – just as Amy had signed up?

'Have you told Perry?' she asked.

'I'll wait till he's back,' Charlotte said. 'Which should have been an hour ago. There must be queues for the ferry.' On cue, Mango's tail began whipping back and forth, signalling the arrival of the Range Rover out front.

'Didn't she bark last night?' Amy said. 'When the activists were trespassing?'

'She's trained not to, at least not more than a single warning bark. We had a dog whisperer in when she was a puppy.' Charlotte petted the animal, ruffling her chest and scratching her throat. 'She might have, though. I don't know. I sleep so much better when Perry's away. Hello, darling.'

Perry appeared in front of them now, portly in shorts and an old-style cricket shirt, radiating bluster. 'You won't believe what I've just seen. Tabitha, cuffed to the ferry chain like a fucking suffragette! Up to her waist in water, holding a placard saying – and I quote – "Sod Off, Second-Home Scum". We were held on the ferry for ages while they tried to get her and her comrades out of the way so we could dock.'

'I thought it was odd for her to make such an early start,' Charlotte said.

Perry threw up his hands. 'Is that all you've got to say? That it explains why she didn't get a lie-in? You're not appalled that she's down there spreading hate about us? Her *hosts*. I thought the fuckers had been given homes now, anyway? Shouldn't they be busy measuring up for curtains?'

'Perry, they're not fuckers. And the KosyKabins aren't going to appear overnight, are they? There'll be a whole load of red tape before they go up.'

'At least Benedict wasn't involved,' Amy said, trying to be helpful, but Perry's scowl only intensified.

'Where is he?'

'Still in bed, I think,' Charlotte said.

They watched as Perry marched back indoors, Mango bouncing at his heel, and shouted up the stairs: 'Benedict! Get out of bed and come down now!' He returned, followed a minute later by Benedict in a pair of frayed jean shorts and nothing else. His skin was a patchwork of white and pink and brown, with a chain of insect bites up his left side, one of which he began to scratch.

'What the actual fuck, Dad? I was asleep!'

'Did you know?' Perry demanded.

'Know *what*?'

'That your girlfriend is down at the ferry attacking second-homers.' He thrust the phone at Benedict like a dagger and the boy took a step back before examining the image.

'Oh.'

'You *did* know?'

'No. Well. She said she was going on a protest, but I didn't know what it was about.'

'There's only one thing people protest about in this place! She's joined Not Just For August – while staying here *for August*!' Perry gave a bark of sardonic laughter. 'Am I *seriously* the only one who appreciates the hypocrisy of that? Well, if she thinks she's going to spend the morning shouting about what cunts we are and then come skipping back up for lunch, she's got another think coming!'

'Sorry, Amy,' Charlotte said.

'No worries,' Amy said.

'We're not in for lunch, anyway,' Benedict said mildly. 'We've got plans.'

Neither he nor Charlotte was remotely flustered by Perry's outburst, Amy noticed. Her own heart was banging like a gong.

'What the hell's happened here?' Perry said, catching sight of the Nook. 'Why's it yellow?'

Charlotte got to her feet. 'I've been trying to tell you, but you've had atrocities of your own to share. It's a sticker attack. It happened overnight.'

The four of them trooped down for an inspection.

'Was this Tabitha as well?' Perry said.

'There's no way it could be the work of one person,' Charlotte reasoned. 'And it's not just us, it's all up the road.'

'Huck and Julien have got the steamer out,' Amy told him. 'It seems to be doing the trick. As soon as they finish ours, they'll be down to do yours.' Over his shoulder, she spied Linus approaching from the footpath and slipped away to brief him. 'Tabitha's on an NJFA protest. Perry's not happy.'

Behind her, she could hear Charlotte appealing to Benedict. 'You did say you might be going to Amsterdam, darling? Maybe today might be a good day? Or tomorrow?'

'We actually thought we might stay on here,' Benedict said. 'The hotels were too expensive.'

'Unlike *this* hotel,' Perry snapped. 'This hotel is free.'

'Perry, it's his home,' Charlotte said firmly.

'*You* can stay,' Perry told Benedict. 'But not her. I want her out. Today. No arguments.'

'Oh, come on, Dad. Where's she meant to go?'

'How about home? She's got plenty of options.'

'She can stay with us,' Linus said, speaking for the first time, and the three Tuckers turned to him as one.

'Linus,' Amy said, but he just placed a hand on her back as if to bring her into line. She could sense the exhilaration in him.

'I mean it. If she wants to stay in Pine Ridge, we'll take her.'

Perry snorted. 'You're welcome to her, mate.'

Linus ignored him, speaking directly to Benedict. 'Just send her over when she gets back from her dissident activities.'

'Okay,' Benedict said, glaring at his father. 'I will.'

*

Amy followed Linus back to the bungalow and into the living room. She could hear Beattie in the bathroom talking in the warm, confiding way she reserved for her friends – 'I know, he's *such* a legend . . . Really? Tell her I'm not down with that as a concept' – either oblivious to or untroubled by the fireworks at the Tuckers'.

'Was that wise?' she said.

'It was worth it to see that pompous bastard lose his mind,' Linus said.

'He'll see it as a betrayal.'

'A betrayal of what? The much-maligned league of millionaire holiday home owners?'

Amy was at a loss. She was damned if she was going to support him on this, and yet . . . If she and Linus allowed themselves to be divided, they would never make this second-home arrangement work. She had a sudden image of them giving up before they'd started. Selling the place with planning permission, even the garage still intact. Queuing for the ferry as the protesters celebrated.

'Why not have the girl stay, anyway?' Linus said. 'She can go in the summerhouse with Beattie. You literally just said yourself she can't stay down there on her own, so this'll put your mind at ease. No one would mess with Tabitha. Plus, she seems to be operating as some sort of double agent, so that should protect us from being targeted in the future.'

All of this was true.

The bathroom door opened and Beattie emerged in a striped

crochet-knit dress, another of her 'fake' designer items that Amy had looked up online and identified as a beach brand sold in Selfridges for £325. 'Mum, when are the boys going to be finished? I want to get back in as soon as possible.'

'Not on your own, Beats,' Linus said. 'It's not safe. You need a roommate.'

Beattie gave him her best death stare. 'No way am I sharing with Huck.'

'Not Huck. Tabitha. She's just been thrown out by her hosts for sedition.'

'What even is that?' Not waiting for an answer, she demanded, 'From when?'

'From whenever she unchains herself from the ferry and makes her way home.'

Beattie turned to Amy for confirmation, eyebrows raised.

'It's a good solution,' Amy said. 'We'll bring a camp bed down for her. It'll be fun having a roomie.'

Beattie stopped just short of rolling her eyes.

'You will explain to her about bolting yourself in at night, won't you?' Amy added.

32

Beattie

The backpack was wedged into the small space between her proper bed and the new uncomfortable-looking portable one her mum had supplied. It had a funny smell and she was a bit squeamish about smells, but the windows only opened a tiny crack so she pushed open the door instead.

'Say if it's not okay,' Tabitha said. 'Ben and I can go up to London or back to Bristol.'

'No, it's fine. I actually think if you weren't here, they'd make me go back up and share with Huck and I seriously don't want that.' Huck and Julien had finished steaming off the stickers, taking most of the paint while they were at it, but her mum needed another trip to buy supplies before she could redo it. 'It's just . . .' She faltered. They'd hung out a lot this trip, but she wasn't sure what Tabitha knew of her private exploits. 'I'm kind of . . . expecting a friend this afternoon.'

'When?'

'Like, half an hour.'

'Thought you were looking good, girl.' Tabitha stretched her arms above her head, steepling her index fingers. 'My shoulders are really sore. So who is he then?'

'He's called Tate, but—'

'I know Tate! From the NJFA meetings.'

'Oh.' Of course. This was why she'd been sent packing by the Tuckers. She'd signed up after going to the housing meeting earlier in the week and getting into a conversation with Robbie. It was pretty awesome, if a bit exhausting, the way she'd thrown herself into it.

'He's like a solid nine, B. Wow. You kept *that* quiet.'

'Because he's got a girlfriend.' Remembering she'd heard her mother tell her father that the Tuckers thought Tabitha 'puritanical', Beattie added: 'You probably think it's really bad, don't you? Sneaking around behind her back.'

Tabitha's forehead crinkled. 'She might know. They could be polyamorous.'

Beattie wasn't clear exactly what this entailed, but she was fairly sure Tate was just cheating old-style. 'Maybe. Have you ever seen her at these meetings? Ellie, she's called.'

'I don't think so. Tate's always with Robbie, kind of like a deputy. They weren't at the ferry this morning – maybe tired after this sticker thing in the night? It's quite hardcore doing this on top of their day jobs. They're total warriors, these guys. Super inspiring.'

She showed Beattie images of her and another activist in the water that morning, the car ferry hovering behind, heavy with dozens of vans and cars, as well as the local bus. Motorists had gathered at the rail with their phones raised. 'I felt bad about the bus,' she said, 'but there's always collateral.'

'Couldn't you have drowned?' Beattie said. 'If you were, like, shackled to the chains?'

'The lock had a safety catch. But the cops didn't know that. Anyway, listen, this shouldn't be for long. Me bunking here. Ben says his dad will change his mind.'

'You'd go back?' Beattie said, surprised. 'What, you mean if he apologized?'

'He doesn't need to apologize,' Tabitha said, bouncing a little on her camp bed. She was always in motion, Beattie noticed, had an unusual amount of energy. 'These older people, it's hard for them to change their views. They grew up in the Dark Ages. I get that. Plus, he's got his addiction issues. They get these intense emotional states, people in recovery. They've been self-medicating and then they have to deal with real feelings, you know? Ben says we can help ourselves from the fridge in the Nook, by the way.'

'Cool. This sounds bad, but I'd rather be in the Nook,' Beattie said. 'It's so much nicer, with the shower room and everything.'

'I'll get Benedict to suggest to his mum that you can use it,' Tabitha said. 'She's totally doting, completely worships him.' She sprang up. 'Right, I'll get out of your way. We all need our conjugal visits, right?'

'What's that?' Beattie asked.

'You know, when prisoners get to see their wives or girlfriends. I don't think they do it in the UK, actually.' Her new roommate hooked her 'Ban Bigots Not Books' tote over her arm. 'Our penal system's not as humane as it should be.'

*

Left alone, Beattie checked her phone again: ten minutes till Tate had his break. The Wi-Fi was dodgy down here so her daily 'gym theft' search was painfully slow to bring up results. Expecting the usual stories from ages ago when some guy in Manchester had had his Rolex stolen by his personal trainer, she was astonished when a BBC link came up from that morning: a video news feature entitled '*Gym Theft Victim Failed by Police*'.

She played the video, her pulse tripping. A reporter introduced the story from a gym reception familiar to Beattie from a visit earlier in the summer:

Reporter: This is the Westminster branch of GymLads, the preserve of the healthy and wealthy, who've been rocked by the news of a brazen theft under their noses . . .

A woman in yoga clothes appeared, sitting in the gym café with a glass of green juice in front of her, people working out on the other side of the glass wall. As she spoke, a caption popped up: 'Amelie, theft victim'.

Amelie: I came back to the changing room after my Pilates class and I saw my locker was open. I knew I'd locked it properly so I was really worried. I went through my stuff and I thought it was just my phone that had been taken, but then I realized it was my bank card as well. Obviously, I didn't have my phone to call the bank but I was with a friend and I borrowed hers and my bank told me there'd been all this spending in Harrods. Literally while I was doing my fitness class! Clothes and shoes and sunglasses and make-up, plus they'd used my card at two cashpoints. I reported it to the police, but they said there's nothing they can do. It took ages for my bank to agree to a refund and the whole thing has really affected my mental health.

The video cut to a police officer from the Met, whose face was as bland as his voice:

Officer: While we have huge sympathy for Amelie, the truth is hundreds of people check in and out of big gym chains every day and we have no way of identifying the thief – or thieves – on the evidence we have. What I will say is that it would be a very brave person who tried this again, now their methods have been exposed by the media.

Now a new face came on, a stressed-looking guy, captioned 'Toby Minter, Action 4 Victims of Crime':

Toby Minter: Sad to say but this is a city where 80 per cent of burglaries go completely unsolved. What we're seeing more and more is the police putting the onus on the victim to do better next time – rather than getting out there and catching these criminals. It's just not good enough.

The Met officer came back on:

Officer: Gymgoers need to be aware of this scam and take measures to protect themselves. The main thing is to never leave your phone and your bank card together in your locker. If you must have both of these items with you when you visit the gym, try to keep them on your person while you work out.

Oh my days, Beattie thought. It really was game over. She inhaled sharply as the screen filled with the words 'How the Gym Thief Steals Thousands in Minutes', before showing a bunch of women in a changing room.

Reporter: Cameras are not allowed in changing rooms, which is why we've filmed this on a set with actors and partly explains how the thief has been able to get away with this crime . . .

Fascinated, she watched the reconstruction of how 'the criminal' had perpetrated her theft, entering the gym through an open barrier, then sauntering into the changing room and eyeing the other women. The camera closed in on one wearing flashy jewellery and designer yoga gear: the victim-to-be. The method was pretty accurately portrayed, though once in possession of the phone and card, the thief was shown hiding in a toilet while she downloaded the banking app, which Beattie would never do.

It was surreal that there was a news story about her. They'd interviewed people and hired actors and everything. She was like, what was that Netflix character? Lupin, that was it.

The whole thing was terrifying – and, weirdly, hot. When Tate arrived and started to make some comment about the scraped exterior of the Niche, she bolted the door and jumped on him and wouldn't let him speak until they'd had sex. Fast and frantic and kind of feral, their best yet.

'You on whizz or something?' he said panting. 'Your heart's really racing.'

'Just adrenaline,' she said.

'Anything wrong?'

'I'm fine.'

She loved how he didn't go on and on, just asked once and then accepted her answer.

He took in the camp bed and rucksack. 'Who's in the extra berth?'

'Tabitha. You know her – she stopped the ferry from docking this morning? The police were there and everything.'

'Oh yeah. I wasn't at that one, but I saw the video. She's a new recruit. Bit of a rebel. You all are, to be fair.'

'All?'

'Yeah, you posh uni girls.'

'I'm not at uni yet.'

'No, but you will be.'

'Of course.' She thought she caught a look of hurt and hurried to correct herself. 'Not that it's for everyone. What were you like at school?'

'Pretty lazy.' Tate raised a hand and ran his fingertips over the nearby wall, tracing the grooves in the timber with the same gentle precision he did when touching her. 'Robbie was the clever one. But I wasn't interested in academic stuff and my mum didn't exactly crack the whip.'

'Lucky you,' Beattie said pouting. 'My mum's a nightmare. Obsessed with grades.'

'She seems all right.'

'*Seems*, yeah.'

'C'mon, I bet she just wants you to be happy.'

'That's what they say, but what they mean is they want you to be happy with all A-stars and an offer from Oxbridge.' She nuzzled him. 'So, go on, tell me.'

'Tell you what?'

'Duh. If you came up here in the dead of night and covered my bedroom in yellow stickers?'

He reached across her for his jeans, lying creased on the floor where he'd stepped out of them, and delved in the pockets. Peeled the back off a sticker and stuck it over her stomach.

She cackled in delight. 'I *knew* it.'

'Didn't last long, though, did they? Thought we might get a bit more mileage than that. Where did your mum even find the builders at the weekend?'

'My brother and his friend did it. Sorry.'

'Doesn't matter, we filmed it.' He showed her the reel, featuring the Niche, the Nook, and a whole load of others around the village, soundtracked with 'Yellow Submarine' and notching up likes in front of their eyes.

'The parentals are *not* going to like that. This is cute.' She admired the childlike sketch of his face on his phone case, the scrawled words, 'Tate's 1st fone'.

'My mate Des did it. Think you met him in the Gull? Works at Retro Studio in Poole.'

'What's that?'

'Tattoos.'

She stroked his left arm, with its cool lotus flower design, the ink vivid pink and blue. 'Did he do these?'

'Most of them, yeah. You ever thought about getting inked?'

'No. I hate pain. But my brother's desperate to get one. You think Des would do it?'

'Has he got ID?'

'No, but he's got cash.' She smirked. 'Thanks to your stickers.'

Checking the time, Tate wriggled to the edge of the bed and began dressing. 'I was a bit worried last night, actually. About waking you. Didn't want to scare you.'

'I sleep really heavily,' Beattie said. 'In London I'm the only one in my house who doesn't wake up when the police helicopters are out.'

'No guilty conscience,' he said. 'I like that in a girl.'

33

Perry

'You have to hand it to them,' Charlotte said to him when Amy texted from the beach with news of a TV crew interviewing holidaymakers at the bar. 'Even the caravan stunt didn't get this much attention.'

They were reading in the snug – well, Charlotte was, he was online – while Huck and the French boy cleansed the Nook of its stickers for a frankly criminal rate of pay that had been shaken on before he'd had a chance to intervene. But they were too late: being the most photogenic of Pine Ridge's summerhouses, its image was all over social media, a symbol of the denounced elite, a laughing stock.

The nationals were starting to pick up on the story too. The *Guardian* website had a piece called *'The Rise of the Third Home'*, illustrated with a close-up on the NJFA sticker and describing Robbie Jevons as a 'rock star of Zoomer activism', which made Perry's blood boil. Spiteful lines proliferated in the comments section:

Boomers have bled this country dry . . .

The evil rich are depriving the poor of basic shelter . . .

These privileged parasites should be forced to sell . . .

And so on. Meanwhile, *Mail Online* had tacked the new photos onto an existing story headlined '*Resentment-on-Sea*', mainly about Devon and Cornwall, but again, Jevons got a namecheck.

NJFA was reposting by the second, coyly fielding compliments without formally claiming responsibility, while the local police had issued some namby-pamby statement about taking criminal damage seriously.

A well-known columnist posted:

Looking to talk to anyone down in Pine Ridge about this anti-holiday home vandalism – DM me! #journorequest

Perry was tempted to get in touch. For fuck's sake, someone had to speak up for them, for their group, their generation. These young people were trying to silence them, intimidate them into thinking common sense was wicked, hard work and success a crime. What had Benedict said? *Don't be that guy.* The kind of guy who ran over members of his own family! Perry loved his son more than life itself but he could be a patronising little fucker.

Speaking of which, he'd just arrived in the room, ignoring Perry as he had done since yesterday's drama and waggling the key to the Moke at Charlotte – 'Okay if we take the Moke over to Sandbanks, Mum?' – as if his girlfriend had not grievously insulted her hosts.

'Not if *we* includes *her*,' Perry growled, and Benedict tossed the key onto his lap with rare petulance.

'Fine, we'll get the bus.'

'Make sure you allow plenty of time – you might find you get held up at the ferry.'

'Perry,' Charlotte berated him, when the boy flounced off.

'What? There's no way I'm indulging the little turncoat like nothing's happened.'

'*Turncoat*? What kind of a word is that?' She closed her book and placed it on the sofa next to her. 'For heaven's sake, if you separate lovers, they'll only want to be together more. It's basic stuff. It's Shakespeare.'

Perry stared at her, not sure why the hairs on his arms were suddenly rising.

'Don't estrange yourself from your only child. This comes up all the time in agony columns – Richard Madeley had one in the *Telegraph* not long ago. Never ask your child to choose between you and their partner because they will always choose their partner. *Always*. Be the man here and concede.' She pulled her hero-teacher-reasons-with-hopeless-delinquent face. 'Really, we should be thanking Linus for taking Tabitha in, otherwise she and Benedict might be sleeping on the beach tonight.'

'Hang on a minute,' Perry said. 'They've both got family homes they could go to. Plus their student rentals sitting empty over the summer.' He brandished his phone, with the 'third home' *Guardian* headline. 'They're the ones with three homes, not us! Besides, we all know Linus only did what he did to spite me.'

'Linus isn't the one who covered the Nook in stickers,' Charlotte pointed out. 'And nor is Tabitha, for that matter.'

'You're right.' Perry jumped to his feet and scooped up the key to the Moke with a little flourish. 'I'm focusing on the wrong person.'

*

He sped up to the caravan park at the vehicle's top speed, scarcely braking as he drove down the central avenue (5 mph? Was that even technically possible?) and spraying gravel in his wake. A band of kids appeared, one with a dirt-spattered face like something out of *Oliver Twist*.

'Looking for Robbie Jevons,' he called to a bloke out on his deck, fag in hand. 'D'you know him?'

Stupid question. Of course he did, Jevons was a *rock star*. 'Think he just got back. Up with the tourers. First right and follow it round.'

The tourers were the ones on wheels in a section at the far end of the park and all looked the same to Perry. 'Which one is Robbie's?' he called to the next person he saw, but before she could reply a voice drifted from the opposite direction.

'Over here, mate.'

It was Napoleon himself. In his mechanic's overalls, sitting under a torn awning at a crap little plastic table, smoking.

Leaving the engine running, Perry jumped out and marched towards him, smacked him hard in the face. He'd been aiming for the nose but got the side of the mouth, felt the sharp edge of a canine on his knuckles, the very pain he'd hoped to deliver, hot and acute at the point of contact, then spreading down his arm. It was the element of surprise as much as the force of the blow that gave him time to dance back and evade any reciprocal swing.

'You fucking lunatic,' Robbie said in a thick, wet voice, and staggered to his feet. The plastic chair he'd been sitting in tipped to the ground behind him.

The kids had caught up with Perry by now and he noticed two of them holding up phones, a sight that characterized all of life's interactions these days. If it wasn't being filmed by a cretin, it wasn't actually happening.

'Be my guest,' he told them. 'Take it to the police and they might finally do something about these people.'

As the kids began to chant the word 'grockle' at him, more in excitement than menace, he slid back into the Moke and put it into gear.

'I like your getaway car,' Robbie sneered, on the gravel now, spitting blood. 'Very gangster.'

Perry gave him the finger and careered out of the park and onto the road without bothering to check for traffic. Put his foot down for a nihilistic rush. The act of violence had not satisfied him as he'd hoped; on the contrary, it had inflamed a greater need. The need to drink. One beer, that was all he wanted. One cold beer. He'd settle for pouring it over his face and lapping what he could of it like an animal.

At the entrance to Pine Ridge Road, he was flagged down by a news reporter. Not some dick with a phone, but a real professional, with a camera guy standing by. The same crew that Amy had seen at the beach bar, perhaps.

'Do you have a minute?' they asked him, all metropolitan charm. 'It's about this stunt with the stickers.'

'Is that cockney rhyming slang?' Perry said, and this time when he came to a halt, he turned the engine off.

*

At home, Charlotte had moved to the kitchen terrace, already on the rosé, a jumble of guidebooks and maps on the table in front of her. At the bottom of the garden, the boys were making good progress on the Nook, now only a third yellow, two thirds a distressed version of the original.

'Looks like it's survived okay,' Perry said, cracking open a Lucky Saint and sinking into the chair opposite her.

'It's not too damaged. But it'll need to be primed before it rains. Where've you been? What happened to your hand?'

He ran the cold can across his inflamed knuckles. 'I punched the bastard.'

'Linus?'

'What? No. Robbie.'

Charlotte looked nonplussed. 'Why?'

'Why? Are you trying to gaslight me, Charlotte? Because it was a damn sight easier than going to Hobbycraft and buying enough stickers to cover his skanky little caravan. Because he fucking deserved it. Because someone needs to stand up to that tinpot Arthur Scargill.'

Charlotte gave a dismissive sigh. 'Is that what you called him? He's far too young to have heard of the miners' strike.'

'I don't care! I'm not tailoring my cultural references to his or any of these jumped-up babies'! If you don't know who Arthur Scargill is, fucking read a history book!'

He was breathing heavily, lungs straining, could see that Charlotte was growing concerned. She pulled the wine bottle out of the ice bucket and there was a euphoric moment when he thought she was going to pass it to him – 'Have a drink, darling. I always knew the time would come when it would be worth sacrificing a year's sobriety' – but this was quickly dashed when she kept the bottle and slid the bucket across the table.

'I suppose he had it coming,' she said.

'Thank you.' He plunged his sore hand into the ice. 'What are you doing with all these maps, anyway?'

'Planning a day trip.' She flashed him a smile, pantomime toothy, entirely artificial. 'You know, like you're supposed to do when you're on holiday.'

'Ah,' Perry said. 'Is that what this is?'

34

Robbie

Tuesday 29 August, 12.30 a.m.

In the narrow zone between Old Beach Road and the dunes, the pines cast black stripes of shadow in the moonlight, an army stunned into silence. Beyond, there's activity – and hours after you'd expect the emergency services to have retreated for the night.

Confirmation that it's real, this death.

The southern half of the beach is taped off and a police car parked across the main entrance. An ambulance idles close by. Through the gap you can see that a white tent's been put up just beyond the water sports hut. Is the body in there or have they already taken it away, steeling themselves for the grim task of identification? Of notifying loved ones and inflicting a lifetime's sorrow.

Other than me, there are no civilians. No gawkers or ghouls – yet. Everyone went home thinking this was just a salvage operation, they thought it was only property that got removed from the face of the earth, not a human life. It'll be different in the morning when word gets out.

When the accusations start.

Light from my phone torch catches Tate sitting at a picnic table on the far side of the car park, and I have a weird sentimental flashback to the pair of us at school. He always had the lonesome thing going on. The lost puppy the girls wanted to cuddle.

And, later, to fuck.

'Yo.' I scoot over to him. 'Why aren't you answering your phone?'

He doesn't reply. As I slide in next to him, he shrinks away, wiping at his face – the idiot's crying! Maybe we *are* back in primary school after all. Just for tonight. Something really bad's happened and we need our mummies to come and sort it out for us.

'It's not her, Tate.'

'Who?'

'You know who.' Then, as the breeze drops and voices carry from the crime scene, 'Please tell me you haven't been over there asking questions?'

He shakes his head. That's something, at least. I can already hear the questions: Why did you go down there in the middle of the night? Getting off on some sick power trip when you saw all the trouble you'd caused?

There's a silence. 'How do you know?' he says, eventually, and I show him the text exchange.

Just checking you're OK?

I'm fine. With Beattie.

'Tabitha. Half an hour ago. So whoever it is, it's not either of them.'

Tate's breathing slows a fraction.

'Ellie's gone back with Shannon. She doesn't know, does she?'

'Don't think so.'

'She seems to think something's wrong, though,' I say.

'Something *is* wrong.' He swings towards me then, as if in

221

aggressive dispute, but when he speaks his words are flat and defeated. 'She's pregnant.'

'What?' For a moment I don't get it. 'Beattie?'

'No. Ellie.'

Ah. Which explains a lot. No need to ask how he feels because it's obvious he's not celebrating. 'What does she want to do?'

'She wants to keep it. She wants me to want her to keep it. She wants to move into a shiny new KosyKabin or whatever the fuck they're called and live miserably ever after.'

'Right. Okay.' His stupid self-pity jars given the circumstances and yet it kills me to see him so morose. An unwelcome thought strikes: the last time I had sex, there was no condom involved, nothing. This could be me.

Don't think about it.

'So Beattie. What's the story there? Just a summer thing?' His silence speaks volumes. 'Come on, Tate. How's that going to work?'

'I don't know. She'll be back at school next week.'

School? He needs to listen to himself. 'Then just be grateful you got away with it. You could've got into deep shit, a girl that age.'

'She's seventeen,' he says, all indignant. 'We've done nothing wrong.'

'Legally. But that's not how her parents will see it, is it? Or Ellie. Especially now. You need to forget about the whole thing. Seriously, we've got bigger issues here.' I pause, breathe the night air, the usual aroma of brine, pine and fried food mixed with diesel fumes. 'We both know why the police are going to focus on you.'

Tate glares at me. 'Fine, so I drove a tractor a couple of times one summer. It's not the same as a backhoe loader or whatever the fuck this is.'

'Yeah, but there can't be that many people who've had that experience and belong to NJFA. You need to have your story all sorted. Let's go through—'

He cuts in: 'I don't need a story! I was working at the bar when it happened.'

Well, you weren't there when we left the beach. 'Can Gav or someone back that up? You were there at the exact time the house went over?'

'Look, I didn't do it,' he groans.

That'll be a no then. I rub my eyes. 'You got any cigs on you?'

He chucks me his pack and I light up. Feel 10 per cent better – until I hear the suck of his breath and I know it's coming. The damning detail I don't want to hear but need to know.

'The thing is, Rob, I was in it. During my break.'

'In what?'

'The house! The summerhouse.'

'You're not for real?' And I remember now, when we were in the Gull, he said there was construction kit up there. *At the old bungalow, I think.* I 'think'! He knew which house it was and he's been sitting on it all night. This is bad. Are they going to find his DNA in the debris? Will the seawater wash it away? No wonder he's been agonising, he probably left the girl in there after shagging her.

I can just picture him doing up his flies as he scurried back down the cliff steps.

'Don't mention that to the police,' I instruct him. 'Make sure she doesn't either. Say you spent your break watching the band. I'll vouch for you.' This should be the end of it, but he's moaning again and I see there's more to come. '*What?*'

'I'm pretty sure I left my phone in there.'

Fuck. If the police find it, they'll start to build a case, look for connections, and the tractor thing will start to look like more than coincidence. But then I think back to the night of the stickers, remember what Shannon said in the pub earlier: *there were two right next to each other.* 'Hang on, there're two summerhouses at this end, aren't there? So maybe it was the other one and not hers? Your phone might still be where you left it.'

I toss my fag end, get to my feet. 'Come on. Let's go and get it back.'

But before he joins me, he hunts down the cigarette end and grinds it out.

'Don't want to start a fire,' he says.

Too late for that, Tate. Way too late.

35

Charlotte

Earlier in August

The moment she heard the note of menace in Benedict's voice, she knew the previous day's trip to Abbotsbury had been no more than that: a one-off interlude in a month of madness. A fleeting redressing of the balance between holiday and socio-political crisis.

'You need to see this video,' he said within seconds of her returning to the house from walking Mango in the woods. Perry was still in bed, she deduced.

'Why do I get the feeling this isn't going to be husky puppies learning how to skateboard?'

'Just watch,' Benedict said.

It was a current affairs feature – or course it was – on the Sky News website and opened with the usual sun-spangled shots of Old Beach: pedalo capers on ultramarine waters, ice cream dribbling down toddlers' chins, teenagers thumping a volleyball back and forth.

Voiceover: This is Pine Ridge on the south coast of England, an easy hop from the bustling city of Bournemouth. On the face of it, it's peaceful, even idyllic . . .

There was a shot of the beach bar, a member of staff bearing a tray of amber beers towards a group of attractive young people.

'Oh,' she said, 'is that Beattie at the bar?'

'Not that,' Benedict said grimly. 'Just wait.'

Voiceover: But these images are a far cry from the scenes that have unfolded over the summer. A war has broken out between locals and second-home owners, with a series of altercations taking place, notably at the ferry . . .

Mobile phone video played, showing the activists throwing their red gloop at 4x4s, followed by footage of Tabitha and her buddies at the ferry dock, hip-deep in water.

Voiceover: Now second-home owners have hit back, accusing locals of vandalism, criminal damage and abuse, which they claim has not been properly investigated by police.

She felt Benedict tense by her side as an all-too-familiar face now appeared on screen, with the caption 'Perry Tucker, holiday home owner'. He was standing on the cliff path in front of Alison and Humphrey's shepherd's hut, which was plastered in those vile stickers, and squinting into the camera.

Perry: We've suffered in silence for long enough and it's time to call this what it is: discrimination. You could own twenty houses and you should still be entitled to the same protection by the police as everyone else. Don't forget those of us with holiday homes pay council tax – soon to be doubled, by the way – to help subsidize community services. Locals claim they are second-class citizens, but I would argue it's the other way around. People like me, who work hard and have earned their time off, are being punished. We're being bullied and intimidated and the police are doing sweet FA about it.

Charlotte sent Benedict an appalled look. It was not so much the sentiment that repelled as the tone: high-handed almost to the point of imperious, choked with fury. How could he not have known he would come across exactly as the viewers would expect: posh, rich, tone-deaf.

Ripe for the guillotine.

When the hell had he done this? Obviously at some point after the sticker attack (at least he had not allowed the producer to use the Nook as his backdrop). A clue lay in the way he'd tucked his right hand into the crook of his left elbow. Soon after he'd walloped Robbie Jevons?

A talking head from the local police now appeared, his tone a good-tempered contrast to Perry's.

Officer: Inevitably you get more petty crime in beach resorts in high season, when the population swells. Thefts, driving infractions, pub brawls – they all tend to increase at this time of year. But as far as the vandalism to property is concerned, the second-home community should rest assured we are using all available manpower to investigate each and every complaint. The idea that one group would be treated differently is completely false.

The camera tracked two uniformed officers on Old Beach as they nodded benignly at holidaymakers and interacted with lifeguards.

Voiceover: There's a noticeable police presence in the village and that will be stepped up further for the annual beach festival on Bank Holiday Monday. In the meantime, both groups insist they want to see a peaceful conclusion to this season of record temperatures – and record crime.

Charlotte handed Benedict his phone. 'Oh dear. Sorry to say this, but Dad's becoming a liability.'

'That's what we think as well.'

She assumed he meant Tabitha and him. Possibly the Shaws too, since Tabitha now shared meals with them and must be privy to their views.

She could only pray there was not some wider band of Perry detractors in Pine Ridge.

*

She tackled him when Benedict left to meet Tabitha, joining him on the veranda of the Nook where he was smoking a cigarette (a rarity these days and often a sign of guilt) and gazing out to the trembling sea. It was the first time since the stickering that she'd chosen to sit here herself, unable to bear how denuded and forlorn the little house looked, fragments of scraped paint caught in the decking.

She was not confident of success as she opened the conversation, not because of the repetitive nature of the game – another ill-advised reprisal, another confrontation – but because of what was different. There was a shift in the dynamic between them this time, a shift of a significance not seen since his drinking days. At the start of the trip, if he had said something inflammatory, she'd generally agreed with him. So united were they in their desire to conserve the status quo, so certain of its benefits, that Benedict had accused them of 'smuggery'.

But now she did not agree with Perry. Words had become acts and acts could not be so easily forgotten – especially by the authorities.

'This isn't the *Voice*, Perry. It's Sky News. It's national. Maybe international.'

'I'm aware of that,' he said.

'You're on the police's radar now. And I wouldn't be surprised if Robbie Jevons has made a complaint against you as well.'

'He won't.' Perry puffed on his cigarette, using his free hand to clear the smoke. 'If anyone's on the police's radar, it's him.'

'Plus there's the speeding thing. That's obviously been formally logged.'

'I couldn't give a crap about that.'

This, Charlotte thought, was part of the problem. He looked as if he couldn't give a crap about quite a few things, when he really ought to. 'Perry, is there something going on with you I need to know about?'

And all at once, even as she asked the question, the answer seemed obvious. Look at the trajectory of the evidence: it hadn't *begun* with demonic rage, rather the demonic rage had developed – alongside secret texts, urgent returns to town.

'These trips back to London . . .' He'd been three times in as many weeks and always on the Friday. Previous volunteer shifts had not fallen neatly on the same day like this. This felt more like an official appointment. 'You're not seeing a doctor, are you? I don't mean for the drinking.' Thanks to years of practice, she was attuned even to his *thoughts* of lapsing. 'For something else.' Cancer would be her first guess since it had claimed both his parents in their sixties. 'Whatever it is, you don't need to go through it alone. I'm here.'

Perry gave her a weary look. 'I'm not ill, Charlotte.'

'What then? What's happened to you this summer?'

'Nothing! I'm just reacting to events.'

'But you're reacting with anger. Punching locals. Feuding with your own son, with our friends. There's barely anyone left you get on with.'

There was a silence. A couple with two young children strolled into view, hands gripped tightly as they registered the sheerness of the drop.

'Sorry,' Perry said, when they'd passed. 'I'll try. I'll try with Benedict, anyway.'

Charlotte regarded him with curiosity. Though she believed he meant it, she did not trust that he would be able to do it. There was an issue he was keeping to himself and it was clear she wasn't going to be able to coax it from him, not yet. Instead, as in previous crises, she reached for the therapy of manual work. It had worked for him better than anything else – just look at his dedication to Keeler House.

'Do you fancy doing me a favour?'

'What?'

She tapped her fingers on a nearby post. 'Repaint this. We've got the paint in stock, I think.'

'Fine,' Perry said. 'But I'm not doing the Shaws'.'

'Amy will want to do theirs.' Charlotte felt herself softening. 'I know this summer has been hard, but there's not much of it left now. I'm sure we're through the worst.'

Was she sure, though? Below, the tide made that growling sound you sometimes heard as it began its return to shore. In the past, she might have stayed to watch the racing currents, the way they doused the skin of the ocean as if tossed from some huge pail just out of range, but not this time. The longer she sat here on the Nook's war-torn deck, the more vulnerable she felt.

Amy had picked up on it straight away, hadn't she, though she hadn't been able to name it, had sublimated it into other anxieties. But how easily defined it was now.

They were targets, all of them. Targets in their own homes.

36

Beattie

She gathered up her bag, beach blankets and towel and stepped out onto the deck of the Niche.

'Mind, darling!' her mum cried out. 'The paint's wet!'

'Like, obviously,' Beattie said, irritated. 'You're literally painting right now.'

She didn't have a problem with her mum redoing the exterior so quickly – she was obsessed and crazy and it kept her attention off Beattie – but it did mean she hadn't been able to invite Tate round, which had led to a last-minute scramble for an alternative location. She'd wondered about the Nook – Benedict had told her where the spare key was, in a weird super-discreet way that made Beattie think Tabitha must have told him about Tate – but when she wandered down to the Tuckers' she found *that* was being painted as well, by Perry.

'Come to lend a hand?' he'd asked her.

Seriously, it was like the oldsters had no idea what a holiday was.

Luckily Tate had had a suggestion: the old pillbox on the far side of the Meadow, which she very much hoped wasn't going to smell of pee.

'Aren't you going the wrong way for the beach?' her mum called after her.

'I'm going to sit in the Meadow for a bit. Do some reading.'

'Have you got sunscreen on? It's deceptively breezy along there.'

'I don't burn,' Beattie said.

'It doesn't mean you won't damage your skin. You'll regret it later.'

'That's like your motto, Mum. *You'll regret it later.*'

Her mum looked hurt and Beattie felt briefly guilty. She needed to go or she risked Tate coming along too closely behind her and her mum noticing. She might put two and two together and make four for once.

'Don't forget you're having my pedicure at The Needles. Three o'clock. There's no way I'll be finished here in time.'

'Okay.' Now she felt even more guilty.

'If they ask, you're eighteen.'

A few minutes later, she arrived at the pillbox, a grey concrete thing clinging to the cliff edge, with a horizontal lookout slit. There was no door and so when Tate arrived, they had sex standing up just inside. He kept craning his neck to the side every so often to check the gap for hikers, which was weird and distracting and she was relieved when it was over and they could just sit on her blankets and chat.

'Can you smell something funny?' she said.

'Like what?'

'Like bodies. But not, you know, ours?'

'It's always smelled like this,' he said wrinkling his nose, which made him look cute and boyish. 'Must've been thousands of people hooking up in here over the years. Shooting up, sometimes, as well.'

'That's so grim.' A slant of sunlight fell through the slit onto their bare feet and noticing her chipped toenails, she had an unwelcome thought. 'I've got a pedicure at The Needles after this – you don't think it will be Ellie doing it, do you?'

At their family's last drinks with the Tuckers, before the dads had fallen out, Charlotte had mentioned how the girl who'd done her facial that day had been moaning about her boyfriend never being around and it *had* to have been Ellie. What with Tate's bar work, his activism, his affair, he couldn't have a lot of time left for his girlfriend.

'I'm not sure she does pedicures,' he said. 'Might be wrong on that. You wouldn't say anything?'

'Are you joking? She'd pull my toenails out!' Beattie remembered Tabitha's take on things. What was it she called it? Polyamorous. 'She definitely doesn't know?'

'No one knows on my side.'

'What, not even Robbie?' It gave Beattie an important feeling to know she was on the radar of the charismatic NJFA leader, who had just been featured in the *Guardian*, according to her mum.

'Nope. And we need to keep it that way. His missus is Ellie's best friend.'

Beattie sighed, suddenly frustrated with the need for secrecy, anonymity. Pine Ridge felt too small for this, like everywhere she looked there were traps. Any minute now, someone they knew could stumble in here and go nuts and make them feel bad just for liking each other.

'What?' Noticing her glum expression, Tate assessed her through narrowed eyes. 'I don't like her more than you, if that's what you're thinking. I think you're fucking awesome. But you'll go back to London soon and I'll still be here, so . . .'

'So you'll need a girlfriend?' she finished.

'I'll need a home. You know I've literally not got a roof over my head without her.'

There was a sullenness to him now, a darkness, and the thought that she'd infected him with her mood made her feel a bit panicky.

She didn't know what he wanted her to say and scoured her mind for a positive.

'You said you might get one of those new micro cabins? Tabitha said they'll be proper registered addresses, not like the caravans.' Beattie had been shocked to learn that temporary residents like Robbie and Tate couldn't use the park's address for banking or benefits or anything else official.

Tate shrugged.

'Or you could always move away?' she suggested.

'Where to?'

'I don't know. London?' She had a vision of the two of them at the club in Soho that she and Sienna and Lexi went to. Dancing and kissing, fingers in each other's hair, their skin oily with sweat. Everyone watching them and saying how amazing they were together. 'They'd love you in London. It'd be so lit.'

He brightened. 'You think?'

'One hundred per cent,' Beattie said.

*

Oh wow. The spa was fully bougie. She was getting serious Bali vibes with all the carved wood and polished conch shells (Bali was her destination of choice for her gap year). Maybe next summer she'd try to get a job here. She'd be eighteen by then and was confident she was just as pretty as the therapists milling around in their tailored green tunics. Not that she had any therapy skills, so she'd need to be on reception, which actually, when she thought about it, might be quite boring. Bar work would be better. Maybe the beach bar, alongside her lover.

But wait, she'd literally just fantasized the entire walk down here about Tate moving up to London; if he did that then next summer he wouldn't be here and Pine Ridge wouldn't be the same without him. Or would she already have flown to Bali by then anyway?

She supposed it depended how much money she banked for her eighteenth.

'Who's my therapist?' she asked the girl on duty.

'Manda. She's running a few minutes late, if you'd like to take a seat.'

Phew. 'Is there a loo I can use?'

'On your left, just through the doors to the changing rooms.'

The loos were shared with the gym users and were very fancy. Green slate tiles and dried flowers, palms shaped like spears and something fluffy and blood-red. Through the glass doors, she glimpsed a bank of lockers and thought, *No*. She couldn't even if she wanted to, she didn't have her shim or her spare phone with her.

But she could always have a little check to see if anyone had left their locker door open, couldn't she? It happened more often than you'd think. People were running late or distracted or thought the lever had slotted into place when it hadn't. Low-hanging fruit for someone like her, someone who had TV reels made about them.

No, Beattie. Just go to the loo.

But the whole time she peed, she felt it. A weird hankering, like hunger but more emotional. Like yearning.

Oh God, she'd heard about this feeling before, from Benedict's dad. She must have an addiction; she must be a . . . what was it? A quick google supplied the answer. A kleptomaniac, that was it.

Great.

She flushed the loo and washed her hands with the gritty citrus handwash and emerged into reception in time to be greeted by her therapist.

'Amy? I'm Manda. Would you like to follow me?'

37

Charlotte

The yoga class was winding down, the instructor adopting hypnotic tones to urge them to 'respect the breath' and invoke all the reasons they should be thankful for their bodies (basically, a list of its parts). The skin on Charlotte's arms gleamed from her earlier massage, mitigating the horrible crinkling she got in certain postures. Not that there wasn't a scientific fascination to ageing, she found, like monitoring the degradation of plant matter. The shrivelling of a potato, for instance.

She caught sight of her fatigued expression in the mirror and thought, *Am I really fifty?* Half a century of breathing and moving and working and parenting and caring and fighting fires and seeking solutions and keeping the peace. It was exhausting. She couldn't manage another year of it, let alone another thirty.

Especially down here, with this new sense of reckoning in the air, even in places with a pro-holidaymaker agenda, like The Needles. She could have sworn her masseuse's manner changed when she'd told her she wasn't a guest at the hotel but had her own place up in the village. You couldn't *see* the resentment, but you could feel its heat in her fingers, like infrared light.

The class finished. She thanked the instructor and went to collect her things from her locker, which opened without her needing to use the code – she obviously hadn't closed it properly;

absentmindedness was another unwelcome symptom of middle age. Exiting the spa, she stopped at the front desk, where the lotions used in the treatments were on sale. 'I want to buy some of the oil Ellie just used in my Swedish? Deep Moisture Retexturizer, she said it was.'

'That's such a gorgeous product.' The girl's smile was genuine as she located it and slid it into a Needles-branded gift bag. 'Thirty-five pounds, please.'

Charlotte opened her wallet, but the card she wanted to use wasn't in its usual slot. She checked the other compartment to no avail.

'Is something wrong?'

'I think I've lost my card. Did I leave it here when I paid for the massage and yoga class?'

'What's the name on it? Charlotte Tucker?'

'No, my maiden name. Miss C Raine.'

'Let me check if it's been handed in.'

But the only things in today's lost property were a yoga top and a water bottle.

'I don't think I closed my locker properly . . .' Charlotte gave a rueful smile. 'You know, brain fog. But the card was definitely in my purse, so I think it must have been stolen.'

At the word 'stolen' the consternation was immediate. 'Is anything else missing?'

The other cards were present and correct and the key to the Moke was still in the zipped pocket where she'd left it.

'Not your phone as well?'

'No, I didn't bring that.'

'Good, because that's a thing now,' the girl said. 'We've got a notice up in the changing rooms, I don't know if you saw it? We're asking people to keep phone and bank cards separate because of the fraud risk. Would you like me to take some details and contact the police?'

But the thought of that useless lot wading in was too much. 'No, it's okay. I'll call my bank from home and get them to cancel it.'

It took five minutes to get back to Cliff View, the traffic into the village lighter than usual. Perry was still at work on the Nook, Benedict, Huck and Julien swiping a shuttlecock backwards and forwards on the lawn. She found her phone and sipped a thyme and citron tea while she waited in the queue for the fraud hotline. She and Perry had premium accounts and she got through after only a brief hold.

'When did you last use it?'

'This afternoon. At The Needles in Pine Ridge.'

'That would be for £122, yes?'

'That's right.'

'There's actually been a contactless payment since then. For £98.'

The contactless limit was £100. 'Really? Where?'

'A shop in Pine Ridge called Fleur. That wasn't you?'

'No, I haven't bought anything from there all summer.'

'We'll make the refund to your account and send an alert to the merchandiser. The card's been cancelled, so whoever's got it won't be able to make any more purchases. We'll send you a new one, it should arrive within twenty-four hours.'

'Thank you.' She'd get Perry to pick it up on his next – and, he'd promised, final – trip back up to London for the mysterious weekly appointment he thought best to conceal from her.

*

Draining her tea, she decided to take a wander down to Fleur. She had nothing planned for the next hour so why not, in the absence of a functioning police force, indulge in a little amateur sleuthing?

She'd forgotten what a lovely shop it was, laid out on two floors of a classic Bird Lane cottage. She'd used it constantly in the early years in an effort to support local businesses, but lately her custom had dropped off. They stocked more beachwear now, high-end swimwear and sarongs, raffia sunhats, sandals with metallic straps. Tubes of French sunscreen were offered at £30 a pop.

She waited for a customer to pay and then approached the counter. 'My card was used here about an hour ago by someone who stole it from me. It's okay,' she said, at the woman's startled face, 'I'm not looking to escalate things. But I wondered if you can remember anything about the person. They spent £98. I don't know how many items that would have been.'

The woman consulted her iPad. 'That must have been the bikini top and the hat. You served them, Chelsea, I think? When I was out back.' She addressed a second staff member, a teen busy stocking cubbyholes with baskets of soaps shaped like mussels.

She came over to join them. 'Bikini top and hat. Yeah. It was a girl.'

'Anything else,' her manager prompted.

'A tourist, maybe?'

'Can you remember how old she was?' Charlotte asked. 'I mean ballpark?'

'Twenties, maybe? She had blonde hair in a ponytail.'

That narrowed it down – to a few hundred people a day.

'Would you recognize her again?'

The youngster looked doubtful. She was plainly not one of those super-recognizers Charlotte had read about who got recruited by GCHQ.

'Can I see exactly what she bought?' At the very least she could look out for the items and confront the girl, vigilante-style.

But the bikini top was black, the only distinguishing detail a trio of beads on the ties. Charlotte pictured herself patrolling the beach ogling women in their twenties in black swimwear. Being called out by Amy for perving.

'And the hat is the same as this one.' The girl held up a white linen bucket hat. Again, standard issue. Charlotte was not familiar with the brand, Briny Baby.

'That same colour?'

'No. Orange.'

'Quite a bright, bold orange,' the manager said.

'Have you sold many of them this summer?'

'I actually think that's the only one we had in that colour.'

'Oh, I remember,' the dope said, suddenly. 'She said she wanted it because it matched her toenails.'

That was more helpful.

38

Tate

'Tate Barlow and Ellie Fletcher?'

'That's us,' Ellie said in the chipper, slightly affected voice he assumed she must have honed for her clients at the spa and made him feel a rush of tenderness for her because she must think who she was and how she spoke wasn't good enough for them.

They followed the greeter to her cubicle in the council's housing department. Liz Hawkins, Housing Officer, read the sign on her desk. There was nothing fake about her broad smile and her accent was Dorset all the way.

'So let's see what you've brought for me.'

Ellie handed over the various documents they'd been asked to supply to prove their long-term residence in Pine Ridge. 'We can show you our reports from the junior school if you like,' she joked.

'Spare me,' Liz Hawkins said with a little wink.

Tate had to admit the council were handling the KosyKabins project exceptionally well. Here they were, just a little over a week since the unveiling, already being processed. There'd been none of the usual procrastination and fobbing off, the expired links and phone numbers that no one ever answered, all designed to break your spirit and move you on. *Hey*, he imagined telling Robbie later, *it's almost as if our campaign's working!*

Liz Hawkins began creating their application on screen. 'Just to confirm, you're expecting a baby?'

'How do you know that?' Tate blurted, and there was a surprised silence.

'Tate, it's on the form,' Ellie said and she and Liz exchanged a 'what are they like?' kind of look, as if all men were simpletons. He knew Liz must be noticing their mismatched attitudes, Ellie's all upbeat and eager to please, his like some hapless bloke in an old movie where he had no choice but to marry the girl with the bun in the oven because it was, like, 1953 and the alternative was life-ruining social stigma.

She showed them the plans for the different KosyKabin types, a more in-depth version of what had been presented at the meeting, and ran through the Net Zero scheme the project was signed up to, the thermal insulation and whatever. Each unit had a smart frontage of grey and yellow – the same yellow as the NJFA stickers, but he didn't point that out – and came with a front patio big enough for a table and chairs. There was no doubt the aesthetic was attractive, the use of space ingenious, but the cabins were tacked right on to each other in an unbroken row; at least in the caravan they had a sense of privacy, no neighbour on the other side of the wall.

'I'm placing you on the list for the family cabin,' Liz Hawkins said, 'which is basically two modules, with that bit more flexibility in the internal space. It can be two-bed to begin with, but if you decide to in the future it can be reconfigured into a three-bed.'

'That's amazing. I can't believe it!' Ellie gushed like they'd won the lottery, like this static by another name was the summit of a girl's dreams. The whole thing felt more and more like make-believe to him. He was still in that old movie, but now he was having difficulty remembering his lines. No one had told him his backstory or where his plot line went next.

Maybe because it wasn't going anywhere.

'Can we see a show flat anywhere?' Ellie asked.

'There's a one-bed on display at the company's office in Somerset,' Liz said.

'Somerset? I bet they're actually made in China,' Tate said, not proud of the mocking note in his voice.

'No, they're manufactured in the West Country,' Liz Hawkins said. 'They've just won a small business award, I believe.'

'Maybe we can get my mum and dad to drive us over?' Ellie said to Tate as if suggesting a visit with Father Christmas to a small child.

'If you can hang on till October, there'll be an open day on the Pine Ridge site itself,' Liz said, and Ellie said she thought they probably could hold on, yes.

'Anything nice planned for the rest of the day?' Liz asked, accompanying them back to reception and her next set of hopefuls.

'Off to see my parents over in Bournemouth,' Ellie said and again self-pity washed over Tate. Days off were supposed to be about gaming and drinking and hanging out with your mates or, this summer at any rate, having incredible sex with DFL goddesses. But not this one.

And next year, none at all. He'd be in a KosyKabin with a screaming baby. A flexible space that in no time at all would be altered to accommodate a second screaming baby. As soon as the babies could speak, they would start fighting and probably he and Ellie would fight too and their neighbours on both sides would ask to be transferred to cabins as far away from them as possible.

The bus got stuck for ages in the queue for the ferry. He felt claustrophobic as the cars came speeding off towards Pine Ridge, all Teslas and Range Rovers and those fuck-off Porsche Cayennes that cost seventy-five grand. Always the same broad-shouldered man at the wheel, the same narrow blonde in the passenger seat, both in this season's Ray-Bans. He imagined Beattie sailing by with her parents, spotting him on the waiting bus and thinking she must have made a mistake.

The bus jerked forwards. At least he'd made Ellie promise not to say anything to her mum and dad about the baby.

*

Phil and Tracey only went and cracked open a bottle of prosecco! They pored over the KosyKabin photos on Ellie's phone and downloaded the floorplans and made lists of spare furniture they had that might fit here and there. A couch. A bed. An old cake stand that might work for toiletries in the shower room.

(A cake stand, for fuck's sake!)

'Make sure you get a contract signed asap,' Phil said. 'Just in case these rumours are true.'

'What rumours?' Ellie said.

'It was in the *Echo* last week. The government's been putting pressure on councils on the south coast to house migrants once the season's over. The hotels all empty out then.'

'They've been in talks with the Staywell chain,' Tracey added.

'We don't mind sharing our village with people in trouble,' Ellie said frostily. Her parents were anti-immigrant, which really bothered her, but Tate didn't rise to it. Tabitha had advised him and the others not to be too hard on the older generation because they weren't *malicious*, only the product of a different time. One day, to their kids, they'd be the bigots.

Or maybe just losers. God, his mood was worsening. He needed to snap out of it before Ellie's parents picked up on it.

'Well, I wouldn't be so quick to support it,' Phil told his daughter. 'These jokers in Westminster don't care about you. Once the Staywell's full, they're going to go, "Hey, they did a good job down there in Pine Ridge, out of our sight. Where else have they got we could use? Oh, look, a whole load of KosyKabins are going up. We'll have those as well, thank you very much."'

'They couldn't do that,' Ellie said, alarmed. 'Could they?'

'Just make sure you keep on top of the application. The slightest delay, you need to question it.' He turned to Tate. 'And I wouldn't get involved in any more of this anti holiday-homes stuff. Keep your nose clean from now on. You don't want to give them a reason to change their minds.'

'You not drinking, Ells?' her mum said, noticing her daughter's untouched glass, and Tate held his breath.

'No, I'm working later,' Ellie said, a rehearsed lie, and he breathed once more.

*

On the bus home, she exuded happiness like a fever. 'We're *so* lucky things have worked out. I'm sure Mum will say she'll help, so I can carry on working.'

He guessed then that she'd told Tracey – presumably at some point after the remark about her not drinking and before they'd left. By now, Phil would know as well and they'd be draining the rest of the prosecco and saying what a beautiful baby their grandchild was going to be with two such attractive parents.

Though the short passage was as smooth as a bowl of milk, he felt suddenly seasick.

But as the bus trundled along Peninsula Road, the ridge on their right, the dunes on their left, the nausea lifted and, in its place came understanding – unexpected and profound. It was to do with the water, he realized. For all the people on Old Beach, both locals and visitors, it was a playground, a reward. It represented fun and pleasure and freedom.

But not him. For him, it meant captivity. He wasn't just trapped by the caravan, by Ellie, by the pregnancy, but also by the sea. It was a forcefield holding him hostage.

They'd love you in London, Beattie had said, and he believed her. He believed *in* her.

The next time he took that ferry, he wasn't coming back.

39

Amy

Refreshed after her sunrise swim, she trod water for a few minutes and drank in the view of the beach, more silver than gold at this hour, the wooded ridge beyond shimmering and alive. A new thing she'd learned from Charlotte: go out early (and not just because dogs were free to roam the beaches). Go out and get your lovely, life-affirming deposit in the bank before your account could be plundered by your enemies. Activists, for instance. Or members of your own family.

As she landed back on shore, she spotted Charlotte coming along the dunes path, frisbee in hand, Mango off the lead just ahead. She waved and collected her towel and the three met in the gleaming fans of the shallows.

'So, I'm looking for a bright orange hat basically,' Charlotte said, having launched into a story of her card being stolen from the changing room at the Needles gym. Not even £100 had been spent on it, but Amy recognized a conscious decision to sweat the small stuff when she saw it. They'd all lost control of the larger issues, even Charlotte.

'Oh, and toenails that match.'

'Toenails that match?'

'That's what the assistant said.' Charlotte threw the frisbee and Mango snatched it in an effortless forward-facing move, hared back for more. 'The woman liked the hat because it matched her nails. I don't get the sense she's a master criminal. More an opportunist. A member of staff maybe?'

'Wouldn't the people in Fleur recognize a local?' Amy said.

'Some of the Needles staff are temporary. And there's a recruitment crisis, as we know. They might have had to take anyone they could get.'

'On that note . . .' Amy gestured towards the headland. 'I have to go back up. The builders are coming this morning to tear down the garage and get their kit on site for Tuesday.'

Amy had, of course, already cleared this with Charlotte and the other neighbours on Pine Ridge Road. Though not strictly allowed to do noisy work until after the bank holiday, the builders were from out of area and proving inflexible – 'If it's not then, we're looking at October, love' – and with the Rickmans away and the neighbours on her other side conveniently leaving this very morning, she'd decided to take the risk.

'I really hope the dust doesn't affect you. But in case it does, Monday night's dinner is our treat.'

They were booked into The Needles for a last supper before both families got on the road the following morning – all except Amy, who would stay to oversee the start of the build.

Of course, neither Linus nor Perry had yet to confirm their attendance at the dinner, superpowers unwilling to be the first to concede ground and lose face.

*

She arrived home as Beattie was emerging from the shower. Rap – gangsta or drill, she wasn't sure she knew the difference – pulsated from the bedroom where Huck had joined Julien for the final weekend, his own room having now been commandeered as an emergency receptacle for the contents of the garage. For all Beattie's negotiations, the boys had ended up sharing anyway.

'Remember the garage is coming down this morning,' she told her daughter. 'There'll be builders milling about, so don't be wandering in and out half naked.'

Beattie said nothing, just slipped on her flip-flops (mercifully not Gucci for £400 but Skechers for a more palatable £30) and set off down the dusty wasteland to the Niche 2.0 (what with its repainting, followed by a trip to B&Q for enhanced security fixtures, life in the bungalow had acquired a Groundhog Day vibe). Amy watched her from the sink – would it kill the others to wash up their mugs? – marvelling at her natural poise, the graceful way her fingers squeezed the ends of her hair, and she wondered if seventeen years of her 'brains over beauty' mantra had made any impact on the girl.

Rinsing the mugs, she stopped dead. The sensation was of bodily possession, a consuming certainty. She dropped the mugs, turned off the tap and found her laptop. Googled – what was the wording she'd seen that time? 'Gym theft', that was it.

A raft of news stories loaded:

London gym thief steals thousands . . .

String of GymLads thefts revealed . . .

**Thief stole phone from locker and
hacked bank account . . .**

She read the first one and then closed the laptop. Went to the bathroom, still steamy from Beattie's shower – and rooted in her toiletries bag for the things she needed. Then she grabbed a roll of bin liners from under the kitchen sink and marched down to the summerhouse. In the distance, a ferry transported normal citizens from A to B and she envied them their smooth crossing, their linearity of purpose.

'Beattie, let me in!'

'Oh hi, Amy.' Tabitha opened up, dressed for the beach in bikini and sarong.

'Sorry, Tabitha, do you mind if I have a quick word with Beattie in private?'

'Of course. I was just heading out. Maybe see you on the beach, B.'

'Yeah. Amazing,' Beattie called from where she sat on the bed, still in her towel. As Amy closed the door behind her, she looked up with theatrical long-suffering. 'What?'

Amy thrust a bottle of nail varnish remover and stack of cotton wool at her. 'Take your nail polish off now. They're not Shellac, are they?'

'No. And no way! They're fire.'

She pulled the expression Amy had grown familiar with this trip: pleased with her own beautification (aka vain), disdainful of challenge. Amy didn't know whether to slap the girl or fold her into a hug and never allow her to make another decision for herself again.

She unscrewed the remover herself and doused the cotton wool in it. 'Do it or I will!'

'Why?' Beattie was starting to look alarmed. She took the pad from Amy, who sank onto Tabitha's camp bed.

'Charlotte had her bank card stolen at the spa the other day. The thief went straight to a shop in the village and bought a hat to match the colour of her toenails – and that colour was orange.'

Thank God neither had been on display in front of Charlotte in the days since, for they'd certainly crossed paths. This was a crisis, but it seemed they'd benefited from the kind of luck that might prevent it from becoming a catastrophe. She thought again of the Google search: she'd worried Beattie might be the victim of crime, not the perpetrator of it. Her naivety made her squirm.

'This is what you've been doing, isn't it? Stealing bank cards from changing rooms in gyms, then buying clothes.'

There was no attempt to deny it, just a dreadful silence filling the space between them, then Beattie brought her left foot onto her right knee and began blotting the colour off her toes. 'It was only a hundred pounds,' she said.

'Because you only had the card. If you'd had her phone too and got access to her account it would have been more, wouldn't it? You'd have bought the whole shop. I read how it's done, Beattie!' Amy wished Beattie *had* found the phone, because surely Charlotte's screensaver would have been a picture of Benedict or Perry or Mango. 'Did you not recognize the name?'

'I can't remember. It wasn't Tucker.'

'She must have an account in her maiden name. Which is good, because it means Perry won't be involved. In case you haven't noticed, he's not a great fan of this family right now.'

One set of toes was free of the orange, bar a soft stain. Beattie began on the other.

Amy's thoughts raced. 'All it takes is for Charlotte to ask at the spa for the names of the clients who've had a pedicure recently . . .'

'But they could have done their own nails at home,' Beattie protested.

'"They" stole the card from the spa, so it'd certainly be worth checking if "they" had got the pedicure there! Thank God the staff didn't call the police, at least not as far as we know.' The colour would have been memorable enough to be matched to Beattie's name – actually Amy's, but that would have won them only limited grace had the police become involved. 'How many times have you done it? Truthfully?'

Beattie wouldn't meet her eye. 'I don't know. Eight. Maybe ten.'

Ten! Jesus. 'We need to get rid of everything that connects you to this. Start getting it all together now. Shoes and sunglasses as well – anything you bought with someone else's money. Including this hat Charlotte's looking for.'

Tearful now, Beattie began assembling her items, including the shim she presumably used for opening the lock – like some basic East End villain. If Amy hadn't intervened like this, what would she have progressed to? Conning pensioners out of their life savings?

'How did you even know how to do this? I've never read about it before now. Who was it who told you? I swear I'll wring their neck.'

'Just . . . This girl on TikTok.'

So her criminal tutor could have been one of a billion people. *Good luck reporting that, Amy.*

Beattie swallowed. 'Don't tell Dad.'

'Oh, believe me, I'm not going to tell anyone. You could get a prison sentence for this. Do you know what would happen if you had that on your record? Forget uni and a great job and all the rest of it. Your life would be ruined.' And being beautiful would be no asset in a young offenders' institute, Amy thought. She knew she needed to calm herself. The police were not about to stage a dawn raid; she had the advantage. 'What phone did you use? Please tell me it wasn't your own?'

Beattie handed over a second iPhone. It looked barely used but it had to go.

'I'll take this and the tool down to a bin in the village. You pack the clothes in these bin liners. Go and get the rest from the house as well. *Now.*'

Down in the village, it felt surreal to be burying evidence of her daughter's crimes as she nodded hello to the shop staff with whom she'd been so assiduous about being on greeting terms. Because she wanted to belong here, be a useful member of the community, not the nurturer of delinquents.

On the way back, she checked the laundry hamper and pulled out the few items of Beattie's she suspected needed to join the pyre. When she returned to the Niche the girl was crying over her bagfuls of beautiful fabrics. The orange hat was there, Amy noted, with relief.

'We can't throw them away, Mum, they're worth thousands!'

'Do not even *think* about selling them. That would be an extra police charge. Fencing or whatever. There must be no trail, do you understand?' Amy paused. 'I don't want them anywhere near here.'

There'd be a skip arriving in a few minutes, might that work? Best not to risk it. Then she remembered the textiles recycling bin near the caravan park. Still a bit close to home, but probably okay. The clothes might be redistributed to outlets across the whole county, maybe further afield. It *was* better that they were used rather than destroyed.

'We'll take them to the recycling bin near the caravan park,' she told Beattie as her phone began ringing. 'Hello, Amy Shaw? Yes, great. I'll be out front in two minutes.' She got to her feet. 'The builders are just outside the village, they'll be here any minute, so I can't give you a lift.'

'It's okay,' Beattie sniffed. 'I'll take them up there myself.'

'They need to all be off the premises this morning.'

'Yes. Sorry, Mum.' With every minute the girl looked months

younger. Uncertain of herself, trusting of her mother. It made Amy feel a complex kind of love, with nostalgia and sorrow and fear mixed together.

'Beattie? When we get back to London, I'm going to set up some counselling. We need to get to the bottom of why you did this.' She hovered in the door. 'All of these things, you could have found nice enough alternatives. Some of them you probably *can* get fakes of, like you told everyone.'

Beattie nodded.

'Why then? Why did you do it?'

Her daughter gave a pathetic shrug. 'Dunno.'

'Just tell me your gut. How did it make you feel when you were doing it?'

'It just . . .' Beattie paused, tears welling once more. 'It was like my heart was *really* beating.'

It was impossible to tell if this was the first time the girl had examined her own motives or the hundredth, but if Amy had to guess she'd opt for the former. 'I'm sure it was,' she said.

40

Beattie

She couldn't do it. It was just too tragic. Yes, it was obvious the clothes had to disappear *temporarily*, but if she could get them back for uni next year then her mum would still be in London while she'd be in some other city and by then the victims – and the police – would have forgotten the whole thing.

She considered stashing them in the Nook while she figured it out – she knew where the key was and her mum would never think to check there – but Charlotte was the last person she needed stumbling on her swag, even if she was careful to dispose of the problematic hat and bikini top.

She grabbed her phone and found her message thread with Tate.

RU in rn? Is E at work?

Y + Y

Can I come over? Need to give U sthg.

OK

She checked her face – how humiliating to have cried like that – and cheered herself with the thought that at least she'd kept back the new iPhone she'd bought in London that last time. There was no way she was chucking that in the recycling. Anyway, she might need it, if she had to go on the run or something. If her life turned into *The End of the F***ing World* or whatever.

Then she walked along the footpath to the Tuckers' place.

Charlotte was on the veranda of the Nook with coffee and her laptop and Beattie felt the involuntary curl of her toes inside her trainers.

'Hi Beattie. Wrecking ball day, I hear?'

Beattie slowed a fraction. 'What?'

'Not literally a wrecking ball. But the garage is coming down, isn't it? Perry's taken Mango out in case she gets anxious.'

'Oh. Yes.' Beattie gave her a quick, grateful smile. 'I was wondering if Benedict's in?'

'Still in bed, I think. Feel free to go up and wake the lazy beggar.'

She padded through the house and up the broad staircase to Benedict's bedroom. 'Sorry,' she said, finding him still under the covers. Even in the gloom she could see that the room was enormous; he was *so* lucky.

'Hi Beats.' He remained prone. 'Does Tabs need something?'

'No, she's out. Can I ask you a favour? Could you drive me to the caravan park?'

'Why? Meeting Elvis?'

'What? Oh, yes, actually. I would walk but I've got this big bag of stuff I need to give him and my mum's like tearing down the garage.'

Benedict sat up, sighing. 'Meet me out front in ten. We'll go in the Moke.'

By the time she reached the street with her bags, a massive

great bulldozer had pulled up at the bungalow, the rest of her family, plus Julien, watching it jerk backwards and forwards into position. Her mother flared her eyes at the sight of Beattie and her bin liners and gestured for her to move out of range before her father noticed her. She dragged the bags past Villa Pino to where Benedict was waiting in the Moke and lugged them onto the back seat.

'Thanks,' she told him, as they pulled away.

He glanced in the rear view. 'Good timing. That looks like it's going to be messy.'

He meant the demolition, of course. 'I know. It's a nightmare. I can't wait to get back to London.' She was slightly spellbound by the yearning in her own voice, like this wasn't her, she was being played by an actor.

Benedict cackled. 'It hasn't been that bad, this summer. We've had a laugh, haven't we? You've had your holiday romance. What's in the bags, anyway?'

'Just a bit of overspill from the summerhouse.'

It made no sense that she'd take them to a tiny caravan, but luckily he'd drawn a different conclusion.

'I hope Tabitha hasn't squeezed you out? I know there's not much space in the Niche.'

'It's fine. I like having her there.'

'Don't forget you can use the Nook this weekend if you're stuck.'

'Thanks. Maybe I will.'

There was a lot of activity at the caravan site entrance. A lorry making a delivery to the shop had blocked the way and several vehicles were waiting to leave. A bunch of pedestrians, one really old and with one of those wheeled Zimmer frame things, hovered like meerkats.

'You okay from here?' Benedict said. 'I need to get back and get changed for paddleboarding. It's The Final Session and we might actually get to strike out a bit.'

She watched as he made a careful three-point turn and then departed. As she dragged the bags around the perimeter path she'd used before, the plastic handles cut painfully into her fingers and she felt emotions rise again, stamped them down. After a while, some guy offered to help her but she politely refused.

Tate was not impressed when he saw her. 'What the fuck? You want me to do your washing or something?'

'No.' She got the bags up the steps, aware that she was all sweaty and gross. 'Can you take them for a few days while I work out what to do with them? It's just some clothes.'

'Beattie, do you see much storage in here?'

'There must be somewhere. Please, Tate. I'm begging you.'

His mouth twitched. 'You're *begging* me. Leave them there, I'll find somewhere.'

*

He didn't seem to feel any differently about her even though she was wearing terrible clothes and old Primark underwear. He was actually, she was starting to realize, kind of insatiable.

'As soon as I've passed my driving test, I'll come down and pick everything up,' she said.

'Yeah, course. But . . . you know what?' His voice had a new optimistic lilt. 'I'm thinking I really will move up to London. Like you said. So I could bring them with me.'

'Seriously?' Joy rushed through her. 'Where will you live?'

'I'd get a room somewhere, I suppose.'

A thought struck. 'One of our neighbours has got this, like, granny flat above their garage? They had Ukrainians in there but I think they've gone now. I could find out if it's free?'

'Amazing. Thought I'd get a bar job while I decided what to do with myself.'

'Maybe you could model,' she said. The ideas were flowing, which was a sign that this whole relocation thing was completely meant to be.

'Not sure about that,' Tate said. 'Don't you have to be six foot or something?'

'You just need to have, you know, a look. I've got cards from scouts, so we could message them or just walk in maybe. I could go in with you, see what they say?'

'All right.' Tate looked pleased. 'Yeah. That could work.'

'*Ça marche*,' she said, which was what Julien said all the time, and which reminded her there was more begging to be done. 'Taaaate . . .?'

He smirked at her, playful, kind of adoring. 'Oh God, Beattie. What now?'

41

Amy

She, Linus, Huck and Julien stood in a line with their back to the street, each wearing dust masks and goggles supplied by the builders. The others couldn't have known how thrilling she found the bone-rattling jangle of the jackhammer, the spectacle of it plunging and lifting, not to mention the spiked bucket shovel of the JCB monster as it scooped the rubble into the world's biggest skip, raising dust clouds thick enough to obscure the worst images of the summer.

Then again, Linus looked like he was relishing it in his own way. Maybe picturing Perry buried in the debris.

'One more paddleboarding lesson and then that's it,' he'd told her in bed that morning.

'What do you mean, "that's it"?'

'I mean, Perry. I never want to see him again.'

She laughed – he had to be joking. 'You can probably avoid him in Dulwich, but not here. We're neighbours.'

'Doesn't mean we have to come down at the same time, though, does it?'

Okay, he wasn't joking. 'You know we're tied to the school holidays. We will be for years.'

'Yeah, but *they're* not. Tabitha said Charlotte said Perry doesn't want to come down in August again. He says the weather's better earlier in the summer and it's not such a bunfight everywhere.'

'Really?' Amy inhaled, her eyebrows lifting. 'What did Tabitha say Charlotte said? *That*'s the only information that counts.'

*

They might have arrived four months later than originally planned, but you couldn't accuse the builders of messing about once on site. Not even an hour had passed before all trace of the garage was gone and the JCB slotted into the gap as if it had belonged there all along. It would remain here over the bank holiday weekend and then on Tuesday colleagues would come to secure the site and start levelling the rear garden and digging foundations for the extension.

It was most people's nightmare, but she was looking forward to being left alone with the builders in dust world.

The JCB driver, Terry, had half an hour to kill and invited Linus and the boys to climb into the cabin and check out the controls, which led to a little photo shoot, Huck and Julien posing like soldiers in a tank.

'These levers here operate the front bucket,' he explained. 'This one up and down and that one side to side.'

'What kind of weight can it lift?' Huck asked.

'Oh, well over five thousand kilos.'

'How much is that?'

'Well, the Niche weighs less than half of that,' Amy said.

'Is that your shed down the bottom?' Terry said.

'Garden room, yes.'

He gave the boys a mischievous grin. 'This bad boy could swat your "garden room" like a fly.'

'Don't go giving them ideas,' Amy laughed.

He was such a natural teacher, they almost forgot about the

paddleboarding until Benedict came by to remind them. Perry had already gone down, he reported. Amy knew from Charlotte that he was still barely speaking to his father, even though Perry had tried to patch things up.

All this conflict! After this last session, which she doubted would be celebrated with a group selfie, let alone a bonding round of beers at the bar, Linus had work to do and the boys planned to game all day, so once Beattie got back from disposing of her stolen goods (she'd been gone *ages*, please God let there not be some new complication), Amy had some time to herself. She was damned if she was going to spend it analysing how her parenting could have gone quite so badly awry – no, she'd reacquaint herself with the architect's plans and browse some high-end fixtures and fittings (ironmongery porn, her friend Julia called it).

'See you on Tuesday,' Terry said, handing her the keys to the JCB. 'Keep these somewhere safe, Amy, yeah?'

'Will do,' she promised.

42

Perry

Later, he blamed the painting job for what happened out in Little Bay that last Friday, or at least as much as the punch-up at the caravan park or the dressing-down from Charlotte that had inevitably followed. Far from being the mind-clearing pursuit he – and certainly she – had hoped, the DIY had in fact facilitated a protracted stewing. All the pent-up fears and frustrations of the last few weeks simmered in the heat and, instead of reducing, expanded.

Clashing with the activists at the ferry. Sharing a home with Benedict again – while he'd worked in the sun like a navvy, the youngster had drifted between mother and lover, barely acknowledging the man who'd paid for the superior education that underpinned his moral high ground. And managing Jordan, who was doing his head in by breaking their rules and leaving voice notes with personal content, demanding to know when they'd be seeing each other again.

Now, at last, weeks since they'd begun, the boys' own paddleboarding adventure – or, as he thought of it, charade – was to conclude and they presented their customary line-up at the water's edge for a final briefing from Rio. Perry stood at one end, Linus and Huck in the middle, with dust in their hair from their garage demolition, and Benedict on the far side, hardly glancing at his father, let alone speaking.

Tabitha and Julien lounged nearby, more in the spirit of having nothing better to do than to mark the occasion. Unlike her childishly petulant boyfriend, Tabitha had no problem making eye contact with Perry and she treated him now to a serene, no-hard-feelings smile, which he, of course, found more infuriating than a shunning. It was a little blustery for spectators to hang around for long – those holidaymakers who'd braved the beach were mainly young families, resolute in their desire for authentic *au bord de la mer* memory-making – and Perry pictured the two of them strolling up to the bar at the first opportunity.

As promised, Rio was taking them further out, down the coast. 'It's a bit whippy out there,' he warned. 'Remember your body will act like a sail, so if you get caught, come down and lie face down on the board with the paddle tucked under you.'

Whippy was the word, Perry thought, as they followed their leader around the headland towards Little Bay. It was easily the bumpiest of their sessions, the waves rugged, the undercurrent powerful. Even so, it was a shock when he felt himself losing control and being borne on a violent gust towards one of the others – Linus, it happened to be – just as a jet ski came skimming towards them. For a few seconds the whack-whack of the jet ski's hull against the swell obliterated all other noise, including Perry's own shouted warning as his board collided with Linus's.

Both tumbled off instantly. There'd been no time to brace and Perry felt his lungs compress with the shock of cold water immersion, aware too of the tug of the leash on his ankle as he floundered. *Breathe*, he reminded himself, as he swallowed and spat seawater, snorted it from his nose. *Don't shut down*. The jet ski had of course buggered off, its wake vanishing fast in the flux and chop of the water.

Only as he got his breath working again did he become aware

that Linus was crying out in pain. Evidently, he'd fallen more awkwardly than Perry had, hitting his shoulder on the edge of the board.

'You all right?' Perry shouted, but by the time he'd reunited himself with his board and struggled back on, he saw that Linus's blow to the shoulder was the least of his worries. The idiot had been separated from his board – he mustn't have attached his leash properly – and it was drifting away from him with the current. As he began swimming after it, bobbing in his PFD, never quite reaching it, Perry struggled to reorientate himself in order to yell once more to Linus or, in the other direction, to Rio, some distance away now with the boys.

He got so far as to open his mouth and gather his voice when something stopped him. Something dissociative and perverse and by anyone's standards, regrettable. He found himself counting silently, slowly, to ten, eyes on the paddle in his hands, and when he looked up again, Linus was further out, a lot further out, still chasing his board. Every so often, his face turned, his cries inaudible by now but a grimace of primitive terror still, just, discernible.

Finally, Perry mobilized, got himself back into calmer waters and joined Rio and the kids.

'What happened?' Rio called to him.

'Got wiped out by a jet ski. But I'm okay.'

'Where's Linus?'

Perry blinked, eyes smarting. 'I thought he was here.'

'No, he was just ahead of you.'

'Maybe the jet ski took him out as well?' Perry suggested.

Benedict and Huck, both with scared eyes and a weather-beaten flush, turned for reassurance to Rio, who produced binoculars from his waterproof pouch and surveyed the horizon.

'Is that him? All the way out there? Where's his board?'

'I don't know,' Perry said hopelessly.

Rio grappled for his phone. 'I'm calling for help. We don't want him drifting into the ferry lanes. Then I'll get the rest of you back to base.'

Hearing the seriousness in his voice (*ferry lanes?*) and seeing at closer quarters the panic on the boys' faces, Perry scanned for potential witnesses. There was no one else out on paddleboards, but what about the sailors of the various small craft seesawing on the swell? Had any of them seen him hesitate the way he had, deliberately neglect to help? No, probably too busy keeping themselves afloat.

He swivelled to look back the way he'd come, but there was no trace of Linus now.

*

The RNLI boat was on its way out even before they'd returned to shore. A small crowd had assembled on Old Beach, though more interesting, perhaps, was the minority who remained on their loungers and deckchairs and stools at the bar, uninterested in the drama. No matter that a fellow human was in trouble.

(Not that he was one to talk.)

Tabitha and Julien rushed to join them, takeout coffees in hand, and Huck used one of their phones to call Amy. Moments later, she and Charlotte came hurrying down the cliff steps.

'Oh my God,' she wailed, 'when I saw the lifeboat, I just had this feeling . . . Didn't I say, Charlotte?'

'You did,' Charlotte confirmed.

Perry knew Amy was neurotic, but on this occasion her instinct for danger had been bang on the money. He watched her grip Huck in a tight hug.

'Darling, you're okay!'

'What's going on?' Charlotte asked Perry.

'Where's Linus?' Amy said at the same time.

'We kind of lost sight of him near Little Bay,' Perry said. 'He's why the boat's gone out.'

'Lost sight of him? How is that possible? He's on a board, moving at a mile an hour. It's not water-skiing!'

'He got, like, swept away,' Huck said with a tremor in his voice.

'He'll be okay,' Perry said. 'He's got his PFD on.'

'I don't even know what that is,' Amy said crossly.

'Personal flotation device. Lifejacket.' In Perry's peripheral vision, Rio hovered, joined by one of the lifeguards.

'It can get really choppy off Little Bay,' Charlotte said. 'It's nowhere near as sheltered as this side of the headland. Where did you lose him, exactly, Perry? Were you quite close to the shore?'

'Not really. I mean, I could see the hotel, but we were a fair way out,' Perry said.

'Where is he?' Amy cried. '*Where is he*?' She was getting hysterical. It didn't help that the tide was starting to wash in with a tremendous roar, the wind creating white crests out to sea.

'I'm sure he's fine,' Charlotte soothed Amy. 'The water's warm, isn't it, Perry? Even further out?'

'Pretty warm,' he agreed, a sentiment contradicted by his own shivering, not to mention the memory of having been robbed of air as the cold squeezed his chest, of having to coach himself to breathe.

'What does that have to do with anything?' Amy asked Charlotte.

'Well, just that he can tread water and won't be at risk of hypothermia.'

'What am I going to tell Beattie?' she wailed, and Huck began to cry. Even the normally nonchalant Julien looked mildly perplexed now. 'How am I going to tell her that her dad—'

'Her dad drifted off and was quickly rescued. *That's* what you'll be telling her,' Charlotte insisted. 'An accident, that's all. Happens all the time.'

Perry felt his wife's gaze move from Amy to him, fixing him with beady attention, and it was now that he felt a swerve inside himself, a swerve from feigned to real alarm. What if Linus didn't just experience an unpleasant scare, as he'd assumed, but got into serious trouble? *Fatal* trouble. What if he, Perry, had played a part in the loss of a man's life?

And, if so, knowing that, would he be able to manage his mind? When the adrenaline had drained and it was just him and his regrets?

The answer was unequivocal and frightening: *Yes, but I would need a drink.*

43

Perry

It took a while, far longer than was comfortable, but Linus was located and picked up by the boat. He'd been blown offshore by almost a mile, one of the volunteers reported to Rio, who relayed the news to the group. He was uninjured, bar a sore shoulder and a stomach full of seawater, and they were on their way back to shore.

There were 20-mph winds out there, apparently, and neither the board nor the paddle had been recovered.

'You won't get in trouble, will you?' Perry asked Rio, noting that the water sports kiosk had suspended business for the foreseeable, red flag flying. 'Let me know if your boss needs a statement or anything.' But the reassurance seemed only to disconcert their instructor, who opted to wait with the lifeguards.

'Why don't I take the boys up to the house,' Charlotte suggested to Amy, 'now we know he's safe. They can have showers and hot drinks. You coming as well, Tabitha? You stay with Amy, Perry,' she added, before he could make any objection.

Not that he would have; he wasn't entirely lacking in perspective. In any case, now it was clear he hadn't contributed to a man's death, he found he was enjoying the drama. And the sting of sand on his skin as he faced the gusts coming off the water, that was pleasurable too. It was a while since he'd felt so alive.

The others trooped after Charlotte, leaving Perry and Amy to their lookout. Before long, a red boat cleared the headland and motored towards Old Beach. A game cheer went up from the beach bar, where staff were following the drama with their customers. Volunteers dragged the boat ashore and those who'd not left to shelter from the elements had their phones out to film as Linus was helped over the side, bringing his feet to terra firma with an ungainly series of stumbles. He submitted to the briefest of embraces from his wife before striding towards Perry, his face florid and grimacing, almost feral.

'I can't believe you did that!' His voice was strained, as if he'd damaged his throat, but the fury was unmistakable.

'Did what?' Perry said, affecting indignation.

'You fucking ploughed into me!'

'It was an accident!' Perry protested. 'I went in as well, didn't you see? Anyway, it was the jet ski's fault, not mine.'

'You *saw* me in the water. You turned away like nothing had happened. You *saw* my leash had come off. You fucking *left me to drown*!' Linus was regaining his normal voice, the volume building, and at the sound of this battery of accusations, the RNLI guys glanced up from their huddle by the water.

Amy intervened. 'Let's talk about this when we've calmed down.'

But Linus's focus remained on Perry. 'Was it because of the girl moving into ours? Or the speeding complaint, was that it?'

'So that *was* you,' Perry said, calmly.

'Of course it was! You're a menace! You should be banned before you kill someone.'

'Banned from where?'

'The road. The sea. The whole fucking village.'

As Amy exclaimed – 'Linus!' – Perry felt his blood fire. His fists clenched, the right one aching horribly, a reminder of his recent fray with Robbie.

'I think you'll find I've been here a lot longer than you have and I've yet to "kill someone", much as you might like that. Face it, you got into difficulties out there because *you* were reckless, not me. Take some accountability, Linus.'

'Accountability? I almost drowned out there!'

'I'm going to say thank you to the RNLI guys,' Amy said. 'Please stop shouting, both of you.'

As she moved away, Linus brought his face right up to Perry's, the salt on his skin almost close enough to taste, his gaze burning. 'You know exactly what you did. I saw it in your eyes.'

Perry stood his ground. 'Oh, you did, did you? You must have better eyesight than me then, because I didn't see a thing.'

A flicker of curiosity crossed Linus's face. 'I think you've got a screw loose. There's something not right. Must be from all those drugs you did in your banker days.'

Perry sucked in his breath, regarded the other man with faux dismay. 'I know you've had a scare, Linus, but it's not good form to mock those in addiction recovery.'

'Mocking's all you're good for,' Linus spat. 'And you know it. Why else would you behave like this if you didn't hate yourself?'

'Fuck you,' Perry said.

*

The house was empty of everyone but Charlotte when he returned, mugs collected by the dishwasher, stained with the remnants of hot chocolate.

'How was he?' she asked.

'To be honest, delusional. Claiming I left him for dead.' Perry gestured to the mugs. 'Can I have one of those?'

Charlotte opened the fridge and took out the milk. 'Did you? Leave him for dead?'

'Of course not. He was in the water and got taken off by a current. Not much I could have done about that, I'm not fucking Poseidon.' He sank into a seat at the table, still in his damp layers from the beach but too tired to go and shower. 'I didn't want to say in front of Amy but it was like a washing machine out there.'

Charlotte poured milk into a pan and fired up the hob. 'So you couldn't have helped?'

'By the time I'd sorted myself out, he was gone. But I *did* help, yes. I alerted Rio, who alerted the coastguard. You run through safety procedures when you start the course and it was all done by the book.'

Charlotte narrowed her eyes. 'Then why does Linus think differently?'

'I don't know! Because he's a paranoid twat?' A commanding sense of injustice rose in Perry then and he honestly couldn't have said if it was real or manufactured. 'Can I just say it would be great to have a conversation with my wife where I wasn't being accused of lying. A bit of support wouldn't go amiss now and then.'

'Okay. Fair enough. I'm sorry.' But she continued to regard him with circumspection as she stirred the milk with a wooden spoon. 'Just be careful, Perry. You can't put a foot wrong now. And, if you do, Linus won't be the only one waiting.'

44

Tate

The rumour about the Staywell had been confirmed. It was top of the agenda at the Friday night NJFA meeting in the Gull, the last scheduled before Monday's festival – and their final stunt of the summer. The migrants would start to arrive the weekend after the bank holiday, Robbie said, at least a hundred of them, bussed in from a processing centre in Kent.

He shared other details he'd gleaned from his sources, his voice thicker, kind of stifled, on account of his having been smacked in the mouth a few days ago. Tate was still doing double-takes when he saw his friend's face all bruised and swollen. Robbie had played it down, said he was pleased not to have lost a tooth, but Tate had seen the video and the DFL who did it was an out-and-out nutter. He'd jumped out of a beach buggy and just flown at Robbie. Any more punches like that and he'd have knocked him unconscious.

He was the same guy who'd thrown Tabitha out, it transpired. Her boyfriend's father. And, according to Rio, he'd also been involved in the paddleboarding accident earlier today, where Beattie's dad got separated from his board and almost drowned. Rio was sore about it, having been suspended from work while reports were written up, his weekend sessions divvied up among the rest of the team. He'd be losing a fair bit of cash because of the incident.

'Apparently, they've had to cancel reservations for a wedding next weekend,' Robbie continued. 'The do is at The Needles, but a lot of guests were booked in to the Staywell. Now they're having to scrabble around for rooms in Poole and Bournemouth.'

'How long will the migrants stay there?' Tabitha asked.

'No idea. Could be months, I guess.'

'Outrageous, when you think of the skanky B&Bs we've been put in over the years,' Rio said.

'You're not wrong,' Robbie agreed, and Tate wondered if he was thinking what *he* was: imagine if his mum had been placed in a nice clean room at the Staywell and not the slum in Crowland where she'd spent her final years. She might still be alive.

A protest group had sprung up to oppose the arrangement, Robbie now reported, and a national refugee support organisation was vocal in countering that opposition. Both intended demonstrating on the day of the festival. 'The refugee group's looking for volunteers down here. They've got the human rights lawyers and all of that but they're a bit light on local support.' He paused. 'Any thoughts?'

Tabitha spoke first, her voice husky with compassion: 'I say we join forces. I mean, we want the same thing, don't we? Humane accommodation for everyone.'

'Well, for locals first,' Rio said, and she turned to him with evangelical eyes.

'But we're all just locals of the world, aren't we? We're all exactly the same.'

Tate was not sure he agreed with this sentiment. Even in this one room there were differences among them. For starters, *she* was not like *them*. Yes, she was a magnetic individual who had developed a following in the short time she'd been involved in their cause, but the fact was she was only here on holiday herself. She'd be gone before the migrants arrived, possibly never to return.

NJFA is not just for August, he thought.

He wondered if their paths would cross in London, perhaps when she was up with her boyfriend, who lived in the same neighbourhood as Beattie's family. Would Tate become Beattie's accepted partner, invited down for the summer as Tabitha had been? (Before she was thrown out by the crazy man, that was.) He'd googled rents and salaries in South London and wondered how the one could possibly cover the other. Then again, Beattie had mentioned a room vacated by Ukrainians, hadn't she, and even if that didn't come off it wasn't like he needed a palace. Just a shed with a bed of his own. Someone's third home.

He pulled his mind back to the present and entered the discussion. 'It can't be a coincidence that this news about the Staywell drops right after they've thrown us a bone about the KosyKabins.'

'I was thinking that,' Robbie said. 'The timing's sus. They knew we'd say if someone gets to live in a hotel it should be us. Though to be fair, I don't think the council gets much notice – or choice.'

'That's what worries me,' Tate said, remembering what Ellie's dad had said. 'I mean, now the government's got these hotel rooms – and I'm not saying that's not a good thing in principle, Tabitha, don't get me wrong – but the next thing might be them wanting first dibs on the KosyKabins. We don't want that.'

'We definitely don't,' Des agreed.

'It's not a question of first dibs,' Tabitha pleaded. 'It's about whose need is greater. Who is literally homeless and who's just looking for an upgrade.'

There was a collective intake of breath. *Just looking for an upgrade*. Easy for her to say with her apparently unlimited accommodation options. Risky too, because she'd unwittingly pushed Robbie's softest button: his loathing of hypocrisy. They all watched as their leader chewed on his swollen lower lip, his gaze darkening as he addressed her.

'Or *maybe* it's about who's literally invested in this issue and who just fancies doing a bit of virtue signalling while they're down here on a fancy holiday.'

Tabitha's eyes blazed with indignation as Robbie's turned blacker still. The two of them stared at each other for a dangerously long time, neither willing to give way. Then Robbie's expression cleared, his decision made. 'Tate's right. We don't get involved in this. We stay in our lane. It's not like we haven't got big plans for Monday already. Let's run through that and then call it a night.'

*

He saw the hat on the table as soon as he stepped into the caravan.

'What's this?' Ellie said.

Bugger, it must have come out of the larger of Beattie's bags, the one that had split when he was shoving it deep into the back of the drawers under the bed.

'It's a pressie,' he said, lightly. 'For you.'

'What was it doing on the floor?'

'I must've knocked it or something. I was in a hurry to get to the meeting. Do you like it?'

Ellie eyeballed him in a new, all-knowing way. 'Don't lie, Tate. I know you didn't buy it for me.'

'What?' His heart gave a horrible judder.

'Someone left it at the bar, did they?'

Perfect! There was no way he'd have come up with that off the top of his head (no pun intended). He feigned a sheepish look. 'They did. But weeks ago. No one's claimed it and it's brand new, so . . .'

'How long are you meant to keep things in lost property?'

'Fuck knows. I can take it back tomorrow if you—'

'No. I like it.' She tried it on in front of the mirror strung with fairy lights, posing and pouting, adjusting the angle till she found the one she liked.

'Looks good on you.' Relief made him kind. 'How are you feeling, babe?'

Ellie's shoulders sank. 'Tired.'

'That's natural, right?'

Hat still on, she stepped towards him. 'Don't go off on one, but I've told my mum our news. I had to. I mean, she'd pretty much guessed.'

'Oh.' This was hardly a surprise and he made no comment. He went to the fridge for a beer, allowing himself a grimace when his back was briefly turned to her.

'Don't you want to know what she said?' Ellie asked.

'I assume she's over the moon, is she?' He eased the tab and put the can to his lips.

'She is. And so am I, Tate.'

He pressed the end of his tongue against the sharp edge of the opening, almost but not quite breaking the skin.

Ellie sighed. It was obvious she saw this whole thing as a long game. Nine months long. 'So how did the meeting go?'

He brightened. 'There's news actually. The Staywell's definitely been requisitioned for migrants. Like your dad said.'

'Oh my God, I thought he was exaggerating.'

'No. They arrive next week.'

'That's so soon!'

'I know. There's going to be a demonstration on Monday during

277

the festival, but we're not getting involved. We'll do our thing early morning and then we'll be done for the summer.'

Ellie removed the hat and turned fretful eyes on him. 'I've been thinking about that. Remember what my dad said? I'm not sure we should take part. What if they—'

Tate cut in. 'It'll be fine. It's not graffiti. It's art.'

'So Robbie says.'

'He's right. It'll go viral, you watch.'

'Even so.' Her hand strayed to her stomach in that weird shielding way you saw with pregnant women. 'We have to get our KosyKabin, Tate.'

'We'll make sure we do.'

And the funny thing was he meant it. Even if he wasn't sticking around, he wanted her somewhere safe. Her and the baby.

45

Perry

Alone in bed, head heavy on the pillow, he closed the latest threatening text from Linus – *If you think you're going to get away with this, you're even crazier than I thought!* – and then tapped the screen to play a newly received voicemail from Jordan:

'So yeah. I just had this like run-in with Trev. I need you to speak to him, Perry, or something fucked-up's gonna go down, I swear.'

He could think of voices he'd prefer to hear on this last Saturday in Pine Ridge. Like Charlotte's, back from her early walk with Mango, telling him she had a cup of tea and a sausage sandwich for him. Or Benedict's, confiding that he and Tabitha had called it a day and he hoped Perry could forgive him for all the unnecessary stress they'd caused him by insisting hot was cold and up was down. Best of all, some reporter's, breaking the news that Robbie Jevons and his merry band of believers had been slapped with restraining orders that prevented them from entering the village during the month of August – in perpetuity.

But no. Jordan. The phrase he'd been repeating when he fell asleep started up once more – *You can't put a foot wrong now* – and he thought how funny it was that a single line could bring him to his senses, achieve what months of soul-searching had not. Not so funny – or surprising – that it should be his wife who'd delivered it, because she'd always been the incisive one, the one who made words count. She'd named his alcoholism long before he'd been able to himself. She'd recognized the link between his work and the addiction, between his ever-younger colleagues and his decades-long conditioning. She'd identified the solution, too.

The difference was these had all been truths, calls to action, whereas this . . . *You can't put a foot wrong* . . . This was a warning. Lying on his back, eyes on the vaulted ceiling, he reflected on other recent Charlotte insights:

If you separate lovers, they'll only want to be together more . . .

You're not seeing a doctor, are you? I don't mean for the drinking . . .

You don't have to do this alone, Perry . . .

He'd been so busy being the most selfish man in the world, he'd neglected to notice he was also the luckiest. Even after ejecting their son's girlfriend, after punching Robbie and giving that TV interview, and after leaving Linus to drown (he knew full well she suspected his version of events to be only that: *his*), he could still count on his wife being on his side.

Just about.

But the affair with Jordan was a crime too far and he knew it. He needed to end it immediately – in person. So urgent was the need, he sent a text back – *I'll be up today, lunch time* – and leapt from the bed. Downstairs, he heard the kitchen door open and Mango's claws skitter across the stone flags, the flow of water from the tap as Charlotte filled the dog bowl. What excuse could he use when he'd already assured her he hadn't needed to make the trip this week, not when they were returning straight after the bank holiday weekend?

As he searched his wardrobe for clean clothes, the answer stared him in the face.

'Do you mind if I take off on my own today?' he said in the kitchen, where Charlotte was sitting at the table slicing a banana. One piece for her, one for the salivating Mango, whose head rested on her lap. Breakfasts began lavishly on these month-long trips, but by this stage of the summer consisted of supermarket croissants and whatever fruit was left in the bowl. 'I think I need to clear my mind,' he added.

This was established code between them for when he was feeling overwhelmed.

'Where are you thinking of going?' she asked.

'I thought maybe Lulworth Cove.'

'It'll be busy. But I think that's a good idea. By the way, I just dropped some flowers round to the bungalow.'

He looked at her blankly and she stopped just short of rolling her eyes. 'For Linus. Our friend who almost drowned?'

'Oh. Yes. Nice idea.'

'I put all our names on the card. For what good it will do.' She slipped the end of the banana to Mango and wiped her hands on kitchen roll. 'Have you heard from him?'

'Who?'

'*Linus.*'

'No. Why?'

'Why do you think?' She was growing frustrated, tired of him. 'Just go on your walk, Perry. Sort your head out.'

*

Should he have needed any further resolve to see his aim through, it was waiting for him on the doormat of Masefield Road: a Notice of Intended Prosecution from the police. At first, he thought it was to do with Linus's complaint in Pine Ridge, but then he saw the registration – Jordan's Astra – and the location, Knights Hill, SE27. Failure to conform with a traffic signal. The idiot must have run a red light. And it was no longer simply a matter of paying a fine, but three points on his licence.

On *Perry's* licence. And in accepting the points as his own he would be committing a separate crime.

Something else Charlotte had said: *You're on the police's radar now.*

He parked on the corner of Ryland Street and walked down to Keeler House, passing what looked like a dead fox in a garden refuse bag. Nearby, someone's food recycling bin had been raided (by a different animal or the unfortunate victim?), grotesque rotting leftovers smeared across the pavement.

He buzzed Jordan, who took his time answering. God, was he even up yet?

'You want to come out? I thought we could get something to eat?' He couldn't risk going in and getting into anything physical. Or arguing in earshot of the other residents. 'I'm in the Range Rover, bottom of the road.'

A good ten minutes passed before Jordan came strolling down and slumped into the passenger seat.

'What the fuck you got on?' he smirked, clocking Perry's get-up.

Perry fired the engine. 'Oh. Just walking gear.'

'Why?'

'It doesn't matter.' Perry pulled into a gap in the stationary traffic, settling inches from the ad on the back of a bus: 'Kill your speed, not your kids!' (*Thank you, nanny state. There I was thinking I should do it the other way around!*) 'So what was the issue with Trev?'

Jordan huffed. 'Fucking threatened me, didn't he?'

'What d'you mean, threatened you?'

'Gonna come for me in the night. Told me there's, like, super-natural shit in the house.'

'Supernatural?' Perry snickered. 'Who does he think he is, Jack Nicholson in *The Shining*?'

But the reference went straight over Jordan's head. 'I thought maybe you could have a word?'

'I can't really get involved, Jordan. I'm just a volunteer.' The traffic was moving again, but now Perry was stuck behind cyclists, riding side by side like other road users didn't exist and then, at the next red light, sailing blithely through. 'You need to tell your support worker. But it sounds to me like he's just messing with you.'

As Jordan grumbled, he drove towards Norwood Road and parked in a side street, scrupulous about paying the correct charge on the correct app. He chose an Italian café that he'd never been to before and didn't think anyone from Dulwich was likely to stumble into. It was two-thirty by now and the lunch-time crowd had thinned. They ordered and Perry produced the NIP.

'I'm sorry, but I have to let them know it was you driving, not me. Otherwise, I'll get the points, which isn't legal.'

Jordan didn't reply. Their coffees were delivered and he began emptying sachets of sugar into his, one after the other. When he reached the sixth, Perry reached out a hand to stop him.

'Jordan, do you understand? I'll need your licence details. You've had it back from the DVLA, I assume? They must have updated your address by now.'

'Yeah. Came in the post last week.' His hand released, Jordan began stirring, causing the foam to slop over the edge of the cup.

'Good.' Perry started to tell him that he intended transferring ownership of the vehicle, how it wouldn't cost Jordan a penny, that he'd just need to call his insurer to register the change, but to his horror the boy started up a terrible groaning.

'What's wrong?' It couldn't be the insurance, because he'd raised that before and not had this ghastly reaction. His heart dropped. 'Please tell me you do actually have a licence?'

'Yeah, I do, but . . .' Jordan's throat bulged as he swallowed air. 'It's just provisional. I never passed my test.'

Jesus. No need to ask how he'd got away with this with his erstwhile employer, because he knew they'd wanted only the bare personal details needed to book him and pay him. Perry folded the document and returned it to the envelope. 'Look, I'll accept the points. But you can't drive again. You need to give me the keys back.'

Their food arrived, along with a pot of Parmesan which Jordan tipped in its entirety over his spaghetti, looking at Perry as if expecting a laugh. Perry had never known him so skittish – or so infuriating. He picked up his own fork, charged with nerves as if he might bend it through willpower alone, and laid it down again. He couldn't face his brick of lasagne, not before he'd said what he'd come to say.

'I'm sorry to do this. I know you're having a tough time. But I can't come and visit you again.'

'Why not?' Jordan said. 'You staying down in Pine Ridge?'

Perry couldn't remember his having ever used the name of the village before. When they'd gone down together, he'd been ferried door to door by Perry, incurious as to the destination; he hadn't even recognized Bournemouth when they'd passed through.

'No, not that. I'm actually going to resign from Helping Homes. Find a role somewhere else.' Seeing Jordan still hadn't understood what he was saying, he added, 'I think that will make it easier for us both. To split, I mean.'

Jordan sucked a rogue end of spaghetti into his mouth. 'Wait. You icing me out because of the points?'

'No, not at all.' Though the casual deception had hardly filled him with confidence in Jordan as a friend, let alone anything more intimate. 'Because this . . . Well, I just think this has run its course.'

That sounded colder than he'd intended and Jordan recoiled. His hand started to shake, the fork clattering on the plate.

'What I mean is I really like being with you, we've obviously . . . got something. But I don't think it's good for either of us. I'm taking advantage of you. And I'm betraying my wife, who I love.' Perry looked at his plate and forced himself to eat. The sauce was grainy, the heat patchy, one mouthful nuclear-hot, the next tepid. After a minute, he became aware of tears leaking from Jordan's eyes. 'Jordan. It's not that bad. You're strong. You don't need me.'

'I've got nothing,' Jordan gulped. 'You don't understand how that feels.'

'I do understand.'

'You fucking don't!' His voice was desperate now, chest heaving. 'Look at everything you've got. The massive house. The Range Rover. That posh place in Pine Ridge.'

Again, the name of the village. It felt pointed, a signal of some sort.

No, you're imagining it.

'I'm very lucky, I know,' Perry said gently. 'But when it comes down to it, everyone's got *something* other people want. It just depends how you look at it.'

Jordan gazed at him with sad, wet eyes. 'What have *I* got?'

'Well, for starters, youth. And good looks. Both of which are worth a lot more than some holiday home. Plus, you're bloody lucky to have got away with the car thing. You could've been up in court over that. Got a fine or even a suspended sentence.'

But words alone were not going to resolve this, at least not words of consolation. Jordan was a man of dark moods and unpredictable impulses; worst-case scenario, he might decide to blackmail Perry or threaten to tell the charity. He was going to need to offer something more substantial.

'Look, I haven't got any cash on me, but I'll drop some round when I'm back in town next week. Enough for the deposit for a studio flat of your own. You can't live with that arsehole upstairs. I'll help you with all the admin, get you settled.'

Jordan, who'd begun flattening his pasta with the back of his fork, raised his gaze, interested.

'But only as a friend, okay? Nothing more. Does that sound all right? Does that sound like a deal?' Perry instantly regretted using that word, making this transactional. 'And I meant it about the car. I'll need the key. Have you got it on you?'

'It's back in the room,' Jordan said. 'Not sure where. Want to come back and help me look for it?'

Perry knew what this meant. Come back and allow himself to be seduced, to weaken and surrender and retract every word of this break-up in some post-coital collapse. Carry on sucking up Jordan's driving misdemeanours until one day he found himself taking the rap for running over someone's pet. Someone's child.

'No, I need to head straight off. If you could find it and put it somewhere safe. I'll collect it from you next week. Wednesday, probably.'

'When you bring the cash,' Jordan said, dry-eyed now.

'Yes. When I bring the cash.'

46

Robbie

Tuesday 29 August, 1 a.m.

Even in normal times life feels precarious in the dead of night. Threatening. The night of the stickers, for instance, we were out for hours and not for a second did the edginess blunt. None of us is nerveless. But tonight, as Tate and I climb the traffic road to the headland – the cliff steps are out of bounds – it feels almost post-apocalyptic. The shops and cafés, so bustling earlier with the festival blow-ins, are desolate now, as if they might never open their doors again.

But maybe that's just me projecting. Maybe I just can't process the idea of everyday life after tonight.

We walk fast, our strides synchronized like our ankles are strapped together for a three-legged race, and soon we're taking a left into Pine Ridge Road, the premium sea-facing properties on our right. Every second driveway is empty, every second residence shuttered for the season, and I think to myself, *This is what it's all about*. This is why we do what we do. It's the last weekend in August and these people have already upped and gone. Many won't be down again till New Year's or even Easter.

Do they *really* not see the iniquity in that?

'Stop!' I slink into the shadows, pulling Tate with me. 'Mate, look.'

Three houses from the end, there's police tape up. A single security light blazes above the front door of the big white house, just as it did when Shannon and I spent the night there, our van illuminated like a UFO. That feels like months ago now. Innocent times. At the edge of the light pool stands a police guard in the same hi-vis tabard as the one down in the car park. He hasn't noticed us yet, his head bent over his phone.

'Why've they got guards everywhere?' Tate whispers.

'Because it's a fucking murder inquiry, isn't it? They can't have people going in and tampering with evidence or whatever.'

'Which house is he guarding?'

'The whole of that end of the road by the looks of it. Let's try the cliff path.'

We double back and continue to the Meadow, turning into the passageway that links the main road to the coastal path. The weather's changed again, the sky half-cleared, and to the south the lines of The Needles are visible. The sea is smooth and low, its surface as glossy as freshly poured tar, and I know without consulting clock or chart that the tide's on the turn once more.

We hit police tape almost straight away, right by a shepherd's hut that's still covered in yellow stickers. They'll have a job getting them off now.

Tate cranes to get a better look down towards the far end.

'Are the police still there?'

'Don't think so. Can't see any lights.'

I reckon the officer we saw will be patrolling, cutting through one of the rear gardens every so often to check. In which case we don't have long.

'What's that?' Tate says and he slips under the tape and scurries a little way down the path. I follow and join him where he's craning over the cliff edge. A few feet down, hanging off a bit of shrub, is a piece of cloth. He reaches, but can't get close enough to hook it.

'Hold my legs, will you?' And he's on his knees, lowering himself onto his front, crawling over the edge.

'Tate!' I crouch, kneel on his calves to stop him sliding. 'You're going to get us both killed.'

'Got it,' he grunts, and I help him back to his feet. His jeans and hoodie are covered in dust, but his only interest is in the item he's rescued. It's green and pink, some ethnic tie-dye-type print.

'What is it? Looks like a sheet.'

'It's a sarong.' His voice gives way. 'It's hers, Robbie. I've seen her wearing it. You don't think—'

'No. Don't be crazy. I showed you Tabitha's text. We know she's fine.'

'She *was* fine. But anything could have happened since that text was sent. I need to know, Rob!' He's losing it again, sounding really pathetic, like, Jeez, a man in love. What has this London Lolita done to the boy? And with Ellie pregnant! But he's right, we *do* need to know something. We need to know where his phone is and get it back.

I grip his arm, wrench him back from the edge – 'You need to calm down, it probably blew down here from her garden' – but then my phone pings. 'Hang about. Message from Shannon.'

'What?' Tate hovers, clutching his stupid sarong.

'She's heard from Ethan. He says the police have an ID and they're trying to contact the family right now. The victim's male. Happy now?'

'Let's see.' Tate snatches my phone and reads it for himself, like he thinks I'm lying or something, and I feel the hairs on my arms rise. The victim is real now. Next time we hear, we'll have a name.

He hands the phone back. 'Weird to say "male" not "man",
d'you think?'

'Why? You don't think . . .?' We look hard at each other, daring
each other to say it.

'Could be a kid,' he says, finally.

'Could be a kid,' I repeat and a deep, deep sorrow fills my
stomach. I think about this morning – yesterday now – and how
euphoric I felt when we stood on the dune path, him and me and
Shannon and the others, looking at the beach below and thinking
how clever we were. How we'd done something special, really
made our mark.

Champions, all of us.

And yet, if I could start today again and do none of it, I wouldn't
hesitate.

PART THREE

47

Tate

They met at first light, the turn of the tide, under-slept but sluiced with adrenaline, equipped with their tools – garden rakes, basically, weighed down with extra lengths of wood – and a scale plan. The core group had all shown up, even those, like him, with long work shifts ahead.

The whole thing was Des's idea. He'd read about this guy who did sand art on a massive scale – Sandbanksy, he was known as, or some other lame pun – and he'd thought, hey, what better way to display *their* message. Instead of defacing what existed, why didn't they create something from scratch?

Initially, they'd planned it for the last day of August. Their season finale, Robbie called it. Then they'd decided the festival was the obvious showcase and they'd studied the tides and figured it could work. They'd need to allow a safe distance from the back of the stage – they didn't want the bands and crew and festival staff trampling all over it – but they'd get several hours of exposure to an enormous audience before it was washed away.

'Make sure everything's spelled right,' Robbie said.

'They're not exactly hard words,' Tabitha said, which drew a grin from the boss. It looked like Robbie was making an effort after that sour exchange at the meeting on Friday.

'You know, this would actually be perfect for the climate crisis,' she said. 'The way it shows how the sea erodes the village.'

'One emergency at a time,' Robbie said then, raising a palm in playful objection. 'No, Tabitha, I don't want to hear how they all intersect. How the migrants are going to be flooded in their beds. It's *way* too early in the day for that.'

Now it was her turn to grin. Of course, she, the only non-local – and non-worker – among them, still planned on going up to the Staywell later to protest against the migrant protesters. You couldn't accuse her of apathy, that was for sure.

They started on the upper stretch of sand, still damp from the receding water, and chased the tide downwards. Tate was allocated to Des's team, working on the intricate art elements, and soon felt the strain in his arms and back. He consoled himself with the thought of Beattie looking down from the clifftop later (much later; she often slept till midday) and seeing what they'd done and going *Wow*.

Wow, these Pine Ridge people are *vibing*.

*

Even before they'd finished, runners and dog walkers were emerging from the village and stopping to take pictures. By the time Rio had operated the drone camera and Robbie had edited the video to upload online, the first festival workers would be arriving, and, on their heels, the revellers themselves.

'You can just tell, can't you?' Robbie said as they stood on the dunes and took a last look before dispersing, some back to bed, some on to their workplaces. That it was going to explode on the socials, he meant.

'The morning light is amazing here, isn't it?' Tabitha said to

Tate, the only one of them to remark on something other than the stunt itself. 'All sweet and pure. Kind of *celestial*.'

He couldn't remember the last time any of them had thought about the quality of the light, let alone used the word 'celestial', but she noticed it and valued it because it was, for her, a temporary gift. He'd feel like that as well, he supposed, when he lived in the capital. When he came back as a visitor, a foreigner. A DFL.

'It really is,' he agreed.

48

Charlotte

Normally the bank holiday arrived at least two weeks earlier than she was ready for it. Ready to leave. But this time . . . Well. The thought of London was more appealing than usual, even her meetings in clients' offices, where she was inevitably something of a senior citizen these days. At least the young 'uns didn't hurl foodstuffs at her or call her a grockle.

The final early morning walks with Mango were to be cherished, however, and since Old Beach was already busy with the festival set-up – there'd be food pop-ups and children's rides and an army of staff reporting for parking marshal duties, not to mention families with young kids descending early – she walked him down the cliff path to Little Bay.

The tide was out and they walked all the way to the water's edge, where the breeze was invigorating. As she threw the ball for Mango and watched her launch herself joyfully at it, all four paws off the ground, Charlotte finally recaptured the glory of space and freedom she'd always associated with Pine Ridge. Of time in the company of the only member of your family who didn't answer back.

She'd asked Perry if he wanted to come, but he was still recovering from Saturday's hike; he'd walked almost twelve miles, apparently, returning to Cliff View with a look of weary relief. 'I'm amazed you haven't got blisters,' she'd said, looking at his pale, unblemished feet sticking out from under the duvet yesterday morning.

Through the pines, the staff minibus came into view, delivering workers. It was a well-oiled machine, The Needles. She remembered when the locals had opposed its opening, but now they scrambled to work there, to get their share of the London overtipping; they accepted it as a vibrant part of the economy.

Everything people objected to and resisted and decried they eventually got used to. Everything was superseded eventually, including opinions. Bob Dylan nailed it in 'The Times They Are a-Changin'.' Fifty years ago. And he was only pointing out what had been known since time immemorial.

It was a process, all of this. No more, no less.

*

Walking back through the Meadow, she saw a figure coming towards her – a woman in an orange hat – and instantly that moment of serenity, of bigger-picture communion, took flight, leaving her once more at the mercy of minuscule personal concerns. *This could be the stolen hat!*

As the girl came closer, she recognized her. 'Excuse me? Ellie, isn't it?'

'Oh. Yes. Hi.' Charlotte having halted smack in the middle of the path, the girl had no choice but to do the same.

'Where did you get that hat?' Charlotte only just stopped herself from humming the melody (her metamorphosis into Perry – the OG wisecracking Perry – was almost complete, it appeared). She was in no mood to explain to a Zoomer that it was once a music hall classic that had them rolling in the aisles. She glanced at the girl's feet, shod in trainers. Too weird to demand she remove them and reveal her toes.

'I was just admiring your hat.'

'Oh. Thanks.' Ellie patted it with her fingers as if she'd forgotten she had it on. 'My boyfriend gave it to me.'

'Can I just ask, is the brand Briny Baby?'

She removed it and checked. 'It is, yes. Sorry, but I'm running a bit late for my shift . . .'

She looked very tired for someone starting her shift, Charlotte thought. 'The reason I ask is my card was stolen and this exact item was bought with it. From Fleur?'

Fear flared in the girl's eyes. 'I don't know anything about your card. My boyfriend got this from lost property at work.'

'Where does he work?'

'The bar on Old Beach.'

'That's convenient,' Charlotte murmured. She'd allowed her tone to stray into sarcasm and the girl grew defensive.

'Wait, are you saying *I* took your card?'

'No.' She mustered a tight smile. 'I'm saying *someone* took my card – and *may* have used it to buy that hat, in which case you *may* be in receipt of stolen goods.'

Ellie thrust it at her. 'Do you want to just take it? I'm really not that bothered and I seriously have to go.'

But Charlotte didn't want the hat and she didn't think a therapist would risk her job for it anyway. What was she going to do then, go to the beach bar, where queues ran into the hundreds on festival day, and demand an investigation?

No, she had to accept that the trail had gone cold. Some chancer had nicked her card, bought a couple of things she'd wanted so little she'd walked off without them, and left town.

*

Perry was drinking his coffee on the veranda of the Nook and, seeing them approach, got up and met them at the gate. He petted Mango, dried his damp hands on his chinos, then said, 'You have to come and see this.'

'What?'

Charlotte followed him to the top of the cliff steps. Below, the stage had been built, crew setting up for what she knew from experience would be a booming sound check, and various food and craft stalls already open for business. A multi-coloured inflatable helter-skelter was new this year and already attracting queues.

'That was quick,' she said. 'I swear it starts earlier every year.'

'No,' Perry said. 'Look past the stage. Can you see it?'

She saw now that the dune path was busier than usual, with regular bursts of silver as raised phone screens reflected the sunlight. 'Is that writing on the sand? What does it say? I can't read it with the stage in the way.'

Perry showed her the aerial pictures circulating on social media. The design, which covered the entire beach down to the water, looked at first to be purely decorative, interlocked Celtic symbols perhaps, but then she saw it was in fact an intricate line drawing of the village streets, from the ridge at the top to the series of curls for water at the bottom. In a few hours' time, the incoming tide would cover those first.

'Wow. I love the map.'

The message – deeply carved in gigantic well-spaced capitals – not so much:

PINE RIDGE
IS NOT FOR SALE
#NJFA

49

Amy

The weather was the stuff of wedding-day fantasies – luminous, cloudless and perfectly still – and she set up breakfast outside in the dirt. Tomorrow, departure day, would be too rushed for them to eat together, so she'd made an effort, gone down to the bakery to pick up freshly squeezed orange juice and cinnamon buns warm from the oven.

Tabitha came up from the Niche, propping a placard against the JCB that read REFUGEES WELCOME on one side and, on the other, NO HUMAN IS TABOO (whatever that meant). The pro-migrant rally she planned to attend wasn't for hours, but she was already prepared. Amy found the girl very impressive.

'Was that you up at the crack of dawn? I mean, I assume it wasn't Beattie.'

'It was me.' Tabitha flashed her that lovely dimpled smile and helped herself to coffee. 'I went to meet some friends on the beach.'

'Is she all right, d'you think? Beattie?' This Amy asked mostly to test the possibility that Beattie had confided in her about the clothes. It had only occurred to Amy after the event that Tabitha might notice the absence of 90 per cent of her room-mate's wardrobe.

'She's fine,' Tabitha said. 'Maybe a bit sad to go home.'

Huck and Julien came slouching out now, both looking the worse for wear, and set about popping painkillers with their orange juice.

'Please tell me you're not hungover, boys?' Amy chided. 'Your vital organs aren't fully developed, you know. You've still got a very limited ability to metabolize alcohol.'

They'd gone into Poole the previous day, returning on the last bus and refusing dinner. *Please, not drugs*, she'd thought, and now thought a second time when she caught the furtive glances between them.

'How was Poole?'

'Dank,' Huck said, which she vaguely understood was not German, but simply meant good.

Linus appeared now in full cycling kit, including the new jersey he'd had delivered the previous week and described as 'aero-optimized'.

'You're not going out on your bike?' Amy said, and he pulled at his sleeves, correcting infinitesimal creases.

'It's been three days, Ames. I'm fine.'

'But they said to give it a week, didn't they? The medics?'

'They meant water sports. This is my last chance to get out before we go back home. All right, kids?'

The boys grunted. Tabitha smiled at something on her phone. Linus poured himself juice and wolfed a cinnamon bun in three bites.

Amy wondered, after this succession of exchanges, what would have happened if she hadn't got up first, if she hadn't fetched the buns and made the coffee, if she hadn't been here to greet each of them with a remark or a question or a caring word. Would any of them have done it instead? Would any of them have even noticed she was gone?

She angled her face to the sun, closed her eyes and conjured a macabre but really quite delicious image of them all surrounding her corpse. Weeping for their loss and saying to each other, 'I wish we'd said thank you.'

50

Tate

There was a point at which the post-stunt ecstasy began to give ground to the agony of not having had enough shut-eye. The terrible realisation that the longest shift of the season stretched ahead. Twelve hours, on a bank holiday, when everyone else was partying.

'It's going to be rammed,' Gav moaned, by way of a briefing. As well as Tate and him, there were three temporary bartenders hired for the day, all students and, they could only hope, not so crap as to be more trouble than they were worth. 'I want you back on time from breaks. Don't go getting lost in the mosh pit, yeah? You're here to work, not play.'

Maybe because of the buzz around the sand art, people had come down early and by eleven there was already a queue at the bar – for alcohol. Usually, the morning was more like a primary school fair: little girls getting their hair braided and arms stamped with flowers and hearts, but this was like the main event right from the start. The live music began at 2 p.m. and would be family-friendly, which was to say bland and underpowered, until the local headliners came on at 5.30 p.m., when it would be just as bland but a lot louder. He knew from having been a reveller in previous years that by then people would be stumbling about pissed. Not for him this time: Gav had a strict no-drinking rule for staff.

Leaving the bar to clear tables, he caught sight of protesters assembling on the near side of the car park. They must be the pro-migrant group because according to the NJFA WhatsApp thread, which pinged constantly with links and screenshots to do with their sand art triumph, the anti faction was already in position at the Staywell. Citizens Against the Elite had joined the antis, apparently, the elite in their sights presumably the government officials who'd requisitioned the hotel rather than the migrants themselves.

'March for Migrants over here!' yelled a woman of about his age but whom he didn't recognize. In fact, he didn't know a single face among them, which suggested Robbie had been right about them being shipped in from out of area. London probably. There were a lot of posh voices and spotless white trainers – a whole bunch of Tabithas, basically. She'd be here any minute too.

More importantly, she'd promised Beattie she'd still be out when Tate went up to see her during his break. They had thirty minutes for their final proper meeting before she went back to London.

After that, things looked a whole lot more complicated, especially since Beattie had texted him last night to tell him her mother had said the Ukrainians' granny flat was now occupied by the owners' grown-up son and his partner. Tate could only guess how challenging it was going to be to find somewhere affordable (the stories in the papers about London rentals were apocalyptically bleak) and it didn't help that both this and the job search would have to be conducted in complete secrecy so as not to tip off Ellie.

Which pretty much made him the lousiest bastard in the universe, but what was he supposed to do? Lead an existence he couldn't connect with, not properly, not in his soul? Perform life, not live it?

Over the bar's sound system one Nineties banger segued into

the next, by Spiller, which happened to be one Tate quite liked: 'Groovejet (If this Ain't Love)'. Maybe he'd ask Beattie to leave him the key to her summerhouse when she went back to London. Just in case the timings didn't quite match up. Ellie could be pretty formidable and she'd be sure to get everyone on her side, all their neighbours at Golden Sands, her family, Shannon . . . Maybe even Robbie too.

He wasn't sure if the adrenaline surge was from terror or anticipation or the double espresso he'd just made himself, but either way it galvanized him sufficiently to earn rare praise from Gav for his dynamism.

'If only everyone was like Tate,' he said.

51

Perry

'You go down with Amy,' he told Charlotte. 'I'll come and find you later.'

He couldn't say what it was that was making him opt out of the festival and stay home alone instead. The instinct to wallow, though he wasn't sure what in? Uncertainty about his unresolved tensions with Linus or, indeed, Benedict? Relief for having rid himself of Jordan? Remorse for having done it so, well, remorselessly?

The boy had phoned multiple times since Saturday and Perry had neither picked up nor returned a single call, stopping just short of blocking him.

Conscious of Charlotte's querying gaze, he considered citing some phantom pain, something beyond his stiffness from 'hiking', but felt too guilty following that exchange in which she had feared he was harbouring a secret diagnosis.

'Worried about seeing Linus?' she said. 'Well, you needn't, because he's off all day on some road race thing.'

'Of course he is.'

'Perry, we should be pleased he's back in the saddle! He could have been psychologically damaged after what happened. Lost his nerve completely.'

'Hmm.' He watched her collect bits and pieces from various

tote bags about the place and transfer them into a different one. Much of women's free time seemed to be taken up with this activity.

'Can you at least walk and feed Mango?' she said. 'I'll probably go straight on to The Needles. You are coming to that, at least?'

'What time's the table booked for?' Perry asked.

'Seven, but we said we'd go early if the band's as awful as last year's.'

'Sure. Okay.' He experienced an abrupt surge of optimism; his emotions today were in a road race of their own, with no clear favourite as to which might cross the finish line first. 'Maybe we can have a nightcap in the Nook when we get back?'

'Yes,' Charlotte said. 'Lovely.'

After she and Benedict had left, he made a cup of tea and did a bit of half-hearted packing. Every so often he found himself drawn to the window overlooking the street, an instinct to defend his turf perhaps for cars arrived frequently on festival day and other bank holidays, drivers either failing to notice the 'No Through Road' signs or hoping for a suspension of parking restrictions (no chance).

He spent five minutes looking for his iPad and when he found it he began drafting an email to Alice, the tenancy leader at Helping Homes responsible for Keeler House:

It is with regret that I must resign as a volunteer owing to . . .

Owing to what? He indulged the absurd and terrible notion of stating the truth, that he'd had an inappropriate sexual relationship with one of their vulnerable tenants. Waiting for the shockwaves to obliterate every part of his life until, one day, having looked up from the abyss, he found he'd been allocated a room in Keeler House himself.

But no, that kind of dramatic irony only happened in novels. He had enough money, enough property, never to have to worry about having a roof over his head. He deleted the draft and closed the app. He'd arrange a meeting instead. As with his exchange with Jordan, he'd uphold the protocols of his unfashionable generation and discuss the withdrawal of his services face to face.

Time passed. Down on the beach, one band finished and another started, this one louder and cheered by what sounded like a full-capacity crowd.

He scrolled through Twitter. Posts about the NJFA sand art had been shared thousands of times and the group already had a photo of it as their header and a pinned post of Robbie being interviewed by BBC South. The injured side his face was saturated by sunlight so you couldn't see the bruising.

Robbie: We thought this would be a brilliant way to share our message with a wider audience. Something positive and creative, you know? It's symbolic, as well. We can't turn the tide on the beach, but we can turn the tide on local homes being sold off to rich Londoners who have no roots in our community . . .

Yeah, yeah, yeah. Perry found himself rewatching the news clip of his own interview, playing it on mute, unable to bear his own outraged plummy tones. The visuals were monstrous enough; he looked so old and jowly. How did life do this, transform you in the blink of an eye from virile and photogenic master of the universe to decrepit has-been? It was as if there'd been some sort of technical error, a glitch that meant you skipped twenty years – the best twenty.

It was just as this thought ran through his head that the doorbell went. A journalist, if he had to guess, or maybe some joker offering him a tenner to park in their drive.

As he opened up, the music boomed from the beach: 'I Love Rock 'n' Roll.' This was actually okay music, maybe he should go down after all—

Then he saw who it was.

'Yeah,' Jordan said. 'Me. Sorry. Can I come in?'

At first, Perry neither replied nor moved aside, fixated on just how bad Jordan looked, the magnitude of the change in him in only two days. Not homeless levels of unkempt, just not taking care of himself – that was the phrase they always used, wasn't it? When people didn't shower or shave or brush their teeth or change their clothes.

The question was, had he been drinking?

He leaned a little closer and caught it, the whiff of cheap whisky. Misinterpreting the move, Jordan pressed against him, gripping him in a hug, his mouth seeking Perry's, and Perry wriggled from him, appalled. They were still on the doorstep and his reluctance to let his visitor in just about beat out his fear that someone might see them. The street was, for now, empty. 'You can't be here,' he said. 'I meant what I said on Saturday. We can't see each other again.'

But Jordan didn't appear to be listening. He had a strange trancelike aura to him that Perry had at first put down to the alcohol, but now saw more closely resembled shock.

'Jordan, what's happened?'

'I've done it,' Jordan said, having to raise his voice a little over the screeched entreaties to put dimes in jukeboxes from below.

'Done what?' Perry said.

'I've killed him. I've killed Trev.'

52

Beattie

She honestly couldn't imagine how she would ever look this good again. The way the light bounced as she appraised herself in the mirror, it was like her skin had gold leaf on it or something. The irony was she was only in a skater skirt and sun top from Urban. Oh, and a pair of pink knickers that had escaped the designer cull, which was probably just as well because her mum would have been out of her mind if she'd laid eyes on them, said they were for a pole dancer or dominatrix or whatever.

Speaking of escaping the cull . . . Her eye caught a splint of teal green under Tabitha's camp bed and, fishing out a pareo, checked the label: Erdem. That was right, Tabitha had borrowed it the day Beattie's mum stormed in and ordered her to start packing.

Balling it up, she left the Niche and set off down the path towards the Meadow. The groan of guitars from the beach, the yelled vocals, receded and swelled as the path curved. Not exactly Reading, which Sienna and Lexi had been to this weekend. Billie Eilish had headlined yesterday and her friends had shared a million pictures and clips from actually pretty close to the stage.

But had they had a dude like Tate waiting in their tent when they got back?

In their dreams.

She hurled the garment over the cliff and scurried back. Reaching the Niche, she had an interesting thought and kept going towards the Nook (she couldn't believe she was using these silly names, even in her head) and located the spare key under the heavy terracotta pot where Benedict had told her it would be. Her mum was reliably out for the duration, as were Huck and Julien, but she didn't need her dad coming back from his bike ride and bothering her in the Niche, seeing if she wanted to walk down to dinner together. He'd been way nicer to Huck and her since he got swept out to sea and had to be rescued, like he'd only now noticed he even had kids. Kept asking if she'd had a good summer and was she feeling prepared for A-level year and if she wanted to go and look at uni campuses together even though she'd already done all of that with her mum.

She let herself into the Nook and gave a little whimper of joy. She'd only ever been on the veranda before, but, oh wow, it was next-level cute, like somewhere you would spend your wedding night. The bed had a semi-circular headboard covered in blue velvet and a duvet in a print of blue and pink butterflies and leaves. As well as the wine fridge, there was a little drinks trolley with vintage glasses and bottles of cocktails.

She texted Tate: *Come to the Nook.* Then, remembering he *definitely* wouldn't know the silly names, she added: *The summerhouse on the end. The romantic one!*

Something special for their final tryst.

She took a bottle of wine from the fridge and opened it, pouring herself a glass and wishing she'd taken Benedict up on his offer earlier – not that it wouldn't have been withdrawn in a heartbeat if his mum found out that the man she was meeting was one of the NJFA inner circle. Tabitha said Benedict had told her Charlotte had hardened since the stickers incident, which was a shame because she was actually a really decent person and had initially been quite pleased about the KosyKabins.

There was a rap on the glass, the door cracked open, and Tate peeked in. 'Fuck. This is swanky.'

'I know.' She moved towards him, feeling her body heat merge with his, an instant doubling of lust. 'Come in and lock the door.'

'It's a mob down there,' Tate said. 'I almost didn't get my break.' He kissed her while he slid his trousers down his thighs, his mouth not leaving hers for a second even as he was stepping out of one leg and then the other.

The music was still really loud with the door closed, some golden oldie finishing to rapturous applause. But in the gap between the cheers and whistles dying down and the next song starting, Beattie caught the sound of raised voices.

She pulled her mouth away. 'Can you hear that?'

'What?'

'Arguing. Fuck, I think it's coming from the house.'

'Ignore it,' Tate said. 'Come back.'

But she was too spooked. She had a weird witchy sense about this stuff. And she didn't like how the drapes over the glass doors kept fluttering and creating gaps where you could probably see in from the footpath. (For this particular suspicion she blamed her mum, who was obsessed with sex pests and peeping Toms and whatever the other one was. Paypigs.)

'Seriously, Tate, can we go to my place after all? No one can see in there.'

'I've just got my trousers off,' he protested.

'Put them back on. Or just bring them.' She giggled, scooped up the wine and glasses. 'Quick!'

Delaying only to replace the key, she led him along the footpath to the Niche. There were no tourists or hikers in either direction, luckily. Everyone would be on the beach.

'Bob the Builder moving in?' Tate said at the sight of the JCB. It looked giant from down here, as tall as the house itself.

'The build starts tomorrow,' she groaned. 'My mum's staying down to, like, project-manage? She's probably gonna sleep in here.'

'Really? Shame. I was going to ask you if I could have a key. You know, in case I get thrown out of my place.'

Beattie checked the blinds and bolted the door. If her dad came hammering, she'd tell him she had period pains. 'You seriously think Ellie would throw you out?'

He shrugged. 'If she found out, yeah. People think she's all sweet and nice but she can get really mad.'

Beattie had a thought. 'Did you see where I put the spare key for the Nook? Under the second biggest plant pot at the side? If you're desperate, you could use that.'

Tate grinned at her. 'Golden.'

53

Perry

They were in the kitchen, doors open, and Perry had stopped shouting long enough to respond to Jordan's increasingly frantic demands for a drink. He fetched two Lucky Saints, could tell from the eagerness with which Jordan took his that he didn't know it was non-alcoholic. The boy couldn't stop his feet moving, a restless shuffle that got on Perry's nerves, and his focus kept freezing for seconds at a time.

'Start again,' Perry said. 'Tell me what happened.'

'I hit him. On the head.'

'Where? What with?'

'In the bathroom. With one of his weights. A dumb-bell or whatever.' There was a brief light of optimism in Jordan's eyes. 'I thought it might look like he slipped and fell? Like he hit his head on the sink?'

I thought it might look like: that sounded frighteningly like premeditation.

'He was definitely dead?'

'I think so.'

'You think so?' Perry's voice rose again. 'If there was any doubt, you should have called an ambulance!'

'No way. I had to get out of there. If he's alive, he'll kill me. But he's not, so yeah.'

He was slurring quite badly, liquid rolling down his chin every time he took a slug, his hand-eye coordination off. This was a nightmare.

'Jordan, concentrate. What did you do with the dumb-bell?'

'I kind of rinsed it off and put it back in his room with the others.'

'What, with your bare hands? That was stupid.'

Jordan looked offended. 'I wiped it with a towel, though, didn't I?'

'Where's the towel?'

'I dumped it.'

'Where?'

'In the bin by the bus stop.'

Not ideal, but at least not inside Keeler House where the police would find it within minutes.

'Why are you here?' Perry asked. 'It's miles from home.'

'I don't have anywhere else to go, do I?' Jordan spoke with feistiness now, even accusation, as if this were in some way Perry's fault. 'I was thinking . . . Can I say I was down here? Like, all day. With you?'

'Jordan, I'm sorry, but I can't have anything to do with this. That wouldn't work anyway – too many people know what my movements have been today. Plus, there'll be a record of the time you bought your ticket, maybe even security footage of you on the train.'

Jordan looked bewildered and Perry felt his pulse skip. 'You didn't get the train. So you, what? You didn't drive the Astra?'

'Had no choice, did I? I know I'm not meant to be using it, but . . .'

But what did that *matter when he'd fucking killed a man?* Perry could feel his thoughts spiralling, and with them his grip on any prospect of his being able to manage this crisis.

Jordan moved to the open door, taking in the picturesque corner plot, the pines and the yew hedge and the freshly painted Nook, its lines sharp against a spotless sky. 'Can't I hide down there?'

'No way. My wife will be back later and she'll want to have drinks there. We leave tomorrow.' Perry remembered his own proposal of a nightcap in the Nook. Could any notion be more quaintly removed from this shitshow?

Too late, he heard what else he'd said, right here and now – *We leave tomorrow* – and sure enough, Jordan's vexed brow was clearing.

'So, wait. If I, like, lie low tonight, sleep in the car maybe, I could come back up tomorrow and stay there then? Just while I work out what to do. Could you leave some food in there for me?'

'No, I couldn't! This is crazy, Jordan, you don't want to be on the run. What you have to do is go back to London right now and talk to the police.'

'And say what?'

'I don't know, explain you got into a fight with him but spin it so it sounds like an accident? Or deny you know anything about it. But the longer you stay away, the more it will look like you did it. Deliberately.' Perry paused to consider how to phrase his next question. Not that Jordan was in any fit state to notice his rank self-interest. 'Look, does anyone at Keeler House know about the Astra?'

'Don't think so.' Jordan drained his beer and turned to Perry with brimming eyes and running nose. Perry tore off a square of kitchen roll and handed it to him.

'You've never given anyone a lift or told them it's yours?'

'No.'

'Where was it parked this morning, when you left? On Ryland Street?'

'No, the next street down. Never any spaces near me.'

Good. If the police checked neighbours' Ring doorbell cameras on the street, there'd would be no evidence of the fugitive Jordan getting into a vehicle with a numberplate traceable to Perry. 'Look, I need to take the keys now, otherwise I'm going to get caught up in this.'

'How am I meant to get away then?' Jordan said.

Get away, not *get back*.

'Jordan, I'm keeping the car. And neither of us mentions you've been driving it, okay? I'll give you cash to get the train back. Go to the police or at the very least go to your room and then cooperate with whatever's going on. If you want to say you've been down here all day, then that's your call. Say you hitchhiked, maybe. Say you'd heard about the festival from me and thought you'd check it out. But we haven't seen each other, okay?'

He collected up cash from various drawers and pockets, added it to what he had in his wallet: £230 in all.

Jordan eyed the notes with dismay. 'You said you'd give me enough to get my own place.'

'When you've got everything squared with the police, I'll give you more.' If he thought he was going to be living anywhere but at His Majesty's Pleasure, he was deluded. Perry felt an overwhelming sadness then for the boy, and a terrible remorse for his own lasciviousness, his own stupidity. 'You have to go. Please. You weren't here, okay?'

He could see the defeat in his eyes, if not total acceptance, as the car keys were finally surrendered. 'How do I even get to the station?'

'There'll be a bus to Poole and Bournemouth from the main road. Down by the beach. Go the back way and down the cliff steps. That's the quickest.'

'I need the toilet first,' Jordan said. 'I know where it is.' And he was out the room and up the stairs before Perry could divert him to the cloakroom on the ground floor.

He waited at the foot of the stairs, running through the information he had, searching for gaps. Finding one.

'Where did you leave it?' he asked, when Jordan returned. 'The car?'

'Up in the car park.'

'Good. Right. Okay.'

'It's out of petrol,' Jordan added.

Of course it was.

54

Beattie

'I have to go back down,' Tate said. 'I'm late. Gav'll be doing his nut.'

They chugged the rest of the wine as they dressed and then he was at the door, fiddling with the bolt. The light poured in, a hard-edged fluorescent rectangle that almost blinded her.

Though she'd planned to go in the other direction, to avoid the festival crowds and walk along the cliff path towards The Needles, she had a weird primal need to prolong their contact. Almost like she had a premonition she'd never see him again. 'I'll come down with you and get the shuttle bus from the beach.'

On the veranda, they both paused at the sight of the sea below. The sun was mellowing, causing a wedge of silver to spread across the water, and suddenly Tate was crooning absent-mindedly under his breath, not the song the band was playing but something else, lyrics she didn't know – about love, about why it feels so good – and the words sparked another profound sensation, this one a kind of knowledge of having peaked. She had peaked, the summer had peaked, life had peaked.

'I'm just gonna say it,' she blurted. 'This has been amazing and I love you.'

He reeled her towards him. 'I love you too.' He kissed her and she felt their connection deep in her abdomen, like a living thing.

They headed for the steps. At the top, you could see the tide coming in, making the crowd bunch together on the sand. A few people were still in the water on pedalos and inflatables and, way out, on boards and cute little sailboats.

This place is okay, she thought. Next summer, when the bungalow looked like it did in those amazing plans her mum had shown her, she'd get Sienna and Lexi down.

'Look.' Tate was gesturing to the zone beyond the stage, to the NJFA sand art. 'The second line is almost gone now.'

He was right, the lower half of the design was covered by water and you could just see the upper part of the map with the top of Bird Lane and the ridge itself, along with the words 'PINE RIDGE'.

'He's such an amazing designer,' Beattie said.

'Des?' He chuckled. 'Let's hope your mum agrees.'

They took the steps single file, him leading. Below the line of the wall, their fingers met, out of sight of hundreds of people, and it felt more illicit than any of the sex they'd had. On the beach, he steered her towards the pines, just out of sight of the bar, and they kissed a last time. Then he left her, weaving through the edge of the crowd, out of range.

She knew she ought to go back to the house and check she'd locked the back door after going in for her shower earlier, but she couldn't be bothered and anyway it would be fine, her dad would be back any minute. Wait, had she even locked the Nook? She'd returned the key to its hiding place, but she had no memory of using it first.

It didn't matter, there'd obviously been someone in the house. She'd leave it to them.

And oh my God, she was starving. She was going to order the lobster burger and then she was going to have a pudding.

That meringue thing Huck had that time she and Tate had been together in the loos.

On Old Beach Road, the Needles shuttle bus was due in five. It was supposed to be for hotel residents only, but no one questioned you when you looked this good.

It wasn't fair, it just was what it was – and who was she to mess with the universe?

55

Perry

'Well, well, well, who'd've thunk it?' a voice said from behind him, with a familiar gloating relish. 'Who is he then?'

Great. Just his fucking luck. Not once all summer had he seen Linus cycle along the clifftop path – and nor had he expected him to be so stupid as to try it, what with it being narrow and rough and the risks to all but pedestrians marked at regular intervals with warning notices.

But now, just when he had something to hide, here the fucker was, dismounting from his precious carbon-fibre bike that you could lift with an index finger. He'd obviously seen enough, if not all of what had just happened to be able to draw a dangerously accurate conclusion. Perry tailing Jordan to the footpath, having not trusted him to actually leave. Jordan, sensing him, turning to meet him, trying one last time to get physical. Then, when Perry turned his mouth away, appealing loudly to be allowed to stay.

'Please, Pez. *Please.*'

'No!' Perry hissed. 'What is wrong with you? *Go.*'

Jordan backed off, almost tripping on a hunk of granite and needing Perry to reach out and steady him. He had never felt so cruel, so wretched, but he had no choice, he could not risk his family being associated with some squalid death in a clearing house, with *murder*, and when Jordan vanished down the steps he could have fallen to his knees and wept with relief.

That was until he became aware of Linus in his peripheral vision. Still, black-clad and shiny, insectile.

'Some local bit of rough?' Linus guessed.

'You have no idea what you're talking about,' Perry muttered.

'Come on, *Pez*. Does Charlotte know?'

'There's nothing *to* know.'

'Oh, I think there is.' Linus gave a delighted cackle. 'Tabitha's gonna love this. Perry Tucker, bi. No, what do the young 'uns call it? Switch hitter, that's it! Careful she doesn't tell Benedict, eh? He might not be quite so thrilled.'

The sound of that arrogant laughter, the sight of him standing there with his precious bike by his side like a pet, caused an explosion of white-hot fury in Perry and suddenly he was seizing the thing and hurling it over the cliff. The tide had come in and it was instantly washed from the rocks into the water, irretrievable. Snarling, he took a step towards his nemesis. 'I should have finished you off out there when I had the chance.'

Still Linus just stood there, motionless, aghast.

'Keep away from me,' Perry said. 'And keep your mouth shut.'

The element of surprise allowed him to get back indoors before Linus could process what had happened and think to retaliate. His breath came in painful gasps as he locked the kitchen doors and pulled down the blinds.

As expected, there soon came hammering and thumping and a succession of furious threats:

'You owe me eight k for that bike, you twat!'

'Come out now or I'll kick the fucking door in!'

'I'll be making a complaint to the police first thing!'

Well, *that* was an empty threat if ever there was one. The police couldn't give a toss about rich people's bikes. They'd take his stupid complaint and file it under 'Elite Whingeing'.

As the banging continued, Perry took a clean tea towel and set about wiping everything he could recall Jordan having touched, including door handles and banisters and even the bathroom taps. If the boy implicated him in Trev's death in some way, made him out to have conspired with him, then Perry would need to deny flat out that he'd seen him down here today.

Quite how he'd persuade Linus to do the same he'd need to figure out sooner rather than later. At least the din at the door had stopped; presumably the idiot had gone home to lick his wounds.

His phone pinged with a notification of a missed call from Jordan and he threw it down on the sofa and grabbed his sunglasses. He needed to find that bloody car and get it out of sight – now.

*

He took the steps, averting his eyes from the handful of people slumped against the cliff wall below. This was the worse-for-wear brigade, the ones who'd lost the use of their legs hours before the party ended. A tribe Perry knew well.

Jordan, too. He knew on a primitive level that the boy would be planning to carry on drinking; the question was would he leave town first? If, for whatever reason, he decided to stay, Perry had little chance of spotting him because every inch of sand between the cliff, the stage and the bar was packed.

Oh God, he'd given a relapsed alcoholic a pocketful of cash and sent him on a route that took him past a bar! The queue was at least fifty deep, however, which might have put him off; scanning it, he could not see him. The only familiar face was Rio, the paddleboard instructor, who, clocking Perry, averted his gaze with barely disguised dislike.

Up on Old Beach Road, he could see Beattie Shaw boarding the Needles shuttle bus, heading to the family dinner he was supposed to be attending himself. He might even have hitched a ride with her – had he not got himself tangled up with a random lover who'd only gone and *killed someone*.

Threading through the pines to the car park, he saw at once how naive he'd been to imagine he could find the Astra. There were hundreds of vehicles, many boxed in, others parked down sandy trails or between trees. To add to the confusion, he couldn't even remember the registration of the thing. For a car he owned! How could he have been so cavalier?

Thinking he might have a better chance at spotting it with a bit of elevation, he climbed to the top of the dunes. The stretch behind the stage, an almost deserted expanse of soft sand and grassy moguls, gave him an excellent view of the remains of the NJFA sand art. Even as a temporary statement, it had outlasted its audience – in person, anyhow. No doubt its image would run and run online.

A little further on, another unwelcome figure cut through the pines from the road and took long vigorous steps to reach a similar vantage point. Tabitha. Once at the top, she put one hand to her forehead to shield her eyes from the sun as she surveyed the festival crowd. From the other dangled a placard that read 'REFUGEES WELCOME!' and, preoccupied though he was, Perry still found the energy to condemn the sheer egotism of the girl for thinking that she, a resident of Bristol and Rutland, was qualified to represent the community of Pine Ridge on this or any issue. Not to mention unwittingly supporting the efforts of criminal people traffickers.

He ducked, concealing himself – he didn't need her reporting to Benedict that he'd been prowling about the dunes looking tortured – and returned to thoughts of the Jordan catastrophe. He was utterly clear that his only route through this nightmare involved lies. The lie that their contact had never breached the prescribed boundaries between resident and volunteer. The lie that he'd not laid eyes on him today. The lie that he knew nothing of Trev's demise and was as horrified as the next man when the news broke. If challenged by any opposing account from Jordan, he'd gently suggest he was a fantasist.

Tabitha's voice carried from where she'd come to a halt about twenty feet away: 'On my way to dinner with the fam. Thought I'd see how the festival's going.'

'Going good, if you like wanky tribute acts,' a male voice said, at least this was what Perry thought he said, it was too low and garbled to be certain. It was Robbie, though, he'd recognize his sarky drawl anywhere.

'I see our message is washing away,' Tabitha said.

'I know. It was so priddy as well.'

'You're high.'

'You're right.'

Tabitha giggled. 'This is hilarious. You're normally so in control.'

'Fuck control.'

Robbie now offered Tabitha 'some of this'. A drink or a joint, Perry guessed, and the yearning bucked inside him then, a wild horse. To be like one of these young people, these hedonists, whose biggest problem was thinking up new ways to tell the grown-ups what an atrocious job they were doing.

He was about to move away, when their voices started up again.

'You know what I've wanted to do to you right from the start?' Robbie said.

325

'Uh, slap me?'

'No.'

'What then?'

Perry didn't catch the next bit, but when he bobbed to his tiptoes, he saw that they were, unbelievably, in a clinch, stretched out together in a half-hidden dimple in the dune. They weren't . . . they weren't going to have sex? In public, like this?

Where would this leave Benedict? He felt an ache at the thought of his boy's future grief. But wait, might he know? This might be how they rolled now ('like, literally'). They had a right not to be challenged to fidelity.

Even in this, his darkest hour, he'd mustered a spark of humour – perhaps all was not lost after all! Maybe he hadn't seen Jordan, maybe he knew nothing about Trev's death, maybe he was just a middle-aged pervert on the beach watching his son's girlfriend have sex with Citizen fucking Smith.

Not that either of them would have the first idea who that was.

*

Sneaking away, he resumed his combing of the car park before heading across Old Beach Road to the sloping streets of the old village. Nothing. He then set off past the Gull down Peninsula Road, along which cars were parked in a tight metallic snake as far as the eye could see. But this was crazy, he couldn't walk all the way to the ferry. And Jordan was not a planner, he would never have thought to ditch the car so far from the village. Phoning him to ask was out of the question, of course, and not only because he didn't have his mobile on him; the call might catch the eye of the police if and when they later examined the boy's phone. No, he needed to come back when the festival was over – which might be better anyway as he had no plan yet as to how to get rid of the thing.

He turned back. By the time he got back home he'd have thought of something and then he could take refuge in total denial.

But he knew better than anyone that the nirvana of total denial was a whole lot easier to reach with a drink in your hand.

In fact, the way he saw it, hadn't drink been invented in the first place for that very purpose?

56

Tate

He wasn't back behind the bar five minutes when he sensed its absence.

They said phones were like an extension of your hand, but to him it was more like an extra layer of skin on his backside. If he wasn't using it, it was in his right-hand back pocket. Always.

All day he'd been aware of the regular *ping, ping, ping* of alerts as the sand art won the NJFA accounts new shares and likes, but suddenly there was nothing. Or was it simply that their fifteen minutes of fame had passed already? They'd done pretty well to make it last the day, after all.

Not that he wasn't proud of what they'd achieved, but no way was he getting involved in politics when he lived in London. It had been a second job this summer, knackering and unquenchable, day after day after day, early mornings and late nights. Fuck *issues*.

A quick pat on the pocket and he found he'd been right first time: his phone wasn't there. Instantly, he felt powerless. Maimed. Ejected from the human race.

Serving his next customer one-handed, he borrowed a phone from one of the student temps – Joe, he was called – to ring his own number. The voicemail clicked in and he spoke in discreet tones, hoping he'd be heard in the guitar-cranking din.

'Beattie, this is me. I think you've got my phone. I'll be at the bar till late, could you bring it down when you get back from dinner?'

Silly, really, because she didn't know his code and so was not going to be able to pick up his voicemail, but he felt an anticipatory pleasure in imagining himself playing it back later, connecting with her after she'd gone.

He signalled to Joe that he was going to try one more time.

This time, the call connected. 'Beattie, is that you?'

No one spoke, but he could hear breathing and, in the background, the song currently being played by the band and blasting in his uncovered ear, a split second out of sync.

'Beats, stop pissing about.'

There was a funny little giggle that didn't sound like her at all. It sounded, actually, *male*. Then the line went dead.

What the fuck? She hadn't . . . She hadn't gone back up and met someone else?

No, why would she do that? She'd gone to meet her family; he'd seen her head towards the road for the bus. He didn't know her number by heart to be able to call and find out but handing the phone back to Joe, he saw that Gav had pissed off somewhere so . . . Maybe he could just nip back up to her room and grab it?

Fighting his way through the mob and up the steps, he soon wished he hadn't bothered because the door to Beattie's room was locked. The blinds were still down, too, so it was impossible to peer in and catch sight of it, know that it would be back in his possession in a few hours.

Below, a new song started, the classic grinding riff from 'Smoke on the Water', followed by the almightiest thunder of drums and guitars he'd ever heard. Seriously, it was like these old guys had fired up a jet engine on stage and finally struck gold.

57

Robbie

Tuesday 29 August, 1.30 a.m.

Tate beams at me, wild and wolfish, as I catch up with him a few feet from the summerhouse that's still standing. The roof and veranda are like those of the one that fell, but this has square windows, not rectangular – I remember now how they shone like panels of silver before the drop. It's painted white, or maybe pale grey, and the moonlight makes it shimmer like the inside of an oyster shell.

They redid that quickly – those stickers are a nightmare to get off.

'This is hers? This is where you left the phone?'

'Yup.'

Mood-swinging man is happy again. He's forgotten for a second that someone is dead. Maybe a child.

'Then let's get in there and find it.'

Easier said than done. There's a heavy orange barrier between us and the section of the path with the gate that accesses the garden, plus more tape across the summerhouse door.

'Why's it taped off if it's not been touched?' Tate says. 'I don't get it.'

'Er, maybe because of *that*,' I say, sweeping my phone torch from left to right.

A section of wooden fence has been flattened into the

neighbouring garden and crushed to pieces, as has a stretch of the more robust-looking fence that runs parallel with it. Deep trenches mark the JCB's short route to the corner garden, where it now sits, yellow and black, with massive tyres and spikes on the bucket, like a giant toy abandoned at bedtime. The driver – the killer – must have just shut off the engine and jumped out once his demolition job was complete, not having time to reverse and return it to its original spot.

How did he flee? On foot? Down the cliff path and past the Meadow, the way Tate and I have just come? Or out the front way, turning down the traffic road into the village? One thing I'm certain of, he didn't take the steps to the beach because by then everyone had turned to look, including the marshals and the police officers already on site.

'So they drove the JCB from this garden to that one. Where was it earlier? When you came up to see Beattie? Was it still here?'

A breeze stirs Tate's floppy fringe. 'It was up near the house – in that gap where the garage used to be. They tore it down the other day.'

Is it good or bad that the JCB is still at the scene? Good in that they might have fingerprints on the levers. Bad in that they might have fingerprints on the levers…

Again, I can predict the police's question: *Did you get your tractor-driving friend and fellow activist to do the honours?* I look at Tate and my gut says no. He's stressed, sure, but his attention's focused on the summerhouse that belongs to Beattie's family. He's probably hoping he'll find her in there, have a little midnight reunion.

'You need to check for the phone,' I remind him. 'I bet that guard out front is patrolling round here as well. He could come any minute.'

'It was locked earlier, but . . .' He vaults the barrier, scissors over the picket fence and rattles the door. 'It's open.'

Suddenly I don't like his chances. The police must have been in there, taken anything of interest.

'Can I use your torch?'

I hand him my phone. 'Don't touch anything with your bare fingers.'

'Too late for that. My prints are all over this place.'

In the torch beam, I catch a glimpse of the space within. Where Tate's been getting his end away these last weeks. Where Tabitha's been sleeping when she's not with Bertie fucking Wooster next door. It's raw wood, with simple furniture, just a bed and a couple of other rustic bits, sheepskin draped all around. (Is that a *cow bell* hanging in the corner?) It's like Marie Antoinette's idea of a hilltop cabin.

'It's not here,' Tate says.

'Okay.' I search for a positive. 'Well, maybe that's good. It means she must have it with her.'

'I need to see her, Rob.'

'She'll be asleep, Tate. They all will.'

'How can anyone sleep knowing someone died right here?'

'She doesn't know yet, remember? None of them do.' God, he's a goldfish tonight. A complete liability.

He closes the door, but rather than heading back for the footpath he legs it up the garden and starts tapping on the first window he comes to.

I sigh, clear the barrier and follow, tripping slightly on the uneven ground, kicking up dirt. By the time I get there, Amy Shaw is at the window and her expression – startled, then angry, then afraid – confirms what we assumed: they think we did this. They probably think we've been planning it all summer and the sand art was a decoy.

'Go away,' she says, opening the window so we can hear each other, but only a crack, and she takes a step back like she thinks we're going to punch it wide open and start assaulting her. 'Go away or I'll call the police guard.'

'We didn't do this, you need to—' I begin, but Tate's already speaking over me, bringing his face close to the crack.

'We're friends of Beattie's. We need to see her. Five minutes, that's all. Please, you have to believe us!' He's rushing his words, so keen to persuade her it's pitiful, but it seems to work because she looks from him to me and steps forward again.

'I don't know what you have or haven't done, but you can't be here. The police don't want anyone in the garden, it's part of the crime scene. What time is it even, anyway?'

'After one,' I tell her, and she frowns like it's later than she thought.

'Something was going on,' she says. 'Earlier. They had some new team arrive. Have you heard anything in the last couple of hours?'

'No,' I lie. 'Sorry. We've been at a mate's place.'

'Is Beattie still up?' Tate asks her. 'Can we see her?'

Amy shakes her head. 'She's not back yet. She went out with her brother and his friend and Tabitha.'

No mention of Tabitha's boyfriend. And I feel guilty for calling him Bertie Wooster, like he's a character, not a real person.

Also, for shagging his woman on the day of his death.

'Do you know where they went?' Tate asks.

'I don't. But if you find them, send them home, will you? I'm texting Beattie now. Ten minutes, then I'll come looking myself.'

And she closes the window, moves into the shadows, done with us.

58

Amy

Monday 28th August

There were four empty places at their table for nine in the Needles brasserie.

The first was for Perry, who was supposed to be coming but, according to Charlotte, might actually be better off staying home since his mood when she'd left him had been 'sketchy'. She'd phoned him to check, but got his voicemail.

The second was for Beattie, who'd texted her imminent ETA, having said her goodbyes to local friends. A royal pain though the girl had been this trip, it was hard not to acknowledge a little clench of pride at her popularity – after all, no one else in the Shaw family had made friends with the locals this summer.

The third was for Tabitha, running late after her March for Migrants. Amy had checked social media to see how the protest had gone, but what coverage there was had not been much shared or commented on, the sand art stunt having sucked most available oxygen. There was a limit to the wider population's interest in one tiny coastal resort, she supposed.

The fourth was for Linus, who Amy was starting to suspect was pulling a Perry and bailing on them.

'There's no point both of them refusing to come,' Charlotte

said, pouring more Chablis into their enormous wineglasses and gesturing to the waitress to bring a second bottle.

'Honestly, I can't imagine what Julien's going to tell his parents when he goes back tomorrow,' Amy said in an undertone.

'If he's anything like a British child, he'll tell them sweet FA. "Did you have a good time, *cheri*?" "*Oui, bien*".'

Amy chuckled, raised a hand in greeting as one of the therapists from the spa passed by the window.

'Oh, I know what I meant to tell you,' Charlotte said with sudden animation. 'I saw the hat! She's the one who was wearing it, that girl you just waved to. Ellie.'

Amy frowned. 'Ellie can't be the thief, she's a lovely girl.'

'She said her boyfriend gave it to her, and he got it from lost property at work. So that's the end of that.'

Even in the face of this clear declaration of closure, Amy hastened to redirect the conversation away from the mystery culprit. 'She's pregnant, actually. Ellie. She told me the other day when she felt unwell during my facial and had to stop. She hasn't even told her manager yet.'

'Who's pregnant?' Beattie said, sliding into the seat opposite. She wore a reassuringly cheap-looking T-shirt emblazoned with the words 'The Answer Is No' and jeans Amy was relieved to recognize from having put through the laundry pre-Gymgate. It occurred to her that superior parents wouldn't treat their criminal offspring to £100-a-head last suppers, they'd leave them at home with a cheese sandwich and the Wi-Fi disabled, but it was the last day of their 'holiday' and she didn't have the energy for superior parenting.

'The therapist I saw in the hat,' Charlotte told Beattie. 'Ellie, she's called. Did your mum tell you about that? My card was stolen from my locker?'

Beattie visibly blanched and Amy prayed Charlotte hadn't

335

noticed. 'Who were you meeting, babes? Did you see much of the band?'

'No one. Yeah. We've run out of wine, Mum.'

'There's another bottle coming,' she protested as Beattie took her glass and tipped half of it into her own, draining it in one swallow. 'Beattie, surely you can wait five minutes!'

The new bottle arrived and Beattie poured herself more. Again, she couldn't get it down her throat fast enough, it was most unedifying (oh God, was this going to be the next thing? A teenage alcohol problem?).

'The answer to what is no?' Benedict asked Beattie, and the boys all started making guesses:

'No, she doesn't know what she wants to do at uni . . .'

'No, she doesn't eat tomatoes . . .'

'No, she isn't disturbed by Jeffrey Dahmer . . .' (this was some sort of inside joke that Amy could not for the life of her fathom).

'*Non, elle ne parle pas français . . .*'

And so on, until she finally cracked and began laughing. She'd definitely been unnerved by that reference to the hat and Amy hoped she wasn't suffering from guilt. Well, she hoped she *was*, but it would be better for all concerned if she kept her feelings hidden.

The sooner the girl was back in London, the better.

Charlotte's phone rang. She rejected the call and raised her glass. 'Here's to an eventful holiday!'

'We survived,' Amy said. Not exactly a ringing endorsement for their first summer in Pine Ridge, but it was the best she could do.

It was as they brought their glasses together that she saw it. Under a clear plastic dressing on the left side of her son's stomach. Black and elaborate, a creature with a bell-shaped head and long curling tentacles, some sort of jellyfish.

A tattoo: swollen and wound-like and no more than a day old.

She heard herself scream, loud enough to turn heads, and Huck, understanding she'd seen, froze. Now everyone at the table looked.

'Oh. My. Days,' Beattie said, glugging her wine.

Benedict whistled. 'Huck, wow. I mean, go big or go home.'

'*Moi aussi*,' Julien said, lifting his T-shirt.

Amy turned instinctively to Charlotte, but there was no smoothing over of this, no rationalising. She felt her breathing grow shallow and her heart pound; there was the sensation of spiders crawling over her skin. As the room began to spin, the other faces at the table rising and falling and coming in and out of view, fellow riders on a waltzer, the questions came tumbling in: How? Where? Who? What was she going to say to Linus? What was she going to say to Julien's parents?

'She's hyperventilating,' Charlotte said, and Amy peered through the blur as her friend fished in her tote and produced a paper bag. Next thing, it had been placed over her nose and mouth and she was being instructed to breathe in and out, in and out, and she became aware of Charlotte's phone ringing again.

'I'd better get this,' Charlotte said. 'Whoever it is, they're not giving up. Make sure she keeps the bag over her face, Ben, will you? Hello, yes?'

As her breathing steadied, Amy's faculties returned and she registered a succession of sensations: the smell of French fries as plates sailed by to the next-door table; Beattie and Huck exchanging a guilty look; Julien tucking his T-shirt into his jeans; on the other side of the window a man cuddling a fluffy blond dog while a woman dipped to her knees to take a photo.

And Charlotte on the phone, her tone altering from exasperation to concern. 'Yes, okay. Give us ten minutes.' She ended the call. 'We need to get the bill and go,' she told them. 'As soon as you're okay, Amy?'

'I think I'm fine,' she croaked. 'Who was it?'

'The police. They're at the house and they want us back asap. There's some sort of emergency.'

59

Charlotte

They returned by foot along the road, struck by how thick the stream of traffic was coming out of the village.

'I thought the festival went on till late?' Amy said.

'It does. Maybe there're in the break between the last band and the DJ?' It was dawning on Charlotte that the faces of the drivers and their passengers were not exactly *stricken*, but remarkably serious. 'This can't be to do with why the police phoned?'

'What did they say again?'

'"Damage to your property".'

They'd already agreed on abandoning their evening that it had to be something substantially worse than stickers or graffiti, since neither had attracted significant police interest and even when investigated had not once led to a charge. A break-in, perhaps? Something worse than paint smeared on their walls? She'd read of terrible attacks in other coastal resorts involving faeces.

'You didn't notice anything at Cliff View when you left, Beattie?' Amy asked, over her shoulder. Her daughter was walking alone, unusually pensive.

'No. Everything looked fine. From the back, anyway.'

'God, I hope it's not a fire?'

'We'd see the smoke,' Charlotte said. 'And Perry would have

339

called me, surely. If he's home.' She'd phoned him twice since receiving the police summons, but he still hadn't picked up.

'Linus as well.' Amy had tried him too, with the same result. 'Maybe they're together?'

'Well, we're here now, so we'll see for ourselves.'

Having expected swirling blue lights, Charlotte found the sight of a lone police car parked near the Shaws' skip both an anticlimax and a relief.

'I thought this was to do with Cliff View?' Amy said. Then, 'Where's the JCB?'

Charlotte assumed her friend had misremembered its location – until they trooped through the gap and into the Shaws' garden and understood at a glance that it was out here that the disaster lay. The vehicle's progress across the Shaws' and Rickmans' gardens was clear from the carnage of flattened fences and devastated flowerbeds – even a few smaller trees had fallen victim – right to its destination on the near side of her own garden, where it straddled the footpath.

'Where's the Nook?' she said, raising her voice to attract the attention of a group of police officers in her garden: 'Where's the Nook?'

One of them approached and explained what a fool could have worked out for himself: the JCB had bulldozed the Nook off the cliff.

Literally in one piece, contents and all.

After her screeched opening question, Charlotte found herself dumbstruck, needing the others to ask the questions for her.

'How was this even possible?' Amy asked.

'Remember the builder telling us?' Huck said. 'It can move over five thousand kilos.'

'What's happening now?' Benedict said. 'What are all these police doing?'

'We're securing the scene,' the officer explained. 'As you'll be aware, the tide's high, so we're conducting a risk assessment to see if we can start removing debris now or if it might be safer to wait till later or even tomorrow.'

'Does that mean the DJ won't be on?' Huck asked.

'Huck!' Amy admonished.

'The festival has finished early,' the officer said. 'Mrs Tucker, can you think of anyone who might have wanted to damage your property?'

The question roused Charlotte from her silence. 'Yes! The NJFA activists, of course! There's been a campaign against us all summer – as you well know. This will have been planned to sabotage the festival. They want to frighten us into selling up. The leader's called Robbie Jevons. You arrested him when he parked his caravan illegally in the drive next door.'

'We're familiar with Mr Jevons. Rest assured we'll be talking to him as a priority first thing in the morning.'

'First thing in the morning? Go and pick him up now! He lives in Golden Sands Park, literally five minutes away!'

'With respect, I'd ask you to leave us to do our job.' The officer turned to Amy. 'The JCB is yours, I gather?'

'Yes. Well, our builders'. They left it on site over the bank holiday.'

'Where were the keys kept?'

'I left them on the windowsill in the kitchen. There's no sign of a break-in, though.'

'Mum?' Beattie spoke for the first time, her voice uncertain. 'I think I might have left the kitchen door open. I came up to the house to use the bathroom before I went down to the Niche to change.'

'Why didn't you lock it before you came to meet us?' Amy asked.

'I . . . I thought Dad was in. Or back any minute. I didn't think he'd go straight from his ride to the hotel. I locked the Niche, though, I think.'

'Okay. Don't worry.'

Charlotte watched as Amy drew her daughter into a hug. She could see what her friend was thinking – that their troubles were negligible compared to what she and Perry were contending with.

Where *was* Perry? He was the only one from either family not to have assembled, because here at least came Linus, evidently having been down by the cliff edge with the police team there. He was still dressed in his black cycling gear, hair flat on his scalp, and bore a dazed look.

'You've obviously seen what's happened? The Nook's been pushed off the cliff.'

'With *our* JCB!' Amy said.

'Looks that way. I couldn't see from the beach.'

'Why were you on the beach? You were supposed to be coming to dinner at—'

'I know, I was about to join you. I got waylaid.' Linus paused. 'What have the police said? Do they know who did it?'

'Not yet, but Charlotte thinks it was the activists. Robbie or one of the others.'

'Robbie's on the beach,' Tabitha said. 'I just saw him.' Charlotte hadn't noticed her arrive and even through her shock she registered how disorientated the girl looked, how glittering. Charlotte looked from her to Linus and wondered. Both late, both oddly giddy.

No, she thought. *Concentrate on the main issue.*

'Robbie might not have driven it himself,' she told the officer, 'but he'll sure as hell be the one behind it. You wait. Where's Perry, does anyone know?'

'You should check the house,' Amy suggested. 'He might've been having a nap, slept through the whole thing?'

Absurd though it sounded, given the scenes of Armageddon in their own garden, this was not beyond the realms of possibility and would also explain why he hadn't been answering his phone. He'd been out of sorts when she'd left him earlier, plus he'd been known to nick one of her sleeping pills when too antsy to sleep. She was about to cut across the flattened boundaries when a second officer prevented her, issuing instructions: 'If we could ask you not to use your rear gardens, but to access your houses from the street. The footpath will be closed to the public till further notice.'

Charlotte had a strong suspicion that the police were going to run this investigation with the same lack of insight or logic as their 'responses' to the summer's earlier crimes. As she and Benedict let themselves into Cliff View, she wondered if she should get legal advice.

'I hope Mango's all right . . .'

This, at least, was promptly answered, for the Labrador launched herself at them the moment they stepped inside and clung to Charlotte's side as they went from room to room. But there was no sign of Perry.

'I'm sure he'll be back the moment he hears,' Benedict said. 'He must have gone off somewhere. Hiking again?'

'Both cars are here, though,' Charlotte pointed out. 'And he wouldn't leave Mango all afternoon without letting me know. I asked him to walk her.'

'He might have changed his mind about dinner and walked over to meet us?'

Charlotte tried his phone again, this time catching the sound of ringing and tracing it to the kitchen, where she found it on the table. When she picked it up, an alert for her missed calls flashed

343

up. But there was nothing sinister about his having gone out without his phone; he wasn't thirteen.

'Let's wait for him here,' she said. 'Or do you want to go back to the Shaws'?'

'No, it's okay, I'll wait with you.'

They fed Mango and then stood at the open kitchen doors with beers, like attendees of some ghoulish drinks party, watching the police at work, trying to decipher snatches of dialogue.

It didn't seem possible. Her beautiful Nook, her pride and joy. Gone, just like that.

60

Amy

Now that it had been established that the JCB keys had been taken from the kitchen, the police wanted them to keep out of it while they collected evidence. It seemed a bit futile, what with all the previous trooping back and forth, but she took a look at the tight zigzags of tape across the three gardens and decided not to add to the chaos.

'Can I at least take some tea things into the living room?'

A bottle of wine as well, maybe.

Other questions were starting to amass. First up, Linus was supposed to be driving the kids back to London in the morning – Julien had a seat booked on the Eurostar mid-afternoon – could that go ahead as planned? Then there were the building works. She had planned to stay on alone to supervise the first week or two, but would the police want to impound the JCB and, if so, how would the builders react to that? It was not the kind of vehicle you had a whole fleet of in reserve. Terry would be furious with her for letting the keys out of her safekeeping (for all she knew, there could be some sort of criminal penalty for her negligence).

And then there were the boys' tattoos. Regardless of when she managed to deliver Julien to his family, she'd need to consider how to present news of this illegal and self-harming act that she'd done nothing to prevent and had inadvertently funded. Should she let

Julien tell his parents himself? Perhaps even beg him to pretend his hosts hadn't known?

One of them still didn't. But she couldn't bring herself to tell Linus, not right now.

Taking the kitchen items and joining the others in the living room, it struck her that the only question that needed answering with any urgency was where everyone was going to sleep tonight. With the Niche out of bounds, Beattie and Tabitha had lost their berths.

'Girls, we'll set up the air bed in here for you. We did bring it down from London, didn't we, Linus?'

'What?' He looked and sounded quite depleted. 'Yeah. It's in the bedroom with the other stuff from the garage.'

'Great, let's do that now.'

'Mum,' Beattie said. 'You're talking like we're going to bed. It's not even nine o'clock!'

'We haven't had dinner,' Huck added. 'We're starving.'

'We're not allowed to use the kitchen,' Amy said. 'I must admit, I've lost my appetite.'

'Shall we go out, Tabs?' Beattie suggested. 'To the pub, maybe?' Amy had the sense that her daughter, having initially been awed by the drama, was now on a mission to escape it, which could not be a good thing.

'Can't we all just stay here? We could watch a movie or play cards?'

'Play cards?' Huck objected. 'It's Julien's last night.'

Biting her tongue, Amy settled for a hard glare. The little toerag was taking advantage of his father's presence – his father's ignorance – to act like he wasn't in the worst of all bad books, pending unprecedented sanctions. (What, like those she'd imposed on Beattie for *her* crimes?) 'I think we ought to stay,' she said. 'The police might need us.'

'Let them go,' Linus said wearily. 'We can answer any questions. Take the boys with you, Beattie. Not the pub, obviously.'

Beattie pouted. 'Where then?'

'Get fish and chips and hang out somewhere.'

'The beach is closed.'

'The Meadow then. Or Little Bay? I don't know.'

'Keep them out of trouble, Tabitha,' Amy said, and the girl nodded, recognising a cry for help when she heard one.

*

She and Linus inflated the bed and dug out sleeping bags for the girls, then, far from waiting up to answer further police queries, Linus said he was going to have a shower and go to bed.

'How was the bike ride?' Amy said, watching him peel off his kit. 'Where *is* the bike? I didn't see it when I was looking for the air bed.'

'Oh,' he said. 'I had an accident. It went over the cliff.'

'What?' Amy gazed at him, appalled. 'What kind of accident?'

'I was cutting back along the cliff and I clipped a rock. I managed to get off in time but the bike went over.'

'Linus!' No point saying it was foolhardy to cycle along there since he'd presumably come to that conclusion himself. No point either saying it paled into insignificance compared to the Nook because that bloody bike had probably cost as much as the Tuckers' summerhouse. This must have been what he meant by having been 'waylaid'. And yet he'd also gone down to the beach, so he couldn't have been *that* distraught. 'Did you hurt yourself?'

'I'm okay,' he said. 'Just shattered.'

'You look terrible. This hasn't been a good week, has it? First the paddleboarding, now this.'

347

It's almost as if someone's got it in for you, she didn't say, because he would only start moaning about Perry and Amy didn't want to do that, not yet.

After Linus had showered and closed the bedroom door, she poured herself a glass of wine and whiled away an hour or so checking social media. There were lots of posts about the incident, pictures of bits of the Nook sticking out of the water, but no proper report yet and no one had captured the building actually falling. She texted Charlotte:

Is Perry back?

No. We're going into the village to look for him.

Need any help?

TY, but am OK. Benedict coming with.

Amy was starting to have a bad feeling about Perry.

About where he might have been when the Nook went off the cliff.

*

It must have been ten-thirty or so when she became aware of raised voices out back. She went out through the front door, evading the guard manning the barriers in the road, and slipped through the gap to peer over the Rickmans' garden to the Tuckers'. What looked like floodlighting was being installed on the other side of the JCB.

'Hello? What's happening?'

348

Hearing her, an officer approached and determined her identity. 'The tide's out enough now for a special team to take a look at the wreckage.'

'What special team? I don't understand. And why's there a guard out front? There wasn't anyone there earlier.'

'We'll update you in the morning. For the time being, if you could go back inside and try to avoid coming into the garden . . .'

Back on the sofa, she watched a bit of TV before nodding off, awakening – she had no idea how much later – at the sound of a knock at the window. Expecting it to be the police guard, she hurried across the room to answer, but even before she opened up, she could tell that the clifftop activity had concluded for the night. The floodlights had been shut off and, apart from the distant rumble of the sea, it was peaceful.

To her horror, the faces of the two activists, Robbie and Tate, came into focus. Heart banging, she hissed for them to leave, but they refused, insisted they were looking for Beattie. It was, she saw, much later than she'd realised.

'If you find them, send them home, will you? I'm texting Beattie now.'

She'd have been more concerned if they weren't with Tabitha, who was as trustworthy as it got. In any case, what were the odds of lightning striking twice in one night?

She checked her phone, texted Beattie to get the boys back at once. Noticed with a new twinge of unease that her last message to Charlotte, sent just before 10 p.m., remained unread:

Did you find Perry?

61

Robbie

Tuesday 29 August, 1.45 a.m.

It's well into the early hours now and Shannon's messaging me, wanting to know where we are and why the fuck we're not back. She's still got Ellie at our place and they're not waiting up any longer. I'll have to kip on the couch – just what I need before a police grilling.

'Any idea where they might be hanging out?' I say to Tate as we sneak from the Shaws' place and put a bit of distance between us and the crime scene. 'The beach is obviously out of bounds and all the bars closed hours ago.'

'The Meadow?' Tate says.

'We'd have seen them on the way. Little Bay, maybe?'

We continue along the footpath and it isn't long before we catch music on the breeze. The urgent pulse and rapid-fire vocals of rap.

'They're in the pillbox,' Tate exclaims. 'I forgot we were there the other day, Beattie and me.'

Of course they were. I remember he used to take Ellie there when she was still living with her parents and he was bunking up with Des and they had nowhere to be alone. Nothing changes.

There's something off about the music and it takes me a second to realize the lyrics are in French. The word *sensible* is repeated over and over: *sen-zee-bluh, sen-zee-bluh.*

I call in through the opening – 'Knock knock!' – and there's the sound of a brief discussion before the music's turned down.

'What?' a female voice calls, presumably Beattie's because Tate's all animated.

'It's me,' he calls. 'Me, Tate.'

She appears in front of us then, in jeans and a hoodie, smudged glitter on her face. Tear stains as well, maybe. She's a completely different creature from the girl who wafted up the lane in her flares and T-Rex shirt and told us she was lost. Had all the blokes' eyes on stalks in the Gull that time she came dressed in the world's tiniest top, hair spilling over her bare shoulders.

'Tate? What are you doing here?'

And I see it in her eyes right then: she doesn't want him to be here. Whatever's happened, whoever's trashed her mate's summerhouse, it's snapped her right out of her little holiday bubble. I glance at Tate, who looks like he might start blurting, and take control.

'We didn't mean to scare you. Apologies. We heard about your summerhouse and wanted to check you were all safe.'

'Oh, Robbie. Hi.' A second figure appears next to Beattie. Tabitha.

'Hey.' It seems completely mad now, what we did in the dunes. Maybe it didn't even happen, maybe my frazzled brain has invented it. (Wouldn't *that* be useful?) I turn back to Beattie. 'So is everyone okay?'

'Yeah, fine. Why?'

'Who is it, Beats?' a slurred male voice asks, and stepping inside, I see two teenage boys sitting against the wall, both vaping. I don't know who the other one is, but one must be the brother, and they look wasted rather than traumatized. They've got booze, empty cans of Pringles, phones and a speaker – not a party, but not a funeral either. They definitely don't know someone's dead.

Beattie's checking her messages – 'We need to get back, Huck. Mum's texted' – and one of the boys makes some incoherent protest in response.

I take a breath and turn to Tabitha. 'What about your boyfriend?'

'Benedict?'

That's his name.

'What about him?' she says.

'You seen him tonight?'

'Earlier, yes. He was with his mum. They were going out to look for his dad, but they'll be back by now.'

Look for his dad. His dad being the posh twat who came storming up to the park and lamped me, the video of which has been seen by, oh, I don't know, maybe a hundred thousand people.

If he's the guy who died, I really am going to be top of the list of suspects.

'What?' Tabitha says. 'Why are you asking this?' And all four faces turn to hear my answer. They look so vulnerable, all of them, just a bunch of kids, clueless about what they're dealing with tonight.

'No reason,' I say. 'Come on, the path's dark now. We'll walk you back.'

We settle into pairs: me and Tabitha up ahead, then the two boys, then Tate and Beattie.

'That thing earlier. It didn't happen,' Tabitha says, sideways.

'Gotcha,' I say, and I wonder if Beattie's saying the same to Tate, and if she is then how he's going to react and if he'll be able to hold himself together tomorrow with the police.

At the top of the Meadow, we trade subdued goodbyes and the

four of them trudge off down Pine Ridge Road while Tate and I continue down the hill.

'Did she have the phone?' I ask.

'Nope.'

Great. This whole detour's been for nothing.

'Did you think—' he begins, but falters at the sudden throb of an engine ahead. We watch, side by side, as a vehicle crests the hill, its headlights dipped. A black estate car, with blacked-out windows and the words 'Private Ambulance' on the bonnet. As it passes us, the driver's eyes remain fixed on the road.

The undertaker, taking the body away.

And, by my reckoning, only one man still unaccounted for.

PART FOUR

62

Robbie

Ellie leaves soon after dawn. From my berth in the living area, I hear the swish of the pocket door opening, the squeak of the tap and trickle of water into a glass. The sound of her swallowing. You don't need to be a bloodhound to scent the heaviness of her mood. What troubles her most, I wonder? Not Tate's fling, because he's a wily son of a bitch and I'd put money on it that she doesn't have a clue about that, so more likely his reluctance about the pregnancy. He's never been one to fake enthusiasm.

Of course, what she *should* be worrying about is the risk of the father of her child being charged in a criminal-damage-turned-murder investigation that might get him sent down for the rest of his twenties, but hey. Priorities, emotions, will be reshuffled today for all of us, that much I can say with confidence.

In any case, the atmosphere feels lighter when she's gone.

I sit up, try to assess my own mental state. I've had five hours' sleep tops, but I feel relatively clear-headed, the hangover stopped in its tracks by all that late-night fresh air. I use the loo, then slouch into the bedroom to join Shannon. There's an indent where Ellie lay, a pillow at the foot of the bed, the two of them top to tail, like schoolgirls on a sleepover.

Speaking of schoolgirls . . . Bloody Beattie Shaw and that fruitless nocturnal quest. Yes, we saw for ourselves that she was alive and kicking, and her brother and mates too, but she was next to useless about the missing phone. Said she hadn't set foot in her crib since their little assignation.

Last assignation – you watch.

'Check the bar,' I told Tate as we finally traipsed down Paradise Avenue, dead on our feet. 'First thing tomorrow, go and have a proper look. I bet it's been there all along.'

I make a mental note to tell him that if the bar's closed today, which it probably will be, what with the pieces of house fished from the sea right next to it being clues not just to criminal damage but to the cause of a man's death, then he should arrange to get the key from Gav and go in anyway.

'You awake, babe?'

Shannon stirs, turns her head. There's gold on her cheekbone from the party make-up she put on for the festival. Her lips are pale and squishy, like a dried apricot. 'Hmm. What?'

'I was thinking. You know yesterday, on the beach, when it all kicked off? Right before I came to find you. You did see me up in the dunes, didn't you?'

'What?' Her eyes are only half closed now. 'I was watching the band.'

'Say you definitely did though, yeah? When they ask you.'

'When who asks me?'

'The police. They'll be here any minute.' I pause, notice how knackered she looks; it's clear her late night was no more successful than my own. 'We think the bloke who died might be that nutter who slugged me. It was his summerhouse that went over and he was the only person missing last night.'

Her eyes open and she raises herself onto her elbow. 'Robbie, there's no way you'll be a suspect. We were literally standing side by side when the thing fell off the cliff!'

'I know, but I can see how this is going to go. They'll fit me up, say I masterminded it. You know, went up to supervise my foot soldier, then slipped back down at the last minute and pretended to be shocked. I've already been arrested once this month,' I add.

She lays gentle fingers on my arm. 'Don't worry. I'll say you were there the whole time. Though you did go AWOL right before, now I think about it.'

I swallow. That was when I was with Tabitha, who I'd prefer not to involve in my alibi. 'Well, don't say that. I was probably just kipping.'

She nods. 'Which "foot soldier", anyway? You don't mean Tate? Wasn't he behind the bar?'

'It turns out he was on his break around then.'

'Where did he go?'

'Nowhere. He stayed on the beach. But it would be good if we both say we saw him. We don't need to have spoken to him or done anything special, just aware that he was there, you know. Gabbing with the girls like usual, general stuff.'

He and Beattie have agreed to deny they met, he told me that when we walked back, but I'm uneasy about her compliance. She looked wasted – would she even remember? Plus there was that coolness towards him, like her loyalties had shifted.

'So what were you two up to last night?' Shannon says. 'Why was he so salty at Rio's?'

'Just stress. Did Ellie say anything?'

A flicker tells me Ellie's confided about the pregnancy, but Shannon shakes her head. She's not giving up her mate's secrets any more than I am mine.

We lie side by side, not speaking, for a long time, her eyes closed again, mine wide open. When it comes, the sound of footsteps crunching on gravel – confident, purposeful steps, maybe two sets – it's actually a relief. Who's first, me or Tate? Or maybe the two of us simultaneously, in adjoining interview rooms, played off against each other like train robbers on TV.

Knuckles rap on the door and I swing my legs off the mattress, plant my feet on the floor. The floor of a caravan never feels completely stable, you're always aware of the layer of air between you and solid ground.

'Here we go,' I say.

63

Perry

'Perry, up!' Charlotte said. 'The police are downstairs. They want to update us. Now.'

Both her touch and the tone of her voice were abrasive as she roused him from a narrow, tubular sleep, and he came to gulping air. As his eyes creaked open, Mango's panting mouth appeared mere inches away, a blunt impression of his wife above.

He tried to lift his head, but pain pinned it to the mattress (he didn't seem to have a pillow). His tongue was the texture of kindling as he used it to part parched lips. 'I can't—'

'You can. You have to. There's water and paracetamol right here. I'm going back down. Come as soon as you can.'

He finally succeeded in getting himself onto his elbows. There was a stain where his mouth had rested on the sheet: drool or vomit. It was pink, which meant he must have at some juncture consumed red wine. Behind the head pain, faces swarmed – scowling, glowering, pleading faces: Benedict's, Charlotte's, Linus's. A memory of something significant hovered, but remained formless.

He could hear voices in the garden below. Not the familiar exclamations of holidaymakers and hikers as they reached the corner and clocked the view, but low and workmanlike, the to-and-fro of people working as a team—

Oh! The Nook!

The Nook had fallen off the cliff: he'd been told this, though he wasn't sure when. The voices must be the police or fire brigade, some kind of salvage operation going on.

Jesus H. Christ, no wonder Charlotte was in a foul mood.

He raised his body painstakingly, limb by limb. He was naked but for his underwear and had a squalid collection of grazes on his arms and knees, including a fresh cut near the yellow bruises on his right knuckles. His stomach was as sore and aching as his head. As he swallowed the painkillers, more shameful images materialized, these ones of himself: being lifted by the armpits from his seat in the bowels of the Gull and transported, feet dragging, through the amused crowd and into the street. Sitting slumped against Benedict on the backseat of the Moke while Charlotte drove and – oh God – turning and folding forwards to spray vomit into the road. The two of them helping him up the stairs and into bed.

Had the police been on the premises last night, too? Was that when he'd learned about the Nook's destruction or had he known earlier, before he'd gone on his bender? Perhaps the news of its destruction was what had prompted said bender? He had no idea.

In the en suite, he emptied his bladder and brushed his teeth. Splashing hot water onto his face, he braved a look in the mirror. Uninjured, but old, so very old, his eyes meek with shame.

Dressing in soft, fresh clothes restored a vague sense of being a civilized mammal. He descended the stairs gingerly, at all times fearful of his knees giving way, and shuffled towards the kitchen, from which voices drifted. The doors to the garden were closed, a surveillant Mango at the glass as a startlingly sizeable team – some in hi-vis jackets, at least two in those white suits you saw on TV – interacted between a massive JCB and a blue-and-white police tent.

At least the light was forgiving, the sun diffused through delicate cloud and giving their yellow kitchen an almost holy glow.

Charlotte, however, looked far from beatific as she registered his arrival. Her eyes were pink and bare of make-up, her neck blotched from stress. 'You're here,' she said, with effortful dispassion.

'Is that the JCB from the Shaws' place?' he said, relieved that his voice sounded normal and not that of a man on the brink of hurling.

'Mr Tucker?'

'Yes.' He noticed for the first time a woman sitting opposite his wife at the table. She was younger than them, carrying quite a bit of extra weight under cotton clothing with an abnormal number of buttons and exhibiting a rampant case of rosacea. Her eyes were of the sharp, fast-moving, missing-nothing variety that felt dangerous, though he couldn't say why. She introduced herself as a detective of some sort, but he missed the name thanks to an excruciating spasm behind his right eye.

He took a seat with his back to the window and the crime-scene worker bees. 'I know about the Nook,' he told the detective, amazed when a series of grown-up, home-owning questions arrived without thought: 'Have you found out who did it? The NJFA crew, I'm guessing? We'll be needing a crime number for the insurance claim. My wife must have explained it was a one of a kind?'

'There's more, Perry,' Charlotte said. Her tone remained neutral, but when she poured him a cup of tea from the pot there was a slight shake in her hand.

'There was a development last night,' the detective said. 'We discovered that someone was in your summerhouse when it came off the cliff and I'm sorry to have to tell you that he was dead when we recovered him. His body was taken to the mortuary overnight.'

'*What?*' Perry recognized the genuine shock in his exclamation.

Unreliable though his memory was this morning, this was, without question, new information. Appalling information. 'That's terrible. Who was it? I mean, it's not anyone we know, is it?' He turned to his wife like a child to its mother. 'We saw everyone afterwards, didn't we?'

'*I* did, yes. The only one missing in action was you.' Her self-control deserted her momentarily and she lashed out: 'Imagine if they'd found the body before we found you, Perry! Imagine how Benedict would have felt, thinking his father was dead!' At the sound of her anguish, Mango came scuttling to her side. 'Not that it's not still a terrible tragedy,' she added to the detective.

'Who was it?' Perry asked.

'I was just telling your wife, we haven't yet had a formal identification, but he had ID on him in the name of Jordan Lynch.'

Perry felt a sensation then that he'd never felt before: the full-body capture of horror, along with a hyper nausea. On top of the hangover, it felt unendurable, as if he might pass out – were it not for the shards of memory now cutting through the pain: his friend on the doorstep, talking of having killed Trev. He'd smashed his head in with a dumb-bell and fled. Fled *here*.

Can I hide in that little house in the garden?

He swallowed bile, acrid and burning. Forced himself to tune back in.

'I don't understand,' Charlotte said. 'Did he have something to do with the Nook going over the cliff? Is he an activist, as well? Maybe he wasn't actually in it? Maybe he drove the JCB and then slipped when he was climbing out?'

'We don't know what his connection is,' said the detective, 'but evidence does suggest he was inside the structure when it fell.'

Perry suppressed an agonized groan.

'What,' Charlotte said, 'so he drowned?'

'We don't know yet. He may have died of his injuries. It was a thirty-foot fall. A post-mortem will establish the cause. How about you, Mr Tucker? Do you know the name Jordan Lynch?'

His mouth opened. A second passed in the same stupefaction, and another. *Please*, he intoned. Then, on the fifth beat, here it came: an almost orgasmic moment of inspiration as he understood he could say anything in the world and Jordan would not be able to contradict it.

He could save himself. Save them all.

64

Perry

'He's not an activist,' he said shakily. 'I know who he is and he's nothing to do with Pine Ridge.' He felt his eyes fill with tears, the childish, wobbling kind that bounced when they fell. 'This is terrible. Terrible. He's a lovely boy.'

'Who is he, Perry?' Charlotte said, clearly unsettled by his outburst.

'He's one of the residents at Keeler House. That's where I volunteer in London,' he told the detective. 'It's accommodation for people who've been homeless or in institutions. Helps get them back on their feet. I don't know if his ID had that address on it but, if not, I can give you all the details.'

The detective scribbled notes. 'Did you know he was in your summerhouse?'

'No. I didn't know he was in Pine Ridge.' Perry paused. This was coming so easily he almost believed it himself. 'But I've told him about this place in the past and, well . . .'

'Well what?' Charlotte prompted.

'I suppose I sort of suggested he could stay here if he had nowhere else to go. I mean, I never for one moment thought he'd take me up on the offer.'

'When did you make this suggestion?' the detective asked.

'A couple of months ago, maybe. He'd fallen out with another resident and was worried he was going to have to leave. He felt quite isolated, I think – he's estranged from his family. A lot of them are. I wanted to reassure him that he wouldn't be homeless. I don't think I even gave him the full address, though. I just said Pine Ridge, up on the corner of the cliff.'

'It would be easy to find from a basic description,' Charlotte said. 'I can't believe you did that without telling me.'

She was right not to believe it, because he wouldn't have made such an offer in a million years, but the only thing that mattered was that the detective believed it.

'So he didn't let you know he planned to visit?' she asked.

'No. Like I say, I had no idea he was in the area.'

'Did he know about the spare key to the Nook?' Charlotte said. 'Did you mention that?'

'I honestly don't remember. I very much doubt it.'

As the detective eyed him, he gulped his tea, which was well-stewed and by now barely tepid. 'You're absolutely sure you didn't see him in Pine Ridge at any time yesterday?'

'Yes. We had the festival, obviously, so the place was packed. I was up here some of the time, but I was on my own, packing. We were supposed to be leaving today.'

Well, *that* wasn't going to happen.

As the painkillers did their work and the nausea began to lift, the sequence of events slotted disquietingly into place. They'd had a drink and argued, right here in the kitchen, and then he'd stalked Jordan down the garden to make sure he left the premises. But the boy must have come back when he'd judged Perry to be safely indoors. He must have found the Nook unlocked or located the key by a lucky guess or maybe he'd even punched the glass door with his fist; it wasn't reinforced.

What would have happened if the Nook had remained in its

spot, Jordan hiding inside? The rest of the party would have trooped back from dinner and set up on the veranda for drinks. Would one of them have spotted him and hauled him out? It would have been calamitous, possibly the catalyst for all kinds of revelations, but not disastrous like this. Not tragic.

He remembered now trying to wipe Jordan's prints from around the house. How successful had that amateur operation been? Likely not very. When it came to light that the boy had killed Trev and fled, which would surely be a working hypothesis the moment news of the two deaths was shared between forces, the police would be back with a vengeance. Well, it was crazy to imagine he could continue any clean-up now. Better to have a suggestion to hand as to how Jordan might have gained access to the main house without any evidence of a break-in. Perhaps Perry had neglected to lock the kitchen doors before heading out? That would work.

'Perry?' Charlotte prompted.

'I was just thinking, I'm not sure he even knew I was down here.'

'Maybe that's the point.' Charlotte turned to the detective. 'Maybe he'd had enough of this other neighbour and thought he'd come down here to squat over the autumn? Thinking *we* were back up in London? Then the activists arrived and he was in the wrong place at the wrong time.' She sighed heavily. 'What I *don't* understand is how he didn't hear a bloody great JCB revving up outside? It literally ploughed through three gardens and tore down two fences, then shovelled under the room he was sitting in. It must have been like an earthquake – how could he not have noticed it?'

Perry cleared his throat. 'He might have passed out.'

There was a silence.

'Oh, hang on a minute,' Charlotte said, getting it. 'Is he the one you told me about? You've had an AA thing going, haven't you?'

'Nothing so formal. We did meet in recovery,' Perry explained to the detective, 'and, like I said, I was on hand if he needed a bit of extra moral support. But given the fact that he didn't get out of the Nook in time, I'm thinking maybe he'd relapsed? That will come out in the post-mortem as well, will it?'

There was no doubt in his mind that Jordan must have got stuck in to the booze the second he saw Charlotte's drinks trolley, spirits of some sort, probably. He'd been slurring on arrival, following almost a year of sobriety; it wouldn't have taken much more to knock him out.

'There's a fridge full of wine down there,' Charlotte said, before he could. 'Was.'

The detective looked up from her notes. 'When *did* you last see him?' she asked Perry.

'The week before last,' he lied. 'On the Friday. I did a number of odd jobs that day, including one in his room. I replaced the mirror over his basin. I can show you our messages if you like?'

'Your phone's here, Perry,' Charlotte said, motioning to the kitchen counter. 'I've recharged it.'

Thank fuck he'd been so strict with Jordan about comms. Deleted the few rogue voicemails. Which reminded him . . . 'You know what? I did miss a few calls from him these last couple of days. I didn't phone back, but I obviously should have.'

The detective's brow knotted. 'You said he'd had a row with another resident?'

'Yes. Trev, he's called.' Perry reminded himself to use the present tense, trying not to think of Trev dead on the bathroom floor – or undergoing a post-mortem of his own. 'He's quite antisocial, treats the shared areas like they're his own. The others are wary of him. He's a big guy, pumped up on steroids, into his weights. If you go and talk to the residents, you'll know him as soon as you see him.'

'Do Jordan's family know what's happened?' Charlotte asked.

'Yes. They've been asked to formally identify the body today.' The detective got to her feet. 'If you'll just excuse me for a second . . . We found some items on Mr Lynch's person that we'd like to show you.'

As she ducked from the room, Charlotte was finally able to laser Perry with the look familiar to him from his drinking days, a look that trembled with conflicting emotions. Pity versus disgust. Compassion versus revulsion. Love versus hate.

And, in this case, aborted terror. Because if it *were* to transpire that alcohol had been a factor in the victim's tragic final acts, then it might just as easily have been Perry in the mortuary now, Charlotte the next of kin identifying his body.

'I'm sorry,' he said. 'I don't know what I was thinking. I was—'

'Here we are.' The detective was back, a transparent evidence bag in her hand, in which a few pieces of jewellery were visible.

'They're mine,' Charlotte said. 'They were in our bedroom. The ring could've been in the bathroom, actually. Do you think this might have been why he came down? To burgle us? How did he get into the house, there aren't any broken windows? You did lock up when you left yesterday, didn't you?' As she turned to Perry her expression said it all: she thought he'd started drinking here, before he went to the pub. He'd left their home unsecured and this semi-vagrant had come in and helped himself.

'I'm not sure,' he said, grateful for the natural way this crucial detail had been seeded. 'It's possible I forgot.'

'How did he get down here?' Charlotte asked the detective. 'If he got the train, he might have spoken to another passenger? There could be some clues there about his state of mind?'

Perry felt his eyes spring open, followed by the stomach valve that allowed vomit to rise up his gullet and into his mouth.

The car! Fuck!

The car Jordan had driven down in. The car that connected him materially to Perry. The car Perry had left Cliff View to find and then forgotten all about as he drank himself senseless.

He pushed back his chair, indicating without words that he needed to get to the bathroom.

He had to find the keys before he drew another breath.

65

Tate

Robbie was still being questioned by the police when he slipped away, which probably looked deliberately evasive on his part, but it wasn't like they couldn't move on to the next activist on their list and come back later. They'd catch up with him eventually.

The sunlight was patchy on the beach, fast-moving stringy cloud overhead, and there were as many emergency vehicles and personnel in the car park as there had been last night. The tent was still up and what must be pieces of wreckage were laid out in neat lines like on an archaeological dig or something.

A guard accompanied him to the beach bar, where he found Gav in manic clean-up mode.

He glanced up from the dishwasher. 'Tate. Did you not get my message? Bar's closed.'

'I don't have my phone, do I? Lost it yesterday. Thought it might've slipped down the side somewhere here.'

'I haven't seen it. You tried ringing it?' Gav wedged a beaker into the dishwasher and kneed the door shut, before producing his own phone to dial Tate's number. He relayed what Tate already knew: 'It's not ringing. Probably just out of juice.'

Tate spent the next twenty minutes searching, even in crevices he hadn't known existed and were pretty grisly, but in vain. Unless the phone had found its way into the bins – which Gav reported had been emptied that morning – it hadn't been mislaid on the premises.

'How long're they going to keep us closed?'

'I don't know.' Gav, scrubbing the sink now, briefly looked up. 'They took the body away last night, so . . .'

Tate feigned ignorance. 'What body?'

Gav lowered his voice. 'I heard the cops talking earlier. Some bloke died. He was inside the house that went over the cliff. They only realized when the tide went out and they saw an arm or something. Gruesome stuff, huh?'

Tate swallowed. Hearing Gav say it made it real in a way it had not been last night, when only he and Robbie and the rest of the crew had known, when he'd been fixated on Beattie. 'Shit. That's bad. Not anyone we know?'

'From London, apparently.' Gav paused his work to eye Tate with irritation. 'Better not be your lot behind all this aggro. If they keep us closed all week, it's gonna lose me a lot of business.'

'Of course it's not us,' Tate said. 'You saw our sand art. *That* was our season finale, not this.'

'Season finale?' Gav gave a humourless chuckle. 'This isn't fucking *Strictly*, you know. There are livelihoods involved here. *Lives*. Time to grow up, mate.'

Tate turned to leave. The conversation was unnerving him. If Gav knew about the fatality, then the other business owners would too, because they had a WhatsApp group. The residents up on the headland must have been told by now, too, including Beattie, and even if she didn't know the victim personally, it had to be distressing for her. He longed to bound up there and comfort her – a feeling he knew he had to conquer. The way she'd acted last night had been discouraging. Something had changed, and not only because her neighbour's summerhouse had been smashed to smithereens; no, something specifically to do with him. When they'd walked the short distance from the pillbox to Pine Ridge Road, she'd not responded when he'd reached for her hand. He'd taken it anyway, but it was limp, like a dead thing, and after a few moments he'd let it go.

At least she'd agreed they definitely wouldn't mention having seen each other that evening, not with the police crawling all over the bungalow, including her bedroom. It seemed impossible that it had been mere hours ago that they'd been gripped together in the humid wooden space, Beattie joking that Tabitha's bulky backpack was like a third person in the room. She'd been more giggly than usual and he had a sweet flash of her closing the door behind them and bolting it, cackling at the sight of him clutching his jeans like a kid who'd—

He jolted as if electrified. *What the fuck?* How could he not have thought of this earlier? They'd ended up in the usual place, but they'd *begun* somewhere else, in the summerhouse that fell. His innards twisted as he remembered undressing there, being chivvied out because Beattie had heard raised voices up at the house.

He must have dropped his phone in there.

Here he was, scratching around the bar, worrying about the bins, and it was probably fifty paces away, laid out on the beach with all the other debris.

Placing him not only in proximity of the crime scene, which was bad enough, but right on the spot marked X.

66

Perry

As he scrambled back up to the bedroom, a series of sickening flashbacks restored more missing pieces to his memory. His futile scanning of the overflowing beach car park (oh, and Tabitha shagging Robbie the activist in the dunes – a minor transgression in the grand scheme of things, if not quite comic relief). His forays through the narrow village streets and off down Peninsula Road. Giving up and doubling back, exhausted, frustrated, tormented by self-loathing for the way he'd treated his friend. His lover. Passing the doors of the Gull as the band finished a song and the sound of the crowd on the beach gasping and screaming. The pavement drinkers craning to see what was going on, then wincing as feedback sliced through the air.

He'd ignored it. He'd thought, *Jordan has killed Trev. He's fucking killed him.* Then he'd eyed the dripping pints in the drinkers' hands and headed for the open door.

On the grounds that he'd later been recovered from the same location and transported directly home, the car key must still be in the pocket of yesterday's clothes, but there was not the expected heap on the armchair by his side of the bed, nor on the floor of the en suite, which meant Charlotte must have removed them, perhaps already washed them. Oh God, had she checked the pockets and found the key?

Wait, there was still the laundry hamper, in its usual place behind the bathroom door. He flipped the lid aside and there they were, right on top! The shirt he'd been wearing, streaked with vomit and what looked like blood (*Please, don't let me have lung cancer . . .*), the trousers bundled beneath and suspiciously damp (fuck, had he pissed himself?). Crucially, though, the pockets still held his wallet, house keys – and the key to the Astra.

He took the items, flushed the loo, and rejoined his wife and the rosy-cheeked detective, all apologies. Charlotte was still hypothesising about the victim's movements before reaching Pine Ridge, getting perilously close to the truth as she asked about CCTV at petrol stations.

'He definitely didn't run a car,' Perry interrupted with conviction. 'There was no way he could afford that. These residents, they don't even have bank accounts when they move in. The charity helps them with all of that.' It wasn't hard to imagine how the dialogue might progress if he admitted to having acquired the car on the dead man's behalf ('Are you this generous with *all* the residents, Mr Tucker?'). It would be immediately established as inappropriate and they'd take his phone and laptop, do those enhanced checks he'd read about where they magically retrieved deleted messages.

The detective looked ready to wrap this up. 'If I could just get a few details about where you both were yesterday evening, then I can leave you to your morning.'

'We went through this last night,' Charlotte said. 'I was at The Needles having drinks with our son and some friends. We planned to have dinner, but obviously that didn't happen.' She listed the names of those present. 'The Shaws are friends from London and now our neighbours here a couple of doors down. Amy and the kids were there but Perry and Linus hadn't arrived yet.'

Linus! Perry was felled by another heart-stopping electrical current of a memory: that altercation on the path! Straight after Jordan had gone – God, had the boy witnessed *that* little drama? Perry had dashed the man's bike into the sea.

And he'd done it *when he was sober.*

He felt once more the rush of inspiration – far less pleasurable than before since this time he *could* be contradicted, but inspired, nonetheless. 'Linus was with me on the beach,' he stated. 'Watching the band. We were running a bit late getting to The Needles.'

To Charlotte's credit, she didn't cry out in disbelief at this assertion, just queried with a doubtful, 'Really?'

'He and I hadn't been getting on that well,' Perry explained to the detective. 'We'd had a falling out over a paddleboarding accident last week. We decided to go down to the festival together and try to sort things out.'

'Did you see anyone you knew?'

He gave a shrug of one shoulder, as if the question didn't warrant the use of two. 'Loads of people, I should think.'

'And you came straight up when you realized what had happened?'

'Actually, no. It was pandemonium on the beach and we got separated. I'm not sure what happened to Linus.'

'He came up,' Charlotte said. 'We saw him when we got back from The Needles.'

'But *you* didn't, Mr Tucker? Why not?'

Perry paused. This was where it could get tricky and his instinct was to stay as close to the truth – emotionally – as he could. 'I wasn't thinking straight. I couldn't handle any more drama.'

'Drama? You mean from this falling out with Linus?'

'No, no. We'd had a good chat. We were cool. I just meant it's been a rough trip generally. I've been . . . struggling.'

'There've been problems with the activists all summer,' Charlotte said. 'Again, I explained all this to your colleagues. We've made numerous complaints. You may have seen Perry on TV talking about it?'

Bless her for sounding supportive of his notoriety and not, in fact, fervently opposed to it. In spite of yesterday's lapse and the grief he knew he had coming, he was supremely grateful for her being here by his side, both now and in the days to come. She'd back him up whatever he said, however he lied, because in a broken-down world, self-preservation overruled other instincts. Survival. *Family* survival.

'And we were right to be scared,' Charlotte added. 'Look what they did next!'

But the detective was not to be led; her eyes remained trained on Perry. 'So you saw your property fall into the sea but decided to remain down below? You didn't think to make sure your family were safe?'

'I didn't see anything from where I was standing. People were saying the cliff had collapsed. I know it sounds bad, but I assumed everyone I knew was at the hotel and I didn't want to have to deal with it . . . It's hard to explain. I just had to get to the pub.'

'In case it wasn't clear a moment ago, Perry is an alcoholic,' Charlotte said, and though her bald tone made him wince he was glad of the declaration, of its implied justifications.

'Which pub did you go to?' the detective asked.

'The Gull.'

'We found him there at about ten-thirty,' Charlotte confirmed. 'The state he was in, there's no question the staff will remember him.'

'We?'

'I was with our son, Benedict.'

'Where's he now?'

'Upstairs.'

'If you could ask him to pop down, Mrs Tucker, so I can have a quick word. In light of your identification of the jewellery, we'll probably want to get forensics into the house.'

Perry swallowed. *Don't panic. You expected this.*

'And if we can also get your prints for purposes of elimination? My colleague Ethan will organize that today.'

Perry said, as casually as he could: 'Can I ask, are we the first to hear about Jordan's death? I mean, besides his family?'

'Yes. As I say, we'll need the formal identification before we release the news and appeal for witnesses. That will be later today, most likely.'

'I'll go and get Benedict up,' Charlotte said.

'No,' Perry said, on his feet once more, this time in a show of helpfulness. 'I'll go.'

*

Even as Benedict was taking his spot at the table, Perry was out the front door and slipping along to the bungalow. Linus – by a stroke of luck – was alone, visible through the window of a room to the right of the front door, and Perry gestured to him to join him. 'Come round here,' he hissed. 'I don't want the police to see us.'

The gap between the right-hand bungalow wall and the fence was narrow, the two men squeezed uncomfortably close together. Linus looked grim; jittery and badly slept, not unlike Perry himself.

'Tell me the truth,' he said. 'Does Amy know?'

'Know what?' Linus said.

'Seriously, we can't waste time pretending. The police will be coming to yours any minute to tell you. This has completely escalated. Someone was in the Nook and he died.'

Linus's eyes bulged with shock; Perry could see an unbroken ring of white around the irises. In the street, the wind stirred the trees, gently rustling the parched leaves and causing in Perry an involuntary ache of nostalgia.

'What . . .?' Linus choked on his question, tried again. 'What do you mean?'

'I *mean*, you fucking killed someone, Linus.'

67

Perry

He knew psychological collapse when he saw it. That last precious glimpse of the outside world before the cell door slammed in your face.

'Who was he?' Linus whispered and then he began to moan, a ghastly animal sound from deep inside.

'The boy you saw me with,' Perry said. 'Listen, there isn't time to get into it, but there's a way for us both to be in the clear. You need to back up what I've just told the police, okay? I wasn't in when he came to the house. I didn't see him, didn't have a clue he was down here. I've said you and I were together on the beach when it happened. Just tell them the same and we're sorted.'

The moans grew louder and Perry tried to shush him, bringing his own face closer, but Linus just stared glassily at him. Had he heard a word Perry had said? 'You need to get a grip, Linus. The police will be here literally in two minutes and you'll need to have your story straight. We're each other's alibi, do you get it? Otherwise, we're both going down. This could be a murder charge or fuck knows what.'

At this, Linus ceased his awful lament and his eyes snapped back into focus, as if returned from hypnosis. 'What do I say exactly? What are the timings and details?'

Perry took a half step back, satisfied he had his attention. 'We went down to the festival for a drink to try to resolve our differences. Let's say about six? We bumped into each other out back. Don't mention what happened with the bike, that sounds bad. Or have you already told Amy?

'Yes, last night. But I just said I fell. I didn't mention you.'

Thankfully, for Linus, the remorse – or humiliation – had been significant even before this news of a death. To confess to another skirmish with Perry, and so soon after the paddleboarding debacle, would have seen him leapfrogging the activists on the list of motivated suspects for the destruction of the Nook, if not in the police's minds, then certainly Amy's.

'Did you tell her you saw me with someone?'

'No.'

'Good. If they show you a photo, you've never seen him in your life.' *This really could work*, Perry thought. *It* had *to*. 'So we keep it simple. We hung out by the bar, talked things over, what happened on Friday, all of that, and agreed on a ceasefire. We listened to the band for a few songs. We heard the furore, but didn't actually see the house go over. Then we got separated in the chaos and you came back up on your own. Probably took you a while, the steps were closed and the streets were packed. Everyone was leaving at once. You don't know what happened to me. The main thing is we were together when it happened. Neither of us could have driven that JCB.'

Linus nodded, both eyes and voice sharp now. 'Good. Yes. What were the band playing?'

'There was a Queen medley, I think. Then, what was it, "Smoke on the Water". That had just finished when it all kicked off.'

'And did we get drinks from the bar?'

'No. The queue was too long, we didn't bother.'

'Right. Were we wearing what we were wearing when we really did see each other?'

'I was.' Perry tried not to picture the vomit-spattered items in the laundry hamper. 'Were you still in your cycling gear when you spoke to the police last night?'

'Yes.'

'Then that's what you were wearing on the beach.' Curiosity made Perry divert from his task: 'Where were you? I mean, straight after? I really *was* down in the village, but where were you?'

'I came back in,' Linus said. 'Waited it out. I was feeling . . .' He couldn't find the adjective. Invincible, Perry guessed. Euphoric. Petrified of himself. 'Then I went out to see what was going on, acted like I'd just arrived. Went back and forth a few times in the same shoes before they taped off the gardens.'

Good. He'd thought it through at least a little, then. Realized that footsteps in one direction only would have been a dead give-away. Not that the investigators would have much to work with, the ground being so dry.

'What if they've found the bike?' Perry wondered. 'It wasn't far from the Nook where it went over.'

Linus nodded. 'I'll tell them what I told Amy. I lost my balance and came off and the bike went over the cliff. Nothing I could do about it. Maybe I mentioned it to you in our little heart-to-heart. It made me realize how easily something awful could happen? Time to lay these petty grievances to rest.'

That's the spirit, Perry thought. Linus's switch from rabbit in the headlights to shrewd tactician was nothing short of remarkable. 'Go back in. I'll find you when the coast's clear and we'll go over the details before we both give proper statements. No texts, okay? We leave all that to Charlotte and Amy.'

'Got it,' Linus said.

*

He found Charlotte and Benedict upstairs on the landing, having just finished up with the police.

'Where've you been?' Charlotte said.

'Sorry. I had to get some air. I really don't feel well.'

They all knew what that meant. He'd been off somewhere spewing his guts out, deserving of every last agonising heave.

'The police are going to come back to us about taking prints and statements,' Charlotte updated him. 'They want us to stay in town until further notice, which is fair enough. We're allowed to pack a few things to take with us, if you want to sort yours out?'

'What do you mean, take with us?' Perry said.

'This is a suspicious death inquiry, Perry, and we now know the victim was in the house. Up here, ransacking the bedrooms! They can't have us traipsing about where he might have been. It's already too late, though, to be honest. We were all moving around last night. Getting you up to bed.' She and Benedict shared a bleak look. 'But we have to cooperate or they'll think we've got something to hide. I'll phone The Needles and see if they've got rooms. I need to let Madeline know what's happened as well. I don't imagine she'll be thrilled to learn her garden's been obliterated by a JCB.'

'This is awful, Dad,' Benedict said, as Charlotte made the call. 'I'm so sorry about your friend.'

'I'm the one who's sorry,' Perry said, with a pathetic break in his voice. 'I'm sorry you saw me in that state. I promise it won't ever be repeated.'

'I'm just so glad it wasn't you in the Nook.' Benedict advanced towards him for a hug and it seemed to Perry that no human contact had ever been so welcome – or so risky. He longed to weep on the shoulder of this decent gentle boy and yet it was crucial he keep himself in check. His son must never know what he'd done, the part he'd played in the death of a man.

384

Charlotte came off the phone. 'They can take us for two nights, but after that they're fully booked for a wedding. Have you spoken to Tabitha yet this morning, Ben? Do let her know she can come with us if she wants to.' She sent Perry a flinty look to pre-empt any objections he might have, though he would scarcely have dared.

'I'll go and tell her,' Benedict said. 'I'll meet you out by the car when Dad's ready.'

After he'd gone, Perry and Charlotte stood for a few moments in exhausted wordlessness.

'How are you feeling?' she said at last.

'Slightly better.'

'Good.'

'I'll go and pack.'

'I'm glad you and Linus made up,' she said as he turned from her. 'The last thing we need is to start blaming each other. We don't want to give the impression there's been some kind of feud.'

Perry just nodded, not sure quite what to say.

'The plods are dense,' Charlotte added, 'but that detective seemed very bright to me.'

'Yes,' he agreed. 'She did.'

68

Tate

'Tate Barlow, you are under arrest on suspicion of the murder of Jordan Lynch on the twenty-eighth of August . . .'

'What the hell?' he spat. 'Who even is that?'

'. . . and of criminal damage to property at Cliff View, Pine Ridge Road, Pine Ridge . . .'

Jesus. Fuck. An interrogation in situ he'd been expecting, but to be arrested and taken in for the formal stuff! And several hours after Robbie – and, briefly, Shannon as well – had been questioned in their caravan in a manner that had bordered on pally, Robbie had reported, though that had almost certainly been a ploy of some sort. But he'd been untroubled enough to apply his wits to Tate's ongoing phone emergency: the new plan was for Shannon to ask Ethan to find out if it had been logged as evidence at the scene.

Well, Tate thought, as he followed his jailors to their car, that answered *that*.

'What's going on? He hasn't done anything!' Ellie shrieked, drawing Robbie and several others from their caravans to remonstrate as Tate was deposited in the back seat. The bastards had come right into the park and pulled up on Paradise Avenue, so everyone could see who they were taking away.

'Phone me as soon as you can, babe,' she called.

'I don't know your number!' he called back, like he had fucking learning difficulties or something, but no one knew anyone's number, did they, and there was just time for her to thrust a Post-it through the driver's open window and hope it found its way to him.

He stared at his lap for the crawl through the park. No way was he going to risk making eye contact with someone's phone camera and have his face splashed all over social media. He imagined Ellie running after the car like in a film – *Wait, you can't take my man!* – but in reality she'd be going straight over to Robbie's for an emergency summit. Thank God for Robbie. He would sort this out. (It would be better if the Post-it had his number on it, not Ellie's).

They took the ridge road out of the village, bound, he presumed, for the ferry and then the police headquarters in Bournemouth. Two positives came to mind. One, at least he wasn't missing work. With any luck, Gav wouldn't even find out about this. Two, he'd been picked up before any public announcement of the fatality had been made (what had they said the guy's name was again? George? No, Jordan. Jordan something). Imagine if there were media at the ferry filming his removal, or at the station capturing his arrival. This was as discreet as it got.

Hark at you, his mother would have said. *Hark at you looking on the bright side.*

It didn't occur to him to plan a call to *her* to ask for her help. She'd been useless when she was down here and she'd be just as useless now.

*

The duty solicitor assigned to him was female and in her thirties but there was not a shred of a possibility that she was going to be seduced by his good looks or soulful allure, not least because she had an accent that marked her out as from a region of England

387

not known for its beauty spots and therefore unencumbered by any prejudices regarding second-home owners. In manner, she was neutral to the point of robotic as she explained, in a brief conflab before the interview took place, that a murder charge was wishful thinking on the police's part, a common opening gambit when what they were really aiming for was manslaughter.

Oh, well, that was all right then.

The questions began, as expected, with his NJFA rap sheet. Incident after incident, warning after warning, concluding with the recent sticker raid. Pictures, including one of the ill-fated summerhouse plastered in yellow, were displayed before him.

'It was just stickers,' he said, stopping short of admitting to having taken part. His throat was dry already, but he didn't like the water they'd provided. It was warm and chemical-tasting, like they'd scooped it out of a toilet cistern.

They brought up his stint at the farm out near Wareham, the tractor driving training he'd received (one frigging day, three years ago!), until reaching, finally, the events of yesterday.

'Talk us through the period between 5 p.m. and 8 p.m.'

'I was working at the beach bar. I went on my break at six and when I got back, I expected to stay till the end of the festival. But obviously the DJ got cancelled and I left a lot earlier, about seven-fifteen, maybe seven-thirty. I went to find my friends in the pub.'

'What did you do in your break?'

Tate had considered how he might answer this, of course, but had unhelpfully reached this juncture without having made a firm decision. The issue was Ellie. Was he ready for her to know he'd spent his break having sex with another woman? And not any old other woman but the teenage daughter of an enemy family, a member of the thieving elite. He thought again of Beattie last night, how reluctant and withdrawn she'd been, and wondered if telling the police – and therefore, inevitably, Ellie – would mark the end of his keeping his options open. Because the option he'd decided to take was starting to look seriously in doubt.

No, for now, it might be better for her not to know.

'Having trouble remembering, Tate?'

'No, not at all.' He raked his fingers over an itch on the back of his neck. 'It wasn't long enough to go home or anything, so I just hung out. Watched the band. Had a cigarette.'

'Were you with anyone?'

'Not anyone in particular, but I saw a lot of my mates.'

'Names?'

'Robbie. Rio.'

'This would be Robbie Jevons and Rio Miller, fellow NJFA activists?'

'Yes. And Shannon was there.'

'This would be Shannon Reynolds, girlfriend of fellow NJFA activist Robbie Jevons.'

Their mocking tone caused a feeling of childish injustice and he could hear the petulance in his tone as he confirmed the names.

The duty solicitor didn't say a word.

They showed him a photograph next. A young guy of about his age, with reddish brown hair and pale eyes. He had a pierced septum and a curl of ink on his neck, maybe the tail of a scorpion or something. Good-looking but kind of unhealthy.

'Do you recognize this man?'

'No.' At the sight of their disbelieving faces, he raised his voice in protest: 'I'm sorry but I don't!'

'You didn't meet him yesterday at the festival?'

'Not that I remember. I suppose he might have come to the bar, but I served hundreds of people, one after the other. You stop seeing individual faces after a while.'

'You're quite sure about that? Have another look.'

He did so out of politeness. 'I really don't know him. What? What am I meant to say?'

They liked *that*, suddenly got all animated. 'Well, you *could* say the two of you conspired to burgle Cliff View together. You *could* say you then argued over your little caper and he threatened to grass you up and you lost your temper and decided to teach him a lesson.'

The solicitor began to object to this, but Tate spoke over her in a spurt, finally grasping the connection: 'Wait, he's not the bloke who died, is he? What did you say his name was?' *When you arrested me on suspicion of his murder . . .* This was deranged, surreal. 'Look, even if I *did* know him and had some reason to hurt him, why wouldn't I just shove him off the cliff with my bare hands? Why come for him with a fucking great JCB? That's mental.' He gave a gruff laugh. 'Or, wait, maybe we were in there doing smack together and he'd passed out? Gave me time to go looking for the JCB keys, huh?'

'You said it, Tate.'

'I was *joking*. For fuck's sake. I was back behind the bar by then!'

They produced something else now, a see-through bag with a mobile phone in it. He felt all the muscles of his face slacken when he saw the case, with 'Tate's 1st fone' etched into the plastic. Even though he'd expected it, it still felt like a fresh disaster.

'Do you know what this is?'

'It's my phone. I lost it yesterday.'

'When, exactly?'

'I don't know, but loads of people can confirm that I was looking for it last night.'

'People like Robbie and Rio and Shannon?'

Tate gave a huff of irritation. He knew they were baiting him and that he was playing into their hands, but he couldn't help it. 'I thought I might have left it at work. My boss Gav will tell you I was down at the bar this morning to have another look. So where was it?'

'Well, that's the thing, Tate. Would there be any particular reason why the victim, this person you've never met in your life, should have your phone in his pocket when he died?'

Tate felt his eyes pop. *In his pocket?* 'I . . . Well . . . He must have nicked it, I suppose.'

'How could he nick it if you've never had any contact with each other?'

'I don't know. There were a million people on the beach, a pick-pocket would've had a field day. Or I might have left it out behind the bar. I rang it,' he said, remembering. 'It was about quarter to seven, maybe, and I was back from my break. I rang it from my colleague's phone and someone picked up.'

This sparked interest. 'What did they say?'

'They didn't speak. I don't know if they even heard me. I could hear the band, though, so whoever it was, they were there, on the beach or in the vicinity.'

'Vicinity,' they repeated, like it was a big word for a dumbo like him to use.

'But it proves I was back behind the bar,' he said. 'Check Joe's phone. The outgoing calls. You'll see the exact time I used it.'

'Joe?'

'My colleague.'

'So your colleague Joe phoned you, did he? Wondering why you were late back from your break, was he?'

'No, you're twisting what I'm saying. Ask him.' But Tate now recollected an unfortunate detail: Joe – hired for the festival day only – had said he was off on holiday the next day. Today. He swallowed. 'What else did he have on him, this Jordan guy? Was this the only stolen thing in his pocket?'

The flicker that preceded their refusal to answer this told him he'd scored a point – for what it was worth, for they quickly resumed in the same disparaging tones.

'You have to admit it's a bit of a coincidence that the phone belonging to a man familiar with the Cliff View summerhouse from a recent act of vandalism should be found inside that same summerhouse following a further act of vandalism?'

'It *is* a coincidence, yes.' Tate gazed covetously at the phone, wondered if it still worked. How long had it been submerged in seawater? The house went off the cliff at about 7 p.m. and the tide was already starting to go out by then, but it was hours before news came through that a body had been found. Presumably they'd removed the SIM for testing and if they could still retrieve stuff then they'd find messages between him and Beattie. Including ones confirming their meeting. *Come to the house on the end*, she'd said, or something like that. *The romantic one.*

Romantic? Never in his life had he found himself in a situation less romantic. He experienced a fresh surge of self-pity, followed by a kick of realism.

'Look,' he said. 'I don't know this bloke, that's the God's honest truth. But I think I have an idea how my phone was in that summerhouse.'

Glances were exchanged, breath exhaled; body language grew friendlier.

'We're all ears, Tate.'

69

Perry

The luxuries of a five-star hotel did little to settle either his nerves or his stomach. Their rooms wouldn't be ready till three, so Benedict and Tabitha explored the facilities while Perry and Charlotte whiled away time and money on a lunch of braised monkfish and fennel that he had to leave the table to throw up.

A voicemail from Alice at Helping Homes added a fresh layer of anxiety:

> 'Sorry to bother you on holiday, but there was a serious incident yesterday at Keeler House involving one of the residents and the police are here. Could you phone us urgently? We're trying to locate Jordan Lynch . . .'

They'd locate him soon enough, he figured, with or without his input.

Once in their room, an extravaganza of exposed stone, white cotton and jewel-coloured velvet that overlooked the pool, they put the TV on and caught up on the news coverage. A presenter spoke to camera from Old Beach, police beavering in the background, broken bits of summerhouse visible on the sand. The camera lingered on a single drenched cushion from their veranda seating, beached like a dead animal.

Reporter: It's a terrifying incident that blows apart the old saying 'safe as houses' . . . In the idyllic village of Pine Ridge, tourists at a beach concert were shocked yesterday when a large summerhouse tumbled off the cliff and into the sea. Thanks to the tall hedge you see behind me, those on the beach were unable, at first, to tell how such a catastrophic event could have occurred, but the answer soon became breathtakingly clear . . .

Drone footage of the clifftop showed the JCB sitting partly on the path and partly where the Nook had been, its shovel poised dramatically above the void, before a selection of gormless 'witnesses' gave their accounts:

Witness 1: Everyone was just stood there staring, like, completely shocked. Then all hell broke loose, didn't it?

Witness 2: We all started running towards the exit and up the dunes. We thought the cliff was collapsing. Once we found out it was deliberate, we were, like, why would anyone do that?

Witness 3: You never know, do you? I mean, I thought it could even be a terrorist attack or something. I feel really bad for this family who probably did nothing to deserve it.

Probably, Perry noted, as the reporter explained that the owners of the building were not available for comment, before signing off.

He'd not been consulted on their media strategy, but no matter.

'This is only the start,' Charlotte said. 'As soon as they announce poor Jordan's death, the place will be swarming.' She'd begun referring to Jordan in this way, as if 'Poor' were his Christian name. She scooped up her phone and started thumbing. 'Loads of texts coming in, people are recognising the house from the news. Right, I *must* let Tim and Madeline know. I gave that trainee officer their number, but I bet he hasn't got round to telling them. He seemed completely out of his depth.'

Perry watched as she tapped away, unable to do anything but sluice ice-cold mineral water from the mini bar down his throat.

'Have you rung Helping Homes?' Charlotte asked, glancing up.

'No, not yet.' He hadn't told her about Alice's voicemail. 'Why?'

'Why? One of the residents has died, Perry. In *your* house. For goodness' sake, how is that going to look if you say nothing?'

'I thought I just heard that saying nothing was our policy?' Her disapproval was starting to piss him off. 'As far as I understand it, I haven't had the police's permission to share that news. When Jordan's identity is confirmed, I'm sure we'll connect as a matter of priority. And have a bit of sympathy, Charlotte. I know I disgraced myself last night and you're very, very disappointed in me, but I've also just found out someone I know has died. I was really fond of Jordan.'

Talk about disingenuous, but it worked like a charm because she instantly backed down.

'It's a lot to process,' she conceded. 'Sorry.'

'Look, I didn't choose to do what I did last night, at least not in the way a non-addict understands choice. You know that. I know you know that.'

Another murmur of concession. She put down her phone. 'I'm going to see if I can get a massage. Shall I book one for you?'

'No, thanks.' From the window, he watched a familiar figure pad along the path towards the pool. 'I think I'll go for a swim.'

*

The pool at The Needles was not blue but green – pine-needle green presumably, the loungers vermilion. Stripey umbrellas remained closed, the cloud having clotted into an alabaster dome, and the humidity was oppressive.

Or maybe it was just him.

Tabitha was doing lengths of a neat technical freestyle, Benedict nowhere to be seen. Perry waited for her to climb out and pick up her towel from a lounger before he approached. She looked at him warily as she towelled her hair.

He came straight to the point. 'Tabitha, with this awful tragedy and the police sniffing around, I thought it might benefit us both if we try to bury the hatchet.'

Her hair now in damp black spikes, she began patting down her arms and legs. 'We don't really use that term any more.'

'Why not?'

'It's offensive to Indigenous Americans.'

'Is it?' He wanted to laugh – no, cry. He wanted to take the wet towel from her, sink his face into it and sob. 'Okay, well, I'm not aware of any Indigenous Americans staying at the hotel, so we should be safe on that score. The thing is, I saw you yesterday at the festival. Up in the dunes with Robbie.'

Her hands went still as she raised her eyes to his, gifting him the unprecedented sight of self-doubt. 'Oh.'

'Don't worry, I'm not going to say anything to Benedict. But if you could return the favour by telling the police you saw Linus and me on the beach, that would be very helpful.'

'Oh-kaaay,' she said, very slowly. He supposed social justice warriors were not familiar with the concept of a deal. A quid pro quo. It was their way or the highway.

'It wouldn't be a lie. I mean, we had to have been down there or we wouldn't have known you were with Robbie, would we?'

Never mind that there would have been enough time for any one of them to have gone back up and committed the grievous act.

She reached for the Needles-branded robe on her lounger and pulled it on, belting it tightly. 'Did Linus see us as well, then?'

'No, actually. Just me and I didn't say anything to him. He was a bit further away, down towards the stage. I'd gone along the dune path to take a leak.' It wasn't the most savoury image, him with his penis in his hand as he witnessed a sex act, but it was the best he could come up with on the spot. 'Look, this isn't in any way a threat, just a request. Whatever you decide, I won't mention it again, okay?'

She sat for a moment on the edge of the lounger, her gaze grazing his face but not quite settling before swivelling her legs up and easing back. How young she looked, how unsoiled.

'Okay,' she said.

*

He didn't swim. Instead, he took the shuttle bus to the village to hunt once more for the car. The longer the bloody thing eluded him, the more 'what-if's plagued him.

Chief among these: what if the police were sufficiently suspicious of his link with Jordan to run some sort of full check on him that included vehicle ownership? They'd see he had a 2004 Astra registered in his name and find it incongruous alongside the 2019 Range Rover and 2021 Peugeot. Also, what if they ran its registration through their number plate recognition technology and got pictures of Jordan at the wheel on his way from South London to the coast?

But no, he was being paranoid. There was no reason for them to do any of this. He and Linus had each other covered and there was now a very good chance Tabitha would back them up.

He alighted on Old Beach Road near the car park, where he was 90 per cent certain Jordan had claimed he'd left the Astra. That was right, he'd added that it was out of petrol, hadn't he? (Should the police follow Charlotte's tip about checking petrol stations, it should be safe on that, if nothing else.) He supposed he ought to be grateful that Jordan hadn't just pulled up at the house – helped no doubt by the forest of extra signs alerting festivalgoers to the penalties payable should they park illegally. He felt a pang of guilt at the thought that the poor boy had been sufficiently scared not to risk another ticket.

Oh my God, the tickets! He felt his heart kick inside his ribcage. Would they be on his record yet? What if the police asked about them?

Stay calm. If push came to shove, he'd say he'd driven the car himself, on the days he'd been working at Keeler House. He'd settled on his story about having bought it for Benedict to use at uni and there was no reason for anyone to challenge this.

He made his way to the far corner of the car park and surveyed the half-empty expanse of bays. There were still police vehicles, the odd media van – Charlotte was right, these would proliferate the moment the fatality was announced – but of course the thousand-plus day trippers had long gone and both the bar and water sports centre were closed, which meant few if any staff cars.

Unlike yesterday, he could be sure he had eyes on every last vehicle, and yet . . . No Astra among them.

An hour later, there was not a single lane, alley or driveway he had not checked in the village, even the hidden spots behind buildings he'd never noticed before and where Jordan couldn't possibly have thought to park. He'd even returned to the car park for a second sweep, but the result was the same as the first. Had he got it wrong about the car park – it wasn't as if he hadn't destroyed

398

enough brain cells between then and now to have misremembered – or had Jordan had some reason to lie?

If so, where *had* he left the car?

And, if not, who had taken it?

70

Beattie

What the fuck. The police were here and they were demanding to know if she'd been in the Nook with Tate yesterday evening. *In front of her mum and dad.*

The first time they'd come, they'd only wanted to speak to her parents. Then they'd found out Huck and Julien had been in the cabin of the JCB that had, it turned out, not only been used to mess up the Nook but also to kill some guy who Benedict's dad knew – probably accidentally, but still, it was chilling – and they'd returned to say none of them were allowed to leave Pine Ridge until the boys gave statements and had their prints taken. Why couldn't they have asked her about this then?

The guy had a manner like a teacher, friendly enough on the surface but ready to trap you the second you made, like, the *tiniest* blunder. 'Did you meet Tate Barlow during his work break yesterday?' he asked.

Though she and Tate had agreed not to mention it, she might have broken that promise had it just been her mum here with her. But her dad was right next to her, giving her weirdly intense vibes, like he'd explode if anything jeopardized their retreat back up to town tomorrow, and she panicked and said no.

'So you weren't with him in the summerhouse that ended up in the water *or* in your own summerhouse?'

'No,' she said. 'I was on the beach.'

'No one was in when I came back from my bike ride,' her dad said in a stern, confirming way. 'The house and garden were empty and the JCB was where the builders left it on Friday.'

'What's your relationship with Tate, Beattie?'

She felt herself flush. 'I haven't got one.'

'You do know him, though, don't you, Beats?' her mum said. 'He came looking for you last night? With Robbie.'

'Aren't those two suspects?' her father interjected, frowning. 'It said on social media you've arrested one of the activists?'

The officer did not reply, keeping his attention on Beattie. 'Did they find you? Last night?'

'Oh. Yes. We were hanging in the pillbox. But they weren't looking for me specifically.' Nervous her mum would contradict her, she stumbled over the word. 'They know Tabitha as well. They just wanted to know we were all okay.'

'So you *are* friends?'

'We've hung out a few times. There aren't that many places to go out here, you get to know people.'

'What did you talk about last night?'

'Nothing much. Just how awful it was about the Nook. We were only together for a few minutes and then my mum texted and we went home.'

'Did Tate seem his usual self?'

Beattie didn't like to think about this. The truth was she'd felt kind of revolted by him. The Tate she'd fallen for was passionate and funny and a bit cocky, not weak and desperate. And to know that his girlfriend was pregnant! That she'd been telling randoms like Beattie's mum about it while *he* hadn't said a word. It was all just a bit *scarring*.

'I suppose,' she said, finally. 'He was the same as everyone else. We were all, you know, shaken.'

'He wasn't looking for something?'

'Oh.' She remembered now he'd lost his phone and she'd promised to check her pockets and bag, which she had not yet done. 'I think he said he'd lost his phone, but none of us had seen it, so . . .'

'But he thought one of you might have?'

'No. It was just, like, mentioned. I don't know.'

There was no challenge to this. Maybe he wasn't trying to catch her out, after all. It was more like he was expecting her to say exactly what she was, that she was just confirming what he already knew. Were they going to ask to take her phone and, if they did, did she have the legal right to refuse? She literally couldn't breathe without it.

'You were on the beach, you said. Until what time?'

'Maybe six-forty? Before this thing happened. I got the bus to The Needles to meet Mum and Dad.'

'She was with us when Charlotte got your call asking us to come back,' her mum said.

And that was that. The police officer didn't point out that the timing of her departure fitted exactly with the end of Tate's break. He didn't demand her phone. He did, however, ask her to stay local for a few days.

'I suppose it's not the end of the world if you stay on with me an extra night or two, Beats,' her mum said. 'Term doesn't start till next week. Is there any news on when you'll be finished with the JCB?' she asked the officer.

There was not.

'God knows when we'll be able to start the build,' she grumbled when he'd left. 'Terry's really pissed off and the delay's going to cost us a fortune. I know it's awful to think about money, but . . .'

She meant because of the guy who died. Which was something else Beattie didn't like to think about. It was completely terrifying how it could have been Tate and her in the Nook when it got pushed off the cliff – they'd been in it less than an hour before. Okay, so the dead guy must have been wasted (her mum had heard from Charlotte that he had a drink problem), but so might they have been! Tate might have dumped the rest of his shift and the two of them fallen asleep, dead to the world.

Two corpses instead of one.

It was all so real in her head it was like a memory from some actual parallel reality.

Which was pretty much how it felt to watch the news, which she and her parents now did, and to see the pictures of their street, along with the first photo issued of the victim. He looked young and scruffy and incredibly sad.

Reporter: This afternoon police confirmed that suspicions of criminal damage have been upgraded to include a murder probe . . .

A police officer came on now, not the one who'd just been in their house, but more senior, standing outside some police building in Bournemouth.

Detective: A life has been lost and we are pursuing the perpetrator of this crime with all the resources at our disposal. Anyone with information that could assist our investigation can call us on 101, report via our website or contact Crimestopppers anonymously.

'They must have arrested Tate,' Beattie's mum said. 'Did you get that impression as well, Linus? Why else would they need to establish his whereabouts?'

'They were very tight-lipped about it, I thought,' her dad said.

'Well, they must have *something* that incriminates him. Maybe they found something in the JCB? This missing phone, d'you think?'

Beattie felt a horrible chill grip her heart. It was suddenly obvious what must have happened: Tate hadn't left his phone in her bedroom like he thought, but in the Nook. They'd left in a hurry – at *her* insistence – and he hadn't noticed he'd put it down somewhere or maybe it just slipped out of his pocket. The police must have found it near the dead guy.

'Ask Perry when you see him in the morning,' her mum told her dad, adding, 'I'm really pleased you're meeting up.'

Beattie's dad shrugged. 'I just wanted to, you know, offer him some support before I leave.'

'That's one good thing, I suppose. This awful death has put our petty fall-outs into perspective.'

Beattie wondered if that included the tattoos, brokered by her with Tate's help to buy Huck's silence over his suspicions about them. Maybe even the clothes as well, and the threatened young offenders' counselling?

'Why don't we all just stay on for the rest of the week?' her mum suggested. 'Julien could just get the train up for his Eurostar?'

'No way,' Beattie's dad said, with the same intense look he'd had earlier. 'You and Beats can stay, but I'm taking the boys back tomorrow whether the police like it or not. They can chase me up the M3, lights flashing, if they like, but I'm not coming back.'

'All right,' Beattie's mum said and laughed. 'They're just doing their job. There's no need to be such a rebel.'

71

Robbie

I'll be on my own at the garage today, so I plan to keep my head down, clear my slate, and knock off at lunch time. I've got a Mini in for a service, plus there's sure to be a couple of DFL finance bros in with a tyre slashing (or even a genuine puncture) and an urgent need to get back to their hedge funds or whatever, but otherwise it should be pretty dead.

The phrase makes me wince slightly.

On my way out, I knock on Tate and Ellie's door. He wasn't back when I tried last night and I haven't heard from him – this missing phone is a pain in the backside – so I haven't had a chance to find out how it went with the police. I admit that I slept like a baby myself. I was basically fucked – there's only so long nervous energy can trick your rhythms.

Ellie comes to the door, hope in her eyes – until she sees it's me and then it vanishes. I'm about to tease her when I notice her face is puffy; she's been crying.

'You all right? Is he up yet?'

'He's not back, Rob. They kept him overnight.'

'In a cell?' This, I was *not* expecting. 'Why didn't you tell us?'

'I didn't hear from him till late.' She takes a band from her wrist and draws her hair into a ponytail. 'Anyway, what could you have done?'

Good question. 'But he called you? What've they got on him?'

'No one saw him on his break. He's basically got no alibi.'

'What? I told them *I* saw him.'

Ellie pulls an unimpressed face. 'He might need more than that.'

'Tell me his exact words, Ellie. It's important.'

She chews her lip and considers. 'I think he said, "What I did in my break hasn't been backed up." Something like that.'

What he did in his break? More like *who*. That's a message for me, right there. Lolita must be denying their fling and he needs me to twist her arm. But how will I get to her when her family are probably in serious protection mode – if she's even still in town? I'm the last person they'll want sniffing around. I swallow a sigh. Please don't tell me I'm going to have to bail on work and go up to London.

'Look, you know they can't keep him for longer than twenty-four hours without charging him. He'll be back by this afternoon.'

'Yeah. Unless they *do* charge him.' Noticing a neighbour ear-wigging, Ellie gestures for me to come in.

I look around, a little stunned. Normally shipshape, the place is in chaos, with everything moved from its original spot, plus stuff that I'm guessing is usually stored out of sight now heaped on the table and both bench seats. It seems an odd time to choose to reorganize, but I suppose she could be making a start on getting ready for the move to the KosyKabin. Or this could be a pregnancy thing – nesting or whatever.

'What's going on? Some kind of sort-out?'

'Try police search. They left it in a right state.'

'Seriously?' Again, I'm a step behind, not a feeling I like. 'What did they take?'

She looks glumly about. 'Computer. Console. A few NJFA bits.'

'Bastards. They'd bloody better give it all back.' I pluck from the nearest pile a shirt that looks familiar. A swirly multi-coloured print, posh label. 'Nice threads. Don't think I've ever seen you in this.'

'It's not mine,' Ellie says. 'None of it is. They found these two bin liners in the drawers in the bedroom and I was like what the fuck? I mean I *said* they were mine, but I've never seen them before in my life. Where d'you think they came from, Rob?' She holds up a bizarre-looking tank top with a fur hood. 'There's some serious designer shit in here.'

'Is it new?'

'Some of the tags are still on, but most of it's been worn. I was thinking, Tate gave me this hat . . . Where is it?' She combs through a different pile and produces a neon-orange sunhat. 'Said he got it from lost property at work. So maybe that's where all this came from as well?'

'No way.' I can't help laughing. 'This is Pine Ridge, not, I don't know, Saint-Tropez.'

Her face is thoughtful. 'It's weird, though. I told you about that DFL bitch who stopped me in the street and said the hat was bought with her stolen card? What was that all about?'

I reach for a piece of white fabric with the word 'VIBING' on it. I've seen this before, as well – on Beattie. One night at the Gull a few weeks ago. Tiny shorts she had on, hair in pigtails. Everyone was gawking at her and she was loving it. All of this is hers, I bet. But why would she and Tate want to stash her clothes here, right under the nose of the woman they've been deceiving?

Ellie's right, it makes no sense.

Unless . . . I feel my blood quicken. Unless it actually could make quite a lot of sense, in which case we might have ourselves a bit of leverage here.

'Ellie . . .' I find myself in a bit of a dilemma. Clearly Tate didn't confess to the affair in their phone conversation – if he had, she'd never be speaking to me like this, she'd be spitting blood, accusing me of covering for him – which means the last thing he intended was for *me* to spill on his behalf. But I'm thinking the situation calls for an executive overrule. Better she's got an unfaithful bastard as the father of her child than a fuckwit doing time for a manslaughter – or whatever it is they'll be threatening him with – he didn't commit.

'Sit down,' I say. 'I need to tell you something.'

She sinks onto a jumble of clothes. 'What?'

'Tate's done something really stupid and you're going to be seriously pissed off. But we can't get him back here unless you know about it.'

Her sad, swollen eyes are fixed on me, twisting my heart. 'Tell me.'

'I will. And then I'm going to need your help.'

72

Perry

The police had made no stipulations about contact between the families – it wasn't as if any of them was a suspect – but even so he arranged to meet Linus for a dog walk in the woods on the far side of the Ridge, where there'd be no chance of their discussion being overheard.

Linus was waiting in the designated spot, dressed in regular clothes for once, not his usual second-skin cycling gear (the ninja theme had lost its lustre, Perry supposed, now he'd committed the ultimate dishonour).

Mango dashed ahead on the broad woodland path, which crackled underfoot after weeks without rain, a tinderbox of roots and sticks and bleached pinecones. 'No barbecuing' signs had been put up at every clearing.

'How're you bearing up?' Perry said with all the warmth he could muster. He was under no illusion that his own penance took its form at least partly in propping up his former enemy.

'I'm okay,' Linus said. It was already clear he was a different man from the one who'd presided over his own barbecue not so long ago, all that tech bro swagger subdued, the whip hand removed.

Finally, Perry's seniority counted for something – if not wisdom, then cunning.

'This man who died, who was he, exactly?'

The past tense brought a cramp to Perry's chest. 'He was a resident at the place where I volunteer. A bit of a lost soul. He came down to ask me for help and I didn't give it to him.'

'So you weren't, you know, together?'

'God no. I think you misread the signs on that one.' Perry paused. 'I feel like a complete heel for sending him packing.'

But also relieved beyond imagination. Relieved that Jordan's own crime – not yet reported by the media as far as he could tell but surely under investigation, the dots between the two deaths, the two police forces, in the process of being joined – stood on their own merits. Demerits.

'Imagine how *I* feel,' Linus said. 'I honestly don't know how I'm going to come to terms with this.'

Perry sent him a cautioning look. 'Don't go all Macbeth on me, Linus. You didn't know he was in there. Even if you'd checked, he might have been in the shower room or crouched out of sight. Benedict and his friends used to hide down there all the time when they were little.'

But Linus took no comfort from this, his tone growing even more haunted. 'I keep thinking about those minutes just before. I don't know what came over me, it was like I blacked out. Went into a dissociative state, you know?'

'I do know.' How often in life it came down to this, Perry thought, to the momentary insanities driven by rage or lust or grief. 'We both know I drove you to it. If I hadn't done what I did with the bike, you wouldn't have done what you did with the Nook.' He gave a mirthless chuckle. 'Mind you, the Nook was Charlotte's baby. If you'd really wanted revenge, you should have totalled the Range Rover.'

Though it would have been just his luck if Jordan had been

sleeping in the back as Linus released the handbrake and watched it roll over the cliff.

Ahead, Mango examined a set of tree roots, squatted to pee.

'How did you even know how to drive the JCB?'

Linus swiped a stone aside with his foot. 'I was there when the builder gave the boys a tutorial. It's not hard once you get it started. I didn't even get the angle right, but it just took the thing down like it was made of cardboard. I was lucky I didn't drive over the cliff after it.'

'You must be a natural,' Perry said, though it was a little early even for gallows humour and neither man smiled. 'What about prints? Have the police taken yours as well?'

'Yes, all of us. Huck and Julien are with the police right now, doing theirs. We all handled the controls. There're probably photos of us in the cabin on Amy's Instagram. She's documenting the build.'

Which was exactly the kind of thing that made holiday-home owners unpopular, Perry thought – *Look how I've taken this humble shack and blessed it with my metropolitan sophistication!* – but all of that paled into insignificance in light of the loss of a man's life. Even Charlotte had accepted the demise of the Nook as a small price to pay for the miracle of their own loved ones having been spared ('To think I said Beattie could use it. What if *she'd* been in there?')

'The only thing that matters is they believe we were on the beach together,' he told Linus. 'An alibi's an alibi.'

It helped that Charlotte and Amy had separately confirmed that their husbands had been busy patching up their differences during the crucial time frame. Meanwhile, Perry's account of his drinking binge had been verified by the staff at the Gull. The emotions of the day, as well as the cumulative stresses of a difficult summer battling the activists – physically, in Robbie's case – seemed to have been accepted as reason enough for him to have plunged so spectacularly off the wagon.

Gradually the gaps were being plugged, the loose ends tied.

All except one. The car. To say time was running out was an understatement: the news of Jordan's death was out and there'd been a photo of him on the TV news last night, no doubt copied and shared thousands of times already. The circus was well and truly underway: both legitimate media and TikTok true detective types would now be invading the village with their cameras, peddling their theories and lies. Not to mention garnering the odd bit of genuine evidence: any one of the festival punters could have a sudden memory of seeing Jordan driving into the village in a white Astra.

Seeing Mango start to double back – she'd been walking the route since she was a puppy – Perry did the same. Linus followed, and for a short while neither spoke.

'So you're leaving this afternoon?' Perry said presently.

'Yep, just me and the boys. Amy'll try to get the build back on track and the police have asked Beattie to stay in town for another day or two.'

Perry looked up. 'Have they? Why?'

'She knows this Tate, apparently. The activist they've arrested?'

'Oh yes. Charlotte says he hasn't been charged yet, though.'

'I hope he never is,' Linus exclaimed with sudden passion.

'Do you?'

'Yes. I mean, he didn't do it, did he?'

Perry inhaled, brow furrowing. 'Try not to say that too loudly, mate.'

Linus glanced about; they were alone. 'Even so. I couldn't live with a miscarriage of justice like that.'

'You'd have to.' Perry fingered the dog lead looped around his neck. 'But don't worry. If he didn't do it, then they'll only have circumstantial evidence. It won't be enough.'

'Enough to make his life miserable for a while, though.'

'Sure, but what's the alternative? A confession from you?' Perry fidgeted with the snap hook, pressing and releasing, then pressing again. As their cars came into sight through the trees, still the only two in range, parked bumper to bumper, he was assailed by the sudden lunatic idea that if he didn't trust Linus to keep his silence then he'd never have a better opportunity—

'Think of the kids, Linus,' he said, extinguishing the thought. 'You've got more than your conscience at stake here.'

Linus nodded, an air of defeat about him now, of *failure*, and Perry knew then that he would never tell. He was simply too much of a coward.

It took one to know one.

73

Beattie

'Darling, you have a visitor.'

Beattie looked up from her Spotify app. Since the departure of her dad, brother and Julien an hour or two ago, she'd spent a melancholy stretch picking through her stuff (her mum thought she was packing) and playing old Lana del Rey on repeat. The mournful lyrics totally pierced her heart, though she couldn't say what it was she mourned the most. Not just her lost fashion treasures, she wasn't *that* sketchy. The poor man who'd died, obviously, though she'd never met him and so it all felt a bit, well, *abstract*.

And Tate, too, of course. She'd been getting serious shit-got-real vibes ever since lying to the police about him and then hearing from her dad that he was definitely the one who'd been arrested yesterday, had probably been sitting there in the police station in, like, *handcuffs*, while the police were here asking her to confirm his alibi. Which she had not done.

Panicking, she'd binned all their messages, deleted his contact, blocked him. Which was stupid because it wasn't like he didn't know where to find her.

'It's Ellie, from the Needles spa.' Her mum lowered her voice. 'If it's anything to do with that business with Charlotte's card, don't say a word, okay?'

'Okay.' Beattie felt a sharp spike of adrenaline as she walked the few steps to the living room, where Ellie sat marooned on the sofa, bits of packing and DIY stuff from the demolished garage heaped all around. She didn't *look* pregnant, or at least not obviously, though she was old – twenty-five maybe – and so had a thicker waist anyway. There was a tremor in her jaw, but whether it was from nerves or fury Beattie had no idea. Her own emotions were trapped in her chest, giving her the frightening sensation of a boa constrictor squeezing her ribcage.

'Hi,' she said, closing the door behind her and standing as far away from the sofa as possible.

Ellie waited a beat before speaking, assessing her. 'You're the famous Beattie, are you? Do you know who I am?'

Beattie nodded. 'Tate's girlfriend.'

'Okay, Beattie.' Ellie said her name with a sneer, as if she was about to let rip, maybe even attack her physically, then made a visible effort to control herself. 'The reason I'm here is I need you to go to the police and tell them the truth about you and Tate on Monday. During his break? I don't know what you've said, but it's obviously not that he was with you, so you've lied, haven't you?'

'I don't . . . I . . .' Beattie began, but immediately faltered. How she wished she was dressed in one of her amazing fashion looks and not her Uniqlo sale tracky bottoms and hoodie. Great clothes didn't just make you feel awesome, they impressed and intimidated other girls.

'Look, I know all about your dumb little hook-up,' Ellie said. 'None of that is important. What's important is that he's in a police cell and you need to get him out of it. You're the only person who can vouch for him during his break. We need you to say you saw him go back to work afterwards.'

Afterwards. Beattie swallowed. 'Can't Robbie—'

'They don't believe Robbie. Those two have been covering each other's arses since nursery.' Ellie sighed through her mouth, her lips jutting out. 'I take it your parents don't know and that's why you haven't just been honest to begin with? They think you're the sweet little virgin, right?'

Beattie said nothing, but felt her cheeks colour.

Ellie's voice sharpened (Beattie found her tone frighteningly quick to change): 'What kind of a person are you, happy for an innocent man to be accused of something you know he didn't do? You don't seem to realize how serious this is. They've got something on him, I don't know what, but it's hardcore.'

Beattie started to tremble, a weakness Ellie spotted and that seemed to fuel another injection of energy.

'Seriously, I haven't got time for your teenage crap!' She reached for a hessian tote bag by her side and extracted a familiar item: Beattie's prized adidas + Gucci dress, hideously crumpled. 'This might change things. I know it's yours – and the other stuff.'

Beattie remembered her mum's caution and felt fear flare inside her. 'That's not mine.'

'Really? Well, whoever it *does* belong to should know that the police were very interested when they raided the caravan yesterday. That's right, Beattie, we were raided. That's how bad this is. Do you really not get it?' Ellie stuffed the dress back in the tote and Beattie felt true grief to see it so unlovingly handled. 'You know, the day of the festival, a neighbour of yours accosted me on my way to work, said I'd used her stolen card to buy stuff from Fleur. Maybe I should find her and show her the rest of this stuff? See if anything else was bought on her card? It might not get Tate off, but it will definitely get *you* thrown into the mix.'

Beattie could bear this no longer. 'I think they must have found his phone in the Nook,' she blurted. 'We were in there for a few minutes before we came here.'

Ellie's forehead creased. 'The Nook, that's—'

'The summerhouse that went over the cliff. We were only there for a few minutes.'

'Tate was in there?' Ellie put a hand to her stomach as if winded. 'Was this other bloke there as well, the one who died?'

'No. No, definitely not.' This was getting scary. 'Like I say, we were only in there for a minute or two, but I think he left his phone there.'

Ellie drew a sharp breath. 'Right. That makes sense. Robbie said it might be to do with the phone. So say all of that to the police. Say where you were and what you did. Come with me now and say it all.'

'Come where?' Beattie said.

'To the police station in Bournemouth. My friend's mum's waiting outside in her car. We'll take you.'

The police station. Where Tate was. If she did what Ellie asked, would they release him on the spot? She had a gruesome vision of them all riding back home together, Tate, Ellie and her squeezed together in the back seat.

'Beattie?' The door eased open and her mum peeked in. Oh God, had she been listening at the door? 'Everything all right in here?'

Ellie raised her eyebrows at Beattie: *your call.*

'Fine.' Beattie smiled at her mum. 'I'm going out. Ellie just needs me to help her with something.'

'She'll be safe with me.' Ellie flashed Beattie's mum a sweet, professional smile and got to her feet. 'Let's go.'

417

74

Perry

'Look at this,' Charlotte said, when he joined her in the brasserie at The Needles for lunch, and she thrust her phone under his nose. After parting from Linus, he'd driven into the village and treated Mango to a second walk in the form of another unsuccessful hunt for the Astra, this time prowling the Staywell's car park and heading almost a mile down Peninsula Road before giving up.

He feigned astonishment at the headline on the *South London Press* website:

Police Called to Tulse Hill Clearing House

Emergency services were called to Keeler House in Ryland Street, Tulse Hill, on Monday following a domestic incident in which a 29-year-old man was taken to King's College Hospital with life-threatening head injuries.

Keeler House is run by Helping Homes, a charity that provides support for those who struggle to maintain long-term accommodation, including former homeless and criminal offenders.

Yesterday, neighbours spoke of conflict between the victim, Trevor Cochrane, and other residents. 'We've been hearing a lot more arguments over the summer,' said one neighbour, who asked

not to be named. 'Maybe it's because of the hot weather, but there
are some volatile characters living there and tempers have been
flaring. We've complained to the charity, but nothing's been done.'

A representative for Helping Homes said the charity is liaising
closely with the victim's medical team and will be cooperating
with the police in any subsequent criminal investigation. 'This is
a very distressing incident and we're all praying we'll have news
soon of a full recovery,' they said.

'He's not dead?' Perry blurted before he could stop himself.

'No, but still, sounds pretty brutal.' Charlotte took back her phone, peered at the screen. 'Trevor. Isn't he the one you said Jordan didn't get on with?'

'Yes. I don't think any of them do, to be honest.'

'They're not the ones who ran off, though, are they?'

Perry paused. Under the table, Mango was sucking water from a large bowl that had materialized as if by magic, as useful things tended to at The Needles. He felt a sudden desire to place his head on (or maybe *under*) one of the half-dozen soft cotton pillows on their bed upstairs. 'What are you saying?' he asked his wife.

'It's obvious, isn't it? Jordan must have whacked this Trevor and fled the scene. He remembers your throwaway offer of somewhere to stay and decides it's as good a place as any to lie low. He arrives and finds the door left open, comes in and nicks a few valuables. A stupid move, by the way, since we could have noticed and called the police, but he was obviously desperate. Then he notices the summerhouse and decides to hide out there.'

Bingo. If Charlotte could conclude this on the basis of a single news article, then the police would have taken the more detailed report and done the same, even if Trev wasn't yet in any fit state to name Jordan as his attacker.

Just so long as none of the witnesses – either inside Keeler House or in neighbouring homes – had anything to say about the perpetrator's relationship with a certain middle-aged volunteer.

While Charlotte studied the menu, he excused himself and found a quiet corner to return Alice's call – finally.

'I just read about Trev,' he said, his horrified concern pitch-perfect. 'I'm sorry not to have called back yesterday, but I was dealing with the situation down here. You've heard about Jordan now, have you?'

'Oh, Perry, yes. The police said they'd asked you not to talk about it until he was identified. What a terrible, terrible tragedy.'

Her genuine grief disarmed him, brought a choke to his voice as he answered variations of the questions the police had asked about Jordan's final hours, giving a brief version of Charlotte's theory about the destruction of the summerhouse being the activists' seasonal swansong. Neither voiced directly the suspicion that Jordan might have been Trev's attacker, but nor did they discuss any other suspects. They agreed to keep in touch as more information was shared by the respective police teams.

Thank God I didn't send her that resignation email, he thought, returning to the table and updating Charlotte. For the first time since this nightmare began, he was aware of hunger. 'Shall we order? I'm starving.'

'Let's wait for Benedict and Tabitha,' she said as the waiter delivered her a large glass of rosé, which he eyed with a blend of envy and shame. 'They're just up in the car park.'

'I didn't know they were joining us. Where've they been?'

'Just into Swanage. Shopping for souvenirs for Tabitha's folks. By the way, the police rang earlier. They wanted us to know that someone has confirmed seeing you and Linus on the beach when the Nook fell. You were never suspects, obviously, but it's good to be formally eliminated.'

'Oh,' Perry said. 'Great.'

They lapsed into silence, she tackling her wine while he processed his conversation with Alice. He began to feel the tingling sensation of having heard something significant, not from Alice, he soon realized, but from Charlotte. The news about Tabitha having come through for him? Welcome, yes, but he didn't think it was that. He replayed their exchange and finally located it among the more innocuous portion of their exchange. Benedict and Tabitha were *up in the car park* . . .

Jordan had used that phrase too, he was certain. He'd parked the Astra *up* in the car park, not *down*. Yet he'd been on the headland at the time, so it could hardly have been natural to label the beach car park 'up'.

'Charlotte? You know the day of the festival?'

She lowered her wineglass. 'I'm hardly likely to forget it, am I?'

'Was there an overspill car park? There usually is, isn't there?'

'Yes, on the far side of the village, but this year they used the field next to the caravan park. You know, where the new KosyKabins are going to be? Why?'

'No reason.' Perry was on his feet again, heart knocking in his ribcage. 'I'm really sorry, but I'm going to have to miss lunch. I'll be back as soon as I can.'

75

Perry

Exhausted though he was by the hours of walking already under his belt, he headed up to Golden Sands on foot on the basis that he might well be leaving again behind the wheel. He tried not to dwell on the police signs that faced the incoming traffic: 'Fatal Incident in Pine Ridge, 28th August. Appeal for witnesses.'

A further sign, hanging from a post on the uphill climb, was a more welcome sight: 'Festival Parking This Way'. He followed the tracks into a field next to the caravan site, where, near the open gates, a board with 'Parking £5' painted on it lay flat on the dirt. The field was almost empty now, but for five or six uncollected vehicles.

And there it was among them, parked at a haphazard angle under a tree in the far corner, the crap old Astra.

Finally.

Now he just needed to get rid of it. Ideally, by driving it into a larger town or city – Poole or Bournemouth – and abandoning it in a side street without parking restrictions. He'd already googled likely spots. The problem was he wasn't sure if it had enough fuel in the tank for that kind of distance and he certainly couldn't fill it up at a petrol station, where CCTV was a given. Maybe he could just find a stretch of open cliff further down the coast and take the handbrake off?

He strolled over and unlocked the driver's door. He'd feared finding all Jordan's worldly possessions stored in it, but the boy had evidently absconded with only the clothes on his back; a denim jacket with a line of grime on the inside collar was the only garment, an empty energy drink can and Subway wrapper strewn nearby. He disposed of the items in the bins by the entrance to the caravan park – no more than a symbolic gesture since the car would have Jordan's DNA all over it – then returned and slipped into the driver's seat.

He turned the key in the ignition – the engine fired after two tries – and checked the tank display: as Jordan had warned, it was on empty. Might there be enough to get to the ridge, to the out-of-the-way spot where he'd parked earlier for his meeting with Linus? Might he then . . . might he set the thing alight?

He reversed, turned, and began crossing the field at a crawl. But he'd not even reached the exit when the engine sputtered – *damn* – and he had no choice but to steer it to the side, brake and repark. He sat for a moment, trying and failing to contain his frustration, then got out, slammed the door and brought his palm down on the roof with a violence that gained him nothing bar another minor hand injury.

What now? Go and get the Range Rover and drive to the nearest petrol station to fill up a can? Extract some petrol from the Range Rover itself? The first carried the risk of being captured on CCTV, while the second would involve a YouTube tutorial since he'd never before had reason to drain a fuel tank. Would he need any tools?

Just then, someone called out to him from the road: 'Need some help?'

He spun, recognising the voice. Robbie Jevons, standing by the fence in oil-streaked grey overalls, his eyes fixed on Perry as he lit a cigarette.

423

Perry was about to tell the bastard to fuck off when he remembered a crucial detail: Robbie was a mechanic. That was when the idea occurred to him. Brilliant or disastrous, he didn't yet know, but the reality was he had no more time to play with. He *had* to get this car out of his hair before the police linked it to Jordan's getaway.

He strode towards the other man before he could change his mind. 'Robbie? Look, I want to offer a belated apology for, you know, that bust-up we had last week. I was out of order.'

Robbie said nothing, just assessed him coolly, smoke curling from between his parted teeth. There were still traces of bruising on his face.

'And, yes, I'm a bit stuck, so if I could take you up on your offer . . .?'

Robbie gestured to the mound opposite the Golden Sands entrance. 'Let's talk up there.' His manner was that of a wise man accepting a supplicant, which irritated Perry but Lord knew beggars couldn't be choosers, and he locked up the car and followed. They sat opposite each other at a rickety old picnic table. There was a degree of extra chill, he noticed. A sense that the season was turning.

'It was your place that went off the cliff?' Robbie said, evidently requiring some sort of update before permitting Perry to plead his case.

'Yes. Our summerhouse.'

'Sorry to hear about the kid who died. Did you know he was in there?'

'No. No, I didn't.' Perry grimaced. 'We were all very shocked.'

'Who did it, do you know yet?'

Perry could barely summon the energy to go through the motions of accusation, not when he was in possession of the truth, but he knew he had to. 'You tell me. My wife's convinced it was you – or one of your crew.'

Robbie exhaled a last flamboyant stream of smoke and dropped his cigarette end to the ground. ''Fraid not. We're all accounted for. The sand art was our deed of the day, why would we want to compete with that? Anyway, we're a pressure group, not a bunch of gangsters. Bit of graffiti or flyposting or whatever, sure, I hold my hands up. But this? No. No way.'

Not long ago, Perry would have lost his mind at this confession, but now he let it pass unremarked. 'What about this bloke they've arrested? Isn't he one of yours?'

'That's a misunderstanding,' Robbie said. 'He won't be charged.' He appeared so certain of this as to be almost inconvenienced by further discussion of it. 'Anyone got a grudge against you? Besides me, of course.'

'Not that I know of,' Perry said.

No one except Linus.

He glanced over his shoulder at the Astra, its registration visible between fence posts. 'So about that offer to help me out . . .' He sucked in his breath, aware that the risk he was about to take was probably his greatest yet – which was saying something.

'Shoot,' Robbie said.

'You won't repeat any of this, will you?'

'Course not.'

'Okay. Well, I need to get rid of it. I won't go into it, but I don't need it any more and I can't sell it or give it away. I was thinking about maybe setting fire to it?'

Robbie tapped his fingers on the table. 'I wouldn't do that. Not around here. The whole place could go up. Why don't you just take it to the scrapyard?'

'I've thought of that. The thing is . . .' Perry paused, choosing his words. 'It would be better if it wasn't, you know, *official*. I don't need the date catching police eyes because it coincides with what went down at the house. Making out there's some connection where there isn't one.'

'Yeah, well. They're good at that.' Robbie was all sympatico now. He was no fool and would understand at once that a car abandoned in the overspill parking for the festival must have arrived on or around the day of said festival. But it was all about common enemies, Perry saw. The joint covering of arses. 'You just need it backdated then, don't you?'

Yes! His brain clung to the 'just': this was going to be possible; this might even be easy! 'That's exactly it. Even just to last week would work.'

Any time before Jordan's fateful drive down to Pine Ridge.

'I can help you out. I know the guy who runs the scrapyard down Swanage way.'

'Would he be willing to, you know, falsify the date?'

'For the right price, yeah. Would've thought.'

'How much?'

'I'll give him a call and find out. Give me five, yeah?' He got to his feet and moved out of earshot. Perry looked down at the sea, from this distance silvery and quite soundless. It was almost ornamental, not quite real.

Robbie returned. 'August the twenty-first all right?'

'Great. How much does he want?'

'Two grand.'

Two grand! Even allowing for a cut for Robbie, it was way more than he should be paying for a bit of business like this, especially as the car had been acquired for free, but it was just money. Money he could deal with. Transactional, not emotional. He thought of the £230 he'd scraped together for Jordan. An insultingly paltry sum. Had it been more, Jordan might have felt equipped to journey on, he might still be alive – albeit wanted by the Met for GBH.

Perry had yet to reflect on whether it benefited him that Trev had survived Jordan's assault (much less how he had come to be a man who weighed another's life in terms of *strategy*).

'When do I take it in?' he said.

'Might be better if I do it,' Robbie said.

Even better. 'It needs petrol.'

'No worries.' Hardly an issue for a mechanic. 'You'll have to go on the DVLA site and tell them it was scrapped on that same date. You'll need the name and address of the scrapyard as well. Let me give you that now.' Robbie dictated the details. In return, Perry gave him the key and agreed the delivery of the cash.

'I'm so grateful.'

'Happy to help,' Robbie said.

Perry slid from the bench, smiling at him for the first time in their short acquaintance. 'I promise I'll do my best to stop Charlotte campaigning against you.'

Robbie shrugged. 'Let her if it makes her feel better. But like I say, we're sorted.'

76

Tate

'You're off the hook, pretty boy.'

Pretty boy? What year was this even? 'Should never have been *on* the hook,' he grumbled. He was sure they'd held him for over twenty-four hours, but no doubt it was near enough for them to get away with it. They'd have some technicality they could pull. The main thing was he wasn't being charged. He wasn't going to Broadstone or some other hellhole prison to wait for a court date that never came.

'Don't push it,' the officer said. 'You've screwed with a lot of people this summer.'

'Screwed with or just screwed?' a colleague said and they chortled away, comedians now it suited them.

He still had no phone. He'd get his back eventually, they said, but it was wrecked from the sea and unusable. He had no clue how he was going to afford to replace it.

He took the bus home, the same route they'd taken when returning from Ellie's parents last week. He smelled like shit. His skin was all grainy and his eyes sticky, like he'd got an infection. He felt sullied, and not just physically.

He got off at Old Beach Road and called in at the Gull, where the crew often met around this time. His spirits lifted at the sight of Robbie sitting alone in the main bar.

'Yo.'

'Tate, my mate! I had a feeling you'd come here first. Spiritual home and all that.'

They exchanged high fives while the barman pulled Tate a pint on the house.

But the euphoria of release was short-lived.

'This is the thing,' Robbie said. 'I had to tell Ellie. It was the only way to get Beattie to spill. She was the one who went and had it out with her. Shannon's mum drove them to the station. They got back a couple of hours ago.'

Tate rubbed his gritty eyes. 'Is there any point me even going back to the park? Can I bunk up with you if she throws me out?'

'Course. But I think you'll be okay. She wouldn't have got involved if she was seriously going to bin you. You'll need every ounce of that legendary sex appeal, mind. Maybe not sex appeal,' Robbie corrected himself, giving Tate a wry look. 'Display of good father material?'

'Don't. Fuck.' Tate thought how quiet it was in the pub. Just when you got used to the high-summer throngs they were gone. As for those who *were* in here, they could well be media and he needed to be careful not to meet anyone's eye. 'Do we still not know who did it?'

Robbie's brow furrowed. 'According to Ethan, they're interviewing the Citizens now.'

'Really? I'm not feeling it,' Tate said. 'They've done nothing this summer. That Staywell protest was the most I've seen of them in months.'

Robbie nodded. 'They've been doing a lot of media this week, though. They've really muscled in. Mind you, I've made the executive decision to not comment on this particular incident, so let them take the flak, eh?'

'Smart.' Tate pulled a rolled-up newspaper from his pocket. The hot-off-the-press new *Voice*, picked up on the bus. 'Speaking of which, did you read this?'

Robbie took it from him and started reading aloud:

Pine Ridge Season Ends on a Dark Note

Details are emerging of the man found dead in the Pine Ridge bank holiday incident.

Twenty-six-year-old Jordan Lynch, who lost his life when a summerhouse was bulldozed off the cliff on Monday during the Old Beach Festival, was a former addict and rough sleeper who resided in South London in the same charity facility where a man was found gravely injured the same day.

Police declined to comment on any connection between the two cases.

He glanced up. 'What the fuck?'

'I know. Ethan kept that to himself.'

'Doubt he's been told. He's only a trainee. And they've probably already sussed he leaks like a sieve. Here we go . . .'

'This is a tragic episode that highlights the culture of "haves" and "have-nots" both in London and the affluent parts of southern England,' said Jacob Plummer of local pressure group Citizens Against the Elite. 'While the "haves" relax in multiple homes with all the security and protection money can buy, the "have-nots" live exposed lives that leave them more vulnerable to crime.'

Once more, Robbie broke off to comment. 'Well, the "haves" are also the victims in this case. *I* would have said it was obvious this was a personal dispute, not an ideological one.'

Pine Ridge has been a hotbed of activism this summer as local groups stepped up their opposition to second homes, with the police called to multiple incidents, including regular disruptions at the toll ferry. The village now finds itself embroiled in the immigration crisis, with locals and tourists alike opposing the housing of illegal migrants in a prime seafront hotel.

'There comes a point when controversy hits a resort where it hurts and I wonder if we might be seeing that with Pine Ridge,' says Suki Markham, assistant travel editor of the Daily Telegraph. *'What most holidaymakers want is to arrive without hassle and then spend a week relaxing. What they* don't *want is to have food thrown at their car on arrival and then watch protesters marching up and down as they lie on the beach.'*

'D'you think they're right? The tourists'll stop coming?' Tate said.

Robbie discarded the paper. 'No way. By Easter, this will all be forgotten. I mean, where's better than Pine Ridge? It's paradise.'

Tate finished his pint. He wasn't sure what he needed more, a second one or a shower. The smell coming off him was *institutional.* 'You said yourself it's paradise lost.'

'Only temporarily. We can get it back. By the time TJ's running around, this will all be a bad dream.'

'TJ?'

'Yeah.' Robbie grinned. 'Tate Junior.'

'Please,' Tate groaned, the pain rooting deep, but Robbie just laughed as if he was faking it.

'You know what I think? I think you'll love it once it's here. Plus now Ellie's doing it, Shannon'll be next.'

But the idea of a star like Robbie being shackled was almost as grotesque as his own predicament. 'Then make it clear to her while you can!'

'Make what clear?' Robbie said.

'That you're not ready. For a baby.'

'Would it be so terrible? They could be in the same school year, like we were.'

Standing here in the Gull in twenty-five years' time, one having just sprung the other from jail. It didn't bear thinking about.

'Your face,' Robbie said, laughing. 'I think you need another drink.'

77

Charlotte

Thursday 31 August

Not so long ago, Pine Ridge had been their place to escape to, but now they queued to escape *from* it. Statements, loose ends and a last breakfast out of the way, Benedict and Tabitha were ready to depart. While Perry brought the Range Rover around from the Needles car park, Charlotte helped them with their backpacks and told them how much she was going to miss them. They agreed once more how unlikely it was that they should be ending their summer at the hotel when they had a holiday home five minutes away.

Charlotte and Perry's own bags were behind reception, their next stop yet to be determined.

'Let us know all's okay in Masefield Road,' she said, hugging Benedict. Before visiting Tabitha's mother in Rutland, they were going to the Dulwich house for a night or two.

Perry had joked privately about Tabitha filling the house with refugee overspill from the Staywell, but Charlotte was well past the point of laughing along with him, even if she was heartened by a last-minute thawing of relations between the two adversaries. When he'd returned from his latest mysterious outing yesterday and joined them for coffee after lunch, he'd been remarkably friendly to the girl, bearing her wildly simplistic monologue about the evils of bank bailouts with a tolerance unthinkable a few weeks ago.

'Mysterious outing' seemed to have become Charlotte's preferred euphemism for her husband's secret foraging for alcohol and was as good as any she'd coined in the past. The minibar in their room was booze-free, he'd requested this himself, but that was almost certainly a red herring. They weren't together twenty-four hours a day, after all, and when she'd nodded off next to him these last couple of nights on the huge Needles mattress, Mango forming an illicit bolster between them, he could for all she knew have slipped from the covers and gone down to the bar for a nightcap.

Doubtless he presumed that in light of a man's death she had parked discussions about his lapse, perhaps even decided to skip over them altogether.

Which was typically hopeful of him, typically overconfident.

*

While Perry was doing the station run, she settled in the residents' snug and returned to the task of trawling Airbnb and the other sites for somewhere for the two of them to stay for the next few nights – bloody hell, £3,000 for a week in Poole in September? They'd be in a tent at this rate. After that, she was needed back in London and Perry would return to Cliff View to clean up whatever mess the police had made and take care of garden repairs.

'They've said two more nights tops,' she'd told Amy when they'd met for an early morning walk. 'God knows what they're still doing in there. At least they've let the kids head back.'

This included Beattie, who'd been given the all clear following some mix-up involving the suspect – this Tate friend of Robbie's – who they'd arrested and then released without charge (hadn't she predicted they'd cock the investigation up?). He'd claimed to have been with Beattie just before the Nook was destroyed, Amy reported, and though Beattie had denied this, Amy wasn't sure what to believe. Her daughter had become quite the enigma to her.

It was a terrible thing to realize that you no longer truly knew a member of your own family, Amy said, and Charlotte had agreed wholeheartedly. 'Whatever Beattie's been up to, it will just be a blip,' she reassured her. 'She'll be back on the A-level treadmill and won't have time for anything else.'

Neither chose to discuss whether the treadmill might be the very reason the youngsters pursued the blips.

Perry returned from the station in good cheer. 'How are you getting on?' He sank into the huge velvet armchair by the window and encouraged Mango to jump up next to him, even though the hotel politely requested guests not allow pets on the furniture.

'Hmm. It's proving a bit tricky. Nowhere takes dogs.'

'This is stupid. Let's just tell the fuzz we have to get back into Cliff View, end of. I bet they don't have a legal right to keep us out of our own property.'

'Maybe. I've had an idea,' Charlotte said. 'I'm going to ask Madeline if we can stay at Villa Pino for a couple of nights. Can I say we'll fix their damaged fences in return? You can do that, can't you?'

Perry smoothed a hand over his scalp. 'Sure. As soon as the police leave us in peace, I'll get started. I just need to let Helping Homes know I'm not going to be available for a while.'

'Is Keeler House still a crime scene as well?'

'I don't know. If it is, it'll be awkward getting the residents rehoused. They've got zero extra capacity in London.'

Charlotte sent her message to Madeline, then changed into her swimming things and went down to the pool. Might as well use the facilities they were paying through the nose for. When she'd done her lengths, she floated on her back for a while and looked at the creamy sky and thought about the Nook. She hadn't said to Perry, and she knew he wouldn't have intuited it, but she didn't actually want to go back to Cliff View, not yet. She didn't want to look out of the kitchen window and see a square of sky where the Nook should be. It had only been a summerhouse, nothing to compare with a human life, but she was grieving it, nonetheless. People connected with places just as they did other people. Fell in and out of love with them.

By the time she was back, Mango was by Perry's feet, the two of them chastised but unrepentant for their sofa crime, and Charlotte had had an answer from Madeline. They could stay as long as they needed and any help from Perry with garden repairs was gratefully received.

I'm not sure I dare come back to Pine Ridge, Madeline texted.

I know the feeling, Charlotte replied.

78

Charlotte

It was almost dusk by the time they left. She'd been comped a skin-tightening, anti-ageing facial as an apology for the stolen card incident and she wasn't going to miss *that*. (To her relief, it was not Ellie who did the treatment, but a lovely girl called Manda.)

They parked in the drive of Villa Pino in the exact spot where Robbie's caravan had once been and she collected the spare key from the lockbox. Oddly, the burglar alarm was already disabled, which reminded her of Amy's fixation earlier in the trip, her observations about mail on the doormat and shutters being open when they should have been closed. Miss Marple eccentricities from a bygone era.

'What's the story with the alarm?' she murmured, seconds before a young woman in a Housekeepers smock and leggings came scurrying down the stairs.

'Mystery solved,' Perry said.

'Can I ask what's going on?' the woman said, wiping her hands on her smock.

Charlotte introduced herself. 'We've had permission from the owners to stay here for a night or two while the police finish up at our place next door.'

'Oh, I didn't get that message.' The woman stood for a moment, discombobulated, then said, 'Which bedroom are you going to use? If you give me twenty minutes, I'll get it ready for you.'

'We don't know yet. You carry on, we'll sort ourselves out.' Charlotte waited for Perry to take Mango to the kitchen to set up her water bowl, before following the woman up the stairs. She stood at a discreet distance and watched her circle the upper landing and head for the second flight of stairs, which Charlotte knew led to the master suite.

'Excuse me?' She was not surprised when the woman backed away from her, subtly barring entry to the upper stairs. 'Can I have a word?'

'What?' She was fretful now and struggling to hide it.

'How long have you been here?'

The woman made a show of checking the smartwatch on her wrist. 'An hour? It's just a routine check.'

'Come on. I'm not stupid.' Charlotte advanced towards her, offering her phone, which displayed her exchange with Madeline:

OK to get the key from Housekeepers? Cx

Haven't used them this year. Spare is in lockbox on side railing, codes for that and the alarm to follow... Mx

'You've been living here all summer, haven't you? Up at the top, I assume. Who are you? Do you actually work for Housekeepers?'

The woman's gaze dipped. 'No, the Staywell. My friend does, though.'

And he or she supplied the key and code – which Tim and Madeline must not have changed since using the agency last summer – along with the branded smock, to be thrown on in the event of an ambush like this one. 'Your friend's squatting here too?

Okay.' Incredible that they'd had the gall to remain with police swarming the clifftop. Charlotte's mind flashed to her dealings over the contactless fraud at Fleur – more Miss Marple nonsense – and she said, 'You know what? Don't tell me anything else. Just get your stuff and go.'

She headed for the main stairs, then turned back. 'Wait. Did you see anything? The day the summerhouse fell into the sea? Did you see the person driving the JCB?'

The girl sucked her lower lip, obviously wishing she had valuable information to trade, maybe even considering fabricating it. 'I was down on the beach. Sorry.'

Not even ten minutes later, she came back down dragging two backpacks not unlike the pair Benedict and Tabitha had slung into the back of the Range Rover a few hours ago; the second belonged to her fellow squatter, presumably.

Charlotte watched her struggle down the drive and into the darkening street and wondered where she intended going. Why were two working people living like this, anyway? She thought again of her son and his girlfriend, with their multiple accommodation options and inflated sense of virtue, and went out into the street after her.

'Wait up. Can I give you a lift somewhere?'

The girl was, she saw, talking into her phone, presumably reporting the development to her partner in crime. She raised a palm to Charlotte. 'It's okay. Thanks.'

'If you're sure.' Charlotte went back inside the big spacious house she'd been loaned for free next door to the big spacious house she owned and wondered if she should feel guilty for turning the squatters out. Of course, it was possible they had a whole roster of unoccupied houses they could use, and maybe the kind of people who did this were also the kind to steal whatever they could find from said houses and Charlotte should, in fact, feel guilty for not having demanded their details and reported them to the Rickmans or the police or both.

She was too exhausted to figure it all out.

And she still had the most difficult job of all to tackle.

79

Perry

Friday 1 September

His wife's timing was impeccable, which was no less than he would have expected of her. She waited till Benedict had left and she waited till she was sufficiently assured by the police that their family had completed all that was required of them to be eliminated from suspicion and accorded victim of crime status.

A status, in his case, achieved thanks to his alliances with his three former *bêtes noires*, Linus, Tabitha and Robbie. He was, in fact, just reading the text from Jevons Motors when Charlotte came to find him lounging in the Rickmans' sitting room with Mango:

Dear Customer, Work on your car is now complete. Regards.

'Do you have a minute?' she said.

Since he was sitting, phone in hand, in front of the wood burner (it was the first day of September and as far as he was concerned summer was over in every sense of the word, including meteorological), a man with no job and no occupation beyond building fences – literally – the question hardly merited an answer.

She perched on a leather footstool a few feet away from him. 'You did meet this Jordan boy, didn't you?'

Perry started, glad he didn't have a drink to spill. 'What d'you mean? When?'

'On Monday. You met him at the house and something happened that put you in that mood.'

He swallowed, fearful of her cool soothsayer's air. 'What mood?'

'The mood to drink.' As a flush of emotion gripped her, she gestured with upturned palms. 'You'd done so well, Perry! Miraculously well, really. To fall off the wagon like that, something really significant must have happened.'

Perry said nothing. Significant was certainly the word. He petted Mango's ears with both hands, not wanting to free them in case he was tempted to cover his face with them and weep.

'You didn't know about the Nook, that was obvious when we found you in the Gull, so it couldn't have been that. I did wonder whether it might have been the relief of sorting things out with Linus – I know that's been stressful, especially when he accused you of trying to drown him. But relief is too positive. You wouldn't drink to celebrate. This had to have been something that made you . . .' She searched for the word. '*Despair.*'

He brought his teeth together, not daring to speak.

'So,' Charlotte continued. 'Was it what I think it was?'

He cleared his throat. 'I don't know what you think it was.'

Her gaze narrowed. 'Some kind of entanglement. More than friends. You'd arranged to meet and that's why you didn't want to spend the afternoon with the rest of us.'

'We didn't arrange to meet.' He knew this would be answer enough. Of her three statements he'd corrected just one.

'What then? Did he turn up a day early? What was the plan, to get me out of the way back to London and install him here? Instead of sneaking back up, which you've obviously been doing all summer, you were going to sneak back down?'

'No, of course not.' Perry let his hands settle on Mango's shoulders and she sent him a look of uncritical devotion; in that moment, she was his only friend in the world. 'You were right before. The police are right. He came down after this thing at Keeler House. He thought he'd killed Trev and wanted me to help him hide.'

Charlotte's brows shot up. This she had not guessed. 'You've known that all along? Why didn't you just say?'

'I didn't want to implicate myself. I begged him to go back and hand himself in. I thought that was what he was going to do, but he must have come back. I swear that's the truth.'

Charlotte's hands came together, not quite wringing, certainly not praying, before she dropped them onto her lap. 'Okay,' she said.

Okay . . .? He couldn't fathom what came next. *Okay, then I'll join you in your lies and we'll say no more about it?* Or *Okay, then I'll leave you to your 'entanglements' and find a divorce lawyer?*

'The time's come, Perry.'

He was breathless. 'For what?'

'For us to go our separate ways.'

He felt the blood drain from him, the muscles in his face slacken, and let out a groan. The self-pity was involuntary, but Charlotte interpreted it as conscious.

'Don't look so sorry for yourself,' she said coolly. 'All of this is your own doing. This whole trip has been a path to self-destruction. I'm just reacting in the only way I can to stop myself getting dragged down with you.'

She was right. He pictured himself four weeks ago, down on the veranda in the setting sun with his overpriced NoLo beers, quipping with Benedict, baiting Tabitha. Casually telling Charlotte he needed to run up to town the next day to help out those in need. A god of hubris.

He'd had this coming, he saw that; what distressed him was

how controlled she was now she'd delivered her verdict. Almost impersonal.

'What?' she said. 'You can't be surprised?'

'No. I just . . . I suppose I . . .'

'You suppose what?'

'I suppose I thought if it happened, if we ever split, there'd be more . . . passion.'

It was the wrong word and he deserved the disdain he received.

'Look where passion got you, Perry.'

This was a typically last word kind of comment from Charlotte and he expected her to make her exit then, to leave him to reflect on his sins. But there was more to come.

'What I'd like to know is . . . What *are* you, Perry?'

The question took him aback. 'You mean . . . am I gay? I—'

'No,' she interrupted. 'Not that. I know that's complicated. What I mean is how do you define yourself – *to* yourself? On a lie detector test or if you had a gun to your head and you were asked what you are, what's the essence of you, what comes first? Father? Husband? Londoner?' She allowed herself a moment of wryness. 'Motorist? Second-homer?'

He knew the answer, but he wasn't sure if he would say it until he heard himself speak, uttering the words as if in solemn pledge:

'I'm a drinker, Charlotte. That's who I am. That comes first.'

*

Because she wanted to contain their usage to one bedroom, they slept in the same bed they had the night before in spite of their agreement to separate. Lying awake, he counted the beds he'd occupied over the last month: Masefield Road, Cliff View, The Needles, Villa Pino.

444

And Jordan's room in Keeler House, of course.

If the police found his prints on the bedposts, he'd tell them that must have been from a DIY job he'd done.

The screws had come loose, that was right.

Another metaphor he preferred not to dwell on.

80

Perry

Some time later

He could only guess what marital estrangement was like when you shared a small flat, or just a room, or a caravan, because it was oppressive enough when you had two homes and no obligation whatsoever to occupy the same one at the same time.

It was over a week since Charlotte had gone back to London and she texted constantly with instructions for his work at Cliff View, beginning with his replacement of the damaged fences, the police having at long last left, taking their enquiries elsewhere. Also with updates on her interactions with the various professionals who now populated the end of their marriage: solicitors, estate agents, wealth advisors, accountants.

Benedict, thank goodness, communicated with him direct – and with a distinct sense of role reversal, as if Perry were the child in need of support and he the adult equipped to give it. *You okay dad? Tabs and I are here for you.* And so on.

Perry enjoyed the outdoor work, except when the wind was particularly savage or the building works at the bungalow made it impossible for him to hear his vintage *Start the Week* podcasts through his earbuds.

Not that he blamed Amy. She was an innocent in all of this and on the occasions that he emerged from his turtle shell of self-absorption he couldn't fail to notice how drawn she looked. Like a cabinet minister who'd walked into her ministry fresh-faced and straight-backed and left it glum and stooped. Nothing to do with being married to a killer – he remained confident that Linus would keep that to himself, in sickness and in health – and everything to do with the build. The crew were not happy bunnies, that was obvious from the grumbles he overheard, mostly to do with the spiralling costs of materials and the knock-on delays caused by the JCB having been impounded. They wanted to sue the police for loss of earnings. They wanted to add 30 per cent to Amy's bill. They wanted to tear up the contract and work instead on a job in Studland, where the client had deep pockets and there was none of this crime-scene bullshit.

The victim was never once mentioned. People only cared about themselves. Okay, so he was no different, but at least he *knew* he was no different and deplored the fact. (Or was that simply the worst of both worlds? To be one of life's bad guys and to know it and hate yourself for it?)

In any case, he *had* sobbed for Jordan – once, freely and extravagantly, with a bottle of Malbec and a several glasses of cognac. He pictured them together constantly: their first time together in Jordan's poky room in Keeler House, their nights here in the spare room and down in the Nook. Thanks to his own strict rules on comms, he had no pictures of his lost friend other than the one the media had used, which he didn't like to examine because it made Jordan look so luckless, so forsaken.

As if he'd already been shown how his story would end.

*

He and Amy had dinner together some evenings, either at The Needles or in the kitchen at Cliff View. It wasn't his preference because it meant he couldn't drink till after they'd parted – he didn't need her pitching in with motivational talk or supplying Charlotte with bulletins – but it was nice to have the company occasionally.

'Any news on Tattoogate?' he asked, on one of their nights. Creamy orzo risotto was on the menu, not his own work but a posh ready meal from the farm shop in Crowland. Even the salad had been tossed by someone else. He wondered if, after twenty-five years as Charlotte's sous-chef, he'd ever bother cooking for himself.

'Not really,' Amy said. She'd already told him that Linus had been uncharacteristically forgiving of Huck's body art, which she put down to the shock of their 'brush' with tragedy (wouldn't *she* like to know?). To have a son with a jellyfish scratched into his skin was a whole lot better than the position the victim's parents were in. Attempts to discover who had done the tattooing had petered out, though she harboured suspicions that Beattie knew more than she was saying.

'Huck says Julien's still kept his hidden,' she said, and this was, for Perry, an interesting detail. How long could the boy get away with it? It was hard enough keeping actions secret, but bodily marks?

'Apparently laser removal is loads better than it used to be, so, I don't know . . .' She pulled a face. 'How are Benedict and Tabitha? Have you heard from them?'

'He checks in most days. All's well in the Land of Idealism, I believe.'

'I like that they're so politically engaged,' Amy said. 'Not every young person is. I know that from my own two.'

'There's a lot to be said for apathy,' Perry said, forking risotto into his mouth. He thought about Tabitha's odd little tryst with Robbie. Would the two of them keep in touch or did what happened in the dunes stay in the dunes? 'I am surprised they seem to be lasting the course, though.'

'I suppose if a couple can get through the summer we just had, they can get through anything.' Realising what she'd said, Amy flushed. 'Oh God. Sorry, Perry. I—'

'No,' he said. 'It's fine. Honestly. I'm fine.'

81

Amy

They said building works were like childbirth (well, Charlotte did) – almost unendurable, but then once done, quickly eclipsed by the joy of new ownership. She looked forward to that day, but for now it was a blood-pressure raising schedule split between Linus and the kids in Dulwich and her new family, the builders – and Perry – in Pine Ridge.

Depending on the weather, she slept either in the Niche, which was pleasurably close to the elements but involved constant trips to the loo in the main house, or the only bedroom with its walls still intact: Huck's, still dank and dusty but at least now featuring an actual window.

She tried to time her arrival in Pine Ridge for the early evening, when the builders had finished for the day and she could assess their (lack of) progress and allow her inevitable kneejerk anger to ease overnight. If the *Voice* was waiting on the doormat, as it was this time, all the better. She poured herself a glass of white wine and settled down to read. There was always something to make your jaw drop and this time was no exception:

Squatter Scandal Rocks Crime-hit Pine Ridge

Workers from a domestic services agency based in Poole have been found to be squatting in the upmarket holiday homes they were servicing.

The deception came to light when Claire Powell, owner of Housekeepers, a domestic services agency that looks after hundreds of properties in the area, answered a call from a client with a house in Pine Ridge and personally attended the property to carry out the request. There she discovered clothes, food and other items belonging to a member of her staff. When questioned, the worker confessed to having been living secretly in the house for several weeks. Powell conducted an internal investigation and uncovered a system of key copying and alarm code sharing among a small number of employees.

'We are horrified,' she told the Voice. *'The staff involved have had their contracts terminated and we've issued apologies and offered compensation to every owner affected.'*

It is believed that at least two dozen properties were abused in this way in Poole and Pine Ridge. Detached properties were more popular because of the lesser risk of discovery by neighbours, as well as those with no or outdated security systems.

Though contacted by the police, none of the owners has decided to press charges, Powell said.

'I know accommodation is a sore point around here,' said one owner of a holiday home on Bird Lane, Pine Ridge, who declined to be named, 'but this really isn't the solution.'

However, Jacob Plummer of pressure group Citizens Against the Elite expressed sympathy for the low-salaried workers. 'Stories like this show just how desperate seasonal workers can get,' he said, adding that when the council's proposed

KosyKabins are made available to locals, the temporary caravan accommodation currently being used to house them should then be offered for those with a legitimate short-term need. 'If we want people to help run our resort in summer, we have to provide somewhere for them to live,' he added.

Amy topped up her wine, the first glass inexplicably already finished.

Editor of House Security website Karen Crawley advises holiday home owners to regularly change their alarm codes and at the very least install cameras at all entry points. 'Security systems that you can monitor remotely are incredibly easy to set up and will give you peace of mind if you are leaving your property empty for any length of time.'

Police said there is no link between the squatting scandal and their ongoing investigation into the destruction of a summer-house bulldozed off the Pine Ridge headland during the August bank holiday festival. A 26-year-old man was found to have been inside the structure at the time and died of injuries caused by the fall.

No charges have yet been brought.

Amazing, she thought, finding the piece online and sharing it with Charlotte: *I bet this is what was going on at Villa Pino...*

Charlotte's reply came a few minutes later: *Maybe.*

*

The same edition included news of an open day at the KosyKabin site, which happened to coincide with Amy's next planned visit.

Curious, she strolled up to have a look. Fine, so it wasn't Le Corbusier, but when she compared the pristine interiors with the pit where she'd woken up that morning, she felt really quite envious.

The girl from the spa was looking around at the same time. Ellie, the one with whom Beattie had disappeared a couple of days after the bank holiday on an errand that had never fully been explained. Also, the one who Charlotte had seen in Beattie's stolen orange hat, the thought of which caused Amy a twinge of anxiety.

'Hi again, Ellie. This is gorgeous, isn't it?'

'Yeah, it's all right.' The girl appeared rather guarded, perhaps mistaking Amy for a competitor for one of the KosyKabins.

'Amy,' she reminded her. 'From the bungalow on Pine Ridge Road? Did you sort things out with Beattie that time?'

'Oh. Absolutely,' Ellie said, recovering. 'She was great. We love Beattie, don't we, babe?'

A dark-haired male who'd been checking out the shower room now stepped into the living area and Amy saw that it was Tate. Tate, who'd turned up at the bungalow on the night of the festival in a state of agitation; Tate, who'd been arrested and who'd fibbed that he'd been with Beattie around the time of the crime. But whatever it was he'd been hiding, it couldn't have been provably criminal, because he'd been released without charge.

She watched as Ellie took his arm, her manner possessive. Amy hadn't known they were a couple. Did that cast fresh light on Ellie's rather fraught discussion with Beattie that day? Perhaps there *had* been something between Beattie and Tate, and this woman – this pregnant woman – had been warning her off?

Oh, Beattie. If the summer was anything to go by, there were bumpy times ahead. Amy had reached out to private therapists for her daughter, put her name on several waiting lists, but even the most expensive ones were full. Everyone needed help, it seemed, bewildered by a changing world. At least she was studying hard; her mocks were only a few months away and her Cambridge application done and dusted (her second choice was Bristol, inspired by Benedict and Tabitha).

'Congratulations again on the baby,' she said. 'When are you due?'

'February,' Ellie said.

'And when will these houses be ready?'

'New Year, they think.'

Amy gave an exclamation of joy. 'It's not often in life you get perfect timing like that!'

'I know. We're so lucky.'

The entire time, Tate didn't say a word, just stood there gripping his phone, which looked like a brand-new iPhone 14 (she didn't allow herself to wonder how he could afford that and yet need subsidized housing; she could only hope he hadn't thieved it from a locker at the gym). No doubt he'd leave the heavy lifting of parenting to Ellie, preferring to meet his mates or play video games or cycle around like a madman before riding his bike over a cliff.

Nothing changed.

It was only as they drifted out of range that it occurred to her that Ellie had been wearing one of Beattie's ill-gotten designer items under her jacket, the tank top with the fur hood. The caravan park residents must have first dibs on the recycling, she thought.

Good for them.

82

Perry

One overcast afternoon, both sets of fence repairs now done, two notifications popped up on Perry's phone that left him feeling as shaky as at any time in this torrid period of residence.

The first was a voicemail from the police. Not the local force, but the Met – which meant it had to be to do with Trev. Could Perry please phone them at his convenience?

Fuck.

The second was a text: no words, just a picture of the Astra parked outside Jevons Motors in Crowland, licence plate visible. This was troubling enough even before he saw the timestamp: *31 August.* Three days after the death of Jordan and a full ten days after the date he'd agreed with Robbie and recorded with the DVLA as having had the thing scrapped.

No sooner had he opened it than a message followed:

Meet me in the Gull at 7

The little bastard had double-crossed him. And, as ever, as Charlotte had so brutally pointed out, Perry had no one but himself to blame.

*

He arrived five minutes early and made a point of enjoying approaching the bar and ordering a proper drink.

'Make that two,' Robbie said behind him, and motioned to the stairs to the upstairs bar.

Perry followed him up with their pints and located him at the table in the bay window. It was dusk and the sight of the pines across the road caused a pang of gratitude, like seeing old friends stand by in case he needed assistance.

'What the hell are you up to?' he said, depositing the drinks and lowering himself into the seat opposite. 'I paid you the two grand. Why didn't you scrap it like we agreed?'

Robbie took a mouthful of his pint, eyes widening as if surprised by Perry's hostility. 'Keep your hair on. It *was* scrapped.'

'And backdated to the twenty-first?'

'Yep. You notified the DVLA like I said?'

'Yes, of course. I did exactly what we agreed.' Unable to delay a moment longer, Perry raised his glass and swallowed a good third of his pint. 'So why am I here? What was that photo all about?'

Robbie licked foam from the corner of his mouth, the previously injured side, healed now. 'Just insurance. In case I needed a favour.'

Perry could have smashed his own head against the wall. How many more times was he going to ask himself how he could have been so stupid? He should just tattoo the question on his forearm. 'Happy to help', my arse. Quite apart from the fact of his having physically assaulted the guy, why would a resentful mechanic who headed a band of criminal activists be happy to help a rich bastard like him? The very type of person he got out of bed every day with the declared aim of annihilating! That meeting at the picnic table, Robbie must have known there and then what he wanted – or at least that he'd be able to think of something soon enough.

'What kind of favour did you have in mind?' He had a dismal flash of Jordan asking him a favour about the car. How relieved he'd been that he hadn't wanted to borrow Perry's own car. It was shameful, contemptible, to have been so ungenerous.

Robbie held his gaze, cool as you like. 'I hear your house is up for sale.'

'Where did you hear that?' As far as Perry was aware, there'd been an exploratory call or two with agents, but that was it. Charlotte had a whole programme of DIY for him to get through before the place could be listed.

'No secrets in Pine Ridge, mate,' Robbie said.

Well, he sincerely hoped *that* wasn't true.

'It will be for sale, yes. When I've finished sorting the garden and a few other things. Charlotte and I are splitting – or did you already know that as well?'

'I didn't. Sorry to hear that.' Robbie gripped his glass, took another deep draught. Perry sensed he was taking his time purely for his own entertainment. 'Anyway, I thought you might like to rent it to me and Shannon instead.'

Perry frowned. 'Instead? I just told you we're getting divorced. It's going on the market.'

'Then make sure the price is nice and high and we'll rent it from you in the meantime. We can't pay market rate, obviously. Her hours are cut right back in the off season.'

'What *can* you pay?'

'A few hundred a month, maybe.'

Perry snorted. 'A few hundred? That won't even cover the electricity bill!'

'Still. It's good PR, yeah. Doing right by the locals.' Robbie smirked at him. 'Come on, it wouldn't be the first time you'd helped someone out for charity, would it? Rest in peace and all that.'

What a poisonous bastard he was. What a tawdry bit of blackmail he'd dreamed up. Perry reached for his retaliatory ammunition – Robbie and Tabitha in the dunes – but rejected it on instinct. Unlike Robbie, he had no photographic evidence, and not only would Robbie deny it, he'd also discover that Perry was the kind of father willing to use his son's private life to wriggle out of trouble. It was grievous enough to have Tabitha know this.

'Look, it doesn't matter what I say. Charlotte is the one you have to convince.'

'*You* have to convince,' Robbie corrected him.

Perry sighed. He supposed he could spin Charlotte some yarn about having struck a deal with Robbie that exempted Cliff View – make that the whole street – from vandalism during the crucial for-sale period. 'It would just have to be until the house sells. Then you'd have to leave.'

'Yeah, you said. Fine.'

They both knew this could be a while and not only because the Tuckers were free, as Robbie suggested, to set the price ambitiously high. Other factors were also to the other man's advantage. First, there was the article in yesterday's *Telegraph*: '*Second-Home Sales Have Fallen Off A Cliff*' (very droll), all about how fewer sales were being agreed owing to new council powers to tax holiday homes. Second, the fact that Cliff View was no longer known as the most covetable house in Pine Ridge but as the house where a young man had died in an incident the police continued to investigate as murder. An infamous death trap. And even if an offer *was* secured, there was still the conveyancing, which could take months.

'I want the picture gone,' he said, his voice little more than a growl. 'Gone from your photos, from the cloud, everywhere.'

'Of course. The moment you hand over the key,' Robbie said.

*

He delayed getting back to the London police till the following afternoon, just before 4 p.m., which was his self-approved time for his first drink. He tried to ignore the smack of his heart and concentrate instead on the vodka and tonic on the table next to him, frivolous and fizzing, his reward for getting through the call.

He practised pitching his tone between concern and cooperation and, when satisfied, dialled. 'Hello there. Perry Tucker returning your call.'

The detective thanked him and got straight to business. 'You're aware that Trevor Cochrane was assaulted in Keeler House on the twenty-eighth of August?'

'Yes, of course. I think I spoke to your colleague that week. I've been a volunteer at the house for almost a year.'

'Would you be able to come in and give a witness statement?'

The thump in his ribcage was turning into a John Bonham drum solo, crashing right through him, roaring in his ears. 'A witness to what? I wasn't actually in town on the twenty-eighth. How is Trev, by the way?'

The detective explained that the victim was recovering well and had now been able to identify his attacker.

This is it. What had Trev seen? The two of them in bed together? Jordan in the car, registration memorized?

Don't cave in, he told himself. *Go down swinging.*

'Ah,' he said. 'Was it . . . Was it Jordan?'

'Any reason you should say that?'

459

'We just assumed it, I suppose. They didn't get on and Jordan turned up here the same day, as I'm sure you know. I didn't actually connect with him, but . . . Well, we know what happened.' Perry gave a heavy, heartsick sigh. 'It's tragic. He had such potential, I thought. Just needed his confidence building up, a decent employer to take a chance on him.'

It was impossible to know whether or not notes were being taken of these not insincere tributes, but he sensed not. The exchange felt reassuringly informal.

'Are you back in London now, Mr Tucker?'

'No, I'm still on the coast. But I could come back if that helps? You mentioned my giving a statement?'

'Yes, we understand Jordan reported an altercation between him and Trevor Cochrane to you?'

Perry had mentioned this in passing to Alice and very much hoped she was the source of this tip. 'Not officially, but he did tell me about an argument they had in the kitchen.'

'It would be useful to get the details of that on record.'

'Okay, if that's helpful. But can I ask why? I mean, Jordan's dead, so you can't bring any charges against him, can you?'

The bottom line was that they wanted to close this down. Get themselves a statistic in their favour for once. He'd be, in effect, submitting evidence against Jordan to help make sure the boy rested not in peace but in ignominy.

Then again, he *had* clobbered Trev with a dumbbell, so it wasn't as if the police were cynically framing an innocent man.

'Of course,' he said. 'Let me get my diary.'

83

Amy

'How're you getting on sleeping in the Niche?' Perry asked, when the two of them next met for dinner at The Needles, where pizzas from a new clay oven were served on the heated terrace under a web of fairy lights. 'It's not too cold in there, is it?'

'It's all right,' Amy said. 'This truffle and artichoke is delicious. How's your nduja?'

'It's good. Spicy. I'd say you're welcome to move into our place, but I don't know if Charlotte told you . . .'

'What? You haven't found a buyer already?'

'No. The market's completely seized up. Apparently, we might not get any bites till spring. But we've got house sitters lined up for when I go back up to London next week.'

Amy looked at him in disbelief. She knew from Charlotte that in their fifteen years of ownership of Cliff View they'd never once let the place or engaged house sitters. 'Really? She didn't tell me, no. Who are they?'

'Locals. Robbie Jevons and his girlfriend Shannon.'

'You mean NJFA Robbie?' Amy's eyebrows lifted. 'Wow. How did that happen? Didn't you punch him?'

'I did,' Perry agreed, eyes on his plate as he redistributed toppings from a particularly overloaded slice. 'But, well, a lot's happened since then, hasn't it? I'm starting to see things from his point of view a bit more. Like you've always said, Amy, there's a lot of nuance to this housing issue.'

'There is,' she said, flattered. 'Well. If that's not a diplomatic coup, I don't know what is.'

'Yes. I believe it is peace for our time,' Perry said, wryly, and she was fairly sure she got the reference. 'Now I recommend you to go home and sleep quietly in your beds.'

'Churchill?'

'Chamberlain.'

'Of course. Sorry,' she said when Perry looked dismayed. 'I noticed he's no longer all over the papers. Robbie, I mean, not Chamberlain. That explains why. All the agitation seems to be from this other group, Citizens Against the Elite.'

'There'll always be someone who disapproves. No matter how hard we try.'

'Haters gonna hate,' Amy agreed, and nibbled on a pizza crust. 'We can only do our best, try to give back when we see an opportunity. Speaking of which, you've inspired Linus, you know. He's signed up for volunteering. Every Saturday, the council's free cycling skills scheme. Beattie's going to do it with him when she's not revising.' She had in fact pre-emptively claimed to be doing so on her UCAS personal statement, but Amy didn't tell him that. For all his faults, Perry did not volunteer simply because it looked good; if anything, his instinct was to play his good works down.

Finished, they sat back in their seats and Perry poured himself another glass from his litre of San Pellegrino. Charlotte had told Amy he was drinking again and asked if she could let her know if she saw any evidence of this, which made Amy feel oddly defensive on Perry's behalf.

'Will you still live in the Masefield Road house when you go back to London?' It was, she knew, large enough for them to make it work, at least in the short term.

'No,' Perry said. 'Charlotte's keeping that. I'm moving into the flat.'

'What flat?'

'We've got a flat in Camberwell, did you not know? It's in Benedict's name, of course.'

'Of course.' To avoid the second-home stamp duty surcharge, she realized. And since banks weren't falling over themselves to offer students mortgages, it meant the property had almost certainly been bought outright.

'We've been renting it out,' Perry said, 'but we've given the tenants notice. I'll base myself there until we're sold up down here and I've got a bit more budget to play with.'

Amy wondered where the tenants would go and had a brief, terrifying vision of the housing-crisis dispossessed swarming the streets of South London, searching for shelter.

She looked at their empty plates and still felt hungry. The nights were drawing in and there was just that instinct to fatten up for winter. 'Shall we have a pudding?' she suggested, signalling to the waiter to bring menus. 'I think we deserve it.'

'Certainly do,' Perry said.

84

Robbie

The French say *la vie est belle* for 'this is the life' – I read that the other day. Well, let me tell you, from where I'm sitting, on a posh wooden chair called an Adirondack (I googled it, always learning), *la vie est* seriously damn *belle*. Just me and Shannon, out on the patch where the summerhouse used to be and where Perry's laid some turf, drinks and a few snacks on the table between us.

I mean, the sea is *right there*. You can hear the tides like breath. Still as a millpond today, but you should have seen it a couple of days ago. So angry. Great tongues of water shooting up at us and then sucking back again.

I'm reading the *Voice*. The Tuckers haven't cancelled their subscription and every week we pick it up off the doormat, read it, then refold it and set it aside with the rest of the mail.

Police 'Exhaust All Leads' in Pine Ridge Inquiry

Police admit they are 'no closer' to finding the person responsible for the death of tourist Jordan Lynch, 26, in Pine Ridge on 28th August.

The investigation began as a criminal damage inquiry when the summerhouse belonging to a property on Pine Ridge Road was shunted into the sea, but escalated into a murder inquiry when Mr Lynch was discovered to have been sleeping in the outbuilding at the time. A post-mortem found he died of head and chest injuries on or soon after impact. A recovering alcoholic, Lynch was revealed to have a blood alcohol content of 200 milligrams per 100 millilitres, an amount likely to have incapacitated him at the time of the incident.

'We have questioned every activist and every builder in the area, looked at every minute of CCTV, exhausted all leads,' said Detective Inspector Nicola Peck, who is leading the inquiry. 'But with large crowds in Pine Ridge for the festival that day, we are sadly in a needle in a haystack situation, with potential witnesses long dispersed. Frustratingly, repeated appeals have failed to bring new evidence to light.' She apologized to the family of Mr Lynch, who are believed to be based in Kent. 'His loved ones deserve to know who was responsible for this horrendous act.'

Activism groups campaigning for a cap on the number of local properties sold as holiday homes have consistently denied any responsibility for the events of the bank holiday weekend. Last month, Not Just for August (NJFA) announced a temporary disbanding of their activities following the council's pledge to fund a development of KosyKabins for local residents, believed to be the first scheme of its kind in the county.

However, continuing incidents of graffiti in the village point to a new bone of contention: the housing of Channel migrants in the Staywell Inn. 'If there is spare housing available, then it should go to those who've spent years on council waiting lists,' said Jacob Plummer of Citizens Against the Elite.

Both locals and second-home owners are said to be united in their objection to the policy and police have confirmed they will be present in number for a planned demonstration next weekend.

There's a big photo from the bank holiday protest, showing the pro and anti groups assembled on opposite sides of the Staywell car park. Is it me or is there a natural focal point in the form of a small, dark-haired woman on the pro side, brandishing her placard with gusto, flashing her perfect dentistry as she hollers towards the camera? A real firebrand.

She'll be prime minister one day, that girl.

*

We've been here almost a month now. Feels like we're in *Downton Abbey* sometimes, having this massive place to ourselves. No servants, though, obvs.

Perry came down for a few days last week to repaint the kitchen – yellow puts buyers off, apparently – and he and I went out for a drink. He's all right, now I've got to know him a bit better. He didn't come from money, it turns out, he made every penny he's got himself. When his parents died, he inherited debts, not trust funds. He really got it when I told him about my mum. 'It's always the wrong one who dies young,' he goes. 'It's never the one you would choose.'

He's actually kind of entertaining, loves a debate. Brexit, immigration, the war on motorists, you name it. 'What's your view on these trigger warnings, Robbie?' he asked me one time.

'Got no need of them personally,' I told him. 'Prefer to just take it all in my stride.'

'That's the spirit. You know, I read that some American university has banned the term because they say it needs a trigger warning of its own. These are people who are offended *in anticipation* of the offence they may or may not be about to feel! Easier if they just don't leave the house, don't you think?'

'I'm with you on that,' I said, laughing.

His wife – soon to be ex – has been down once or twice as well, to meet agents and check we're recycling properly, putting the bins out on the right day. She doesn't like me hanging up my overalls in the 'laundry room' but otherwise she's happy with how we're keeping the place.

We've submitted to the occasional viewing, of course, made ourselves scarce so we can't lower the tone, but so far, no one's come back with an offer. Which is just how we like it.

How Des likes it as well. He's subletting the caravan from us while we're here. He didn't make the cut for a KosyKabin, but is hopeful for the next tranche. Tate's been in there with him now and then, on the nights when Ellie decides she hasn't *quite* forgiven him.

It's been one long game of musical beds, let me tell you.

'Cheers, babe.' I take a hunk of olive bread and smear it with the pâté Shannon brought home from the deli. Crab and samphire, really tasty. 'I could get used to this.'

'I know.' But she inhales deeply, like there's something bothering her. *Haunting* her.

'What?'

'I just think it's really bad.' She gestures to the newspaper. 'How someone got away with murder like that. Right here. Right where we're sitting, Rob.'

She's said before that it gives her the creeps to sit down here. She prefers to be in the house.

Mind you, there's not much choice if you're home during the week, when the builders up at the bungalow are working, drills and hammers and angle grinders driving you out of your mind. Amy's told Shannon if they exceed the permitted hours by even a single minute then she wants to know about it. She's been very apologetic about it, bringing us flowers and wine and all sorts.

The husband never comes down. Amy told Shannon she's worried he's been spooked by everything that's happened but she expects to get him back onside when he claps eyes on the 'architectural glory' of the finished house.

I have to say I wonder about that.

You see Tate told me something interesting – once he was back in the land of the living, reconciled to his future as a family man and able to view the summer with a bit of perspective. Reacquainted with a working phone. (Now *that* is a story in itself. The day after his release, a brand-new iPhone was left for him at the Golden Sands office, with a note saying '*I'm sorry, Bx*'. Which was obviously impossible to explain to Ellie, so we told her it was a donation from an NJFA supporter who'd heard about his heroic incarceration.)

Anyway, he told me he'd remembered something from the evening of the summerhouse incident. As he and Beattie had left their little love nest, he'd looked back down the footpath and seen a figure on a bike in the distance. He didn't know who it was at the time, thought so little of it he didn't even mention it when he was being grilled by the cops, but a few weeks later when he was stalking Beattie's Instagram (okay, so he's *almost* reconciled to his future as a family man), he saw a picture of her with this same guy, in the same kit and all. They were teaching homeless people to cycle – which makes no sense, so maybe he got that bit wrong – and he saw from the post that it was her father.

'Didn't you ever meet Linus?' I said, confirming his identity with a single glance.

He gave a sad, crooked smile. 'It was never a "meet the parents" kind of thing, was it, me and her?'

Anyway, the point is it couldn't have been even half an hour after this sighting on the cliff path that someone climbed into the JCB parked on *his own property* and took out a neighbour's summerhouse.

Sure, he'll have an alibi – don't we all? – and anyway I'm not looking to put the man behind bars. I'm just thinking, once they finish their building works up there, once the 'architectural glory' is open for business, I might come up with a proposal to house-sit there next. You know, if timings work out.

Actually, the more I think about it the more convinced I am we could make it happen. I mean, it's not like the family will be down in Pine Ridge that much themselves.

Not outside of August, anyway.

Acknowledgements

I have a whole new publishing team for *Our Holiday* and, as I write this, our adventure is just beginning. My editor and publisher, Kate Mills of HQ, has herded this rowdy cast of Pine Ridge residents and holidaymakers with such insight and humour – I'm very excited to be working together on this and future books!

A huge thank you to the whole HQ team, including Lisa Milton, Joanna Rose, Anna Derkacz, Claire Brett, Georgina Green, Lauren Trabucchi, Kate Oakley, Brogan Furey, Emily Burns, Sarah Lundy, and Rachael Nazarko. And thank you to copyeditor Cari Rosen and proofreader Gabriella Nemeth.

Wholehearted gratitude, as ever, to the brilliant Sheila Crowley and the rest of the crack Curtis Brown crew: Moi Lanne Wetzel-Liao, Rachel Goldblatt, Katie MacGowan, Aoife MacIntyre, and Tanja Goossens.

Thank you so much to Luke Speed of Speed Literary and Talent Management for all that you do for me and my stories.

Thank you to Into the Breach for research and to Dawn Wilkins and Harry Wright for advice about Dorset.

A special thank you to the tireless news journos of the UK press, whose reporting of the holiday-home issue has been an invaluable resource during the writing of this book. While *Our*

Holiday may at times read as satire, believe me it is in fact a fairly measured portrait of the dilemma.

As ever, I'd like to thank each and every bookseller, librarian, reviewer, blogger, influencer, book group member, festival organiser, moderator and volunteer, not to mention fellow author, who has helped get this finished product into your hands. The year 2024 marks the twenty year anniversary of my being a published author and there is an elite band of you who've read every one of my sixteen previous books (and one novella): I salute you! If this is your first book of mine or your seventeenth, it's a pleasure to entertain you.

KARIN Slaughter's

CRIME CLUB

© Alison Rosa

Dear Readers,

Louise Candlish, the bestselling author of edge-of-your-seat thrillers like *Our House*, has returned with an incisive and twisty novel about second-home owners clashing with local people.

Summer in the beautiful coastal town of Pine Ridge promises beach days, good wine, and an influx of wealthy Londoners escaping the city. Charlotte and Perry have owned their holiday home there for years, and with their London neighbours Amy and Linus joining them, it promises to be a summer like no other.

But resentment is starting to build amongst the locals, many of whom can't afford one house, let alone two. Led by the charismatic Robbie, a protest group forms, planning harmless but disruptive stunts to make their feelings known.

But then the stunts start to take on a sharper edge. As tensions bubble over between the locals and the visitors, the fallout will tear apart marriages, shatter friendships, and leave one person dead.

Our Holiday will grip you from the first page. I can't wait to hear what you think.

Karin

READING GROUP QUESTIONS

Warning: contains spoilers

1. What did you think of the beginning of the book? Did the narrative follow the path you expected from the opening chapter?

2. Do you think the stunts that Robbie's group perform are an effective way of drawing attention to their cause, or are they more retaliatory?

3. Some of the characters seem conflicted about their role in worsening the housing crisis in Pine Ridge – Amy wants to be 'part of the solution, not the problem', and Charlotte wryly notes that Tabitha critiques wealth hoarders while drinking their pricy wine. Are you sympathetic to this inner conflict or, like Robbie, do you think it's hypocritical?

4. What do you think about the animosity between Linus and Perry? Do you think they're justified in their dislike of each other?

5. How did you think Beattie was getting money for her designer clothes? Were you surprised by the revelation that she was stealing?

6. Perry describes the teenagers and the adults as 'two generations divided by a common language'. Do you think the linguistic misunderstandings are the driver of generational conflict in the novel, or do they simply highlight deeper division? What other divisions did you notice?

7. Which characters would you most and least like to have dinner with at The Needles? Why?

8. Do you think that limiting or penalising second-home ownership would alleviate the housing crisis? What other solutions might there be?

9. Who did you think the dead body would turn out to be, and who did you suspect would be to blame? How did your suspicions change as the novel developed?

10. Have you read any Louise Candlish books before? If so, how does *Our Holiday* compare? And if not, was it what you expected?

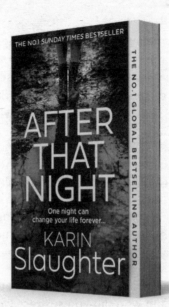

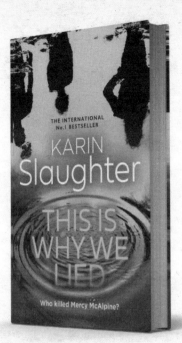

THE INTERNATIONAL
No.1 BESTSELLER

KARIN
Slaughter

THIS IS
WHY WE
LIED

Who killed Mercy McAlpine?

Everyone here is a liar, but only one of us is a killer...

Welcome to the McAlpine Lodge: a remote mountain getaway, it's the height of escapist luxury living.

Except that everyone here is lying. Lying about their past. Lying to their family. Lying to themselves.

Then one night, Mercy McAlpine – until now the good daughter – threatens to expose everybody's secrets. Just hours later, Mercy is dead.

In an area this remote, it's easy to get away with murder. But Will Trent and Sara Linton – investigator and medical examiner for the GBI – are here on their honeymoon.

And now, with the killer poised to strike again, the holiday of a lifetime becomes a race against the clock...

OUR NEXT
KILLER READ

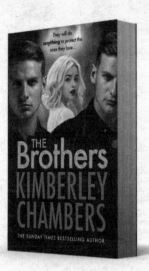

MEET THE BOND BROTHERS.
You don't want to be on the wrong side of this family...

Beau Bond hates fiercely and loves hard. He'll do
anything to protect his twin Brett, and his girlfriend Jolene.

Brett is a survivor. He's always followed his brother's
lead, even if it means he's lived to regret it.

As Beau and Jolene get hitched, their feuding families
must put their differences aside.

But the brothers have a dark secret that could cause
a war between both sides... and what better place to
reveal all than at a wedding...

When their past sins resurface to threaten those closest
to them, will the brothers still have each other's backs?

A brand-new series from the Queen of Gangland Crime!

ONE PLACE. MANY STORIES

Bold, innovative and
empowering publishing.

FOLLOW US ON:

@HQStories